BECKER

A HARRY BECKER MYSTERY

GORDON REID

Printed in Australia
Cover design by Shawline Publishing Group Pty Ltd
First Printing: Sept 2021

Shawline Publishing Group Pty Ltd
www.shawlinepublishing.com.au

Paperback ISBN- 9781922594624
Ebook ISBN- 9781922594617

A catalogue record for this book is available from the National Library of Australia

For Amanda

CHAPTER 1

WHEN SHE CALLED, the dog began to bark. She was on the back porch and the dog was with Becker and the two kids at the creek. They were her kids, a girl and a boy. Becker hadn't heard what she'd said, she being a woman, who never raised her voice, even in anger. A gentle woman with a kindly smile. A lovely wife, you couldn't ask for better. He began walking up to her, some fifty yards. The dog was a young kelpie, very playful, very noisy. He began to follow, but the boy called him and threw a stick, so the dog stopped, undecided.

Half way up, Becker tried again. 'Robyn? What did you say?' She answered, something about a visitor. The dog barked again, then whined, one short cry, as if worried. As if it sensed trouble. Or loss. Or bewilderment. Hard to say with a dog. But something was going to happen. The dog knew it, the way birds are said to know there is going to be an earthquake. It was October 1995.

He was close enough now. 'What did you say?'

'There is someone to see you, Harry.'

'Who?'

'An old man. He says you are his brother.'

'I don't have a brother.'

'I know, Harry.' She shrugged. 'He sounds like an Italian.'

'An Italian?'

'You'd better speak to him.'

Becker reached her, waiting on the porch. 'Where is he?'

'Out front, holding onto a post.' She meant a verandah post.

'Yeah?'

'He looks exhausted.'

'Does he have a name?'

She opened the screen door for him. 'Alfredo.'

'Alfredo?'

'That's what he said, Alfredo.'

Becker went cold. He'd thought he'd never see Alfredo Scarafini again. He'd last seen him at the funeral in Canberra, when they'd buried his sister, Evelyn Crowley. The Italian's sister, not Becker's. He was rattled for a few seconds, his heart jumping. Alfredo was the Mafia. But Alfredo was stupid, he talked too much. That's why people were looking for him. People from Melbourne, the kind who never tell you they are coming.

Becker walked into the house. It was one of those old, simple designs you found all over Australia years ago, both in the towns and in the bush. Looking from the front, a corridor ran right down the middle—on the left-hand side three bedrooms, on the right a living room, a large kitchen, in which they also dined, a bathroom and toilet all in one and finally a laundry by the back door. A seven-roomed house, if you call a laundry a room. It was a deep laundry, with a big cupboard at the end. For storage, but not very secure. Anyone could break in.

He walked through, while Robyn went down to the creek—nominally to keep an eye on the kids, but not to overhear. That would have been impolite. In her opinion, nosy wives were the worst kind. Usually wrecked their own marriages. She knew things had happened he did not want to talk about, but the past is always following you. Like a hungry dog, only a few paces behind. She had her own past and never complained about others having pasts they did not want to talk about.

He stepped onto the front verandah, his heart going *bang, bang, bang*. A man was hanging onto a post with one hand, a foot on a step. In the other hand was a cigarette. Behind him was the peppercorn tree, big and old and twisted and ugly. Beyond the tree was the stock-rail fence and out there in the wide world was the highway, heavy trucks thundering past. Then a big four-wheel drive pulling a caravan. Then two utilities, each with a dog on the back, barking at nothing.

'What do you want, Alfredo?'

'You know me. We brother.'

'Yeah?'

The Italian looked tired, sick and afraid.

'We got talk. Things they bad, you know.'

'That's too bad.'

'Too bad for you, my frien', you don' help brother.'

'You're not my brother.'

'You my brother. We got have some talk.'

'What about?'

The old man didn't answer. He wasn't really old—only ten years older than Evelyn, but he'd looked bad at her funeral. That was only five months ago, but he looked much worse now.

'Have a seat,' Becker said. He pointed to one of the outdoor chairs.

'Not here, no. Somebody—' He was panting. He was scared, you could see. 'We go in house,' he said.

Alfredo was bad news. The police had been looking for him since that trouble in Canberra—not to charge him with anything, but to look after him, put him into protective custody, get him to talk, do a deal. Before someone else found him. To shut him up.

'You don't want to be seen?'

The old man mumbled something, eyes cast down. It was obvious he was on the run.

'How'd you know where to find me?'

'I ask 'round. You not hard find.'

No, Becker thought, not hard at all. No doubt the Italian community knew exactly where he was. He could have been killed any time since he'd left Canberra. Maybe someone had decided he wasn't important enough. Not worth the price of a bullet.

He didn't want Robyn to see him. She'd ask questions. He'd have to explain. Then his whole world would come tumbling down.

'All right, come in. But get rid of that cigarette first.'

The Italian did so the way he had done at the funeral. Dropped it onto the gravel, then gently toed it in with a shoe, a black shoe. In Canberra it had been shiny. Now it was grey like Alfredo himself, like his eyes—grey, worn out. On the run eyes.

Becker opened the front screen door and showed him into the living room. He fell onto a couch packed with soft, fluffy cushions—something Robyn had found in a fabrics store in Wagga. She was always buying stuff for the place. Not junk, mind you. Nothing fussy or finicky. Delighted to live in a house like this. Old-fashioned, reconditioned. A smart, historic homestead called *Nil Desperandum* on one square mile of top-class farmland fifteen kilometres west of Wagga Wagga.

Becker waited. His heart was still going. He told himself he had to relax, but that made it go faster.

Alfredo sat, holding his stick and his hat, staring out the window at the front gate. His breathing was bad—short and shallow and wheezing. Probably had emphysema, lung cancer too. The way he smoked, non-stop. His mouth hung open, teeth yellow and uneven and of little use now. No doubt his gums were rotten. He needed a good dentist.

'Who's chasing you, Alfredo?'

'Some fella,' he said.

'What fella?'

'Young fella on bike.'

'A motorbike?'

'Yes, red bike, big bike.'

'What's his name?'

Alfredo shrugged.

'What's he look like?'

Another shrug.

'How do you know?'

'Some people, they say he asking.'

'Asking about you?'

No reply.

'Where was this?'

Alfredo coughed. 'Griffith.'

'In Griffith?'

Again, no answer. Becker was surprised. Griffith was the last place in Australia for an Italian on the run. It was full of Italians. But who else would have him? A man who'd tried to be a big man with the Mafia down in Melbourne. And had talked too much. Walking up and down Sydney Road, Brunswick, with his chest stuck out, telling everyone he was a big man now. He was in the Mafia, so you'd better look out. All because he'd told them about a top man in a top bank, who was laundering mob money for a fee. And his sister was married to that man. Now Evelyn was dead, for talking to a cop. If you're in, you're in for life. You never talk. Or, if you do, you're dead. It was as simple as that.

'Can I get you something? Brandy? Whiskey?'

'No, no, my frien'—'

'What do you want?'

He thought about it. 'My sister, you love her, eh?'

'You mean Evelyn?'

'Evalina, we call her. She good girl, everybody love her.'

'I've heard that before.'

'She help me. She got money, lotsa money. You got her money, eh?'

'Half of it.'

'Half? She no give to me nothing, her brother.'

'That's too bad.'

'Who get other half?'

'Christine's adoptive parents.'

'Christine?'

'The daughter she had to give up seventeen years ago.'

Alfredo thought about this, panting. He did not like it. He had to get money, fast. Someone was going to kill him. 'You got money, you help me like brother.'

'Evelyn was not your sister and you're not my brother.'

'She my sister.'

'She was your cousin, she told me.'

'No, no, she my sister, I know. You love her, you go bed with her. In my country that mean you brother.'

Becker waited. The back door opened, then footsteps in the hall. Robyn looked in. 'Hello? Tea, anyone?'

He waved at her to go away, well away. So she withdrew. Outside, he heard her speaking to the kids near the house. Gradually the voices faded. Alfredo sighed. It was more like a long, drawn-out gasp. At last, he breathed in.

'She my sister,' he said again.

'What do you mean?'

'My father, her father.'

'Yeah?'

'He have her mother, Eva.'

'Your father had sex with Evelyn's mother?'

'Yes, Antonio he write for Ennio take her to Napoli, put her on ship for Australia. They arrive one night, ship go next day. That night he take her to hotel near ship. That night he go in her room and he have her.'

'Jesus, you mean he raped his own brother's *fiancé*?' Becker thought about it. This explained something about Evelyn, although he was not sure what. 'Evelyn was born in Australia,' he said. 'You came later.'

'*Si*, Eva, she *gravida* she arrive.'

'*Gravida?*'

'What you say, preg—'

'Pregnant?'

'*Si*, pregnant.'

'Did Antonio know this?'

'No, she make him have her first night. She so much ashame. Eight month, she have baby.'

'And that was Evelyn?'

'*Si*, Evalina, we call her.'

'So Ennio was her father? Who was also your father?'

'*Si*.'

'Then what happened?'

'Antonio, he got job Shepparton. He put fruit in tins, you know. Then after a while, they come down.'

'To Melbourne?'

'*Si*, everybody set up shop Sydney Road, Brunswick. Have good time we think. But Eva, one day she jump in fron' tram.'

'A tram?'

'She get hit, awful.'

'Jesus!'

'Everybody rush out, too horrible for to look.'

'She did it deliberately?'

'*Si*, deliberate. She no want live wi' Ennio, work wi' him. She frighten' alla time.'

Becker did not ask why. It was pretty obvious. Quite possibly, she'd dreamed of killing him. But she could not, not her husband's brother. His big brother.

'How old was Evelyn?'

'Seven, eight, I think. She go school. Antonio, he love her, he adore her. She beautiful gel, speak beautiful. Every day he take her school an' every afternoon he bring her home. St Margaret Mary, Mitchell Street. Then, she get more bigger, he send her Loreto Toorak, you know? For boarder. Very nice school, very nice gels. Come home weekend.'

Becker shook his head. Now he understood Evelyn better. She was the child of a graceful and loving mother and a brutal pig of a rapist. Maybe that was why Evelyn, if the circumstances were right, could kill. *For three or four seconds I wanted him dead,* she had said. *I deliberately pushed him over. I murdered him.* She'd been referring to a man in Melbourne who had done her wrong. Would not marry her when she told him that she was pregnant. She had the child, that was Christine.

'What do you want, Alfredo?'

'Gotta get out.'

'Of Australia?'

'Go somewhere, maybe America, maybe Argentina.'

'You've got friends there?'

'Some people help.'

Becker thought about it. This man was not going anywhere—not to America or Argentina or wherever Italians on the run hoped to find sanctuary. He was going to die soon. Or, if he didn't die, he would be a cot case, breathing from an oxygen mask.

Alfredo Scarafini was a cheap crook, a liar and an ignorant, grasping peasant. He and his evil father had used Evelyn years ago, when they'd deceived a young bank manager in Melbourne. If they'd not done that, this peasant wouldn't be in a mess now, on the run from the mob. He was disgusting, and yet he was human to some degree. Back in Canberra, he'd tried to save Evelyn. And she would have helped him.

'What do you want?'

'Hun'red thousan' dollar.'

'One-hundred-thousand?'

'Yes.'

'That'll set you up?'

'Get me there, maybe hospital, maybe quiet life. Me, I no old man. Maybe I get better.'

'Maybe, maybe not.'

'Eh?' The Italian tried to sit up straight. He looked directly at Becker, but failed. His eyes could not quite make it. 'You help? You put me on plane?'

Becker did not reply. It would be worth one-hundred-thousand dollars to get rid of him, but getting him to Sydney and putting him on an aircraft would be hard enough. A passport? Alfredo was probably on a wanted list. As soon as his mugshot popped up on a screen, bells would start ringing.

'When do you want the money?'

'Maybe today? You go in bank an' get money. You drive Sydney?'

'I don't know about that. Got a bank account?'

'Yes, *si*.'

'Credit card?'

'*Si*, I got card.'

'I'll put the money in your account today. Then I'll put you on a plane in Wagga. You'll have to look after yourself in Sydney. Okay?'

The old man, who was not an old man, thought about it. 'Okay.'

'Can you drive so far? To Wagga?'

'Got no car. Fella bring me this place. Got loada stuff for Wagga.'

'A truckie?'

'Yes.'

'Where's the fella now?'

'He go on. He got tomato, lettuce, avocado.'

'Okay, I'll drive you. Got a passport?'

'One I got Griffith. Cost lotta money.'

'A false one? They might pick it up at the airport.'

'I take risk.'

'The police want to talk to you.'

'I never talk.'

'Why don't you give yourself up? They'll offer you immunity, if you tell them everything you know about the bank. How you controlled that poor bastard, the manager. I know, I was a cop once. They'd want to know how Crowley was moving the money out?'

Alfredo did not answer, but his eyes did. They said no.

Becker tried again.

'Do a deal with the police, they'll love you. They'll get you out of the country under a false name. The *Carabinieri* know all about you. They'll protect you if you go back to Italy.'

'No, no—' He was shaking his head. 'They kill me I talk, some people.'

'Looks like they're going to kill you anyway.'

No response. This wreck was not going far. Probably wouldn't make it to Los Angeles or New York or wherever he was going. Might not make it even to Sydney.

'You should be in hospital, Alfredo.'

'No, no hospital. They look hospital.'

'Yeah, we look hospital,' a voice said.

It came from the hall. A skinny kid was standing there wearing a black leather jacket, the kind bikies wore. He was holding a steel-grey helmet in one hand and a Browning automatic in the other. It was a .32 automatic with fitted silencer screwed on. He looked no more than fifteen or sixteen, but he must have been older. Evelyn had said that Giancarlo had been shot by a kid on a motorbike. In Sydney Road, Brunswick, of all places—in broad daylight. As quick and cheeky and cheery as that.

He had light-brown curls around his face. It was a baby sort of face, one that would never mature. His skin was sallow, dry, toneless. He was a real psycho, you could see. Cold-blooded, and crazy like a jumping jack.

Becker jumped up.

'Sit down, pal.'

Becker refused. 'Who are you?'

'You don't need to know.'

The kid went to Alfredo.

'How're you doin', Alfredo? It *is* Alfredo, ain't it?'

He pulled out a photograph and showed it to Becker. It was Alfredo in a hat and dark glasses, taken quite recently, a candid shot in a busy street—probably the main street of Griffith. Someone had ratted on him. The kid smiled at Becker and then at Alfredo, back and forth several times, as if waiting for approval.

He waved the Browning at Alfredo.

'Been givin' people the run around, eh, pal? Tried to hide out? What's that dumb place? Griffith? Not too many pals there, eh, Alfredo? Some wanta make a quick buck? Get on the phone, make a call. You never rilly know, do you? Who's a friend and who ain't.'

He sounded like someone in a B-grade movie from the forties. Becker tried to keep him talking. Keep him talking and hope that Robyn did not reappear.

'Why're you doing this?'

'Why am I doin' this?'

'Yeah, why?'

'You're askin' me why I'm doin' this? You? You're the dickhead back in Canberra that was lyin' on his back snorin', weren't you? Lying there, dead to the world and this dame is on her side beside you, eh?' He giggled or snuffled or grunted. 'Pity, wasn't it?'

Becker was tempted to say, What was a pity?

He didn't get a chance.

'To see her lyin' there, dead to the world. Didn't have a silencer then. All I had to do was pick up a pillow and wrap it around and pull the trigger. Popped her. Really popped her, didn't I? Straight through the skull. With two cops sittin' in a car outside. And one dead in the laundry. Great joke, eh? And you, missed the whole fuckin' show, didn't you?'

He was laughing. He was real crazy, you could see.

'Thought of poppin' you too, but you can't do that, can you? No-one said to do that. You've got to stick to the rules. Do what the customer wants. Never anyone else. That'd be murder, wouldn't it? But a job is a job, eh? Just business, ain't it, old man?'

He pointed the gun at Alfredo, slumped on the sofa, resigned. The old man knew it was inevitable. Had probably seen it done himself, back home. Up in the hills overlooking Reggio. Overlooking the Strait of Messina. Overlooking Etna in the distance, smoking.

'How d'you want it, old man?'

No answer.

'Not fussy, eh? So long, pal.'

Three bullets, straight into the chest. No explosions, just a solid *phttt*, like someone sneezing. Or, suppressing a cough.

Becker tried to jump him, but failed.

'How much are they paying you?' he said.

'How much are they payin' me? You're askin' how much?'

'I'll pay the same. You'll get double the amount.'

'Yeah?'

'For only one job.'

The kid's eyes brightened. 'Double for one job?'

'Yeah, you let me go and tell them there were no witnesses.'

'Tell who?'

'The people who sent you.'

'What if they hear?'

'They won't hear. I'll tell no-one, not the cops, no-one.'

'What about Alfredo?'

'I'll bury him on the property. Or dump him in the river. No-one'll know.'

'Ah, I dunno. If they hear—'

'I'll pay you three times.'

'Ah…' He scratched his own head with the point of the barrel. He was that crazy.

'We'll clear out, disappear,' Becker said.

'Ah, shit, man—'

'Whatever you want!'

'Ah, I dunno. A job's a job, ain't it?'

Becker glanced around. Hoping for a chance, make a break for it. Thought he saw something in the doorway. Or Someone. No time to check. The kid was raising the Browning. Negotiations had ended.

'So long, pal.'

He fired. Just one shot, *bang*. That's all it took.

CHAPTER 2

AT LEAST, THAT'S what Becker thought. So did the kid. But he had *not* fired. He staggered, then caught his balance. Stood there puzzled, disbelief in his eyes. A little defective like him, wondering what had gone wrong. His eyes glazed over, then recovered, his knees sagged but did not recover. The helmet fell, then he fell. Lay there like a child, holding his chest. Stunned and frightened. His face fading to white like a big close up in a bad movie, in which the punk always gets it in the end.

Chook was standing in the doorway, holding a Colt .38 in both hands. A flat automatic, ten shots, definitely not police issue. Not for Canberra cops at that time, anyway. They all had the Smith and Wesson police special. She was a Canberra cop.

'Thought you'd need some help,' she said.

Neither spoke for a while. When you are a cop, the first killing is a *not* a shock. You've been expecting it for years, ever since you signed on. Now it was done. She looked relieved, even pleased. But tired. She walked in.

'Is he dead?' Becker asked.

She kneeled down, put two fingers to his throat and waited maybe ten seconds. 'He is now,' she said and stood up. She was a tall blond with a ponytail. 'Goodbye, shit,' she said.

He thought she was going to give him another bullet. Or at least kick him. Or, it. He wasn't a him anymore—nothing more than a dead thing lying on a floor. A dead thing with a human shape, now worth no more than what you could get at a garage sale for a heap of trash.

The kid was the one who'd killed Polly, when he'd come in over the back fence

at night to avoid the patrol car out front. He'd rattled a broom or something, got her
to investigate. Popped her there and then in the chest. A lovely girl like Polly. Anna
Politis was her name. They called her Pollyanna, or Polly.

They'd been pals and partners, Polly and Chook. They did shifts together. They'd
been given the job of protecting Evelyn and Becker until the police could get them out
of Canberra. Hopefully out of the country. Make them disappear. Off to see the world
and to have a good time. Together.

'Jesus, Chook—'

She uncocked the Colt, put it away. Not in a holster on a hip or under an arm,
but in a pocket of her leather jacket. She wasn't carrying the usual police gear on her
belt. Not on duty, obviously.

'Where'd you spring from?'

She was panting.

'Yeah, well, I heard that—heard that the slug—the slug that hit Polly and the one
Giancarlo took down in Melbourne came from the same weapon—' She took a deep
breath. 'So, I took some leave, flew down there and asked around. Used to ride with
bikies, as you know—'

She sounded a bit nostalgic. Or fatalistic or regretful. It was hard to say.

'Anyway, I looked up some of them and one or two knew about him, knew he'd
done the hit on Giancarlo. Even where he lived, but he'd gone.' She took another
breath. 'To Griffith, I found out. On his big, red, dirt bike. So, I hired a car and drove
up there. Heard Alfredo had been living there, but he'd gone too. Trying to get out of
the country, someone said. Didn't have the money. That's when I thought of you. He
was sure to touch you for a handout.'

'How'd you know where to find me?'

'Everyone knows where to find you, Harry.' Already she'd pulled out a phone.
'I've got to make a call.'

He knew she had to. Soon the place would be crawling with police. State police
first, then the Federal. This could go on for days. Robyn would be horrified. The
kids too. Everything was about to come tumbling down. Goodbye to his beautiful
rural dream.

He was starting to shake. 'What am I going to tell them?'

'Tell who?' she said.

He didn't answer. He walked out, found himself in the kitchen, went to a
window. Robyn was throwing a ball, the kids catching. The dog was barking, trying
to intercept. Then, it did. Leaped in the air, ran off with the ball. The boy went after
it, shouting. Everyone laughing—even the dog, which plunged into the creek. The
stupid boy went in after him.

Chook joined him at the window. She hadn't made the call yet.

'I had to shoot him, Harry.'

'Yeah, I know.'

'He was going to kill you.'

'I know.'

'I'm sorry, mate.'

'If they see this—'

'A lovely family,' she said.

'At least they didn't hear,' he said.

He felt sick in the guts. He couldn't keep them out of the house. Robyn was sure to walk up. Already she'd glanced at the house, seen him at the window. The kids would be following. She'd say, 'Harry? What's happened here? Who is this woman? Who are these men? Is that blood?'

Robyn glanced again. A quick glance, trying not to be nosey.

The shaking was bad now. His hands were shaking, his legs too. An icy sort of wobble had reached his guts. He was going to fall, he knew. Chook put a hand on him.

'Don't worry,' she said. 'I've got a car.'

He didn't understand.

It was horrible. It shouldn't be this way. They'd had it so good. Their own farm, set to carry black Angus. It was a good life, good kids. The birds singing, the dog chasing the ball. In and out of the water, splashing. Robyn laughing. Such a good-natured woman.

'You go down there and hold 'em for five or ten,' Chook said.

He still didn't understand. 'What are you going to do?'

'Best you don't know.' She pushed him. 'Go on, I'll clean up here. You'll have to take care of the bike. It's by the gate.'

He didn't know what she was saying. What bike?

For a moment he thought he was going to vomit. But he hung onto the kitchen bench. He was a cop, not a good one, but a cop all the same. Or, at least he had been a cop in Sydney. Before he'd been kicked out for corruption. Taking bribes at the Cross. Fled to Canberra. Met Evelyn Crowley. Now she was dead. Left him three million dollars. So, here he was, back home in Wagga. Or, not actually in Wagga Wagga, but on a farm and looking out of the kitchen window and seeing that it was all going to collapse.

'Go on,' Chook said, and nudged him. Then disappeared.

Going down, he had to feel with his feet. He couldn't get his lids open, not properly open. He was ashamed and afraid and felt like he'd wrecked everything. Because he knew or had known a man named Alfredo Scarafini. But, somehow he made it, fifty yards to the creek. The boy had come out, dripping wet, ball in hand, throwing it to his sister. She was the sensible one, all of eleven. He was nine and a real tearaway. Dripping wet and laughing.

Robyn was watching him come down. 'Are you okay, Harry?'

'What? Ah, yeah.'

'Who was the old man?'

'Only some bloke. He—' He had to think fast. 'He wanted me to take him to Wagga. Seemed to think I was his brother.'

'Poor man, he looked done in.'

'Yeah, he was.'

'Where is he now?'

'Oh, he got a lift—with a woman.'

She must have seen Chook.

'The one at the kitchen window? Who was she?'

'No idea. Said she knew him. Heard he'd wandered off.'

Robyn watched him. He was not telling the truth, she knew.

'So all's well that ends well?'

Becker did not answer. They might get away with it. If not, Chook could be in serious trouble—interfering with evidence, removing bodies. A good friend. At the funeral in Canberra she'd shaken his hand and said: Any time you feel like a drink, Harry—. But he'd not taken up the offer. He'd felt pretty rotten then. Wanted to kill himself. Was going to do it, but Evelyn's lawyer had come up to him at the funeral and said she'd left him half her money, three million dollars. So he'd come back to Wagga, bought a farm. Met up again with a girl he'd met in Canberra. A Wagga girl herself. Asked her to marry him. And here they were, pretending that nothing had happened. But he never told her about Evelyn's money. Simply said he'd taken a bullet in the line of duty and had received a fat payout from the police and had decided to spend it on a farm. Even so, he seemed to have a lot of money—much more than the three-hundred and ninety thousand dollars he'd paid for the farm. But she never asked him about that.

'What do you think?' Robyn said.

'About what?'

When she'd called, he'd been thinking of damming the creek to get enough depth for the kids to have a canoe. But she'd already warned him that the neighbours down-stream might not like that. Taking their water.

'The creek,' she said. 'It could be a weir, not a dam. The same volume of water would flow over it. No-one would be deprived.'

She was a farmer's daughter. Must know what she was talking about.

'Yeah? Okay, let's do that.'

When they went back to the house, he noticed blood on the carpet, only a few small spots. Nothing else. If anyone asked, he'd say the old man had had a nosebleed. He'd been worried about burnt propellant, the smell. But Chook had thought of that too. Several windows were open, the front door too.

He looked out front. No sign of a car. Walked up, as casually as you like, to the gate to close it—and to check. Sure enough, a big red Honda bike was propped against a tree, the kind able to conquer a mountain without busting a spring. He'd have to do something about it, before a nosy cop in a cruiser came by, spotted it. Checked the registration. He'd wheel it down the highway and then ride it down a dirt track to the river, where he and the kids sometimes fished, trying to catch a cod. With a picnic hamper and a hot thermos. Dragonflies skimming the rippling surface. Yes, he'd push it in. But what if the key was not in it? It was too big to fit in the boot of his own car, Evelyn's car. How was he going to get it there?

Later, after lunch, he went to the gate again, nominally to check for mail. The bike had gone. He looked up and down; still no bike. Somebody had nicked it.

Becker was surprised, then mildly indignant. This was rural Australia. You didn't do that sort of thing in the bush. It was a matter of honour. As for Anastacia Babchuk, he hoped he'd never see her again.

But he did. Eventually.

CHAPTER 3

IT WAS A good property, with a lot of history. Back in 1838, John Kettle had built a two-roomed hut out of split yellow-box, split by axes or forced apart by hammers and wedges, trimmed with adzes, then roofed with bark sheets, the men sleeping in bunks in one room and eating and yarning in the other, which served as the kitchen and living room. Although, during shearing times, the extra men had to sleep on the verandah or in tents. It was rough in those days, very rough, a hard life, for most men a wanderer's life, going from one squatter's spread to the next, looking for jobs. Many men died on the tracks across the western plains. But many hung on, tried to settle down, get a bit of land for themselves and their wives and kids if they had any. Kettle made some money out of wool, soon replaced the hut with a house built out of pit-sawn logs, which lasted until 1910, when the present weatherboard was erected. By then *Nil Desperandum* was an established property, profitable and prospective. Until the government decided to cut up such pastoral spreads, give the veterans of the first world war a chance. The blocks were good for wheat and sheep, perhaps dairy farms, but not much else. At least they were somewhere to live, while you waited for something else to turn up. Which it usually did, in one form or other.

A few weeks later.

Becker was standing back, looking at the rear of the house. It had verandahs on three sides. There was only a porch over the back door. He'd suggested they add a verandah along the back wall. It would make the house look complete, like a real homestead, traditional. But Robyn had objected that the back of the house faced south. It was in shade all year round. If they added a verandah, there would be even less light in the back rooms, particularly in winter.

The back door opened.

She came out, smiling, even happy for him. As if she had good news.

'Ah,' she said. 'You have *another* visitor.'

A man walked out, right behind her. He was in uniform and wore a blue cloth cap. About the same age as Becker, fair and fresh and friendly the way the police are when they want to talk to you. A quick smile too. A warm, businesslike handshake was sure to come. Suddenly everything had become concentrated, like the .38 Smith and Wesson pistol on his right hip.

Already the stranger was stepping down, a hand out, beaming as if it were nothing but a social call. Nothing to worry about.

'Harry, this is Barry.'

Barry? he thought. Barry who? He did not know of any Barry. Not in Wagga Wagga or in Canberra or anywhere in his past, except his cousin, Barry Barnes, who had been a little bastard, always throwing stones. And starting fights at school. And driving his mother mad—Harry Becker's mother, now in a place in Wagga, where they looked after her kind of case, the worrying kind and the forlorn and the widowed. Unable to distinguish the real from the unreal the way she was even at her age, just gone sixty.

He reached out, accepted the handshake, not with relish but with a tingle of fear, which he hoped the stranger in blue wouldn't sense. Although he knew he would. He'd see it in your eyes, in your frown and in the untrusting grasp of his hand, a rough hand certain of the law. This man might know all about you, or might not. But he'd like to know more.

'Barry?' he said.

'Barnes,' the cop said. Two stripes on his shoulders.

'Barry Barnes?'

'Yeah, remember me, don't you?'

Becker was confused. He had a cousin who was a cop and he'd appeared out of nowhere. Grinning and shaking his hand like a man who'd been looking for him all his life. And now had found him.

'He's your cousin,' Robyn said.

'Yeah, I remember now,' he said. 'Barry Barnes.'

'Sorry to bust on you like this, mate, but I was passin' and thought I'd say hullo. Hope I'm not interrupting anythin'. You know what it's like, a couple of cousins, who haven't seen each other for—how long is it? Fifteen years? Big surprise, eh?'

'Sixteen now,' Becker said.

'Sixteen, is it? How's Aunt Iris?'

'She's at Kirralee now.'

Barnes stiffened as if shocked, which was only an act. Everyone in the district knew about Iris Becker, who'd gone mad. Not suddenly, but quickly enough over a few years. It was sad to see. At first, no-one had thought it all that serious. But it was, insidiously. The CO at Kapooka barracks had come to the house and told her himself, hat in his hand, respectfully that her husband was dead. The chaplain was with him, looking sorrowful, as if he did not like doing the job, but he'd promised God he would, so he had to do it. The CO's driver was standing at ease by the car. They all looked ready to rush forward to catch her if she fainted. With the shock. But she did not. She'd been expecting this, ever since he'd left. Even before that, when he'd come home one evening and said he'd volunteered again. Volunteered? she'd said, as if that was the worst thing a man could do to his wife. Harry Becker had stood behind his mother, listening. He'd been nine then. A good boy, always ready to do things for her. Running to the shop, chopping kindling, drying up after dinner.

Not like his dreadful cousin, Barry Barnes, always throwing stones and getting into trouble with the police. A real tearaway, he was. And what happened to him? You wouldn't believe it. Grew up and stopped being stupid long enough to get into the police. Must have been thirty when he got in. They must have been desperate. But that was later, well after young Harry himself had joined. And gone to Sydney and then to Canberra. Now he was back, loaded with money, everyone said. And married a lovely girl, Robyn Sheldrake, who used to work for a dentist in Baylis Street. Widow of that bloke, Arnold Sheldrake, who piled his truck up against a big gum on the road near Tarcutta. Not a skid mark to be seen anywhere, according to the investigating officers. Must have gone to sleep at the wheel.

'Yeah, I heard,' Barnes said. He was two or three inches short of Becker, who was an inch under six feet. Nuggetty sort of build, good strong arms, quick eyes and a knowing expression. Like those of a pet dog, your own pet dog, looking at you and not at you, eyes never still, always scanning the scene, trying to work out what you are going to do next, not missing one detail.

'Was passing and thought I'd drop in and see if you were at home, say hullo. That sort of thing. As a matter of fact, I should be back at the station now. Had to do a run to Griffith, nothin' important. But bein' on duty, you know—'

He turned this way and that, still holding his cap, twisting in his boots, big boots, hard boots, ideal for kicking heads, as they used to say at the Cross, when Becker had worked there. A rough place, King's Cross. Blokes shagging sheilas up against walls down dingy lanes and creeps from every part of the world trying to look tough and important and malicious but nervous at the same time. Because they had a few dollars to spend before someone killed them for it.

'I'll walk out with you,' Becker said.

'Ah, yeah, thanks, mate.'

They followed Barnes through the house, Robyn following. 'Nice place, you've got here,' he said. At the front door he turned, a hand out again. 'Nice to see you after all these years, Harry.'

They shook again. Just a gesture, one cop to another. Becker was uneasy. Something, he felt, had happened. He was being checked out.

'Goodbye, Robyn.'

'Oh, it's wonderful to see you, Barry. I've never met any of Harry's relatives, except his mother who is, you know—' She stumbled. 'You must come and see us again, when you've got more time. Are you married?'

'Married?' Barnes reacted as if he'd been accused of something. 'Yeah, yeah, Maria is her name—' He was going to say something more, but baulked.

'I'll walk up with you,' Becker said.

Outside the gate stood a big, red police car, a highway-patrol vehicle, a Holden V8. With the blue and white check along the side. Very high speed, very aggressive.

The visitor paused. Looked back quickly, perhaps to be sure Robyn was at a safe distance.

'Mate, you wouldn't know anything about a mountain bike, would you? A big, red Honda?'

Becker was stunned. He knew he'd be asked one day. Had always thought he'd have some sort of answer ready. But he didn't.

'A Honda?'

'Yeah, a big, red one.'

'I don't think so.'

'The reason I ask is we picked up some kids recently, out at Wybilonga. You been there? A deadbeat dump now. Did a stint there once, bugger of a job. One-cop town. Y'never get any sleep, all the bloody punch-ups. Shops all closed except one and the pub could be delicensed any minute. Full of Abos and their kids, full black and half-castes, you know the sort of place. Well, we caught some black kids ridin' a big, red Honda bike. The kind you see kids ridin' in championships on TV, kickin' up dust like mad. Anyway, they couldn't explain the bike.'

'What did they say?'

'Nothing. You know what they're like. So, we worked on 'em. Eventually it came out, especially when one of the blackfellers came out and told 'em to 'fess up. Old Arthur Goorawoy it was. Used to know him, not a bad sort of bloke for a boong.

Anyway, they said they found it, along this road. They'd been hitchin' back home from Wagga. Reckoned it was outside a place with white rails and a new green roof and a smart car parked under a big pepper tree. They looked around and couldn't see anyone. Reckoned someone must've chucked it away. They always say that, so fuckin' innocent. Anyway, they took it, just for a joyride, they said.'

'And never brought it back?'

'That's right.'

Barnes was watching him; his mouth and his small blue eyes screwed up in a gesture of confident advantage. 'It sounds like this place,' he said at last.

Becker had had time to think. It was better not to deny it. If there was one thing a citizen had to know, it was this: Never lie to a cop. They always know when you are lying. If they know you are, you'll never get rid of them.

'Yeah, I remember now. Must have been a few weeks ago.'

'Any idea who left it?'

'No idea. I thought it must've been left by someone who'd run out of gas. And walked back to the gas station at the turn-off.'

'That looks like three kilos. Funny they didn't knock on your door and ask for some.'

'Maybe they did, but no-one home. Or, we were all out back, maybe at the creek.'

Becker shrugged, hoping he was getting away with it. 'I saw it when I came up to the gate to check for mail. Later, I came up again to see if it was still there, but it'd gone.'

'No idea who owned it?' Barnes asked.

'No idea at all.'

Barnes was smiling. 'Belonged to some kid from Melbourne. Disappeared late in September.'

'Yeah?'

'Wanted for murder.'

'Murder?'

'Yeah, a job he did in Melbourne. Quite brazen, they reckon.'

Becker froze. 'Melbourne?'

'Yeah, walked into some Dago joint one day, where all the smart Dagos hang out, and popped a bloke. They reckon the Mafia's top echelon has lunch there every Friday.'

'Yeah?'

'Straight through the back of the head, while eatin' with some mates from Griffith.'

'Griffith?'

'A lot of money in Griffith, eh?'

'You mean drugs?'

'Yeah. Anyway, the bloke got away on a big, red, Honda mountain bike.'

'Yeah?'

'And it turns out that this is the bike.'

'Someone got the number?'

'No, they had to check on everyone who had such a bike. Everyone in Victoria. Got themselves a few likely candidates, then had to narrow that down with the rough description they had. Some thin kid with a helmet. Not much to go on was it? Except he said, Hi ho, Silver?'

'Anyone can say, Hi ho, Silver.'

'That's right mate. So, this might not be the bike at all, might it? But it's funny, ain't it?'

'What's funny?'

'That a guy, who does hits on people, rides a such a bike and it turns up here.'

'I don't see the connection.'

'Yeah, well, Ballistics have worked it out that the guy, who did the job in Melbourne, used a gun also used to kill a female cop and a rich dame in Canberra.'

Becker froze. Truth was getting closer and closer.

'And the lady in Canberra was a lady, who you'd been seein' a bit of, so they say. And that lady had a lot of money. And now she's dead. You see the connection?'

'The connection?' He could hardly breathe. He lived in a world of fear. It was all about to come undone, what he'd been trying to hide from Robyn. Hide from the world.

'Yeah, mate. The lady is dead. And the bike owned by the possible killer turns up here.'

'What are you saying?'

'I ain't sayin' anything, mate. I'm just tellin' y' what it looks like.'

'Are you trying to say I hired a man to kill a woman? To get her money?'

'What?' Barnes jumped back, mock shock all over his face. 'Jesus, mate, spare the thought. I ain't tryin' to do anything'. Just pointin' out how it could look. For your sake, right?'

Becker said nothing. His heart had stopped, although strangely, he was still alive.

Barnes patted him on a shoulder.

'Anyway, for your information,' he said, 'the bloke's name was Medich, Branko Medich.'

'Who?'

'The owner of that bike. Makes y'wonder, don't it?'

'Wonder?'

'What happened to Medich.'

'I've no idea.'

Barnes smiled. Or did not smile, but grimaced. He had that kind of mouth. Every time he tried to smile it went up on one side. Like a crooked penny.

'Don't worry, Harry. We ain't gonna search your property, dig up the place.' He went to his car. 'If you hear anything, give us a ring, will y'?' He got in, looking back. 'Nice place you've got here. Must be worth a bit, eh?'

Then, with a wave and a click of his tongue, he drove off. A sort of smile too. It was the kind of smile you'd expect from a man who thought he was onto a good thing.

CHAPTER 4

HE DIDN'T KNOW what to do. No-one would believe it was a coincidence. He should never have gone along with Chook. She'd saved Robyn and the kids from the horror—the place crawling with cops, the murder of Alfredo and the killing of that little defective. But it was too risky. Something would go wrong. It always does.

Late that day his mobile phone went off.

'Becker,' he said.

'How are you, Harry?'

He had to think. 'Chook?' Then realised his mistake. 'I'm sorry, I meant Stacey.'

'The same,' she said.

'Where are you?'

'At home, in the Currawong flats, lying on the bed, reading a John le Carré and enjoying a Jack Daniels.'

He knew what she meant. The Currawong flats were a big, bald and unprepossessing block put up in the sixties by the Federal government to accommodate public servants being brought to Canberra from Melbourne. But later, as housing improved, the transferees had moved out and anyone from anywhere had a place there now. Even a cop on a motorbike. It was where Chook and Polly Politis had lived in a one-bedroom flat with a double bed, from which they could look over the grand car parks of the CBD. They'd lived there in some sort of harmony, forever quarrelling but always friends. And lovers, Becker had thought. He was not sure. Chook had said at the funeral in Canberra: 'I'm not a dyke, but Polly is the only person I've ever truly loved.' Then she shook his hand and walked off.

'What's happened?' he said.

'I have something for you.'

'What?'

'Best not to say.'

He understood. Anyone could be listening. There had been a few loose ends. No doubt the Federal police were interested in him now, possibly in her too. Why had the red Honda been found parked outside his place? What had happened to the kid? He'd never returned to some cheap rat-hole in Melbourne, where he'd dreamed of making a killing out of killing. Being someone, being fast and smart and ruthless and making a show of it. What had he done in Melbourne? It took nerve to walk into a place in full view of diners and plug a bloke. No-one except Becker and Chook knew what had happened to the kid. And he did not know what she'd done. How had she disposed of his body? Both bodies, in fact. He did not know. And did not really want to know. The less he knew, the better.

'You gonna be in town tomorrow?'

'In Wagga? You want to see me?'

'As I said, I have something for you.'

He had a fair idea what it would be—his own sidearm, an old Smith and Wesson .38 revolver.

'You mean my piece?'

'It's no longer needed as evidence,' she said.

'I don't want it.'

'It's registered to you.'

'I don't want to see it again.'

'I think you should, for safety's sake.'

He baulked. 'What do you mean?'

'I'll tell you tomorrow.'

Next day was Saturday. When he told Robyn, he said he was going to town to see Tommy Thomkins about boring for water. Tommy was an old stock and station agent in Fitzmaurice Street. Becker had worked for Tommy long ago, before he joined the police. The old windmill had gone but, even if it hadn't, it would be inadequate. He had cattle and cattle needed water. No cows or heifers, only weaners. His plan was to buy in weaners, fatten them up, then a year or two later send them to market. Hope to get double what he paid for them. That was his plan, but he wasn't allowing for farm costs. He didn't care much about costs, as long as the farm paid for itself. He wasn't worried about money. After all, Evelyn had had a lot of shares in the Royal Bank and he'd inherited half of them. And the bank was paying better than ten percent. But cattle drank a lot of water—and the creek would be unreliable in time of drought. The squeaky old Southern Cross windmill had gone years ago and the old bore would be too small to supply cattle in a drought. He'd need a new bore and an electric pump, a powerful pump. And new troughs and new yards. He was determined to make the *Nil Desperandum* drought-proof.

Robyn said she and the kids would come with him. He couldn't think of a way to stop her without making her suspicious. So they went in to Wagga. He was still driving the BMW he'd inherited from Evelyn Crowley. He would never give it up.

Each time he sat behind the wheel, he was with her again, Evelyn. And they were setting off, her driving, head up, smiling, as happy as a kid going on a picnic. They were going to escape to Perth, but it had never happened. If he had his way, he'd be buried in it, so he could in some twisted way be with her still. He had bought a four-wheel-drive Nissan, which they used for ordinary farm work and in which Robyn took the kids to the local school at the turnoff to Lockhart. There was a local school bus, but still she liked to take them. See that they got there safely. Also, she liked to be at the school, doing things. Like helping in the tuck shop and the library. Or merely chatting to other women.

Next year, the girl, Wendy, would be twelve and would be going to Wagga Wagga High School. She was a good kid, who rarely said anything, but smiled shyly or laughed with her mouth shut. When she did speak, it was mostly to her mother secretly, a hand to her mouth—smiling at Becker as if he were an unfathomable mystery. Which of course, he was. He'd told Robyn he'd been retired from the Sydney police force after being shot in the line of duty and had received a big payout. Which was not true. He'd been shot before he could tell someone high up what was happening at Kings Cross—the corruption, the payoffs, the killings. But Wendy understood her mother was mad about him and that they were somehow miraculously lucky.

The boy was nine and a bit of a rascal, always making a lot of noise, but you got used to him. He told all his mates at school Becker was a millionaire—which was true. But Becker never said so. In fact, he said nothing about money. He was nervous about his good fortune, which might at any moment go flying out the window. That was one reason why he was worried about seeing Anastacia Babchuk again. She was a Federal cop, and she'd killed a man and not reported it. And she didn't seem to be concerned about it.

He dropped them at Grace Brothers to do some shopping, but did not go to see Tommy Thomkins in Fitzmaurice Street. Instead, he walked up Baylis Street to the Hovell, which was not a hovel but a hotel named after William Hovell, who, with Hamilton Hume in 1827, pioneered a route from Yass, north of the present day Canberra, all the way down to Port Phillip. In the old days when wool was king the Hovell had been the only place to stay in Wagga. By the 1970s it had become pretty well musty and beery and rundown. But not long ago someone had got their hands on it and tarted it up. Now, in 1995, it looked like a fairly high-class boozer. Even so, the Hovell was a violent pub, especially on Friday and Saturday nights. Which was half its attraction.

When Becker walked in, Chook was sitting at a table near the front window, holding a beer. Didn't move or change her expression when she saw him, not a flicker. She was not a chicken, far from it. She was a senior constable, who'd worked mainly in witness protection when Becker had known her in Canberra. Dressed now more or less in her working gear—leather jacket, t-shirt, blue jeans, hair pulled back, not in a ponytail this time, but in a knot at the base of her skull. Hair the same pale gold—the kind you'd expect to go white pretty soon. Footwear different, however. Instead of police work boots, she was wearing motor-cycle boots. She was very tall, and had broad shoulders, slim hips and no noticeable breasts. Looked more like a male truck driver than a woman—the kind you might see driving a road train across the back-blocks of Queensland, a hundred sheep up behind. She had everything a truckie would have—except the suntan, the dick and the tattoos. She was called Chook because of the common *mis*pronunciation of her family name, Babchuk, which in Ukraine is pronounced Bab*chuck*, not *chook*. She hated the nickname and often threatened to shoot anyone who called her Chook, but she never did. At first sight you would have thought her a hard-faced bitch you'd never want to know. But Chook was all right, once you got to know her. Full name was Anastacia Babchuk, which she knew was a mouthful, so normally she went by Stacey Babchuck.

She lifted her glass in a casual sort of salute.

'What can I get you, Harry?'

'What are you drinking?'

'Just a Hahn.'

He'd never had Hahn beer, but he said the same. She raised a hand and a girl in an apron wiping another table came over. 'Yes, ma'am?'

'Another Hahn, honey,' Chook said, 'and don't spill it this time.'

The girl quivered. 'I'm sorry, sir. I'm terribly sorry. It's my first day.'

Anastacia nodded, her eyes following the girl. She was so fresh-faced she looked no more than sixteen, but must have been at least eighteen. You could not employ anyone under eighteen in a place that sold liquor. It was the law.

Becker was amused. 'She thinks you are a man,' he said.

'She wouldn't be the first,' Chook said.

She had a mannish sort of voice, not exactly male, but like the voice a young man might have if he had a sore throat. Not much tone to it, but hard and sharp and clear enough.

'How'd you get here?' he asked.

'Rode,' she said, taking a sip. 'On the hog.'

'Hog?'

'Harley, on my way to Melbourne.'

'Business again?'

'You could say that.'

'Police?'

'Personal.'

'Anything to do with—'

Becker could not quite say it. He looked around, but they were well out of ear-shot. There were only a few other drinkers in the room, plus the pretty girl and the barman filling their glasses.

'You could say that.'

Becker was afraid, although neither was saying anything that could later be pinned on them.

'You don't mean—'

The girl came back with the beers balanced on a small silver tray. Very carefully, she set them down, glasses full to the brim, topped with foam. Did not spill a drop this time. She looked up at Stacey, waiting. The big cop nodded. The girl smiled. It was a sweet smile, anxious to please. They waited for her to depart.

'You don't mean it?'

'I mean it.'

Becker was shocked. Chook would not leave it alone. He didn't want to get involved, but he was involved if not legally then morally. He owed her one. Without her, his marriage would be ruined. If Robyn knew what had really happened at the farm, she'd be horrified—a woman like her, incapable of thinking ill of anyone.

'You aren't going to—?'

She nodded. 'Yeah.'

'You mean get one of them?'

Nodded again.

'Jesus, Stacey!'

'I've been thinking about it a long time.'

'You mean terminating?'

He looked around. The girl was now quite near, looking out of a window, perhaps hoping to see someone. Chook's lips moved, as if saying 'yeah' again, but no sound came out. Becker didn't know what to say except to whisper, 'Don't do it. For Christ's sake, don't do it!'

'Just one, the *capo dei capi* as they call him, the big chief.'

'The fat man? The one who was there when they shot Vince?'

'Yeah.'

'This bloke called Terracini?'

'That's him.'

'He's the *capo*? Down in Melbourne?'

Babchuk shrugged. 'Maybe.'

'Why isn't he behind bars? You've got his card. Buster found it by the lake. That puts him there, where they killed Torrence.'

'He says someone stole it.'

'You believe that?'

'Nope.'

'And Adams won't talk?'

'Not in a thousand years.'

Adams had been the cop who'd killed Torrence. Actually, the cop who'd pulled the trigger. He was at the lake in Canberra with Torrence and the fat man. Torrence wanted more money for spying on Evelyn Crowley. But the fat man thought he'd become a liability. Asking too much and knowing too much. So, the fat man had given Adams the nod and Adams had gone behind Torrence and shot him in the back and then in the head—just to make sure. Then had pushed him into the lake, late at night. The Mafia had wanted to know what Mrs Crowley was going to do. She was talking to an ex-cop named Becker. Was she telling him what was going on at the Royal Bank? Where her husband was a big noise. Through which they were laundering millions, sending it to Italy. But where in Italy? That's what the police had wanted to know. So did the *Carabinieri* in Rome. From the police's point of view, the problem had been to get someone to talk before the Mafia woke up that they were being watched. As it had turned out, Evelyn had known next to nothing. But they killed her none the less.

'And you're going to kill him? Terracini?'

'If he turns out to be the one.'

'You think he ordered the hit on Evelyn?'

'Maybe.'

'How?'

'I know where to find him.'

'Where?'

'South Yarra.'

'What's he do?'

'Runs a lingerie shop in Chapel Street, Prahran.'

'A lingerie shop?'

'Who'd have thought of that? The Mafia running a lingerie shop? It's a perfect cover.'

'Jesus, Chook.'

'His wife does the selling and he does the books. Which leaves him plenty of time for other interests.'

'Such as?'

'One of them's an import business in South Melbourne.'

'Importing tomato cans from Italy—full of coke, I suppose?'

'Something like that.'

Becker's heart was wriggling. 'Ah, Jesus, Stacey!'

'He killed Evelyn too, remember.'

The girl had gone back to the bar.

Becker leaned forward, whispering: 'Let it go. You don't know what you'd be up against! Look, Evelyn told me, it's not one bloke, it's a whole family, maybe more than one family. There'd be too many. You can't kill 'em all. And anyway, the Melbourne cops'd soon see a pattern. Or someone would talk, suggesting who might be doing it. For revenge, you hear? It's too fucking obvious.'

Babchuk had been drinking while he'd made his little speech. She took her time, put down the glass and thought about it.

'I don't care,' she said, 'even if I do die.'

'Don't be stupid.'

The girl ran to the window again, looked out. Then hurried back to the bar. Babchuk watched her all the way. 'I was like that once,' she said, 'young and innocent. Not pretty, nothing much at all. A tearaway, couldn't get on with my folks. Then, after Mum died, I ran away, only eighteen. Ganged up with some bikies down in Melbourne. I was a bikie's moll, riding up back, hanging onto his cock for dear life. Yeah, I was fucked stupid some nights, and not always by the same bloke. I was mad, high on drugs and booze and Christ knows what else, for a year or two.'

She was fiddling with the empty glass.

The girl came over. 'Can I get you something else?'

'Not for me, honey.' She looked at Becker, who shook his head.

The girl danced away, again running to the window, again disappointed.

'What happened then?'

'I tried to run away with another guy. He wasn't a piece of shit like the others. In fact, he was a cop.'

'Working undercover?'

'Yeah, a new guy named Red. Must have had another name, but I never heard it.' She glanced out the window. 'I think I was in love with him, as much as I could have been in love with any man then. We didn't have sex. I couldn't then, I was as sick as a dog. He told me to get out, there was going to be a raid. But they shot him, the others I mean. They must have woken up to him. I broke down. The cops came, State and Federal, a joint operation. They grabbed me, sent me to hospital, the Austin in Heidelburg. Pumped be full of anti-biotics, but that did not work, not completely. They didn't want to operate, but they did. It was touch and go, so a specialist told me. Then I got over it, slowly but surely. After two weeks at the Austin, a man came to see me. He was the one who'd led the raid. I was pretty scared, but he said nothing would happen to me, if I helped them. So I helped them. Told them everything I knew.'

She drank some Hahn. He waited.

'I had a private room at the Austin. They took it all down, everything I said on tape. I was there nearly four weeks, then they took me to a place in Greensborough for people who'd suffered heavy trauma. Weaned me off drugs—except the occasional joint, but that's only for professional reasons. To get people talking, like having a beer.

'One day, the guy who'd rescued me came in and said I was coming along fine. The doctors were pleased with me. The commissioner was pleased with me. Because of me they'd been able to break the ring. Two million dollars' worth of coke at street level had been seized. Plus, thousands in cash and a lot of weapons, some of them really nasty, like assault rifles and machine pistols. I said, "What's going to become of me now?" He looked at me for a while, sort of smiling. Then he said he'd like me to meet someone.

'He went out and came back with an old man wearing a very good suit and a pol-ka-dot bow tie and grey hair brushed straight back without a part. He had a dark-grey little moustache and looked like a very old Errol Flynn.

"You've done a splendid job, my dear," he said.

"Everyone is thrilled. How about joining us?"

"The cops?" I said.

"The Federal Police," he said.

"You'll be quite safe. Part of a family."'

'How did you feel about that?'

'Astonished, but that's what I wanted, a family.'

She was gazing at nothing. Or everything in her life. As she'd been speaking, she'd been tapping her glass on the table.

The girl appeared again, pushed by the barman. 'You're sure you won't have another?'

They looked at each other. The poor kid, she was trying. 'A Jack Daniels,' Becker said, 'on the rocks.'

'And you, sir?'

She was addressing Babchuk, who'd been about to decline. After all, she had to ride to Melbourne today, but changed her mind. 'Make mine a Jack too,' she said. 'No rocks.'

The girl dashed off.

They had a couple of whiskeys, tossing them down. Becker checked his watch. It was ten to twelve. 'I have to go,' he said.

'So do I,' she said.

Chook stood up, picking up her helmet. It had been sitting on the floor on the other side.

Becker paid for both and they walked out. 'Where's your bike?'

'Up here a bit.'

He hoped she'd forgotten about the Smith and Wesson, but she had not. Chook went to the Harley, opened a saddlebag and pulled out a fat parcel, not big but heavy. Becker took it, alarmed. Something bad would come of this. It was a snub-nosed Smith and Wesson .38, a Police Special, barrel only two inches. Easy to draw and fire quickly, but reliable only up to about ten yards—if you were lucky. As she'd bent, her jacket had opened. Becker saw the butt of the Colt .38 under her left arm. The automatic with which she'd killed the kid. She caught him looking, said nothing. But she smiled.

'You don't like guns, Harry?'

'It reminds me too much of Canberra.'

'Yeah? Everything reminds me of Canberra.'

He knew what she meant. Polly had been her partner. They'd been detailed to protect him and Evelyn until the Feds could get them out of Canberra. But they had failed. Polly was dead and so was Evelyn. One great operational fuck-up if ever there was one.

'And this—' She pulled a folded form from a pocket in her jacket. 'This is for you to sign and post back to Canberra. To prove you received it.'

Chook put on her helmet, then extended a hand. She had a grip like a pipe wrench.

'So long, Harry,' she said.

Then stepped onto the big, black bike and pressed a button. Immediately the engine sprang into life, began to purr sweetly, discreetly. He watched. She was a good woman, but revengeful, scary. Taking the law into her own hands. Yet he admired her, a braver human than he would ever be.

'Have a good trip,' he said.

Anastacia Babchuk had a chiselled sort of face, long narrow eyes when she smiled. High cheekbones, something Asiatic about them. And her nose, it was square cut, like a small hatchet. Her eyes were disconcerting. Unnaturally blue, bright, shining. Made you feel that something not quite human was watching you. Becker didn't know much about Ukrainians, but thought they were some sort of Slavs in eastern Europe, who'd had a bad time during the war. Everyone had a bad time in any sort of war, he knew. His father had been killed in Vietnam.

'Nice to see you again,' she said.

Then she was gone.

He went to the BMW and stowed the parcel in the boot. When he closed it, a woman said: 'Excuse me.' It was a parking inspector, the woman who'd caught him on his first day back in Wagga. That had been outside the Gumnut cafe, this was outside the Hovell.

'I haven't been here an hour,' he said.

She pointed at a sign over his head. 'It says quite clearly, No Parking Loading Zone.'

'Loading zone?'

'This is where they deliver the barrels,' she said.

She was a fine figure of a woman, certainly not the kind to argue with. Quite handsome in her smart uniform. She raised her pen and pad, looking at his NSW plate. 'So, you're one of us now? I'm not letting you off this time.'

He was going to protest, but what did it matter about a few dollars fine? After all, he was probably the richest man in the district in terms of ready cash, if only people knew. But they would never know. They must never know about Evelyn.

Just then, the girl ran out. 'Mum, Mum, I've been watching out for you. I got the job!' Then she saw Becker. 'I was right, wasn't I, sir?'

'Didn't spill a drop,' he said.

'All right,' her mother said, 'but next time you won't be so lucky.'

CHAPTER 5

THE FIRST THING Becker had to do was hide the revolver, but he had no idea where. Any place he chose in the house would certainly be discovered by Robyn, who spent much of her days polishing and cleaning and putting things away. Worse, it might well be found by one of the children, or both. Even if he did find a place to hide it, he might need it in a hurry. He could hide it in the machinery shed or even dig a hole among the trees. And it would be tragic for his family if, under threat of death, he couldn't remember which tree. He tended to hang onto it, still loaded. He vacillated, wanted to keep it ready at hand, and yet wanted to get rid of it. Robyn would ask why he had a revolver. What was he afraid of? He'd have to tell her some lie, as he'd already lied about the mysterious woman at the kitchen window that day.

Becker walked down to the Gumnut cafe. Usually, when in town, they had lunch at the Gumnut. They were already seated when he arrived, looking pre-occupied and worried, as if something bad had happened, or was about to happen.

'Beat you to it, didn't we, kids?' she'd said brightly, almost adoringly. She thought he was the most splendid of men, the right age, only three years older than she, and well-mannered. And, being a retired policeman, was in many ways a man of the world, a world she did not know, but was anxious to hear about. She was always waiting for him to say something about his past. But all he'd said was he'd been married. He'd been in the police force, he'd taken a bullet in the line of duty. And he'd been paid off. None of which was untrue, but he did not tell her about the other things. And never mentioned Evelyn.

'Harry?'

He was thinking of something, she knew. He was always thinking of something, like a man who had done something of which he should have been proud but wasn't, like a man who'd been to war and never wanted to talk about it. Her father was like that. No-one mentioned the war.

'Harry?'

'Oh, sorry, what?'

They were sitting in the corner, where he'd been when she'd spotted him on that day months ago, eating a chicken and mushroom pie, thoughtfully looking out the window at nothing. And she'd gone in and said nervously, because she was full of shame for having stood him up back in Canberra, Excuse me, are you Harry Becker?

'We saw you, didn't we, kids?'

'Yeah!' the boy said. They were waiting for a salad and bruschetta each for him and her, and apple pie with lots of cream for the kids.

'At the Hovell,' she explained.

He jumped a little, trying to cover it. He'd been caught out.

'Oh, yeah—' He couldn't think fast enough.

'The tall blonde who came for the old man?'

He was surprised. She had not previously described Chook as a tall blonde. She must have seen more of the visitor than he'd thought.

'Tall? Was she?'

'Yes, dear, she was taller than you.'

Of course, that was it. Chook had been standing beside him at the window. And she really was taller than he. Over six feet.

'Ah, yeah, I'd been down to see Tommy, but he was not there. His girl was there and I could have waited a while, but I knew I had to meet you. So, I came back. Thought I'd have a drink while waiting. Walked in and there she was, the same woman and—' He was beginning to blush. He'd not gone down to Fitzmaurice Street to see Tommy. He hated having to lie. He didn't want to lie to her, but he didn't want her to know the truth about Chook. That would lead to everything that had gone wrong in Canberra. If she found out, she'd wonder what the hell sort of man she had married. She might want to clear out, get away from him, take her kids and run.

They were staring at him, all three.

'So you had to say hullo?'

'Yeah, especially as she had seen me. And so I had to buy her a drink and—' He dried up. He could not go on lying. Not to a good woman like Robyn. He didn't love her, but he liked her immensely. She was what he'd needed. Especially after what had happened in Canberra.

A waitress appeared, holding the two bruschettas. He waited while she served them.

'Thanks, Heather,' Robyn said.

'I'll be back in a tick, children,' the woman said, smiling. They were all such pleasant women at the Gumnut. He picked up a knife and a fork, not sure whether it was the right way to attack bruschetta.

'You can cut it and then pick it up in your hands,' she said. 'No-one will mind.'

'Oh, right.' He'd promised himself he'd never lie to his new wife. Now he'd done it.

'So?'

'What?'

The waitress came back with the ice creams, each with a wafer and a cherry on top.

'Hooray!' the boy said. 'I'm gonna eat the cherry first.'

'Going to,' his mother said. 'Not gonna.' She'd made her first cut into her food. 'Harry?'

'Yeah?'

'What happened to the old man?'

'What happened? Yeah, well, he wanted to go to Los Angeles.'

'Los Angeles?'

'He had relatives there, so he said.'

'Did he?'

'She said it was all in his mind. He was, you know—'

'Wandering?'

'Yeah.'

She finished a mouthful. 'She knew him, then?'

'Yeah, she did. She'd been asked to find him, check along the road. He was hitching rides to Wagga to get on a plane to go to—'

'Los Angeles?'

'To Sydney first then to Los Angeles.'

'Did he have any money?'

'None at all. He wanted me to give him a hundred-thousand dollars.'

'A hundred-thousand?'

'Yeah, well, he was crazy.'

'The poor man.'

He was relaxed now, lying quite easily. He thought he was safe. They ate in silence for a while, the children watching them. Already they were halfway through the ice cream. The boy had eaten both the wafer and the cherry first. The girl was saving hers for last.

'Like Mum,' he added involuntarily, but it was what he thought of his mother. Also, it was a change of subject.

He'd taken Robyn to Kirralee twice to see her, the first time before they were married. Robyn had wanted to invite her to the church wedding. She was a strong Anglican, but Becker had talked her out of it. Iris would be an embarrassment, not knowing what was going on and sure to ask more than once: Who is that girl holding his arm at the altar? Is it Shirley Bascombe? Or his cousin, Biddy Barnes, the one who fell off her bike and smashed all her teeth?

And the second time was when she'd had a stroke. She'd been in hospital then, but she'd not known him. All she could do was lie there and grunt now and then to herself. Or call for the nurse, asking quite loudly: Where was her pink cardigan? She'd looked everywhere, but could not find it. Someone must have stolen it. Ignoring her son and her new daughter-in-law, as if they must be visiting someone else and had wandered into the wrong ward.

Pitiful to see. They shouldn't go that way, as mad as they might be. Even if they'd had a bad life, wracked with worry, and she being a war widow. All because of those dreadful Asians.

Robyn was watching him. She too knew about war. Her own father had been at Tobruk. They'd held out there for six months against the Africa Corps. But he never talked about the war. And he never went to an RSL club, to drink beer and play the pokies. He'd been a wheat farmer out Lockhart way. Three years ago he'd given up, walked off, couldn't take it any longer. The long dry and the debts. He'd moved to Wagga with his wife and settled in a small weatherboard near the railway station. Settled down to playing bowls by day and listening to freight trains in the night.

'I'm sorry,' she said, touching his hand.

They finished the meal in silence, the kids watching them. They knew something had happened they didn't understand. But they sensed it, in the way a pet dog will sense it, feel it, worry about it with you.

'I've finished mine, Mum,' the boy said. 'Can I have another?'

'May I have another. No, you may not, Terry.'

'That was lovely, Mum,' the girl said. She always ate slowly, and spoke slowly, and thought slowly. She was not unintelligent, just thoughtful and watchful. Wendy never asked for more or complained about anything. Like her mother, she was thankful for what the good Lord provided in His wisdom each day.

'Coffee, Harry?'

'No, er, well, perhaps I'd better.' It was not that he needed coffee to keep himself awake. He had whiskey on his breath and Robyn would have noticed. He was thinking about Chook. If she found the fat man—the man who'd ordered the hit on Polly—she would kill him.

Robyn ordered two long blacks, then returned to the subject tactfully.

'So, does she live in Wagga, then?'

'Who? Oh, the woman? No, no, in Griffith, where the old boy lived. He was Italian.'

'Was she Italian?'

She was being nosy, against all her rules. But she had to ask.

'Italian? Oh, no. Not everyone in Griffith is Italian.'

'So, what was she doing in Wagga?'

'I didn't ask. Shopping, I suppose. Or business. Anything.'

She seized an arm, patted him. Trying to smile reassuringly.

'I'm not being jealous, Harry,' she said. 'I just wonder happened to the old man.'

'Yeah, sure.'

'Please believe me, Harry.'

He nodded, eating.

'Please, dear,' she said again

He chewed and nodded. 'No problems, Robbie. It's all right.'

But it was not all right. He knew it and she knew it. And the kids looking at them knew it was not, but they didn't know why.

She loved him. It was not fair he was so often far away. Thinking about something terrible or something wonderful, it was hard to say. She accepted him as she found him, thankful for every day with him. After what had happened to her first husband—a terrible smash on the Hume Highway going south, the truck bursting into flames—she knew God had understood her grief, had taken pity on her and sent her a good man named Harry Becker. But there still remained the man in Canberra. She had fled from him. He was a Vietnam vet, and he might turn up at any time. But she could face him next time. She was now married to a former policeman who looked tough and had tough friends.

That was the thing about Harry Becker. She felt safe.

When they arrived home, they were surprised. The big, red Holden was parked near the gate, which was closed as they'd left it. It looked menacingly official, a hefty red car with a blue checked pattern along the sides. Sirens and lights and antennas piled up on top like a battery, not so much of firepower as of authority. The law has called and you'd better have your story straight before you open your mouth.

'Jesus,' Becker said.

The boy hopped out and opened the gate. They could hear the dog barking behind the house. He wasn't as smart as the dog Becker had encountered when he'd visited this place nearly twenty years ago. When he was working for Tommy Thomkins, stock and station agent in Wagga. This dog couldn't open and close gates, but he was a good watchdog. He was a nut-brown kelpie named Nutty and he was barking frantically, aggressively.

They were getting out of the BMW when Barnes appeared from one side.

'Ah, g'day,' he said. 'Thought I heard y's.'

Becker did not reply, but Robyn did. 'Oh, hullo, Barry. How are you?'

'Great,' he said. 'Yeah, great. Was just passin', you know, an' thought I'd drop in again. See how y's are gettin' on.'

He walked up cheerily, his hard, thin, crusty lips open, grinning like something from the depths of an ocean. His arms out too, walking like a gunfighter out of an old movie. The revolver on his right hip sticking out, loosely, floppily. Which was what he wanted you to see. He was an undersized cop with the over-sized confidence of a man with a badge and a gun.

'Knocked on the door, but no response, so went 'round the back, thinkin' y's'd be there. Nice dog, but. Nearly took a bite out of me. Nice place you've got, anyone can see. Can I help y' with y'shoppin'?'

He was ready to take a bag or two, but Robyn said, 'I'm right, Barry.'

'Y'sure?'

'She's right,' Becker said, stiff with unfriendliness.

He went to the door, opened it for his wife and the two kids to pass. He was going to close the door, but Barnes immediately followed, wiping his boots on the coir mat. Being thoughtful, like a welcome visitor.

'By gee,' he said, y've got a nice place here, haven't y'? All them cows. Counted forty. Prime condition b'the look of 'em. They'd be worth a bit, I bet.'

Becker said, 'You must have counted some twice. There are only thirty-five. And they're not cows, they're weaners.'

'Weaners?'

'Yeah, calves that have been weaned.'

Robyn cut in. 'Would you like a cup of tea, Barry?'

'Gee, Robyn. You gonna have one?'

'We've just had coffee.'

'Have y'? In that case, don't worry about me.'

He'd taken off his blue cap and was banging it and whacking it from one hand to the other. Dancing too in his scraped and greying with age clunky boots, the kind who never kept still. His eyes going like mad, peering at this and that. Adding it all up. 'No, no,' he added, 'just called in t'say we'd love t'come and have lunch some time. That is,' he added, 'if the invitation's still open.'

'Oh, yes, of course. I'm sure you and Harry have a lot to talk about. He said you and he were at school together.'

'Yeah, we were. Great mates, weren't we?'

Becker did not answer.

'Really?'

'Anyway, like I said, we'd love to come, Maria an' me. Just name the day, and we'll be here. I was tellin' her about y's. What a beautiful place y'had. Really enthusiastic, she is. Thinks she might know you from somewhere. Told her she's sure to be wrong.'

'Maria?' Becker said.

'Yeah, from Griffith. Been married only three or four years. No kids yet, but.'

'She's Italian?'

'Yeah, right.'

'Maria who?'

'Terracini,' the cop said.

CHAPTER 6

HE STILL DIDN'T know what to do with the pistol. It was still hidden under the spare tyre in the boot of the BMW. Then he got a bright idea. It was the dogs which gave it to him. They'd appeared one night, harassing the weaners. Pretty fierce they were, trying to bring one down. Must have been four or five of them, hunting as a pack. He'd gone out, heard Nutty barking furiously. Thought of letting him loose on them, but changed his mind. They'd probably tear him to pieces. So, he'd run to the BMW, got out the Smith and Wesson. Rushed back in the dark, almost falling over in the creek. Accidentally discharging a shot, which went anywhere in the dark. Rushed into the paddock among the cattle, among the dogs. He'd fired away at them. Then, seen one dog, eyes gleaming in the moonlight, snarling at him. So, he'd fired at the yes. Terrible howl. Rushed at the rest, firing until out of rounds. He'd stood still, not daring to move. They could have rushed at him, torn his throat out. But they'd gone. He'd slept on the verandah that night, Nutty by his side. Ears up listening. Come dawn, he'd checked. No sign of any dogs. Not the one he'd hit. Maybe he'd slunk off. Maybe the others had eaten him.

He told Robyn it was his old service pistol. Which, of course, it was not. You don't get to keep your pistol if you are a cop. Maybe she knew that, maybe not.

She didn't like what she saw. 'Oh, Harry, that thing frightens me.'

'I'll get rid of it.'

'What about the dogs?'

'I'll get a rifle.'

She couldn't argue against that, she knew. She'd been a farm girl. Her own father had had a rifle, when he'd had a wheat block out west at Wybilonga. That was years ago, before he'd had to walk off. Give up, sell the farm to pay his debts. He'd tried to teach her to shoot when she'd been a girl, but she never did learn. She'd had a brother once, but he had shot himself. She was the one who'd found him. No-one knew why he had done it. There had been a girl, they knew. Or they thought there had been a girl, but eventually it came out. The girl was married. It looked like suicide, a broken heart.

But was it suicide? The police weren't too sure. He may have been murdered and his death made to *look* like suicide. The bullet had definitely come from his own gun. But who pulled the trigger? She was sixteen, when she'd found his body in the she-oaks at the bottom of the hill, propped against a tree. A spindly, smelly sort of tree that looked as if God couldn't make up his mind what to do with she-oaks, now that he had created them. They didn't look like anything at all. And about them always was that smell, that strange smell of rotting wood. The smell she always association with death.

Her big brother had been her secret love. The kind of man she dreamed of marry-ing one day. A quiet, dependable man.

Next day, Becker went to town and bought a lever-action Winchester—not the famous Model 73, the gun which supposedly had won the West—but its successor, the Model 94, a centre-fire carbine, still with the lever action. It was quite a fan-cy-looking weapon. He could have bought a modern Winchester at less than half the price, but it had a cheap-looking stock, composite. Somehow, he felt that a gentleman farmer like himself should not be seen with anything cheap. Besides, it could hold only three to four shells, whereas the 94 carbine held seven. And he might need seven one day. As for the Smith and Wesson, he locked it in the glove box of the BMW. And did not tell Robyn.

He was uneasy. His creep of a cousin was still hanging around, dropping in when he wasn't wanted. Becker had a bad feeling about him—and anyone else he may have been linked up with. Such as his wife in Griffith. Lots of Italians in Griffith. And, he feared, many of them had by now heard of him.

When she saw the Winchester, Robyn had a fit. 'Harry? What is that? Oh, sorry, I mean *why* have you brought that thing home? A rifle, a great big evil-looking rifle. So shiny too. It looks alive!'

'For the dogs,' he said. 'And the rabbits and the duffers.'

'Duffers?'

'Cattle duffers.' He meant rustlers. 'A bloke a few miles down the road lost six one night.'

She was horrified. 'You mean you'd shoot a man?'

'Any man who steals cattle is worth shooting.'

'Oh, Harry, do be careful.'

'I'm never careful,' he said.

He'd said that to Evelyn Crowley soon after he'd met her. She'd asked him to do a job for her, find out who was blackmailing her. And everything had followed. But it was all in the past. 'I do what I have to do,' he said.

'Yes,' she said, 'yes.' Wiping her hands on the apron. 'If you think so, dear. Where will you put it? They have to be locked away, don't they?'

'In the laundry.'

'In the laundry. In a cupboard? With the linen?'

'No, don't worry. I'll get a locker built, a strong locker instead of that cupboard.'

'Oh, Harry, I'm sorry to be so jumpy. I hate guns, the awful things that can happen, accidents and—'

'No need to worry,' he said.

'If you think so, dear.'

He went to the laundry and locked the rifle away, along with a box of cartridges. Then he went to the bathroom, washed his hands. It was lunchtime. When he came back, she was standing with hands clasped across her belly.

'I have some news,' she said.

He thought she was going to say she was pregnant. Several times she'd asked him whether he'd like a baby, at the same time saying she knew he might not wish to take on the burden of another dependent. Aware, she was, that he had three children in Sydney, or two if you allowed that the first had not been his child. But it was not that at all.

'They're coming to lunch.'

'Who's coming?'

'Your cousin and his wife.'

'Oh, Jesus!'

'Harry, have I done the wrong thing?'

'You shouldn't have invited them in the first place, Rob.'

'She rang just then. I couldn't stop her—his wife, I mean. She was gushing like a galloping goof, so happy to be invited, she said. They'd love to come to lunch. He was not working this weekend, either day. What day would it be?'

'What did you say?'

'I said Sunday would be the best.'

'Jesus, Rob, I can't stand the bloke, I never could.'

'I felt I couldn't say no, after inviting them. Oh, dear, what have I done?'

She looked as though she'd burst into tears. He was sorry. He had hurt her, this good woman. He went to her, put his arms about her, even patted her, kissed her on the neck. 'No-one's going to hurt you.'

Maria Terracini was overbearingly affectionate, grasping Robyn and kissing her—as though, suddenly, they were sisters. As soon as she'd walked in, she'd set out to inspect the house, every room and nook and cranny. She plunged in, squealing, 'Ah, gee, ain't this beautiful? What a lot you've done to this old dump. We used to laugh when we was passing, didn't we, Barry? Hey, come and look at this, love, a bath with gold taps! Oh, my god, you must be loaded, mustn't they, love? And look at the kitchen, stainless everywhere. We couldn't afford that, could we? Ah, you've got a Miele! Everyone says they're the best, but cost an arm and a leg. We've only got a Samsung. Always breaking down, isn't it, Barry?'

Him following and grinning and poking at everything with his smoky-pokey little eyes. She was long and loud and loutish. Her poky little husband following her everywhere, even when she was opening Robyn's wardrobes and fingering her clothes, saying, 'Can I just have a quick look?' All he could say was 'Mmm' and 'Yeah' and 'Jesus, eh?' and 'This is nice, ain't it, darl?' They were the cousins from hell, no doubt about it. They had arrived a quarter of an hour early, as though they'd raced at high speed to get there early, be the first to have a peek.

They'd invited two neighbouring couples, farmers who did not rush anything. And who arrived with house-warming presents, tentatively offered. And smiling with the warmth of people who'd been on the land a long time. And knew their manners. Or, if they had not, then eager to learn. They knew the way you did things in the bush—with care and grace and consideration in the bad times and with an all-pervading thankfulness in the good.

The first were an old couple from across the road, Jeff and Florence Jessup, not one minute too early and the others were a Hank and Anika van der Bruggen, who'd migrated from the Netherlands and worked forty years as pastry cooks until they'd saved enough to buy a bit of Australia—six-hundred and forty acres next door on the eastern side, the earth so rich you could eat it.

Everything went reasonably well, considering. Robyn had managed to get together a menu able to satisfy, after days of worrying she would make of a mess of her first luncheon as a rich man's wife and lady of his house—so much that at one stage Becker had offered to hire a caterer so she could sit back and play the gracious hostess while he looked after the drinks. But she would not have that. It would look like failure on her part.

They ate well and she didn't drop anything in the kitchen, in which she was helped by the busybody woman from Griffith who talked non-stop, telling her about the beautiful Italian dishes she could cook, but her stupid husband didn't like them. He ate only beef steak and boiled potatoes and cabbage and carrots and mustard sauce. So fussy with his food, she said. She didn't know why she'd married him. No-one left until three o'clock, thanking them for their hospitality and saying they must come and have a drink soon, certainly before Christmas. And then they left, the neighbours. But not the new-found cousins. While his garrulous wife was helping Robyn clean up in the kitchen, Barnes hopped a bit closer. From one chair to another.

'Jesus, mate, while the ladies are out of the room, could you give me a minute?'

'What for?'

'A private talk. I can see you aren't strapped for cash at the moment.' Barnes coughed into a loose-knit hand, cleared his throat, raspingly dry despite all the Johnny Walker he'd consumed. 'I don't suppose you could help us out, could you?'

'What kind of help?' Becker could have refused straight out, but he wanted to know what this little crawler was up to.

'Ah, well, you see, things are a bit tight at the moment. I mean, I'm a bit over-committed. You know how it is, a big mortgage, lots of stuff on hire-purchase and a bit of a problem with some people.'

'What people?'

'Ah, you know, her old man, who lent the money for a deposit, a few other debts here and there. Nothing too big, but Maria keeps naggin' at me. You've got to pay your debts, she says. If you don't they'll come around and—' He didn't finish, screwed up his dry and scungy little mouth the way some men shrug, a little rattle of the head too. He was an urger, a creature who'd work on you until he got what he wanted, one way or another.

'How much?'

'Aw, you know, ten-thousand if you can spare it, maybe fifteen.'

'You want me to lend you fifteen-thousand?'

'If you can spare it, mate. You'd get it back, no worries.'

Becker stared at him, this cocky little nobody in a cop's uniform when he was on duty, prowling up and down a highway each day, trying to catch someone at something illegal, all to gain a few pats on the head. And trying to get a promotion. Probably all he ever got for hiding around corners or behind bushes to catch the occasional speeding hoon or a truckie with an overweight load. And the accidents, trucks run off the road and head–on collisions. The filthy mess, the blood. The vomit, the screaming. And dragging drunks out of cars and kids screaming their heads off. Ten years of that, every day. And what had he got for his trouble? Nothing, still a low-grade constable after ten years in the service. In fact, he was now forty years of age, a failed cop going nowhere. Becker knew he and Barnes were the same, except that he'd been caught and kicked out, whereas Barnes was still in there. Hanging on by his fingernails by the sound of it.

'No,' he said.

'No?' Barnes jumped as if he'd been hit. 'No?'

'Not one dollar.'

'Eh?'

'Get out,' Becker said.

'Eh?'

'Piss off before I hit you again.'

'Eh? By Christ—' Barnes jumped to his feet, his face livid. 'You can't talk to a bloke like that.'

'Can't I?' Becker was on his feet too. 'Take your woman and clear off. Never come here again. Get her out of here. I can't stand her yapping voice, and I can't stand you. I never could.' Becker reached for him. 'Go on, get out!'

'What? Ah, Jesus, what a good mate you turned out to be. I mean, I'm your fuckin' cousin. You understand? I'm family. Don't you forget it!'

Becker pushed him, steering him out. His wife rushed out. 'What is it? What's wrong? What's he gone and done to you, love?' She turned on Becker. 'Why're you pushin' him?'

'Just shut up and get out.'

'What?'

'Get out!'

'What? What? You can't talk to us like that. What sort of a cousin are you?'

'One who doesn't forget.'

'What? What d'y'mean?'

'This little bastard used to beat me up at school. He hated me because my dad was a soldier, a sergeant. This brainless little fuckwit liked to belt me in the guts, in the solar plexus. He like to see me cry. He was a fucking creep, a brainless nobody. I cry baby. His dad used to beat him up. I saw him once, on the ground, crying, asking for mercy while the old man was kicking him. Kicking him, you understand. Whereas, my father, my father never hit me or kicked me of insulted me or made me cry. He was a soldier. A soldier would never do such a thing.'

'What?' she said again. Maria Barnes did not have much vocabulary. She was more expression that verbose. All face and fury and bad breath. Her mouth went back so that if you were there, you would have seen long thin, twisted, horsy teeth. Almost out of the gums. Red gums, infected, you could see. And her eyes, they had gone back into her head. As if in retreat, like a crab into a shell. Creepy crawly sort of eyes. On stalks with frightened rage.

'You can't talk to him like that,' she said.

'Just clear out before I throw you out, the pair of you.'

She retreated backwards out the front door.

'You can't speak to us like that. You'll see.'

Barnes was already out the door, his pinched little eyes full of hate and humiliation.

'Come on, love,' he said, 'we're gettin' out.'

'What?'

'Grab y'bag and move y'self.'

'What? Jesus, we was havin' a lovely time, wasn't we, Robbie?'

'Are you bloody comin' or not?'

She grabbed her bag and hugged and puffed her way out. Robyn followed her husband onto the front verandah, watching them run for it. To a colourless Datsun, which had seen better days.

'Harry, what is it? What is it?'

He did not answer, watching until they'd fled in a cloud of angry noise and angry smoke.

'Harry, please, what is it? Did I do something wrong?'

'I beat him up at school. He'd been picking on me for years, because I was a little kid. Then I grew up and he did not. I had the reach on him. One day I beat the shit out of him.'

She was trembling, yet trying to work it out.

'But, you got even, didn't you? There's no problem now, is there?'

Becker thought about it, sniffing the air as if for any lingering odour.

'You never get even,' he said.

He didn't mean it that way.

He meant that Barnes was going to get even.

CHAPTER 7

HE WAS SCARED again. In Canberra he'd been scared, always afraid someone was going to hit him. A bullet from nowhere, or a road accident. Or maybe a knife in the guts one cold night on his rounds, checking places downtown, banks, car showrooms, department stores, warehouses. Those bleak and comfortless night rounds. A watchman's job. He'd come down to that. He used to be a cop in Sydney. In Canberra he'd been a nobody who worked by night, trying to make enough money to support his wife and family in Sydney. She wasn't his wife now. She'd divorced him after he'd been kicked out of the police force for corruption. Which was a big joke. Her old man was a locksmith who'd done time. He used to open safes without permission, in the dead of night. He'd hated Becker, a man who, in a rash and good-hearted moment, had saved his daughter from ignominy and possible suicide or at least a good thrashing for getting herself pregnant, by offering to marry her. They had never thanked him, not even young Adeline. Who'd divorce him when he'd been kicked out of the police without a pension. Only his contributions plus accumulated interest.

He'd thought of going back to Wagga Wagga, his hometown. But people there would know him, would ask about him. Want to know why he wasn't still a cop. So, he'd hidden himself away in Canberra. Hidden from the light of day, working at night, twelve hours a day, five days a week. Sleeping by day. Or trying to sleep. Normally he'd get out of bed about one o'clock, get dressed to go to town, have some lunch. He'd been sitting in Garema Place, eating hamburger one day in April last year. He'd finished the burger. Got up, walked to a bin to throw in the paper bag, then had spotted the handbag. A shiny bag, a quality bag, a Gucci. No woman would throw away a bag like that.

Self-consciously, he'd lifted it out. People were sitting around at tables and under the plane trees. He'd opened it. As he'd guessed, she had been mugged. Her bag snatched. No purse, no keys. But a letter, which had been opened. Addressed to Evelyn Crowley, who lived in Empire Circuit, Forrest. Anyone who lived in Forrest was sure to be worth a packet. There might be a reward...

His thoughts tended to wander. Sometimes memories came back for no reason at all, like dreams you don't want to dream. The kind of memories which keep knocking at your mind. Shouting at you, Hey, don't forget me!

One Friday night at the Cross he was called to a trouble in Roslyn Gardens—not to be confused with Roslyn Street, which ran down from Darlinghurst Road to the gardens at the bottom of the street, where there was a terrace of three-storey houses, one at least of which was known to be a brothel. Some of the boys went in there for a freebie. Even Whitford himself, blatantly. Everyone one who lived at the Cross in those days knew about the police. No-one complained.

Operations had received a call from someone living opposite, reporting a woman was screaming her head off in the street. Trying to run across the gardens, but a man was trying to drag her back. But the screamer, who sounded young and foreign, she was crying and shouting over and over in some incomprehensible lingo. Which sounded Chinese or similar.

The bloke was shouting something at her. Only one word, it seemed. Some sort of order, a barking type of order, really snappy. And a woman in a red dress with a high black collar was running out of the whorehouse and yelling at the girl and then running back inside, then outside again. The racket was going on and on.

People at a party across the road were getting irritated. And ringing the police, and saying you've got to come and do something about this racket! Not to do something to help this poor girl, mind you. They didn't give a stuff about her, only about the unseemly behaviour.

The Cross in those days was a fairly quiet place, especially off the main drags like Darlinghurst Road and Macleay Street. Some respectable people lived there, particularly down in Elizabeth Bay, by the water. Grand old homes with terrific harbour views, occupied by important people. Like bookmakers and speculative builders and senior cops, and politicians who were in it for the money and stuff the voting public.

Becker arrived within minutes of the call, sirens going and red and blue lights flashing. By which time some pedestrians and gawkers from the country, and dealers who'd been drawn to the spectacle from the park, where they had been so inconsiderately disturbed, had gathered. Becker jumped out of the patrol car and ran at the melee, which was probably the smallest melee the Cross had ever seen, but also possibly the noisiest.

The girl was still screaming and saying over and over one word, unintelligible to him, but sounded like 'No, no, no!' in anyone's language. Of course, it could have been 'Help, help, help!', but that's beside the point. He jumped out of the car and went over, charging into the fray. Alone, he was that night. His buddy's wife was having a baby. He'd been working his arse off, looking after smashes, break and enterings, drunken brawls and all the usual problems in and near the Cross on a Saturday night.

'What the hell?' he'd said. 'What the hell is going on? What's wrong with her?'

The girl, who looked about sixteen but was probably a few years older, she being some sort of Asian in a short dress, slit down the side, was rolling on the ground.

And bawling her head off, although not so loudly.

The man in a white shirt and black pants was trying to get her to her feet, but she refused.

'What's going on?' Becker said again. White shirt was holding her with one hand, while trying to deal with Becker.

'She all okay,' he said. 'No much problem.'

'So why the hell is she crying?'

White shirt had a fat round head like a football and straight black hair sticking out each side and long slits for eyes. 'Ha? Ha?' he was saying, which probably meant 'What? What?'

'Why is she crying?' Becker demanded, at the same time signalling the bystanders to keep back.

'She okay,' white shirt said.

'Take your hand off her,' Becker said. The girl was almost quiet now, looking up at Becker through her tears, as if slowly realising some sort of help in a strange uniform had arrived.

'No, no, she okay now,' the Chinese guy said. 'She no feel good. She got bad news.'

'What kind of bad news?'

'Ah, bad news from China.'

'She's Chinese?'

'Yes, she okay now. We take her in house.'

'Which house?' Becker asked. He had to ask several times, because the boss man didn't seem to want to answer. 'That place there?' Becker asked, pointing at the brothel. 'Did she run out of that place?' It was a three-story terrace, well-known for nice, clean, Asian girls.

'Yeah,' one of the spectators said, giggling. And rolling his eyes. He was high on something. So was the girl with him, not a pro by the look of her. She didn't have the short skirt and thigh-length boots of the professional. Probably a couple who'd decided the Cross was the place to be on a Saturday night. So they'd better have a snort while they were there. Get into the mood of things.

Becker was trying to get the Asian girl to her feet, but the boss man was trying to drag her away.

'Get your hands off!' Becker said. 'That's an order! Release her or by Jesus I'll arrest you!'

During all this, red dress had been running in and out of the brothel. She stuck her nose in, yelling her ten cents' worth, but Becker told her to shut up. She kept yelling at him, as if he were committing some awful public outrage. Even shaking her fists at him. And snapping at the man, one word over and over. It sounded like 'Wiffor' or 'What for'.

White shirt then released the girl.

Gently, Becker got her to her feet.

'What's your name?' She tried to say something, but it meant nothing. 'I am police, you understand? Police?' She nodded. 'Are they hurting you? Do you work in that place?' He pointed at it.

She did not reply, scared stiff as she was, glancing about rapidly like a cornered fox. For a moment Becker thought she was going to run, anywhere to escape. But she did not, especially as he spoke as slowly and soothingly and sympathetically as he could. 'Do you need help?'

She didn't seem to understand. 'You want to go back there?' He pointed at the house.

Now she seemed to get the message. Shook her head. The poor kid, probably fresh off an aircraft from Hong Kong a few days ago, thinking she was going to get a good job in a Chinese takeaway, instead found herself in a place of ill-fame.

'You want to go with me?' He pointed to the car, the lights still revolving. 'Go car with me?'

She seemed uncertain, then nodded.

'You want police help?' Probably she didn't understand a word he was saying. But the car, it got her. 'Keep back,' he said.

The boss man and the woman tried again to grab her.

Becker tapped his sidearm, hard. They jumped back.

Cautiously he led the girl to the car, opened it. Told her to get in. Or indicated to get in. She hesitated. The woman in the long dress was snarling at her.

For the first time Becker noticed that the woman was holding a small black mobile.

The girl hesitated for a moment then got in, almost dived in.

'The party's over,' Becker said to the small crowd. 'Break it up!'

He was about to slam the door on the girl when something screamed at him.

It was a single blast from a car, an angry blast. It had come hurtling out of nowhere. Not a marked patrol car but unmarked.

Next thing Becker knew, Whitford was bearing down on him.

Torrence was at the wheel. Torrence took his time getting out, as if in no hurry. And grinning in his habitual way as if everything was a great big joke.

But Whitford, he used his full weight, not only physical weight, or weight of authority, but personality. Which was vicious when he was in the mood. And he was in the mood that night.

He barked at Becker. 'What the hell're you doin'? What the fuckin' hell?' This was trouble, Becker knew. 'What are you doin' with that girl?' Whitford demanded.

'Taking her to the station, sir.'

'What the fuck for?'

'She asked for help.'

'What do you mean, help?'

Becker froze.

He'd worked for Whitford for a year or two then—a good-natured boy from the bush, who believed in the rule of law. But Whitford was a law unto himself.

'Get that girl out of that car at once!'

Becker baulked, but obeyed. He sensed what had happened. The woman in red had phoned Whitford. It was a private deal. If you ever have any trouble with the police, call me on this number. He'd made a lot of money that way, although Becker had not known then how much.

'Yes, sir.'

He opened the door and indicated for the girl to get out.

She was startled, afraid. Something had gone terribly wrong. Australia was not what she had expected. Everyone comes to Australia and makes lots of money. She was going to make lots of money, but not for herself. She'd get a few dollars and a bowl of rice each day.

Respectfully Becker waited for her to get out, a hand to an arm. He felt rotten. It shouldn't be this way. The woman in red came forward, took control. The girl was terrified, but fatalistic.

The Chinese, he thought, were like that. You did what you were told, even in Australia.

He watched as they took her back. Slow steps, head down, probably fighting fresh tears. Not screaming now, no fight left. Whitford followed them to the steps, having a word with the operators. Then he returned to Becker and took him by an ear.

'Never do that again,' he said. 'If you're ever called to intervene in anything like that, call me first. Understand?'

'Yes, sir.'

'Get back on the road. There's a bloodbath on Darlinghurst Road—one football team stuck into another.'

'Yes, sir.'

Through all this Torrence had been standing back, smiling, a hand on his weapon. He was a cool customer. Becker said to him: 'What'll become of her?'

Torrence shrugged. 'A pretty girl in a *cheongsam*? She'll be fucked to death in two or three months,' he said. 'Or, if not actually dead, she'll wish she was.'

Becker did nothing about it. He'd failed to do a lot of things back in those days at the Cross. He couldn't forget it. The Cross was with him for life. He could do nothing about it. The Cross was his own cross. He'd got fed up with it, the corruption. He'd decided to go to the top and report what he'd seen and heard. But one night, while taking out his trash, he'd been shot. Whacked in a shoulder, his right shoulder. He'd survived. But he'd been kicked out of the force for his troubles.

A voice was calling him. It was her voice. His wife was calling from the back door, and chuckling, embarrassed. He woke up, but too late. He'd been cleaning the Winchester on the back porch, but had not finished cleaning it. In fact, he'd forgotten it. He must have been holding it in mid-air for several minutes, an oil cloth in the other hand. Immobile.

'Harry,' she said, 'what are you thinking about? Sitting there, frozen like a statue.'

He jumped. He was like that, he knew. Always thinking about something.

Always thinking of the Cross and what had gone wrong here.

Or, it was Canberra and what had happened there. What had happened to Evelyn.

Or, it was about his mother and what she had said to his father, because he was going back to Vietnam. He didn't know what she'd said. That was years ago, when he was a kid.

Robyn came and sat beside him. Leaned against him.

'A penny for your thoughts,' she said.

CHAPTER 8

HE PRACTISED NEARLY every day with the rifle. He had plenty of room, a whole square mile. He'd go right up to the back fence, hide behind a few trees and blast away at tin cans, bottles and even a crude target he'd made out of a few pieces of deal board he'd found in the shed, nailing it to a tree. There he'd blast away, usually missing at first.

The manufacturer claimed the 94 was fast to the shoulder and comfortable. But Becker didn't find that to be so. He was right-handed but slow. Any impact on the right shoulder hurt. On an impulse, he tried the left side. Surprisingly, that was a lot better. He could use his right hand to work the lever and the trigger, one-two, one-two, one-two, getting faster each day until it was automatic. You had to sight and fire instantly. Becker was not sure he'd ever get it right, get it perfect. To save himself, or at least save someone. He didn't matter all that much, he knew.

Eventually he took Terry with him. A cheeky kid, as bright-eyed as a budgerigar and as chirpy. He begged to be allowed to have a go with the big rifle, but Becker refused. Robyn would have been horrified. They began to range far afield, hoping to spot a rabbit or pot a crow. Which they did. But they never saw a wild dog, not that they really expected to do so, such animals being very wary of humans and tended to appear at dusk. Some of them were part-dingo, the native dog, very aggressive and known to attack small children.

School had broken up for the long summer vacation—six weeks in which to do nothing in particular. Robyn had tentatively asked whether they were going to do anything during the school holidays. Like what? he'd asked. Well, dear, I thought you might like to go somewhere, like Canberra. That's not far from the coast, is it? We could go down there and the kids could run on a beach and splash and sun-bathe and make sand castles and, well, enjoy themselves.

He didn't wish to return to Canberra so soon, even if he would be going back a very different man, a fortunate man, thanks to Evelyn Crowley. Who had left him half the money she'd inherited from that devious little husband of hers, who couldn't take it any longer. He'd been moving millions for the Calabrian mafia thorough the Royal Bank, of which he was a big shot. Moving the stuff in such a way that no-one could work out how he was doing it or where it was going, not the Federal police and not even the *Carabinieri*. He'd gone for the high jump, eight stories down to the pavement in downtown Canberra. Surprising the shoppers landing at their feet, *splat!*

Left him half her money in bonds and shares and property and paintings, the sense of which Evelyn had thought was not there on the walls of that posh house in quiet and comfortable Forrest, where nothing ever happened that you'd want to write home about—except the killing of a lovely girl, Christine, only seventeen and longing to meet her birth mother. The other half was to go to Christine, but she died a day *before* her mother. It ended up going to the girl's adoptive parents instead. That's how Evelyn had changed it, as they were trying to flee Canberra.

To meet her, embrace her, kiss her and admire her.

He might see her, even though she was dead, once again in Garema Place, the occasional gusts of cold wind unravelling her rich-brown hair. Like a fruit cake just out of an oven, luscious. She, standing and twisting on a caballero heel, at the same time delicately pulling strands away from her face with her long and elegant Italian fingers and saying, almost shyly: 'Would you like to dine with me?'

Becker said: 'Not Canberra.'

'Sydney, then?'

'Not Sydney either.'

'Because of Adeline? And the kids down there?'

'No, not that.'

She was propped up on one elbow in the pearly darkness, watching him, lying flat on his back, one hand behind his head, his nose and chin and Adam's apple being silhouetted against the hall light intruding through the open door. It was always open to hear one of them cry in the night, the boy in particular, crying out, Dad! Although he had not seen the conflagration, he seemed to know something awful had happened to his father in the truck going south on the Hume Highway that day two years ago.

'Harry, six weeks is a long time for kids to muck around, even on a farm. And it gets so hot, the poor things.'

'Kosciusko,' he said, pronouncing it as it is spelt and not Kosciosko, as a nation of indolent yobs, even educated professors, would have it. Although, according to an out-of-work Pole he'd met in a bar in Canberra one lonely night, it was pronounced 'Koshyoosko' in Poland. You couldn't expect even a professor to know that or, if he did, would not pronounce it correctly—because no-one in this lackadaisical country cared a fuck about getting anything exactly right. Every university student he'd ever met was interested in one thing. How to make a motza in the fastest time possible. Who cared about the English language or any other language? Who cared who Kosciusko was named after? You can't eat History, can you?

'Kosciusko?' she said. 'Why Kosciusko? In summer?'

'It's cool up there, thousands of feet up.'

'There's no snow in summer.'

'You don't need snow in a place like that. I've been there more than once. It's grand. The valleys are high and wide and echoing. And the chair-lifts, they go all day, the kids thrilled to be soaring hundreds of feet up, up and up and up to Crackenback.'

'Crackenback?' She'd never heard of the place.

'It's a range, six-thousand feet up.'

'Is it near Kosciusko?'

'About twenty-five k's from Jindabyne. But, you can drive most of the way.'

'What do you do, then?'

'You walk, nine kilometres.'

'Nine kilometres to the top of Australia?' she said, flopping back on her pillow. 'We could never walk that distance. Not there and back. I mean the kids couldn't.'

'There's a lot more to see,' he said, turning over. He'd been thinking of Barnes, trying to calculate what a resentful little thug like him would do.

The bastard was sure to ask around, among cops he knew, about Becker. Hoping to discover something on him, something dirty. Something he could use. He was sure to hear about what happened in Sydney. And in Canberra too. Try again to get his hands on fifteen-thousand dollars, and never have to pay it back.

'Oh, Harry, how wonderful,' she said.

She lay there with an arm over her eyes, thinking about it, the fun and the echoes and the chairlifts. It was too good to be true. She had a considerate husband. Even now, after four months, she couldn't believe her good luck. Being kind and smart and willing to accept a stranger at a checkout in Canberra for what he was—a decent sort of chap, a bit shy and perhaps none too happy, smart in a rough way, not well dressed. But his face had lit up when she'd said, 'Hullo?' And smiled at him. And said before he could reply, 'How are *you* today?' As though she knew him well, if only from a distance or casually or incidentally for some reason. He had registered with her. And he'd smiled as though he couldn't believe she had actually remembered him and was willing to chat, as she'd flashed his stuff at the barcode reader and handed it to him. Which had happened a few times, developing a rapport, if that was the right word.

Until the last time, when he'd asked her to have coffee with him. And, surprised, she'd said, 'All right.' Which she'd done that afternoon when she knocked off. She always knocked off at two, so she'd be home well before for the kids. She'd liked him. There was a certain gentleness about him. And a sorrow.

They'd gone to Gus Petersilka's place on Bunda Street, where she'd had to keep an eye out in case Martie walked in and caught her—because he thought he owned her. That's what he'd said last time. I own you, Robbie, so don't you forget it.

She reached out a hand to touch him. 'Harry, thank you.'

He did not respond; he was asleep. Or, to put it another way, he was both asleep and not asleep. Even dead to the world, he couldn't stop thinking about Barnes.

They went to the snowfields after Christmas. They couldn't go before Christmas, they had obligations. Most of all, to her parents. Bob and Muriel Elliott had had a place at Wybilonga, out past Lockhart, well past, out in the broad wheat lands, at the end of a railway line. Before you reached the town, you could see tall and slowly deteriorating concrete silos, three rows of them, built nearly one-hundred years ago, rising up into the bleached and furious and relentless sky, which was never quite blue out there on the plains, but a smeary sort of nothingness, in which you might make out a cloud or two way up high, or not so much a cloud as a nimbus, which some angry apology for a cloud God had tried to rub out but had failed. This was the land of failure, especially in summer.

Old Bob had had a place out there, a mile or so south of the creek which seldom ran. In fact, in the old days, when Bob was a kid, you could drive a horse and buggy over it. And the dust and heat in summer terrible. The place was called The Pines, which was a bit of a joke, the pines really being a clump or copse or cover of she-oaks about an acre in area, which were not oaks at all but casuarinas. If you know that variety of tree, it's not much good for anything, not timber or firewood of even shade. Its leaves are not leaves but a scruffy and desiccated bunch of needles, among which hung clumps of hard, thick, knobbly seed pods—much like something dead caught up there, perhaps a bat or a bird or even a cat someone had shot in a moment of rage. And that smell, the smell like rotting wood and some sort of spirit, perhaps turpentine. No, not that strong. It was the smell of slow but inevitable and yet digni-fied disintegration.

Whenever Becker had them to tea or, on one occasion, to lunch, they reminded him of that smell. Not that they were a smelly old couple. Muriel smelled like soap, fresh Lifebuoy, and Bob smelled not so much of tobacco, which he smoked after every bite or sip, but of a wheat field when it's golden or just past golden. Something of the earth, which is changing slowly and sinking back into its sandy brown past.

After lunch, well into the afternoon, he found Bob sitting on the eastern verandah, out of the sun and watching the cows, the long black shadows creeping across the grass to catch them up in their own kind of sensual darkness. And Bob was smoking.

'I want to thank you, Harry,' he said.

'We love to have you. The kids love to see you.'

'For what you've done for her,' he said.

'She's worth it.'

Bob thought about his next words. 'Has she told you yet?'

'About her husband? All I know is he had a smash on the Hume, heading for Melbourne—'

'That's right.'

'And went to sleep at the wheel.'

Bob simply said, 'Hmmm.'

'You don't think so?'

'There were no skid or brake marks, you know.'

'There wouldn't be if he was asleep.'

'And there wouldn't be if he were awake.'

Becker was surprised. 'You mean he could have deliberately driven it into a tree?'

'Could have.'

'Jesus, Bob, why would a man do a thing like that. Burn himself to death?'

'Yes, why?'

'You think it was deliberate?'

Bob did not answer. He was more than seventy. He must have been, because Robyn was born when he was forty and she was now thirty-five. He'd had other children, but no mention was made of them. Bob did not look all that old. He must have been a handsome man once. Had a good head, almost patrician, and thin, white hair carefully combed across his scalp. But he'd been well exposed, a farmer all his life. When he turned and looked at you, you could see the bumps on the whites of his eyes and the yellowness in the corners. Too much sun. Too much hard yacker. And too much faith in the goodness of the Lord.

He'd walked off five years ago, during the drought. There always was a drought, every seven years, according to the Bible and every seven years according to conventional wisdom. Walked off with only a few bob in his pocket, after paying off the bank and buying the small weatherboard in Wagga, up near the railway station and the rattling trains in the night. A good man, one you could depend on, even if it cost him an arm and a leg. A softly spoken man, with an edge of good diction to his voice.

Bob did not answer, but after a while, scratching an ear, he said: 'Why would he want to leave a girl like Robyn?'

No more was said about the matter.

That was Christmas. Two days later, they packed up and left Bob and Muriel in charge and drove along the Snowy Mountains Highway, up and up through the great national park, eventually reaching Jindabyne. They could not get a place at Thredbo up in the high country, every so-called chalet had gone, booked out months in advance, and the hotel was big and bleak and noisy with boozers and boasters and blow-ins from about every part of south-eastern Australia looking for a good time, where they could relax and drink themselves stupid. They went to other places, like Bateman's Bay and ate fish and chips from a paper roll and watched the fishing boats coming in over the bar. And down to Merimbula, and paddled in the lagoon. And had a joy ride in a light aircraft. All of them, even though Robyn was scared stiff. It being her first flight.

Then they came home, happy but anxious. Bob Elliott said nothing whatever had happened. But there had been one small thing. A strange man walking through the property, slowly and casually as if he had a perfect right and did not need to ask anyone's permission, holding a rifle, a long-barrelled model with scope on top. As if he were a hunter. There was nothing worth shooting around here, no wild deer or horses or pigs or anything a hunter would want.

Bob had gone out and asked him what he'd wanted. The man, anywhere between forty and fifty, had simply said, 'Nothing'. And walked on, shuffling and scuffing his way through the grass, long now but drying out fast, there not having been good rain for a month, the summer settling on the land like a hot-press you might see in a steam laundry.

Bob had watched him, strolling to the front fence, where there was no car or truck or other form of conveyance as far as he could see. Having climbed through the wire fence, the nonchalant and indifferent fellow had ambled off down the road.

Becker wasn't greatly worried. You had to expect that sort of thing in the country, people out for a day's hunting, although in the district there was nothing worthwhile taking a shot at. But, still, they did it. If you had spent a lot of hard-earned money on a hunting rifle, you had to kill something, hadn't you?

A few days later he was out walking with the boy, thinking he might let him hold the Winchester. Terry was now ten, about the same age as he himself when his father had died. He would slowly and carefully introduce the boy to hunting. If he was going to live on a farm, he had to learn some day.

They'd walked up the creek to the top fence, which wasn't high ground at all, the country around there being almost flat, it being a riverine plain flooded by great silt-bearing torrents over millions of years and would grow anything. They went to his shooting ground, where Becker took a few shots at the old target, now mangled and splintered and shot almost to pieces and practised his speed.

Then he said, 'Want to hold it? Get the feel of it?'

'Yeah!' the boy yelled. He was always yelling, rowdy. But you got used to it. 'Can I really?'

'Come here. Look, take it this way, one hand under the stock behind the trigger and the other under the forearm. And feel the weight. It's much too heavy for you. Hold it, get used to it, feel it, take it as if it's a baby, gently. Now lift it a bit, let it down, lift it. Then turn it this way and—'

There was a shot, an ear-splitting shot.

It could *not* have come from the Winchester, the magazine of which he'd taken out. And there was nothing in the breech, he'd double-checked. Bark chips fell, one piece hitting an ear. The boy jumped, shocked, scared.

'What the hell?' Becker pulled him down, guessing the shot had come from up the hill, although there was no real hill, a gentle rise or swell like a stationary wave in the endless land. He crouched over the boy, dragging him behind the tree.

On the ground lay fresh chips of the bark and sappy flesh of the yellow box, shattered and disfigured by an idiot.

Becker looked out, one eye, then two.

He could see nothing.

Not a soul, not a shape, except a few trees and an occasional wattle bush.

The shot could have come, he realised, from farther upstream, over the back fence. The shooter must be behind a tree or bunkered down in the creek bed, not wet for weeks. He could not be lying or squatting in there. That was a wheat field and his neighbour had finished harvesting more than a month ago.

The field was totally bare except for the stubble, dotting the slope with twisted and battered stalks looking like thousands of crippled stick figures on a battlefield. Becker stood up slowly, wishing the Winchester had a scope. He'd bought it, not for hunting, but for close-range protection.

'Terry, crouch down low and get back to the house. Duck from tree to tree as fast as you can. I'll follow you.'

They did that, the boy ducking and Becker creeping backwards, loading the few shells left in a pocket, covering the boy, his gaze jumping from spot to spot in case the fellow showed up. He had a good mind to shoot the bastard and apologise later. But the bastard did not show. Either he had slipped away unseen or he was still up there lying low in the creek.

Nothing more happened. Then he walked back, mostly backwards, from tree to tree until there were so many trees between him and the marksman that he thought he was safe. Then dashed to the back door.

He was not going to tell Robyn, but the boy couldn't keep his mouth shut. She came out to meet them. 'Oh, Harry, who would do a thing like that? Right at you, just above your head?'

'I don't know,' he said. 'But if he comes back, I'll shoot him.'

CHAPTER 9

HE HADN'T HEARD from Anastacia for weeks and it worried him. Not that he'd really thought he should have heard. She was not going to tell him on a phone that she'd killed someone. She wasn't that stupid. She'd said, or at least had hinted, she was going to Melbourne to find the man, whose name had been on the credit card picked up by Buster Keaton after Vincent Torrence had been popped one night by the lake. The Feds had already interviewed the man, a businessman in Melbourne, who sold bras and girdles and gee strings and other pretty unmentionables in Chapel Street, but he'd said someone had stolen his card. He had nothing to do with any shooting in Canberra. He wasn't even in Canberra at the time, he'd said.

So, who was the fat man?

What had happened? Had she found him? Had she killed him or not? Not a word. Not a hint or a whisper or nudge or story in *The Daily Bulletin*, which usually ran hot wire stories as they used to be called. There was nothing, not a skerrick. Nor in the interstates held at the local library. He dared not make inquiries; people might wonder why. That was the last thing he wanted. He could call a mate and ask him to check with Melbourne. He didn't have any mates in any force, except old Bob Fricker at Queanbeyan. Fricker would have been reluctant to help, he being only two years from retirement.

Still, he was edgy. He was, in effect, a party to a murder, if in fact the crime had been committed. She had not committed a crime when she'd shot the kid. That was okay, she'd done her duty in saving him from death. But disposing of a body without notifying the authorities was a crime, although perhaps not serious. She'd get a scolding from her superiors, if they found out she'd done all this in secret. But the real problem was that he knew what she had intended to do in Melbourne—kill a man. And if she did kill him, he would be an accessory before the fact. And that would be serious. He had no doubt that she would kill him, if convinced he was the *capo*, the one who'd ordered the hits on Torrence and Evelyn. The one who'd killed Polly Politis in order to get at Evelyn. Babchuk was going to get satisfaction. There'd be no stopping her. She seemed to be a woman of cold-blooded rage.

Toward the end of the long school break, Becker saw the hunter.

He'd been watching an electrician installing the new pump above the eastern side of the creek, when he looked up and saw the man.

He was walking across the property, slightly downhill. Must have jumped a fence up there, followed the creek. Average height, a bit porky and had a beard. Not any kind of beard, but one about two inches long with a little curl at the point. Not exactly a van Dyke, a bit too scruffy for that. And a moustache, which at that distance looked gingery, like Becker's own moustache, but not so dark. Like the beard, it was more grey than gingery.

'Nearly there,' the electrician said.

'Excuse me a minute.'

Becker went after the stranger, to intercept him, to ask what the hell he was doing on private property? But he had to be careful. This man was holding a long-barrelled rifle with a telescopic. Holding it in his right hand on his right side, so Becker could not see it well. But he knew it was a very powerful rifle, something you saw Americans in movies using to bring down deer. The man did not stop. He kept on walking toward the fence and the highway. The more Becker increased his step, the more the intruder edged away. Increasing his own step. Watching Becker warily. Glancing at Becker, then at the road he was heading for. Then back at Becker, then at the road. Increasing speed. Eyes going back and forth. Like a scared kid about to break into a run, but he didn't. He kept going.

'Hey, you!' Becker said.

The fellow twisted or jumped or jerked at the call. But he did not reply.

Then he was at the fence. Grabbed a wire and slipped under. Cut through some young wattles and climbed a small bank and onto the highway.

Becker called from the fence: 'Come back here!'

No answer. He could hear the man behind the wattles, or at least sense him. But couldn't make him out. Just an impression of a thick and sturdy creature, standing still and breathing, and watching out. Not more than a few feet away.

'I want to talk to you.'

A tourist bus went by, swishingly, gravel flying, faces at the glass.

'Are you the bloke who shot at me a few days ago?'

No reply, only the breathing. Heavy breathing, like that of a man who had trouble breathing with his mouth jammed shut. Almost snorting.

'Are you the one? Nearly blew my head off up the creek? And frighted the wits out of the boy?'

Becker was edging along the fence to get a better view.

The man wore a cap, not a hunter's cap but some sort of old-fashioned headgear. Raggy, Becker thought. Not a scarf, not a turban. Like they used to wear in the jungle, because of the sweat. In Vietnam.

'You been in a war?'

Suddenly he could see the man, standing side-on.

Rifle elevated, pressed against his chest as regulations specified, in case you shot a foot off or shot a buddy. Whiskered, and fat in the face and body and tired of living. There was an eye, looking at Becker. It was the eye you saw in the face of a small child, perhaps six or seven, scared he's going to get a whipping. He's done wrong. Or, he hasn't done wrong and doesn't know why everyone is looking at him like that. It was a frightened eye, wide open and crazy. The kind of eye you wouldn't want to look into too deeply for fear of seeing yourself, scared witless, never knowing where the bullet would come from or when. Or who'd shot it.

And when it did come, you wouldn't even know you'd been shot. You were so scared. All you knew was feet, perhaps in boots and perhaps not, were approaching through the bush and bamboo and everlasting slush. And a rifle pointing down, probingly.

You're looking up, afraid the face is not an Australian face, but something below a *red* sweat band and some sort of slanty eyes and sloping head. And an enigmatic smile, like the smile on a skinny and dirty and ill-fed peasant, holding a Soviet-made Mosin-Nagant carbine, staring at you.

And thinking something you would never know before he fired. Straight through the skull. This man had that sort of stand and stanch, like a man waiting stock-still under cover, unsure whether he should twist around and open fire or run for his life. Crash out of there.

'You were in Nam?' Becker asked.

The guy did not answer, but he breathed as if it were a release, Vietnam.

'My old man was in Nam,' Becker said, hands on the top wire. 'In '68,' he added. 'You there then?'

The man made some sort of sound, maybe a quick snort. Perhaps a snuffle. May have, for a moment, taken his hand off the trigger, relaxed a little, perhaps opened his mouth to say something. Changed his mind.

'He didn't come back,' Becker said.

Then thought he should add something, like 'Poor bastard,' or 'Bloody shame, that' or 'We all miss him' or 'But that's life.' Anything you could say was pretentious, as though you didn't have a hole inside you, a cavern.

'What outfit were you in?'

Then the man said something, not a word. More like a last gasp.

Early in his first posting, Becker had had to go to a man who'd smashed up on the road out south of Cootamundra. The car was pushed in at the front and the driver had been jolted out, just his head. The rest of him was tangled in shattered steel. Across the road a truck was on its side, crates of oranges and lemons and grapefruit spilled. There was no sign of its driver. Must have been thrown out, or crawled out and stumbled into the scrub, and perhaps died. The man in the car was not left much of a man. His legs were mangled and held tight in the desolation.

'You okay, mate?' Becker had said, he being then only a young copper, straight out of Goulburn college.

It was the most stupid thing he had ever said. The man was gasping, mouth and eyes wide open. He tried to answer, no doubt not to answer such a foolish question, but to say something like: Get me out of here! Or perhaps he knew already he was not going to get out, unless they cut off his legs. Even if they did, he was doomed because his pelvis and his spine had been crushed. He'd gasped something, over and over. In the distance, a siren was wailing, getting closer and closer.

Becker had kneeled down and said, 'Hang on, mate. They'll be here soon.'

He was dead before the ambos could stick a needle in him.

The man behind the bushes did not try again.

'You want to come in and have a beer?' Becker asked.

Already the fellow was departing.

He walked away unseen. Becker waited, hoping he'd come back and have a beer and talk about Vietnam, but he did not. When he climbed through the fence and the wattles onto the road, the man had walked some distance. A slow, slovenly sort of walk, hopelessly. The rifle held high, not on a shoulder, but held like a man would do when walking through water, a lot of it, mud and slush and water lilies.

Becker walked up to the house, thinking he would tell Robyn to be careful. There was a fellow walking about with a high-powered rifle. She was not at home. She'd taken Wendy into Wagga for her first day at high school and had said she'd do some shopping, provisions for a week. She'd not returned yet. When she did, he did not tell her.

She was always jumpy, scared of guns. Scared of men with guns.

The electrician called: 'I think we've done it.'

Becker went over. The pump was to be housed in a small cabinet by the new troughs.

'Ready?' he asked.

The electrician grinned. 'Want to be the first to start it?'

Becker bent down.

'Press that button.'

He pressed it.

They waited. At first, nothing happened. Not even a sound from the pump.

'Is it working?'

'It's working, I can feel it.' He had a hand on it. 'Listen!'

Becker listened. Nothing at first, then a gasping sound, rising in a faint crescendo. Something was coming up. Coming up fast.

'Here she comes!'

It shot out of the pipe, a two-inch pipe. Ample capacity. Shot across the earth. Toward the troughs. Water everywhere. All they had to do now was connect it up. Connect it to the cattle troughs, connect it to the house, so that if it never rained again, they would have water, at least water to wash with and to water the garden and the fruit trees and even to cook with and drink, if it was not too hard. He'd get a water softener, try that. So that you could shampoo your hair and brush your teeth, if need be, in bore water. He was close to getting what he wanted: a model farm, in which every eventuality had been covered.

Becker jumped back, splashed. Delighted.

'You've done it!' he said.

The electrician was still squatting by the gleaming pump. A hand on it. Feeling the vibration, soft, purring. Very sweet. Not a wobble anywhere. He was grinning up at Becker. He was happy.

It was a great day.

'Now you're drought-proofed,' he said.

CHAPTER 10

EACH SUNDAY MORNING, they would go to church, all five of them. That is, Robyn and the two kids and her mother and father. They would meet Bob and Muriel at St Paul's Anglican Church in Turvey Park, it being only a few blocks to walk for them. Becker would drop Robyn and the children at the church, then clear out. He'd go out to Kirralee, which is in the east, on the way to Forest Hill, where the aircraft came in. It was one of those homes for people who could no longer manage, both at home and themselves. It was spread out, three rugged blocks and an administrative centre. With an office and a sign on the wall. Our commitment, it said: Care, Comfort and Christ. Then, underneath, a long spiel about dignity, support, respect and devotion to the needs of those who, in fact, had no need of anything but a clear answer to the unanswerable question: How much longer?

Becker opened the door and went in.

Normally, the manager was at church, although occasionally he was called to a crisis and couldn't make it. He did have an understudy, but she was not there that day The office was bare. Becker tapped a bell. He heard a rustle off stage. There was an attached flat, the manager living on site. A hustle and a putting of something aside, a clinking of a cup, the flip of a crisp little napkin and a quick little cough.

The manager was at morning tea. He came out, wiping a crumb from his authoritative lips and smelling of tea and milk.

If there was one thing Becker could not stand the smell of, it was milky tea. It reminded him of his mother sitting at the kitchen table, staring out the window and smoking and saying: 'Why do they do it? Why do they go off and get themselves killed?' And the steam rising from the cup on the table and mixing in and being with the vaporous nature of things. And the fervent belief in the unbelievable.

'Ah, Mr Becker!'

He was a solid and stolid man, always dressed in a dark-blue suit, white shirt and blue tie, although he did now and then permit himself a blue and red tie or a blue and grey with a dash of something not quite perceptible. A busy man, courteous to a fault and having all the decency and dedication of a self-important nobody.

'Is it your mother again?' he said, dispensing with a last crumb.

'How is she?'

'How is your mother? How is your good mother? Well, I must say she's more or less as she was.'

'As she was what?'

'When you were last here? When was that?'

'Last month.'

'Oh, yes, a Sunday too, as I recall. Well—she is, she is, how should I put it? Quite well for a person with her troubles, you know. We must all be thankful for that.'

'In other words, just as bad?'

'Bad? Oh, no, no! Bad is not a word we use here. She is, like so many others, getting on a bit—'

'She's only sixty.'

'Yes, but, in her condition—'

'She has dementia. Is that what you're saying?'

'Dementia? Oh, we do not use that word either. If anyone of them were to hear you say they are demented—'

'But she is, isn't she? She doesn't recognise me, tells me to go away. Thinks I'm someone else. Thinks I'm Tony Leesham, who flew helicopters in Vietnam. And went down in flames. And won a DSO.'

The manager understood perfectly. He sympathised completely. He was about to say God in his mercy brought peace to the suffering, but he did not. God's grace would be wasted on a man like this Becker, a rough sort of fellow. A bent copper and no-good reject, who'd rejected the grace of God and the hope of the Saviour.

'What can I say?'

'She's dying slowly and dementedly. You could say that.'

'We are all dying, Mr Becker.'

'Not fast enough in some cases.'

The manager was shocked. 'How can you say that about your own mother?'

'She's been dying since the day she was born.'

It was a cruel thing to say, he knew. But that was how it was.

Some are born to die and some are born to fly, if only for a few days or nights or hours. Just like Evelyn Crowley. Happy as a lark when they'd loaded up quickly and got out, off in the BMW. Off to a better world, where there was fishing and forests and good wine and fresh food and a long beach, fresh and windy and challenging, south of Perth. On the other side of the continent. They'd never got there. She'd seen the girl sitting on the old seat in the park, the dog snuffling among the fallen leaves, the red leaves. The blood-red leaves. And the girl had been watching them, both thrilled and afraid. The girl was her lost daughter, Christine. "Don't stop," he'd said. But it was too late. Evelyn was getting out of the car and walking across. The girl was smiling, unbelieving that she was about to meet her real mother. Then two shots, *bang, bang*. The girl was dead. The bastards had missed Evelyn and hit her daughter. Straight through her skull.

Becker was leaning on the counter, on his knuckles. And staring at the manager. Not actually staring at him. There was so little to see. Nothing but a puffed-up functionary in a blue-serge suit. Still searching with his tongue for one last crumb. His belly was full of faith and his eyes full of ebullient sincerity. Quite suddenly and with the adroitness of a fervent believer, he changed his tune.

'I know,' he said, leaning to some undignified extent on the counter, on one elbow, offering a knowing ear. 'Please believe me, Mr Becker, I know, we all know, what it is like for the families. The frustration, the long waiting for something to happen, to get better, but as you know, there is no better and no hope. I mean, unless you *believe*. Then, then, there is hope. The pure joy of knowing at last that we are to be lifted to another place, where there is no toil and tears and indignity and befouling of oneself and the pain and the pills—the awful indignity some of them have to endure and the anger.'

'The anger?'

'It's so common what we, the staff, who want only to ease them gently into the arms of the Lord, have to put up with. Only last Christmas, in fact it was on Christmas Eve, a certain lady—I'm not saying it was your own dear mother—said to me I was a bully! A bully? My word, Henry—May I call you Henry? I was startled. That anyone would say a thing like that to me? To me? A devoted servant of our Lord Jesus Christ? And on Christmas Eve at that!'

His eyes were popping, his blood-red cheeks near to bursting. 'I was shocked to the core of my soul!'

Becker was staring at this fatuous fool, quite calmly.

'You don't have a soul.'

'What?'

'You don't know what a soul is. You don't know until you've seen something so bad it hurts. Like seeing a beautiful girl whacked in the head by some shithead trying to kill her mother. Right there in front of her eyes.'

The manager jumped back, agape.

'What?'

'I saw that happen, in Canberra.'

'What?'

Becker stared at the Manager, or not actually stared at him. Or not at him, but at something in a blue serge suit. He was going to say a lot more, really rant at the stupid, sanctimonious bastard, but he did not. He walked out.

He went down the path to the common room. Most of them were there, some with visitors. Others fast asleep, leaning over, almost falling out of their chairs, held only by the fast and puffy cushions on fast and stuffy chairs. Old chairs and old bodies, barely hanging on. In a corner, a woman was staring at a television set. There was no sound. The screen was full of zigs and zags.

She was asleep. He began to move to his mother, but stopped. What was the point? How do you communicate and comfort and try to understand someone who does not recognise you and tells you to go away? Last time she'd told him she was going to England to see the Queen, tell her something must be done about the food. Always curried potatoes for breakfast and raspberry jam on Sundays. Nothing for tea.

Becker went back to the church and waited. Tapped the wheel of the BMW, waiting. What had happened to Barnes? Nothing since that confrontation before Christmas. He'd gone silent. Desperate, or a con man? Or a fool who'd borrowed too much money and couldn't pay it back? Pay up or you're in trouble.

What about his crass wife? She was Italian. Lots of Italians in Griffith. She would have relatives. Had they backed Barnes in some unlawful caper which had gone wrong? No deal, no profit and no future if you don't pay up? He didn't know. He didn't much care. He didn't want to see Barnes again. But he knew he would.

They came out in dribs and droves, then a whole family, followed by a crowd. Then he saw her and smiled. He did not love Robyn, but he liked her immensely. She was the right woman for him. A decent country girl, who would never do anything wrong, never ask for anything she did not really need. But he'd always tell her to go to town and buy whatever she wanted, for herself or for the kids or the house, and each time she'd been surprised, like every day was Christmas day, the world being so bright and bountiful.

'Oh, Harry,' she said, getting in. 'How was she?'

He waited until they were in and belted-up. Then he let off the brake and eased the car into a roll, in some sort of stately finality, out of the yard and onto the street, before answering. Not the kids; they had to walk. It was not far to the little weatherboard by the station.

'Much the same,' he said.

'The same?'

'Never says much.'

'Oh, poor Iris.'

'What's that, dear?' Muriel said in the back.

'Poor Harry, he tries so hard to help her, don't you, dear?'

She reached over and pressed his hand on the gear change, warm under hers. 'My dear man,' she said.

They went back to the house by the railway and had lunch. It was very much the same lunch they always had on Sundays, roast beef sandwiches and soup. Muriel never cooked on Sunday, it being the Lord's day. A woman was entitled to one day off. And biscuits, and nut roll for the kids.

Bob Elliott was a studious man. He read the local paper and listened to the radio. Read the *Weekly Times* each week to check the prices of wheat and wool and maize and canola and fat cattle. He was a help to Becker. He knew so much, like a neglected book, which has opened after some years of its own volition to unburden its facts and experiences and wisdom.

It was a good lunch, even with milky tea.

Then they drove home—Becker, Robyn and the two kids, the boy slapping a knee and occasionally slapping his sister's knee and humming something unintelligible, even occasionally kicking the back of Becker's seat. It was irritating. Overactive, but he'd grow out of it. Turn into some kind of a man one day.

Nutty was barking in the background. Straining at his leash. Always tied up while they were absent. He couldn't be trusted not to run away. He loved to go exploring by himself and was not as intelligent as his grandfather, the one which could open and close gates and had had enough sense not to run away. It was not Nutty's normal bark, not welcoming. But urgent, as if he knew something they did not. And wanted to warn them.

They went up the steps and opened the front door, the kids first and then Robyn. She stopped, surprised. So quickly Becker bumped into her.

'What is it?' he said.

'Oh!'

'What is it?'

He pushed past her.

A man was sitting on the sofa in the living room, the sofa on which the kid had shot Alfredo in the guts three times. It was the man with the hunting rifle and the scope. He was holding it across his knees, and looking lost and tired and worn-out like a man who has suffered too long. And has made up his mind.

'Martie!' she gasped. 'What are you doing here?'

CHAPTER 11

BECKER DID NOT jump or say anything at first. He was an instinctive sort of man. He did what had to be done to survive, often without thinking. Now and then he failed, but he was still alive. He went to the man, a hand out. Not offering to shake but to make a gesture, as if saying not to worry. No-one was going to hurt him. It had been a part of his police training. Don't do anything to provoke a man with a gun. Try to be natural and friendly and interested. Try to get him talking. Try to be sympathetic.

'G'day, mate. Been here long?'

The man did not reply. His eyes moved from one to the other, not with precision or purpose, but like a child following whatever moved. He was dressed more or less as Becker had last seen him, even with the sweatband around his head. It may not have been the same band; it looked a little cleaner, as if cleaned for the occasion. Like dropping in on friends on a Sunday afternoon.

'Oh, Martie,' Robyn said again.

She had stepped back a foot or two, shielding the children. At the same time trying to back out slowly, ushering them with a hand behind her back. Becker was signalling her not to move, not to run.

'Been to church,' he said. 'Sorry to keep you waiting.'

There was something about the pale-grey eyes, leaden eyes. Perhaps a flicker of surprise and gratitude and relief. That he wouldn't have to do anything, that it might work out after all. Becker had moved in front of Robyn, still backing up. Even so, she was able to speak. 'Martie, what brings you here? Way out here to Wagga. I mean, *here* to where we live?'

He breathed, perhaps hopefully. He might well have said something, but Wendy the girl said, 'Mum, I've got to wee.'

'What? Oh, no, you should have gone at Nanna's.'

'I didn't know then.'

Becker was watching his hand on the rifle. One finger was on the trigger. And wondering if perhaps he could not speak. Maybe he was a dumb man, all ears and eyes and nothing to say, except what he had to say with a bullet. Then he recalled Robyn saying at the Gumnut that day they'd re-encountered each other last year: 'He hit me. He slapped my face. I jumped back against the wall. He came at me. You bitch, he said. Then, he… he…' The man could talk then, and that was only a few months ago.

'I told you,' he said. 'Told you I'd find you.'

Robyn shook. 'Yes, yes.'

'And y'wouldn't believe me.'

'I know, I know. It was difficult, Martie. I mean, I tried, didn't I? I tried to be good for you.' She was shaking, her hands up imploringly. And yet spread as if to shield the kids. Perhaps catch a bullet.

'Mum, I've got to go!'

'What? Just a minute, Wiggles.'

They called her Wiggles, because she was always wiggling and wobbling, being a smoochy sort of girl, a smiley girl. Even wiggling while talking. Or chewing an apple. Sometimes she'd stand with one foot on the other, wiggling. Which is not quite the same thing as wriggling. You can wiggle your bottom, but you can't wriggle it.

'It's all right,' Becker said. 'Off you go.'

She hesitated. The man was watching her, a finger still on the trigger.

'Don't worry.'

Becker was going to jump him, when the girl was out. Grab the rifle.

'Go on, love,' Robyn said.

The girl went. The man had tightened a hand around the stock, as though he were going to lift the rifle. Becker walked around, thinking. Trying to look nonchalant. He snapped his fingers.

'Would you like a drink, mate?'

The man looked about fifty years of age—and aged before his time. His hair was grey with some residual ginger. His beard was all grey. It was uncut and indecisive. It could have been a smart beard once, but it was pretty ragged now. Looked chewed in the corners of his pinkish brown and blistered mouth. He opened his mouth, showing the tips of broken and ground-down teeth. Not many. His forehead was spotted and scratched, little cuts here and there. Possibly scratched with worry when he could not sleep, and even when driving a cab. His ears were burnt and lumpy. Maybe they'd seen too much sun.

Robyn was staring at him, not so much because he was holding a rifle and could wipe them out at any second, but because she was sorry. She had once loved him after a fashion. Now he was on the edge. Pushed there by hurt and misery and indecision and pulled by the wide-open chasm of despair. She hurt for him.

He seemed to reply. Then he spoke: 'Don't worry 'bout me.'

Robyn had an inspiration. 'Would you like some nut roll? Remember? I used to make it. The way Mum does, with walnuts and ginger and lots of butter on it. Would you?'

'Ah—,' he said.

'I brought some home,' she said.

'Yeah, I might.'

She went out, taking the boy with her. He soon reappeared at the corner, peering. Becker could hear her whispering, urging him to come away. But he would not. He wanted to see. If the boy would do as he was told, if he'd got out of range, Becker thought he might have a chance, all of them now being out of the room. He could jump the man, wrench the rifle from his grip. But the rifle was pointing directly at the stupid boy at the door. Also, he couldn't see the safety catch. Was it on or off? If it was off, too risky. Anything could happen, one shot leading to another. Everyone screaming.

'I'm going to have tea,' Becker said.

'Me too,' the man said.

He was wearing a big hunting jacket, no doubt a handful of cartridges in one of the deep pockets, probably the right. He was right-handed, at least his right hand was on the trigger. And the jacket was floppy and sprawly—voluminous, you might say. Waterproof gabardine. Looked as though it'd had some use. Most likely he didn't do a lot of shooting, not a keen hunter at all. Only now and then. When he went for a walk to think about things. And to shoot at whatever came his way.

Most likely he roamed the Brindabellas Ranges west of Canberra, or went up around Yass looking for quail or down to Jerangle, up high among the rocks and scrubby reaches of high hills. Not so much mountains as granite peaks, bleak and barren and forlorn and abandoned. Except by the wedgetails soaring up high, gloriously free and eagle-eyed. Becker didn't know why he thought about the Jerangles. Perhaps it was one of those unrelated thoughts you have, when someone is sitting three or four feet from you with a loaded rifle. Finger on the trigger.

'Ever go up on the Jerangles?' Becker asked.

'Yeah, been up there. Nothin' much there, but.'

'Wasted sort of country, isn't it?'

'Yeah, wasted.'

Becker crossed his legs. He could hear movement in the kitchen. Not much. Robyn could have cleared out, run for her life, gasping into her phone: 'For god's sake, come quickly, there's a madman in the house and he has a gun—' But she had not; she was still there. He couldn't hear Wendy. Perhaps she'd been sent flying to the nearest neighbour. He hoped not. If this nutter knew, he'd probably go wild, jumping up and screaming: Why'd you do that? Why'd y' go and do that?

'Yeah, I used to do a bit,' Becker said. 'Not when I was in Canberra, but here with my Dad.'

The eyes changed, a flicker of interest.

'Pretty young, though. Only eight or nine. Down to Uranquinty and even as far down as The Rock. Ever been there?'

A shake of the head.

'Bloody high, goes straight up, sticking out of the plain like something bursting out from the earth and going up and up, the way a whale breaks the surface.'

'Yeah?'

'We did a bit of shooting there. Only a twenty-two. Couldn't have held anything any bigger, not at my age. Nine, it was.'

The man almost nodded or shrugged.

'Dad was at Kapooka.'

'Yeah?'

'Ever been there?'

'Yeah, before we went.'

'Which outfit?'

'Ah—'

Robyn entered with a tray. 'Here we are,' she said, and set it on a coffee table. 'Tea and nut roll and brownies and some shortbread. They're bought ones, I'm sorry—the shortbreads I mean. How do you like it, Martie?'

'As it comes, I reckon.'

'Milk? Yes, of course, I should remember. And there's sugar.'

She pushed a bowl closer. He watched her, serving. His eyes went up and down, momentarily catching her legs and ankles and shoes and the edge of her skirt. They were the leaden eyes of deep depression.

'Thanks, Rob.'

It took some time to serve them all, but she did, even the boy standing back and chewing a brownie. The girl was not there, except for an eye and a nose and a finger or two, now and then at the door.

'So,' Becker said, 'which outfit?'

'Sixth battalion RAR.'

'Sixth, eh? When was that?'

'August '66.'

'In Phuoc Tuy?'

'Yeah. You know Phuoc Tuy?'

'Never been there. My dad was there, though.'

'When?'

'Two years later, Seventh Battalion.'

'Officer, was he?'

'Sergeant. He'd been there in '64, training unit. Didn't have to go again, but he volunteered.'

'Volunteered?'

'Thought he'd like to see some more action, I suppose.'

The man shook his head, as if he couldn't believe anyone would have volunteered to go to Vietnam. 'How long?'

'Pardon?'

'Was he there?'

'Oh, three months.'

'Hit, was he?'

'Yeah.'

'Killed?'

'Yeah.'

'Ah, Jesus!'

He put down his cup and rubbed his mouth with the back of a hand. Then bit it. His eyes closed. His face, as much as you could see of it, had turned white. His teeth, when he stopped biting, were red. His lips were red. He'd drawn blood.

They waited, watching. There was nothing they could do but wait, sipping their tea.

'You okay, mate?'

'Eh? Yeah, yeah. Gets me sometimes. Used to scare Rob. She'd think I was mad. Had to go to the hospital, out to Concord, in Sydney. See a doc. Got over it, in a day or two. You never forget, but.'

'I know.'

'Another cup, Martie?'

'No thanks, Rob.'

'A biscuit?'

He waved a hand. 'Ah, no, no!'

'Feel like a beer, mate?'

'Ah, no, no.' He waved both hands. 'I'm right now.'

Becker thought the time had arrived. The man's hands were off the rifle. One quick lunge and he could get it. But what if he did not?

'What company were you in? In the Sixth, I mean.'

'Eh? Ah, Delta.'

'Delta?' Becker remembered something. 'Wasn't that the outfit that copped it at Long Tan? In a rubber plantation?'

'Yeah, that was it.'

'Were you in that fight?"

'Yeah, I was.'

'Some battle, they say.'

'Yeah, nearly wiped us out.'

'Killed eighteen?'

'Seventeen of us. One in the APCs that come and rescued us.'

'But you killed a lot of them?'

'Eh? Oh, I don't know. We had to count 'em afterwards. Headquarters wanted to know. It was… It was… I dunno.' He was going white again.

Becker was going to change the subject, but the man came out with it.

'Next day we had to count 'em. Got up to two-hundred and fifty and gave up. Night was comin' on and we didn't know exactly where the main force was. Some blokes said as many as three-thousand could be out there beyond the plantation.'

'You found two-hundred and fifty bodies?'

'Yeah, bits of 'em. Plus, another five-hundred or so over the next two weeks.'

'One Australian company killed nearly eight-hundred VC?'

'Yeah, well, it was the artillery. Blew 'em to bits.'

Becker was surprised.

'How close were you? To them, I mean.'

'In the thick of it? Ah, one or two hundred yards, I reckon.'

'Jesus, that was close. With all that fire coming down.'

'Yeah, close. Had to hide behind the trees to avoid the shrapnel at one or two stages. They were working the shells closer and closer to us.'

'Christ, that's amazing.'

'We were calling them up, on the radio. Giving the co-ordinates. We'd see a few slopes in a bunch and we'd bring 'em fifty yards left or twenty yards closer. And the ordnance would hit, exactly. It was pinpoint.'

'Amazing accuracy.'

'Yeah, the gunners, they saved us. Lost only seventeen out of a whole company.'

'Boy, that was brave.'

'It was the gunners,' he said again.

'Yeah.'

'Fuckin' geniuses, they were.'

He was shaking now, a hand to his head, eyes closed. Becker tried to change the subject, get off war. But the man wouldn't let him.

'You get used to losin' your mates, but you never get used to seein' hundreds—'

'You want a beer, Martie?'

'No, no thanks. 'I'd better be—'

'A whiskey?'

'No, mate, I'm fine.'

He wasn't fine, you could see. He had sort of seized up, waited as if holding his breath. His eyes closed, he went white in the face, as if hit by a convulsion which would not come out and shake him and rattle him. But it did not come. He breathed out.

'Sorry,' he said. 'It gets yer.'

'That's all right, mate.'

He looked at his watch, then at Robyn, then at the boy. Who'd stopped chewing long ago, but his mouth hung open. He'd never heard such a story. He'd tell it at school tomorrow. The man looked at Becker. Some sort of decision passed across his eyes. Unsteadily, he rose. 'Only dropped in to see y's, see how y's are gettin' on, and...' He didn't seem able to get his tongue around it, an apology. 'Givin' you a fright that day. Up the creek. Should've known better.'

'The shot? Ah, anyone can make a mistake.'

He stumbled, clutching the rifle. 'Better be gettin' along.'

'I'm sorry, Martie,' Robyn said.

He was heading for the door. But turned slowly, gazing at Robyn and Becker and the boy and finally at the girl at the door. Then back to Robyn.

'I'll be right,' he said.

They followed him to the door.

'Where's your car, Martie?'

'What? Ah, down the road a bit, up a lane.'

Becker followed him onto the verandah, helped him down the steps. Walked with him to the gate, where he looked back. One last glance at Robyn.

Almost smiled, almost waved.

'Thanks, mate,' he said and walked off, much the same way he'd done the day Becker had climbed onto the road and watched him depart. A faltering walk, uncertain. Becker watched until he disappeared back into history.

Late that day, as the sun was going down, there was a knock at the front door.

Becker went to it. Barnes was standing there in uniform. Behind him, the patrol car stood at the gate, lights flashing.

'What?'

'There's a bloke,' he said, 'up a lane. Down the road.'

'A bloke?'

'Sittin' in a car.'

'So?'

'Dead, shot dead. Straight up and under.'

'Up and under what?'

'His chin.'

'Oh, Christ.'

'You know anything?'

Becker felt sick. He'd seen a lot of bad sights in his life. He did not want to see this one. They had failed. They had failed a man who couldn't take it any more. Maybe Robyn was his last resort. Without her, he was no-one. Better to get it over with.

'How'd he do it?'

'With a rifle. Straight up and through the roof.'

'A rag around his head?'

'Yeah, know him, do y'?'

'His name's Martin Scowcroft. He's a Vietnam vet.'

'Friend of yours, is he?'

'Robyn used to know him.'

'Visiting y's, was he?'

Becker did not answer.

'You want to come down and have a look?'

'No thanks.'

Barnes began to back off, but paused.

'Someone's got to identify him.'

'Okay, I'll come.'

He closed the door and did not tell anyone where he was going.

'Trouble seems to like you,' Barnes said.

'Yeah?'

'Heard you had a bit in Canberra.'

Becker didn't say anything. Barnes got into the patrol wagon, but Becker did not. He walked down the highway to the lane in the thickening night. And the oncoming lights.

CHAPTER 12

THE STRANGE THING was, Robyn wanted to go. She had to go, she said—back to Canberra. For his sake. They argued for a day or two. She'd been in love with Martin once, or thought she was. She'd said she'd marry him, although she'd not told her parents. Nor made any formal arrangements. But could not have gone through with it; a man often so depressed and so far away, unable to say what was troubling him. Harry too was like that, silent and thoughtful and faraway. But Harry was not violent. He was comforting. Never raised his voice or scolded or complained or said a bad word about anyone. And supported her parents in town and the kids, paying school fees and trips and books and plenty of pocket money. And walked with them and talked to them. In his own quiet way.

She'd known that Martin had been in the war and had been disabled out. Medical reasons, although he'd never quite said what medical reasons. Agent Orange, she'd thought. Perhaps that was it. Maybe it was mental. He'd go to Sydney now and then to see someone about it—a psychiatrist, she thought. He'd had such bad dreams. In bed he'd doze off, then jump. It seemed impossible to jump when you're flat on your back, but he could. As if hit, whacked in the night. A bullet coming out of nowhere. She did not know whether he really loved her, or wanted to lie in her arms and cry soundlessly. Eyes shut tight, as if afraid to open them.

Sometimes she'd thought all he wanted was the sex, the relief. She didn't mind the sex, but he'd get rough, too rough. It was as though he was fighting her, shoving it up and up and grunting and crying, a squealy sort of cry. As if he had to do it, but couldn't unless he shoved it right up her, hard. 'Marty,' she used to say, 'Martie, not so hard, please. You're hurting.' But he never seemed to hear. He'd been in a bad way, she realised now. The poor man, it must have been the war. But it had got too much. She had to get out of Canberra. Go back home, back to Wagga Wagga. Or else something terrible would happen. She felt it, she knew it.

She'd begun making excuses and saying she had to see a friend, or was working back, doing the night shift to help out someone else who had a date. The end had come that night when he burst in, wanting to know where she was going. With Helen Sedgwick, she'd said. And he'd said, 'You're lying, you bitch!' And grabbed her and rammed her up against the wall and did it. Or not exactly did it, but thrust himself at her, as if he were really doing it, penetrating but not getting it in. Hurting her too, making her cry.

Then he'd quit in a fit of rage. Saying, 'If you ever go off with someone else, I'll follow you, I'll find you...'

She was lying on their bed, three days later. The funeral was to be the next day, a Thursday, in Canberra. He had family of some kind up in Yass and Boorowa. Both good farming districts, especially for fine wool, north-west of Canberra. Not many friends, perhaps an Army mate or two. There wouldn't be many there, she thought. A man like that.

'You don't have to go, Rob.'

'That poor man,' she said, 'so lonely. If I'd been able to do something for him...'

'He was gone,' he said. 'Far gone.'

She was looking up at him, sitting beside her and holding a hand.

'You were wonderful, Harry. Such calmness. You saved us, didn't you?'

'Ah, you get used to it. You're trained for it.'

'Was he really going to kill us?'

'Ah, hell, no. He just wanted someone to talk to. They all do.'

'He had a rifle.'

'He was a hunter.'

'All those bodies he said. Hundreds and hundreds cut to pieces. What would they have done? Picked up the pieces? Put them in bags? Dug graves, buried them?'

'Left them for the VC to steal away in the night, I suppose.'

She winced. 'Oh, Harry.'

She clutched his hand in both of hers, her nails biting in. 'I'm so glad I've got you.' She sighed. 'I'm such a fool. I would have gone to pieces, if you hadn't been there.'

'Come on.' He tapped her. 'What'll we do with the kids?'

'If we go? Oh, I've spoken to Mum and Dad and Hank and Anika.'

She was referring to the Dutch couple on the farm next door. An old wheat farm, it was. They had the Dutch Oven bakery in Baylis Street, down by the park and the lagoon. And coffee too, if you wanted it. You could sit outside at little tables and drink it or wander off into the park and feed the water hens or the ducks. They had fresh bread hot out of the oven every day except Sunday, crowds sure to be lined up for a loaf or a birthday cake or a strudel or a raspberry treat or a sticky bun for tea. Doing well, they were. Such a lovely couple, two sons and two daughters-in-law running the shop—and they, not too old. Mid-sixties, he thought. Working out the rest of their lives on the farm, milling their own wheat and holding the flour for six weeks to let it age to get that extra taste and nutrition, which no one in Wagga had at that time.

'Okay?' he said.

'Yes,' she said, 'any time, they said.'

'What time's the funeral?'

'Two thirty.'

'At Norwood Park?'

'Yes, the crematorium, not the cemetery.'

'We'll have to leave soon after ten. That is, if we're to have lunch first.'

That's what they did. The girl went in early on the school bus to Wagga and they left it to Anika or Hank or both to pick up the boy from school and endure him until they returned home late in the afternoon. It felt strange for both, going back to Canberra, if for only a few hours. It was an easy run in the BMW, cool and bright. The countryside around Yass and Murrumbateman looked happy, well cared for, well fed, contented. They'd had more rain over summer than had the wheat lands out west.

When they crossed the border and entered the national capital, both were calm. Coasted down and down several miles, to Northbourne Avenue, which looked somehow narrower and jammier with more traffic and lights and signs of prosperity than when they'd both left, she before him by a month or two, last year. The capital had a quiet, business-like air about it. Not an exciting city, but respectable, well laid out. And the lake, it was always the lake. Which got you in, although quite artificial, a dam on a small stream with a wobbly sort of name, Molonglo.

It was the same, picturesque lake, the roads, the leisurely ways, the bridges and the Carillion. And up high, across the lake, the hill, where sat, or sat in, the new Parliament House, something like a half-buried ziggurat. A coat-hanger of a flagpole on top. Our flag waving proudly, invitingly, as though saying, Nice to see you again. Where the hell have you been?

They drove around for a while, looking and thinking. Becker's eyes would fly to Commonwealth Park, almost against their will. The park where, in the middle of the night, they'd killed Torrence, one in the back and one through the head. And had pushed him into the water, *splash!* To be found by a jogger early next morning. The event having been witnessed by some disgraced school teacher and professional deadbeat named Buster, sleeping rough. Who'd seen them and understood enough to tell Becker for twenty dollars what he had heard or misheard. You could not be sure with Buster. His brain was pretty well shot by then.

They'd killed Torrence and tried to pin the hit on him, Harry Becker. Who had nothing whatever to do with the whole business, except that he knew a woman named Evelyn Crowley. And Mrs Crowley knew too much about was going on in the Royal Bank of Australia, where her husband was pretty big in international operations. And did a lot of travelling. Moving millions, nay billions, around the world. Who'd be a good friend to have if you wanted to move money you did not want the police to know about.

'Where do you want to have lunch?' he said.

'Where would you like?' She was like that. Always let him choose. Not that she was weak or servile. Whatever he wanted, he would get. She saw to it.

They ended up at Gus Petersilka's joint on Bunda Street, where they'd had orange cake and coffee that day months ago, almost a year. She hadn't wished to sit outside. Hadn't wanted to be seen, that was obvious. By whom? Now he knew. Martin Scowcroft, whom they were to farewell today. Farewell to the flames, and the misery of the lonely and forgotten and rejected.

As they went in, two female cops came out, smiling and talking. One was the senior constable who'd pulled Becker out of his car outside Evelyn's place when they'd tried to escape Canberra. It had blown up. Not Canberra, but the old clanking and clunking Holden. It had been a good old car, 300-thousand on the clock.

The woman in blue looked at him as they'd passed. He should have thanked her. She'd risked her life to save him. Had been awarded a medal for her bravery, so he'd heard. But, if he had, he'd have had to explain to Robyn.

'Will this do, Harry? Out here? On the street?' Then, as she sat: 'Who was that?'

'Oh, just a cop I knew.'

'In Canberra?'

It was a silly question, she knew. They were *in* Canberra.

'Yeah,' he said. A girl had appeared with a menu, an order book, a bottle of water and two glasses.

'Hullo, how are we today? What would you like?'

They looked. 'I'll have the john dory,' he said.

'And you, ma'am?'

'The same, please, and—' She smiled, twinkling. 'Orange cake,' she said. 'If I may.'

'And you, sir?'

'Yeah, sure.'

Robyn laughed. 'You remember?'

'Yeah, sure.'

'I didn't want to eat too much,' she said. 'I didn't want you to think me a pig. That day, our first date.'

'I gobbled mine,' he said. 'Talking,' he added.

She rubbed a foot against his leg under the table. Then realised that it was the first time she'd ever done that with any man. Only sexy girls did things like that in public. But she did not care now.

'I think I was in love with you then,' she said.

'Yeah?'

'I used to look at you, when you'd come to the register with your shopping.'

'Yeah?'

'And when you went to another girl, I was sorry.'

'Yeah?'

'I used to wonder how old you were. And why you shopped after lunch. Used to wonder what sort of job you had. Must be a night worker, I thought. Perhaps a policeman. He looks like a policeman.'

'What do policemen look like?'

'Sure of themselves. And well-mannered. Men, you can trust. Firm but respectful. Not like—like—'

His phone rang. He dragged it out, wondering.

'Yeah?' he said.

'Harry?'

'Yeah?'

'Heard you were back,' she said.

He stood up slowly, suddenly apprehensive. He both wanted to, and did not want to, hear from Anastacia Babchuk. She had gone to Melbourne to kill someone. He feared the worst. She had done it. And she was going to tell him all about it. Knowing he would not talk, because they were in each other's debt. Chook had saved his marriage by removing two dead bodies from the farm. While Chook herself would be in serious trouble, if he broke down under interrogation and told the police. You never knew when they might have heard something about two bodies, which had popped up somewhere.

'Hi,' he said, moving, only two or three steps away from Robyn. Pretending to be searching for a better signal.

'Can you speak?'

'Well, the reception's not too good here. We're on Bunda Street at—at—'

'Gus's place, I know.'

'Do you? Yeah, well—'

'Can you get away?'

'Well, it's a bit awkward. We're here for a funeral, and—'

'What time's the funeral?'

'Two thirty.'

'At Norwood?'

'Yeah.'

'Can you get her to do some shopping?'

'Oh, I don't know.'

'The time's now five to one. I'll be in El Rancho at one thirty.'

'I… I don't know about that.' He looked around. The girl was coming with two plates, smiling.

'Something has come up, Harry.'

'Yeah? Well… I'll see what I can do. I think… I think Robyn *does* want to do some shopping.'

'El Rancho at one thirty,' she said. 'Enjoy your lunch.'

He put the phone away and sat slowly. What had come up? Jesus, what now?

Robyn was making room for the fish.

'You guys not having anything to drink?' the girl asked.

'Coffee later,' he said.

'You look worried, Harry.'

'Ah, some guy I used to know.'

'Back here?'

'Yeah, wants to buy me a drink.'

'And I'm to do some shopping?'

'Yeah, do you mind?'

'Of course not, dear.'

The El Rancho was the same, only worse—dark and subdued, not only the lighting but the mood. If you could call it a mood. The buffalo horns were still on a wall behind the bar and the pictures of rodeos and snow-covered peaks were the same. Chook was sprawled in a corner, long legs stuck out and one arm along the back of another chair. In her free hand was a whiskey glass. Becker remembered she drank Jack Daniels, bought one and went over. There were only two or three other women, plus the usual male lushes sitting there, hoping something would happen. But it rarely did.

'How tall are you?'

She almost smiled. 'Six foot two and eyes of blue.'

She did indeed have eyes of blue, the kind you couldn't look at for more than a couple of seconds without looking away. The kind that could stare you down. Her leather jacket was open, zipped only at the waist. He glimpsed the butt of something nasty under her left arm. Maybe that was deliberate. Like she was saying to the whole bar, Any trouble and you're dead. That was her habitual pose. Polly had once said that Chook was a kick boxer. And had added: If you want to give her any cheek, Harry, hang onto your teeth.

'I once knew a girl,' he said.

'Yeah?'

'At school, back in Wagga. Must've been six feet.'

'What happened?'

'She was coming along the street one day. Someone started chiacking her.'

'Saying?'

'Tall girls never get a bloke, so—'

'And?'

'They never get a poke!'

She laughed. 'Yeah, I used to get that, too. How did she react?'

'Went crazy, raised her hands like a grizzly bear and went for us, teeth bared and brutal and bleeding. Or, we thought they soon would be.'

'What'd you do?'

'Ran like buggery.'

She laughed. And tossed down her whiskey.

'How old were you at this time?'

'Twelve.'

'Cheeky little bastard. 'Nice to see you, Harry.'

'What's happened?'

She pulled in her legs, sat up and leaned forward, arms folded. But always leaving her right-hand fingers, or at least fingertips, just inside her open jacket. A habit, you might say.

'Know a bloke called Barry Barnes?'

CHAPTER 13

BECKER WAS SURPRISED and relieved. They weren't going to talk about Melbourne. They were going to talk about Barnes. After they'd wrapped up the job in the lane, he'd said it was a terrible shock, especially for Robyn. Scowcroft was a Vietnam vet and some of them went through hell, even thirty years ago. He'd been in love with her, but she was not interested in him. Disappointed love, that's all it was. But Barnes hadn't seemed to be interested in the details. He'd said, as he'd left, out of the corner of his mouth: I don't need your fuckin' money now. And had looked at him that way he had, aggressively with his little blue eyes going grey and washed out. And meaningfully, as if saying, Understand? Like the two-bit bully he was, and always would be, to the end.

'Yeah,' Becker said, 'he's a sort of cousin. And a cop.'

'What sort of a cousin?'

'A second cousin on my mother's side.'

Chook smirked. She was a good smirker. 'Not a good record, has he? Still a base-grade struggling after ten years.'

'He's not too bright.'

'And not too careful, is he?'

'How do you mean?'

'He talks too much. Word gets around. It's his wife. Apparently, she can't keep her mouth shut.'

'About what?'

'What do you think?'

'Drugs?'

'Yeah, he's working with some truckies, loaded with fruit and vegetables.'

'Delivering here? In Canberra?'

'All over the place. Even down in Melbourne.'

Becker sat back. 'So that's it?'

'That's what?'

'He was pestering me for money, twenty grand. Later he put it up to thirty, then forty. He was going to tell people what I'd done in Sydney. Even hinted he knew more than that.'

'The bank and Evelyn?'

'I think so.'

'How would be know her husband was laundering money for the Mafia?'

'I don't know. Maybe some cop has been talking to him.'

Chook shook her head. 'Yeah,' she said, 'that can happen.' She flipped back the leather cover on her watch. It was one of those watches in a leather case like officers in old wartime movies used to consult as they counted down the time to going over the top.

'Drink up, Harry.'

He did so. 'Hey, why are you, a Canberra cop, interested in Barry Barnes, a Wagga cop?'

'I'm not a Canberra cop.' Her left hand dived inside her jacket and came out with a new warrant card. She opened it with one finger. He saw a photo of her in civvies. There was the usual wording, but one word stood out: *agent*.

'You're a federal agent?'

'Yeah, love undercover work, so they gave me a transfer.'

'Good for you.'

'Now I go everywhere, man, look at everything, man!' She sang it like the Tenter-field Traveller did.

'Promotion?'

'Yeah, not bad.'

'Sergeant?'

'We don't have ranks. Everyone's an agent, like in the FBI. But the money's good, equal to sergeant.'

She glanced at her watch. 'How long do we have?'

'Another ten minutes.'

'You haven't said why you're interested in Barnes.'

She grinned or smirked or shook her head ruefully.

'Some information came in,' she said.

'Yeah?'

'He's doing a deal with truckies.'

'He's crazy. Those guys talk, when they're caught overloaded or driving more than eleven hours.'

'I know. They offer cops a deal, information for a little tolerance.'

'What's he doing?'

'Getting them to carry soft stuff.'

'Drugs?'

'Only weed at this stage.'

'So, that's why he doesn't need my help any longer?'

'We're still checking, but I may have to drop in on you some day, have another look around Wagga.'

'Yeah?'

Becker was scared. He didn't want to see her again, not in Wagga, anyway. People would notice. Robyn might notice. Chook tended to stand out in a crowd.

She was watching him, amused.

'What's the matter?' he asked.

She dropped her voice. Around them, people were staring. In a place like the El Rancho, there was little else to do. 'You haven't asked about Melbourne.'

Becker had to swallow his fear. 'How did it go?'

'I looked up at that guy.'

'The one in the lingerie shop? The fat man?'

'He wasn't fat. He was a short and grisly little nobody with a bad heart. And he wasn't in Canberra that day they killed Torrence.'

'How did his card get there, on the ground, under the light? By the lake?'

'He lent it to someone.'

'The fat man?'

'Yeah, so his name would not appear on the passenger manifest.'

'Pretty smart. But the fat man lost it. Which led you to the shopkeeper. Who was worried and told the fat man he had to get it back?'

'Looks like it.'

'So, what did you do?'

'Some more checking, looked up company records. He doesn't own the business.'

'Who does?'

'She does, his wife. He does the books.'

'And what's her name?'

'Terracini.'

Becker gulped. 'Terracini?'

'Yeah, why?'

'That's Barnes's wife's name.'

Chook shrugged. 'Terracini? Common enough name among Italians, isn't it? Could be related, though.'

'Yeah, but what if they're closely related?'

'Where does this Mrs Barnes live?'

'In Wagga, but she has family in Griffith.'

'Does she, indeed?'

'A connection?'

'Maybe.' Chook looked at her watch again. 'You've got five minutes.'

'What did you do? When you found the shop?'

'Walked in and asked for a bra. The grubby little jerk was behind the counter, looking for something. He looked me up and down and said something to his wife, who came over. What size? she said. I said, what's the biggest you've got? They looked at each other. I know I don't have much up here, mostly pectorals, not fat. You're not one of those funny men, are you? she said. Me? A transvestite? I said. We have some funny types come in, she said. Theatricals, they call themselves. You want to see my fanny? I said. In front of all these people? Two girls were serving women of all shapes and sizes and ages, behind displays and counters and fascinated smiles. The old bitch gasped in a modestly frantic way, no doubt thinking this could cost millions if I really was someone famous like Danny Larue. And up yours too, darling, I said, and walked out.'

Becker laughed. 'You didn't blast anyone in Melbourne?'

'Only some officious arsehole, who wanted to ticket me for parking in a Police Vehicles Only zone. It was outside the local cop shop. I am the police, I wanted to say, but I didn't. Anyway, I was there on private business, and I didn't want people to know why.'

'Okay,' Becker said. 'I'd better be getting back.'

'To Gus's? Before she spots you. Jealous type, is she?'

They got up and walked to the door. 'She's an angel.' Becker couldn't think of anything less corny. Chook put a hand on the door and pulled. It opened.

'Thanks, Harry,' she said. 'This might be the link we need. I might call you again, put a little proposition to you. If you're interested.'

'Yeah, sure.' He knew he had to do it, whatever it was she had in mind. He was tied to her now. 'Well, Chook—' He'd done it again. 'I mean Stacey.'

'That's okay.' She tapped him on a shoulder. 'Thanks for seeing me.'

'I'd better run before—,' he began to say. Standing by the bin where it had all begun was his wife, smiling.

'Hullo,' she said. 'Had a nice chat?'

'Oh, ah—' He didn't know what to say. It was like being caught in bed with another woman. 'Rob? Been for a walk?'

'Went into David Jones, couldn't think of anything to buy, came out, bought an ice cream and sat and watched the children on the merry-go-round.'

'Ah, yeah, well, this is—' Suddenly he couldn't think of Chook's name. He didn't have to, Chook herself stepped forward, a hand out. 'How are you, Robyn? I'm Anastacia.'

Robyn was surprised. But she accepted the handshake, surprisingly gentle.

'Anna—?'

'Stacia, but you can call me Stacey. We used to work together. Where was that, Harry? Canberra?'

He couldn't think fast enough. His wife now knew about Chook. He'd have a lot of explaining to do.

'Yeah, saw you two go into Gus's and thought I'd try to say a word before you disappeared.'

Robyn was studying her. 'Were you the one at the back window—'

'That's right. Was passing and thought I'd drop in. Found he had a visitor, an old bloke looking for a lift to Wagga. Gave him one, sent him on his way. Wanted to get to Sydney. Didn't have a cent. Mind wandering, I reckon.'

'Oh, the poor man. He said he was Harry's brother.'

'Brother? Didn't look anything like Harry, did he?'

'I wonder who he was?'

'We may never know.'

Chook shrugged, grinning. She could look quite happy now and then. Very matey, very much in control. She shook with Becker.

'Nice to see you again, Harry. So long Robyn. Must run.'

Then she was off, vanishing in the lunchtime crowd. Always a crowd in Garema Place, even when it was empty. A crowd of memories. They walked back to the car.

'What a tall woman,' she said.

'She's a kick-boxer.' He couldn't think of anything more intelligent to say.

Robyn Laughed. 'A kick boxer? What on earth is that?'

He did not answer, worried. Thinking about what she'd said: Wanted to get to Sydney. How did Chook know Alfredo had wanted to get to Sydney? Had in fact wanted to get to Los Angeles, people looking for him, afraid he'd talk. That was before the kid had turned up. Or had she turned up sometime before he'd appeared. Hopped out of sight, then crept in behind him. Then calmly executed him. Gave him one for Polly. But why wait so long, listening to the kid talk, let him put three slugs into Alfredo?

He was still thinking about it while they drove up to Norwood Park. Very few were at the service. The usual people from a few miles away, like Gunning and Crookwell, and a little place called Laggan. Becker had been to Laggan on one of his wandering trips, when he had to get out of Canberra for a few hours. Nothing there but half a dozen old houses, some crooked stone walls, a broken-down mill, some potato fields. Good potatoes came from Laggan. They'd have to have Irish potatoes in a place with a name like Laggan. An old man had been leaning on a rusty gate, smoking a pipe and looking up and down the road, waiting for something to turn up. Not that it mattered what turned up, as long as it did. Plus, a boy on a bike, doing circles.

So they sang a few hymns and an old man, who could have been the same old man, said a few words about Martin Scowcroft. How he'd always been a good boy, a friend of everyone in the district. And had served his country. That was the important thing, he had *served*. The old man was wearing a medal, very old, tarnished and drab and dark brown, almost black with age. He must have won it in the desert or in the jungles of the last big war. More than twenty years before Long Tan. Everyone looked around, but no-one else wanted to speak or, if they wanted, dared not. Then they looked at the funeral director, who looked at the old man, who nodded, not without a sort of cry, a snuffling squeak.

As if of its own mind, the coffin moved back and through the curtains and disappeared. Carrying Martin Scowcroft to his last firefight.

Driving home, Robyn was more than usually quiet. She was fretting, he knew. Now and then she would blow her nose, not so much to clear it as to wipe away a tear or wipe at least a shadow of a tear, starting to brim. They'd just passed Yass, when she spoke.

'Harry, why do you think he did it?'

'In his car? Up the lane?'

'Oh, no, no, I don't mean that. He'd left us and walked down the road. He must have been thinking that, when he walked out. Because I would never go with him, not now—'

'I don't know what was in his mind.'

'I can't stop thinking. When you and Terry came running home that day after that shot up the creek, I had a feeling. I don't know why, but I thought, I just thought, it might be him. Shooting at you, to kill you—'

'Forget, it Rob.'

'So he could come and drag me back to Canberra and I'd somehow feel I'd have to go with him, because we'd had a relationship. That's what they called it nowadays, don't they? It sounds so cold and matter of fact, doesn't it?'

'Stop thinking about it.'

'I can't, I can't, I can't!'

He eased off on the pedal and began to edge over.

'What are you doing, dear?'

'Going to stop for a while. There's a comfort stop here.'

There were trees and a few cars parked beside a small building, which everyone knew. Men one end and women the other.

'Oh, no,' she said. 'Please don't, I'm so sorry. I don't have your strength and calmness and pressure under fire or whatever policemen have, always knowing what to do.'

He drove in slowly and stopped, uncertain. He'd intended to put an arm about her and let her blub for a while—until she got herself together, the way women do. But she said: 'No, no, I feel better now.'

'You're sure?'

'Yes, yes.'

'We can stop at the next town and have a cup. Or at a pub and have something. Might calm you down or give you a break or—'

'Oh, no, no. I've had my little cry.'

'Sure?'

'Yes, dear. I know I'm sentimental. If I didn't have you—If you'd not been so calm and in control, he would have killed us, wouldn't he? All of us.'

He wanted to say it was just part of the job, looking after women and children. But he didn't. She was looking directly at him now.

'I love you, Harry. I really and truly love you—'

She was rubbing his left leg, not sensuously but gratefully.

'My dear man.'

They drove on, around the northern end of the Brindabellas, and began the run along the Hume toward the south, thinking not about the funeral but what Chook had said about a little operation. A drugs bust? He was not sure. He didn't wish to get involved. Yet, whatever it was, he had to do it. She had risked her job for him and them and had done something no cop who played by the book would ever do. Dispose of two bodies and, apparently, she'd got away with it. Where had she disposed of them? And how? He did not know. He might never know.

Back in Canberra, he'd walked up to a door of a posh sort of house. He'd pushed a bell button and waited. Nothing had happened. He'd pushed again. Then the inner door had opened, a solid door, not the kind you could break down. A shape was standing there behind the screen door, the security door. It was a woman, or it looked like a woman, but he could see only a face. A fascinating face, the kind that you see passing by, maybe on a train like they said in the song. Or footsteps in the night. It was not a complete woman, just a lot of dots seen through a screen, suggesting a woman. Good afternoon, ma'am, he'd said. Are you Mrs Crowley? Yes, I am, she'd said. I think I have something of yours. He'd held up the bag. Oh, so you have…

They drove on and on. He began to think about Arnold Sheldrake, who'd driven down this same highway, time after time, fighting to keep his eyes open. Until one day, he couldn't resist. He'd gone to sleep, and veered off and gone over. Over and over and hit a tree. The truck bursting into flames. The conflagration, horrific, some witnesses had said, *Whoosh!* What had old Bob said? There were no brake or skid marks? And: Who would want to leave a beautiful girl like that? Why did he say leave? Did he know something?

Becker straightened up and breathed deeper and willed himself to steer straight and true. They had to get home before it got too late. It was past five o'clock now. The kids would be wondering. Asking each few minutes when they'd be home. And Muriel would be making scones and cocoa for them. Except that only Wendy was with Bob and Muriel in Wagga, whereas Terry was with Hank and Anika next door to the farm. No doubt getting up to no good, whatever he was doing. He wanted to grow up and be a soldier and have guns and shoot at everything. Which everyone thought stupid. But he was a boy and would grow out of it. Or so they hoped.

Becker relaxed, wide awake. His wife was beside him and all was right with the world. She was sitting up straight now, her hands on her bag on her lap. Her head up, as if she'd got over it, and could see straight and calmly into the sullen hills and dales and the westering sun lingering over the limitless plains of wheat and wool. And fat cattle.

'If only I could have done something for him,' she said.

CHAPTER 14

IT WAS A good day. Not a cloud in the sky and the sun not too hot or bright, a cool breeze fluttering up from the south, and birds having a ball in the trees. You could almost imagine fish jumping in the creek. There were no fish, of course, but there were yabbies. Small crustaceans you could eat if you were desperate, or doing it for the fun, boiling them in an old pot. The kids were down there with two boys, grandchildren of Hank and Anika, trying to catch yabbies, enough for a feed between four, but not much luck, the creek being down now. It had been a long, dry summer. But there was hope, the end of summer having about it a comfortable intimacy, like a bed out of which you have just arisen, and would like to go to for a few minutes more. Putting in the weir, as Robyn had suggested, soon after she had arrived, had worked for a while. A weir made of loose rocks, gathered in the hills to the south, had held enough water back in the good times. Not now, not after six weeks without good rain. But it didn't matter.

The neighbours didn't have a creek, and a creek attracted kids like bees to nectar. In the background, the radio was playing and Nat King Cole was singing: *Roll on those lazy, hazy days of summer...*' It was Bob Elliott's birthday. They were all out there on the eastern verandah, away from the sun. Including Anika and Hank.

Robyn had wanted to invite Bert Henschke from the western side. Bert was a garrulous old man who talked a lot, but never said anything really intelligible. His face and figure were worn and eroded in the way an old fence post is worn and weathered and splintery and dangerous to touch. His loose and feathery hair hadn't had the mother's caress of a comb or brush or a lick and spit in years. And, if he did have anything intelligible to say, it was only when he was arguing with God. Or talking to his dog. It was an awful dog named Blue. A blue heeler, a cattle dog which is really blue. Or is not blue, but grey. The blue being a chromatic effect. And with black and tan markings. Fortunately, Bert had not turned up.

They'd had a good lunch, a cold salad made by Robyn augmented by sweets and delicacies and special treats from the cake shop in town—all free of charge, Anika and Robyn being as thick as thieves. Even though Anika was thirty years older. They smiled and chatted, often looking over their shoulders, saying secret things, the like of which you could guess, if you could be bothered. Becker could not. Never listened to gossip, on principle. He said and thought and believed only what could be proved to be true and would, he hoped, stand up in court. In which case, if it couldn't, he wasn't interested in gossip.

Robyn and Anika had been whispering in the kitchen, when Muriel was outside and he'd heard, through the window, a drop in chatter, a certain hush. In which Anika had said: 'Really? Are you really? Oh, darling, how long?'

Becker had taken no notice. Perhaps he'd not wanted to notice. Not yet prepared for it. Instead, he was trying to listen to old Bob, who was talking about the first world war and the first soldier-settlers. In those days, the big pastoral spreads had been cut up and allocated to men who, before the war, hadn't had a hope in hell of ever owning a piece of Australia—the country for which they had fought and died. And had come home wounded or legless or gassed. From Flanders' fields, including Passchendaele. Or, as it was officially known, the third Battle of Ypres, which the boys had called Wipers, in which the British had suffered 275,000 casualties—if you included the Canadians and the Australians.

'That's what it was like,' Bob was saying. 'It was done so the returning boys had a chance.'

'Your father was one of doze?' Hank asked. 'He came back vounded? And was allocated?'

'He came back, not wounded or legless or anything like that, but shocked.'

'Shell-shocked, you mean?'

'No, shocked by what he'd seen at Passchendaele.'

'It must have been awful,' Robyn said, setting down tea. Bob always had tea in a pot, never coffee. He was like that, old-fashioned. And it had to be real tea-leaves, not those bags you bounced.

'It was, my dear.'

'He got himself a block out at Vybilonga?' Hank asked.

'As a returned serviceman? No, he got that after the war, but he was not eligible for the soldier-settler scheme.'

Bob was sitting back, eyes half-closed. His face was handsome and, in some lights, patrician. Not a rough and ready retired farmer, but a man who had known people and known things. Not so much about the first world war, which was well before he was born, not so much about the second, in which he'd been a captain with a DSO, as what it meant to be a decent human being. And officer and a gentleman, you might have said of him. He had about him the air of an educated man, although he'd never been to any college or university or subscribed to any would-be intellectual club or political cause. It was his care and precision and the love of words. He never dropping his aitches or his 'g's'. And his careful reading, slow and thoughtful, of the *Sydney Morning Herald* on a Saturday, even the literary pages, made much of his day.

Hank was mystified.

'Your father did not qualify? A man who had served? In France?'

'No, no,' he said. He had a habit, plucking away at his eyebrows, particularly the right, searching for and finding at least one hair. Then thoughtfully looking at the hair as if it were important to know whether it was black or grey. It was a sign. He had so little to do with his life now, he had to pick and fiddle, if only to fill in time.

'His wife, my mother, at the time had too much money.'

'Ah, she vass ay rich girl, dis girl?'

'She was indeed a girl, when he met her, only eighteen.'

'And she voss an heiress?' Hank pronounced it 'hair-ess'.

'No, not at all.'

'Then how, if you do not mind my asking, Bob, did she get the money?'

'Ah, yes...' He was not going to tell them, but he did. He told them the story of Caitlin Maguire, an Irish girl, or not so much an Irish girl, as the daughter of a dirt-poor farmer near Derrinallum in the so-called Western District of Victoria not long before the first big war. Poor, more than poor, only just hanging on, eating potatoes and spinach and onions and herbs and drinking milk. Not much else, perhaps some beets and onions and herbs and shallots. Marvellously rich land, it would grow any-thing, including fat cattle and some of the best Corriedale sheep in the world, fluffy white and contented. Her father had a few acres, not too far from Derrinallum. When she'd turned eighteen, she got a position at Canley Vale, a big, old, pastoral spread near Mount Elephant. It was owned by Sir Ralph Mountford, who had two sons.

The first was a thorough young bastard. It was said he'd whipped a man in the main Street of Derrinallum—a man who'd laughed at him in his Derby cut of clothes and his spit and polished boots and his cocky little trilby. By contrast his young brother, Christopher, was a slow, dreamy sort of youth, who'd been at university or was still at university in Melbourne, no-one was it was quite clear. He used to spend a lot of time at home, mooning about the place, sitting under trees and reading the

metaphysical poets. And thinking about the loveliness of the world into which he'd
been born. And the mystery of young beauties like Caitlin Maguire.

Then, something bad happened, everybody knew. The elder son, Roderick, had
been arrested or, if not arrested, questioned by the police regarding a certain matter.
No-one knew exactly what. But, his father suddenly ordered him to join up and get
out of the country as fast as possible. War had been declared against Germany only a
few weeks ago.

So off to Egypt he went, this young heir to the Mountford fortune. Thank God,
everyone said. Free at last of that strutting and rutting young buck from Canley Vale.
Yes, rutting. He was noted for it. Down in Melbourne every week or so shouting
everyone to a drink at Young and Jackson's, or at the theatre kissing chorus girls and
often, it was said. The life of the party at a famous house of ill-fame in East Melbourne. But, to everyone's surprise, he returned a few months later. Apparently, he'd
accidentally shot himself in an arm in Egypt during exercises near the Pyramids. None
the less, he returned in a high mood, as if he were some sort of hero. But he was not.
No-one welcomed him back. If they saw him in the street, they turned away. They
knew about the police.

A terrible shock awaited Roderick. His father had disinherited him. Not a penny
would he get when the old man died. This enraged him. He became abusive and
violent. Sir Ralph told him to clear out—never show his face in Derrinallum again.
Roderick went back to Melbourne, became a drunken fool and ribald clown. Running
up debts, dishonouring the family. That did not stop him. He went on spending. Had
to borrow from all sorts of people. They paid up, not for his sake, but for his father's.
To save him from the shame of having a debtor son. An insolvent son. A gaol-able son.
But, one night the police found him dead drunk in the gutter outside the Melbourne
Club, which had shut its doors in his face. They let him sleep it off in a cell. Then
hauled him into petty sessions next day. Fined ten pounds, drunk and disorderly. His
name in *The Age*. Sir Ralph was horrified; he had a reprobate son. He died of shame,
everyone said. A grand old man like that.

Still, they did not know what had set off this disaster in the first place.

'So, Bob, what happened?'

'This left young Christopher as the sole heir. But, a few weeks after receiving the
deeds to the property, he killed himself. Everyone was astounded. My father was the
groom. He came into the kitchen one cold morning and found all the staff in a panic.
Young Caitlin had only then arrived and was putting on her pinafore and her mop
cap. On the table was a letter Mrs Lane, the housekeeper, had been reading. She had
got to one point, then had thrown it down in horror and hurried upstairs. Father said,
'What has happened?' No-one had any idea. They stood around, longing to pick up

the letter, but dared not. There was an envelope lying by the letter. It was addressed to: 'She who knows my heart.' The envelope had not been sealed. They were all puzzled. What did it mean? Who was 'she'? Then Mrs Lane came down the stairs slowly.

'It's the young master,' she said. 'I think he's taken his life.' Everyone was shocked.

'Yes', she said, 'There's a blue bottle on the floor by his bed.'

'They all gasped. They knew what that meant. Poisons came in blue bottles back in those days. Mrs Lane said to go about your business, then resumed reading the letter. When she got to the end, she was the one to gasp. Even cried out. A real squeal. Slowly she put the letter back in the envelope and handed it to young Caitlin. 'I think this is meant for you,' she said. Caitlin was amazed. 'Me?' she said. Mrs Lane was barely able to speak. But she managed to say: 'It would seem that you, Caitlin Maguire, are now the mistress of Canley Vale.'

'Caitlin fainted, but Father managed to catch her. They carried her to a couch and called the doctor—for the young master, not Caitlin, who'd revived by the time he'd arrived. Then came the police, who demanded to see the letter. Then Sir Ralph's solicitor came and read it and said, 'No doubt about it. It's perfectly clear. Miss Maguire is the sole heir.'

Anika was amazed. 'But how, please, Mister Bob, is it that *you* have the letter?'

'Caitlin was my mother.'

'Oh, how amazing! But, please, Bob, what did she do with the money?'

'It took a while. Roderick, of course, challenged the will in court. Christopher had not left a will. He claimed the letter was a fraud—that Caitlin had poisoned Christopher and written the letter. But all the experts proved him wrong. It was his handwriting and the court accepted that it his last testament.'

'And then?'

'There were all sorts of debts left over from the great drought from 1898 that went on for ten years. The Federation Drought, they called it. Horrible, devastating. But, in the final wash up, she had some ten to fifteen-thousand pounds.'

'Oh, such a lot of money it must have been in those days?'

'Yes, it was. And she married Walter Elliot.'

'Oh, what a lovely story! And they lived happily ever after? In the big house with the wonderful view of the Elephant?'

'No, no, she sold it. They came up to the Riverina, looking for a new life. And bought a wheat block a mile or so south of Wybilonga.'

'They lived happy ever after on their wheat?'

'For a while, in the twenties. They bought up three other blocks, contiguous. One great big wheat farm, but things were going bad. The market in England was collapsing. They stopped buying. The farmers, the graziers too, went broke. My father and mother had to sell off three blocks in the great crash. But they survived, just survived on what was left.'

'And tell me, Mister Bob, who was Caitlin?'

Everyone laughed, or smiled politely. Anika was a bit dumb at times.

'She was my mother.'

'Your mother? Oh, how marvellous! And Walter?'

'Anika—' Hank said.

'Isn't he wonderful, Hank? He tells such beautiful stories. Oh!'

She jumped up and ran across and hugged and kissed old Bob, kissed him on his perfectly combed hair and even on his forehead and on his nose. 'Thank you, thank you—'

'Annie, it is four o'clock!'

'So sorry! So sorry!'

She ran to Robyn and kissed her and then to Becker, who hadn't said a word or moved an inch during the telling. Then to Muriel—shy on a settee, pale in her summery chiffon, flowers of reticent green and gold—with more hugs and kisses and finally to the children. And seized her own two boys, saying, 'Now, off! Now off and sank you!' But remembering, running back to Robyn for another kiss, but also whispering. 'I am so *happy* for you, darling!' Then they were gone, all four. Into the dazzle and delight of the diminishing day.

Robyn was passing with a tray, cleaning up. Becker said: 'What was all that all about?'

'What, dear?'

'The whispering?'

'Oh, nothing. I'll tell you tonight.'

'Why not now?'

Just then, his phone went off. 'Hullo?'

'Can you speak?'

'What? Oh, yeah, in a minute.'

'We have to meet,' Chook said.

'Where?' he said.

He stepped away, turning a little as if seeking a better signal. He did that often. She was not offended. She never would be. As a girl, only fourteen of fifteen, she'd once watched an old movie on TV called *All This and Heaven Too*. She liked to think that was what she had now. She didn't mind his secret calls. He was a man of mystery, but it did not matter. That was half the attraction. She'd known he was mysterious when she'd first seen him. They'd got talking at the checkout and he'd baulked as if about to say something. His body had stiffened. Then relaxed. He'd tried to smile and said: 'How much is that?' She'd taken his money and given him the change. Watching him, amused. Men were always asking her for a date. But she could not, because of Martie. Then he'd finally got it out: 'Would you like to have coffee somewhere?'

And she had said, on an impulse: 'Yes, I would.'

Surprising herself.

CHAPTER 15

A MAN AND a woman were sitting on a bench in the Memorial Gardens. Men had died here, metaphorically speaking. Golden roses were fading to creamy at the tips. Lushly beautiful like Evelyn, when she'd been standing at her kitchen bench, making toast and coffee for him, glancing at him. He'd just got out of her bed, surprised he was still alive, and had gone to the kitchen. She had tried to be bright and sparkling, but he could see she was worried. She'd had a call from Melbourne. Something happened? he'd asked. Giancarlo is dead, she'd said. Giancarlo was Alfredo's young brother, the one who talked too much. He'd been popped in Sydney Road by a kid on a motorbike. A kid wearing a full helmet and dark glasses. Like in the movies, except that the kid did not have a driver. He'd done it all himself, just hopped off the bike a few yards along the street and waited for Giancarlo to come up, and smiling at him. A nice matey smile…

'What do you think?' Chook said.

She was leaning back, waiting for an answer. Becker was sitting forward, fiddling with his hands. And thinking there was no way out. It was a matter of honour.

'It's dangerous,' he said.

'Not if we're smart. You've got to remember, mate, this is the Federal Police. There are a lot of us. We have the organisation, the equipment and the authority.'

'I don't think he'd fall for it. And, even if he did, it might take a long time to get through to the *capo*.'

'So what? Either we go after him, or we don't. You know what I'm saying?'

'Yeah, I know.'

'I mean, if we do get to the *capo*, we can cut the balls out of the whole fucking organisation.'

'You're taking on the Mafia,' Becker said.

'So what? We'll take 'em on. We'll do to them what the *Carabinieri* and the investigating magistrates did to the fucking Mafia in Sicily. They cleaned 'em out. We'll do the same. Right out of this country.'

'What if Barnes doesn't play along?'

'Look, Harry, I said we'll get him by the balls. He'll have to play along. He's got no alternative. We'll use him to find his supplier, then we move on from that little maggot to the next maggot and then the next until we get to the *capo dei capi*. Then *bingo!* a big raid. Twenty or thirty going in. Big pictures on TV and in the press. Federal Police Smash Mafia in Australia! Great headline, eh?'

Becker sat up, hands on hips, stretched a little. They'd walked in the gardens, looking at the memorials to the dead and the not yet entirely forgotten. And the relics, like a field gun and a mortar and a three-bladed propeller off some warplane on a stand. And listened to the band from Kapooka playing to the Sunday afternoon crowd. Getting a big round of applause. But other sacrifices, other memories, hung in the air. On walls around the Eternal flame were plaques bearing more than two-thousand names. He'd gone again to one of them, moved in close, peered at the words: C V Becker, KIA, Vietnam 1962-75. It was always the same and told him nothing new. Not how it felt to know you were shot and you had only seconds to live. He'd been shot once, in a shoulder. But he'd had a terrible feeling that he was going to live. At that, this was the beginning.

'Barnes is a piece of shit,' Becker said. 'He'd go to pieces, tell *them* what we're doing. He'd be more frightened of them than of us. Anyway, his wife would soon wake up—if he co-operated.'

Chook laughed. 'She already knows.'

'What?'

'Knows he's dealing. She's the one who fixed it for him. How to get into it, how to solve his financial problems. Her family's notorious in the Griffith area. They are supplying it to him. And he's fixing it with truckies. All those big interstate trucks, B-doubles some of them, taking stuff out of the farms and the wineries.'

'How do you know all this about her family?'

'Maria Terracini? We have a contact there.'

'A mole? In her family?'

'Not exactly *her* family.'

Becker thought about it. 'They kill them, you know. If they talk.'

'She's a pretty game girl.'

'A girl?'

'Well, not exactly a girl now.'

'She has a family?'

'Maybe.'

'Who is the mole?'

'You don't need to know, mate.'

'Okay,' Becker said. He could not get out of it, not after what Chook had done for him and his wife and the baby now on the way. 'So, this mole gives him a packet?'

'That's it.'

'And he thinks it's coming from someone big in Griffith?'

'Correct.'

'But it's really coming from confiscated stuff you have in bond?'

'Correct.'

'Then you nab him?'

'Correct again.'

'And put the screws on him?'

'To put it mildly, yes.'

'Half a kilo of happy dust? Wouldn't Barnes think that was too much? That's a lot of dust for a peripheral player like him.'

'His wife will tell him it's okay. And they're going to be rich, very rich. No more money troubles.'

'And she has connections?'

'Let's say her relatives have.'

'A long way up the line?'

'Far enough.'

Becker did not like it. 'Where do I come into this?'

'You're the supplier.'

'What?' Becker nearly jumped over the moon. There was one, a few days past half full, a bright white moon up there in the blue sky.

'That's right. You hand it to her.'

'The mole?'

'That's right.'

'And the mole gives it to his wife?'

'Yep.'

'And his wife gives it to Barnes?'

'Yep.'

'Where does this happen?'

'In Griffith.'

'Exactly where?'

'In a motel. The mole works there. It's a big place, very pretentious, called *The Capriano*.'

'Why the hell is she doing this?'

'She has her reasons.' Chook stood up. 'I've got things to do, Harry.'

They walked back together. In the background, through the trees, the band was playing the famous Eric Bogle number. No-one was singing or cheering or chatting, not even the kids. They'd been told to hush up and listen very respectfully to a very sad song even if there were no words today, about men coming back from a war, some of them legless, some eyeless and some hopeless. All shot out. The tune was: *And the Band played Waltzing Matilda…*

Becker was not happy.

'Why bring Barnes into this at all?'

'In case the big deal goes wrong.'

'You're gonna make him talk? That's why he has to have the dope?'

'Exactly.'

'Dope which you supply, the police?'

'Right again.'

'Isn't this like entrapment?'

'It sure would smell of it.'

'He could wriggle out of any charges.'

'Right again. That's why we have to offer an inducement. He tells us what he knows and we drop charges.'

'But if it goes to court and it is revealed that you have supplied the dope, you'll be in the shit.'

'Perfectly expressed, old boy. What's why it won't go to court.'

'And what if he doesn't talk?'

'We simply tell the press he has been charged. Make him sweat for weeks, months. That will ruin his career.'

'Or drive him mad.'

'There is that possibility.'

'He's a puffed up little phoney, a bully boy, a crook at heart.'

'I love kicking creeps like that.'

Becker was not impressed. 'Ah, gee, Chook, this sounds too risky to me. Anything could go wrong.'

'It usually does, dear boy. But, with a little bit of luck, it won't.'

They had reached the Harley parked in the street.

'Why don't you hand the coke directly to this woman? Why bring me into it?'

'She is watched night and day. And they know us, we're often in Griffith, talking to people, valuable contacts. But, the same people talk, trying to make double deals. You never know whether you can trust them. But, they don't know you, Harry.'

'So, how are you going to do it?'

'Right under their noses. Out in the open, with them watching.'

'How will she know where to find me?'

'You'll be staying there, Room No. 12.'

'She's gonna come to my room?'

'That's right, after dinner.'

'Why?'

'To have a bit of nookie.'

'What?'

'But really to pick up the dope.'

'Ah, Jesus, I don't like this.'

'You worry too much for a cop.'

'I'm not a cop. I'm out of all that.' They walked on a few paces. He was not out of it, he knew. He would never be out of it. 'How will I know her?'

'She'll find you. She'll have a photo. And another thing, the top button of her blouse will be undone.'

'Why?'

'To show her crucifix. If you can see the crucifix, it's okay to go ahead. If you can't, the whole deal's off. That's why we need Barnes, as fall back.'

'Jesus, this is getting serious.'

Chook nodded. 'It is.'

'So, after pretending we've had a bit of nookie, she departs with half a kilo in her bag?'

'Yeah, after she's handed over a certain document.'

'What document?'

'Ah-ha!'

'I don't like this. Anyone watching would be suspicious.'

'Yeah, suspicious that she's gonna run away with you. Big scandal, she's gonna run away with A bloke nobody knows, who's not Italian and not even Catholic. Shock and horror running through the community! What is Angelo going to do about it?'

'You mean he might kill me?'

'It's possible.'

'What?'

Chook laughed. 'Don't worry, mate, once we have that document, he won't want to touch anybody.'

Becker laughed. Or he tried to laugh. In fact, he was scared stiff. 'This idea is so corny it'll never work.'

She was mounting the Harley. 'Don't worry, old boy. It *will* work because it *is* so corny. Italians love romance, especially an intriguing romance with a touch of danger. But it's all part of a trap.'

'For her father?'

'Yeah, her father.'

'Jesus, what has he done to her?'

'Not to *her*, someone else.'

'Who?'

'Her sister.'

'What happened to her sister?'

'Maybe she'll tell you, while you're having a bit of nookie.'

'I'm not going to have a bit of nookie with some strange woman.'

'Pity. She's quite beautiful. I wouldn't mind screwing her myself.'

'Who is this woman?'

Chook hesitated. 'Promise not to tell? Not even Robyn?'

Becker nodded.

'Angelica Cosco.'

'What?' This time Becker did jump over the moon. Or his heart did. 'You mean Angelo's daughter?'

'That's correct.'

'Jesus, he's the *capo* in Griffith.'

'Not quite. Old Mario Pescii is the *capo* in this part of the world. Angelo's the hard man, the enforcer.'

'You've penetrated that high?'

'Yep.'

'How did you do that?'

'She came to us.'

'Angelo Cosco's daughter came to you? Why?'

Chook pressed a button on the Harley.

'He killed her sister.'

CHAPTER 16

AND THAT, MORE or less, is what happened. Becker arrived about seven and checked in. He'd told Robyn he'd been called to give evidence at a court hearing called for Sunday, which any fool knows is almost never held on a Sunday, unless there is some urgency. You can't hold someone for more than twenty-four hours without one. But she'd not queried it, she being she. He'd asked her, as he'd paused at the door, as if realising he had not asked her something he should have asked long ago, early in their marriage, instead of taking her for granted: 'Do you love me, Robbie?' Surprised, starry-eyed, she answered: 'Love you? I revere you.'

As Chook had said, it was a big room, already crowded. He was met at the door by a woman in a long red skirt and a cream blouse, standing behind a lectern, checking reservations, who showed him to his table some distance from the door, handing him the menu with a smile. He felt alone, very obvious and very set up.

A waitress came, bustling. You could see it was going to be a bustling sort of night. Already a group at a near table was shouting, laughing and saluting each other. They looked Italian, Italians from the far south. They had the heavy, stocky and almost featureless aspect of the assiduous farmer, the noble but dogged peasant and the get-rich graspers of a hard-working and hard-drinking tradition.

'Now, sir, what would you like?'

She didn't look like any sort of woman who was going to suggest they get together after dinner, or sooner. She looked perfectly ordinary, not Italian at all. Fair and tawny, a hard-working woman with sunburnt arms. He had noticed that *saltimbocca* was on the menu. Evelyn had said she was going to make it. *Gnocci* too, if she had time. Would he like to dine with her? He had declined, not wanting to get so close to her. She had dangerous friends.

'I'll have the *saltimbocca*,' he said. 'Do you have *gnocci*?'

'No, sir, not normally. We could make it, but it takes about twenty minutes.'

'Just the *saltimbocca*.'

'Anything to drink, sir?'

'Oh, what is that winery you see driving in from the east?'

'At Yenda? That's Yellowtail, sir. I used to work there, during the harvest.'

'You must have been busy?'

'Frantic, sir. Would you like a Yellowtail?'

'Do they have a light, dry red?'

She hurried away. Did not seem to be the woman. Did not bend down to intimate anything. Nor was her top button undone. He was embarrassed. He should have got a paper and sat there reading it. Or not reading it. Only pretending. At least that would have made him feel better.

Then, at the next table, sudden excitement. An old man had arrived. Everyone at the table had stood in welcome, gasping with respect, ready with their smiles and cheers, one or two clapping. He was bent and lined and wobbly, grinning in a vaguely childish way, waving a stick and escorted by the lady in red on one side and a buffoon in a party hat on the other. It must have been the old man's birthday. He sat too quickly, almost fell. Doddery, on his way out. On his last legs.

He was family, you could see. An old man, a patriarch, perhaps a don, but not in the Godfather sense. Nothing but a wobbly old man, grinning, not all his teeth there. All rushing to help him, but unnecessarily, the lady in red already having pulled out a chair, a hand under an elbow. Others reached for his shoulders, his stick.

The waitress came back with the Yellowtail. Showed him the label. He nodded and she poured. So he sat there drinking, waiting. He was not a heavy drinker.

At a table not far away sat a couple—a solid young man with a crew cut and a tight grey suit, a well-dressed woman with beads or pearls. He was not sure. Her blond hair kept falling over one eye as she drank soup. Probably *minestrone*, he thought. The man's back was to Becker, but the woman was drinking quickly and glancing at him.

At first he avoided her eyes, sure she was amused to see a solitary male. No girl to romance tonight? Oh, poor man. When he looked back, she was seriously smiling. Quite deliberate, he thought. She winked. Then she looked from him to the group at the big table and back again. As though pointing with her eyes. Now, he realised. He had backup. Chook had thought of everything.

The same waitress appeared. 'And here's your *saltimbocca*,' she said.

So, he ate and he waited.

A small group in informal costumes appeared. As Chook had said, it was a violin, a bass, a clarinet, a concertina and a tinkling piano. They began with *Arrivederchi Roma,* and kept going for what seemed to be forever, the diners and the drunks and the children and everyone singing along. So, he sat back, pretended to be a connoisseur of light red wine, and listened. And thought about what might have been if they'd got away. Gone to Perth like she'd said. Full of enthusiasm, like a kid going on a picnic. And driving in her own car, which was now his car, the BMW. Off to see the world with lots of lovely cash, millions of it. Then the squeal of brakes and *Bang, bang*!

'Excuse me, sir—'

Another woman was standing beside him, not actually beside him, but behind his right shoulder. Very close, so close that he could not clearly see her, very personal. But he could sense her, in the way he could sense Evelyn and not Robyn.

'How is the barramundi?' she asked.

'The barramundi? Oh, it's—It's fine. Just what I wanted.'

'I'm so pleased, sir.'

He'd already seen her, a tall straight brunette at the other end of the room, briskly serving. Smiling as if she knew every guest personally. Now and then bending down, a hand on a shoulder, occasionally laughing. Like a good woman, very polite. Very welcoming. Now her face was only a few inches from his. The top button of her blouse was undone, so he could see an inch or two of cleavage. But also a small gold crucifix.

'I am Angelina,' she said. 'Please call me if you need anything.'

She walked away briskly, leaving nothing but her presence. And her voice, it was like Evelyn Crowley's voice, dark and earthy. A gritty sort of voice, from the deep south.

He ate and sipped more light red. When he'd finished, he ordered a dessert.

She suggested a *tiramisu*. He'd never had it, so she had to explain. Lady fingers dipped in coffee layered with whipped eggs, sugar and mascarpone cheese, and soaked in Marsala wine. He waited for that to come, then ordered coffee, long black.

'That sounds fine,' he said.

'Thank you, sir. Shall I charge that your room?'

He was going to protest that he'd pay cash, but woke up.

'Oh, sure, if you like.'

'What number, sir?'

He showed her the key.

'Thank you, sir.'

Becker finished about eight thirty and went back to his room. Watched a program on the ABC on the dangers of atmospheric pollution. Several times he thought he'd switch over to something more dramatic, such as *Hey Hey It's Saturday*. Then he realised that he'd thought quite the opposite when walking with Evelyn Crowley by the lake in Canberra.

Back in those days, when he respectfully thought of her as Mrs Crowley. She was some woman then, walking along, her skirt swinging with her steps, her handbag held before her body, bouncing off her knees, off her thighs. Her heels, her high heels tapping musically on the concrete like a measured tympani, as they'd walked on and on, slowly, casually. Toward the High Court and the National Gallery, and talking. Chatting. She had opened up then and said she'd been to a concert, a symphony concert, which had been wonderful. They'd played something by some fellow called Sibelius and, in the last movement, there had been swans flying away, sixteen of them, over a lake. And the music had gone up with them and she'd said: Sometimes I wish I could fly away with those swans—up and up into limitless nothingness—and never come back…

Suddenly, a knock at the door. It was a few minutes after ten. He must have been asleep in the chair. It must have been the wine. He'd not slept well last night. Wide awake for hours, worrying.

He went to the door.

'Who is it?'

A woman replied. But it could have been anyone. He opened the door, only an inch or two.

She was standing there.

Coming along the corridor behind her were three women and a man, laughing. One was singing the old Dean Martin song: *Volare, oh oh/ E cantare, oh oh oh oh oh ho/ No wonder my happy heart sings…* She lingered, making sure she'd been seen. That was part of the plan. She walked in.

'Hullo,' he said.

'I hope there has been no misunderstanding,' she said.

'It'll take only a minute.'

'Oh, no, it must take longer, if it is to work.'

'Yeah, of course.' Then he corrected himself: 'Yes.' He didn't know why he did that. It must have been the situation. You didn't say, 'Yeah' to a woman you didn't know, but is trusting you with her life.

'I am to give you something,' she said.

'Yes.'

'And you are to give me something?'

'That's right.'

He opened his bag and took out the package wrapped in plastic. She accepted it gingerly, as if it would explode or burst into flame. 'It is worth so much money?' she asked.

He was surprised. Her family dealt in drugs, but perhaps she was never told anything about that. In fact, maybe a grand silence was maintained at home. No one was told anything they did not need to know.

'About a hundred-thousand,' he said. 'On the street.'

'Dollars? Oh, my God.'

She looked like a young woman, who really did believe in God. She had done up the top button, but he could still see the crucifix, the golden top of it. And the chain.

'You'd better put that away,' he said.

'Yes, yes, of course.' She had a large leather handbag, into which she placed the package—carefully tucking it down, securing it as if handling dynamite. Then took something out.

'This is for you.'

It was a long, sealed envelope, the business type. No name or address on it. Becker put it in a jacket pocket.

'What shall we do now?' she said.

'Just talk.'

'What shall we talk about?'

'About you, I guess.'

'About me?'

'Why are you doing this?'

'Oh, I don't think—' She glanced at the door, listening. She seemed nervous and yet excited. She was getting out. The police had everything arranged. They would look after her. And they were the Federal Police. That's what she had wanted. When her sister had gone to the local police, the State police, something awful had happened.

He went to the bedside radio, turned it on. Found some more music, classical music. He left it on low, but not too low, hoping no-one could hear them.

'You like Prokofiev?' she asked.

'Is that what it is?'

'Yes, *Romeo and Juliet*.' Then she added: 'I love it. So dramatic, so cruel and so unhappy.'

She was nervous, tight, wary.

'What do you do?'

'Oh, I—' She looked around, took a seat. Becker sat on the edge of the bed. 'I teach music, in the high school.'

'And why are you doing this?'

'Why?' She shrugged, tightly. 'Someone has to do it.'

'What if your father hears about this?'

'He *will* hear about it.'

'What are you going to tell him?'

She shrugged again. 'I'll be gone by then.'

'Gone where?'

She didn't answer. Her eyes flicked from him to the door, then back. Maybe she'd been instructed not to say. Not to tell a soul. Not even him.

'I hope he will be dead by then.'

'Why would he be dead?'

'If he gives them what they want, he will not live long.'

'Give who? The police?'

She nodded.

'Someone will kill him?'

'*Si*, kill him.'

Becker was startled. He'd never heard a woman say such a thing.

'And if they do not?'

'Then I will be dead.'

'He will kill you?'

'No, I will do it myself.'

'How will you do it?'

'With the acid.'

'Acid?'

'That's what they did to Connie.'

'Connie?'

'Concetta, my sister. She went to the police. But she spoke to the wrong man.'

'Here in Griffith?'

She nodded. She looked tired and frightened.

'They killed her with acid? A woman? Why acid?'

'It's what they do, back in the old country. To a woman, if she talks. They make her drink the acid.' She shuddered, a hand to her throat.

'What kind of acid?'

'The hydrochloric, you call it.'

'Your father, why didn't he stop them?'

'He was responsible, along with the rest of them.'

'Who?'

'*Gli capi*.' Becker didn't have enough Italian, but he thought she was referring to important people. Thought too he was getting the picture.

'He went along with it? The murder of his own daughter?'

'*Si*,' she said.

He was shocked. 'Did *he* do it? Your father? With the acid?'

'No, not him.' She paused. This was hurting her, he could see.

'Someone else?'

'*Mio fratello*,' she said.

'What's that?'

'My brother.'

'Your brother did it? Why your brother?'

'It was a matter of the family's honour, he said.'

'Who said? Your father?'

'Yes, to toughen him up. To make him understand what he must do, if ever the time comes.'

Becker didn't know what to say, so he changed the subject.

'Why did Connie go to the police?'

'She was in love with someone, a good man.'

'An Italian?'

'*Si*, he refused to kill someone. Walk up behind a man in the dark and shoot him. He said he could not do it. It was dishonourable to shoot a man in the back. Also, he did not know the man. He had nothing against the man.'

'And?'

'He said he was going to go to the police.'

'And?'

'They killed him.'

'Killed her boyfriend?'

'*Si*, he was found floating in a ditch.' She meant an irrigation channel. 'Face down,' she added, putting a hand to her throat again. On one finger was a gold ring.

'You're married?'

'No,' she said. 'I wear it to keep the men away.'

'You don't wish to marry?'

She looked away, then back at Becker. 'I am about to marry the Lord Jesus Christ, if all goes well. If they can hide me away.'

'You're going to be a nun?'

'They have promised to get me away, hide me.'

'The police? Who said?'

'The tall one, she said it was all arranged.'

'You mean Anastacia?'

'*Si*, Anastacia.'

Now he understood. They'd pick her up in a few minutes, probably at the back door. Perhaps she wouldn't have packed a bag. She would need none of her clothes where she was going. She'd slip out, a car would be waiting, possibly Chook driving. There would be a long trip through the night, not to the Griffith airport but to another, maybe Wagga, maybe to Sydney, where, next morning, she would fly away. Up, up and away to some far nunnery, where she would take the veil. Free of men forever. And never show her face again. It was neat, the thought. Very neat. He had to hand it to Chook, she was smart. He stood up.

'I think we've taken long enough,' he said.

'*Si, si.*' She rose too, clutching her handbag. It was a heavy bag, not because of the package but personal belongings. Some toiletries, some underwear and perhaps a few mementoes of what she was leaving. He went to the door, turned the handle.

'Good luck, Angelina,' he said.

'There is something—,' she said.

'Something?'

'I have to do. Before I go.'

She seemed uncertain, perhaps embarrassed. But she stepped forward and kissed him on a cheek.

'Thank you,' she said. 'Now I must go.'

'Where are you going to meet Maria?'

'Outside, in the back lane. In her car.'

'Then she takes it back to Wagga? Tonight?'

'Yes.'

'And where do you meet Anastacia?'

'In the lane too. She will be watching. When Maria is gone, she will pick me up.'

'Then off to a new life?'

'*Si,*' she said. Angelina looked at the door, but hesitated. As if uncertain. It was now twenty past ten.

'Why are you doing this?' she asked.

'I used to be a bad man, but I rolled over.'

'Rolled over? What does that mean?'

'I decided to go to the commissioner, tell him what I had done.'

'Ah, *uno penitento?*'

'What does that mean?'

'A penitent. I am *una penitenta*, but I shall pay my penitence to God.'

On Monday Becker took a call. He was in the paddock with Nutty. He used to bark at the cattle, which would lower their heads and flick their tails warningly. Nutty was a tan kelpie, a sheep dog born and bred. Not a particularly bright one, but it had finally dawned on him cattle were not sheep. He now followed Becker around, happily sniffing. He had a good nose, especially for finding dead things, where you would never expect to find a dead magpie or a dead man. One day they'd been out walking, Becker and Nutty. Suddenly, Nutty had raised his nose, began sniffing, deeper and deeper. Then he took off along the lane and around a corner. They went three or four-hundred yards, Nutty getting more and more excited, wagging his tail. Then they saw a man. He was very old, like a swaggie of old, sitting by a fireplace. Made of stones and some sticks and ashes. There was an old blackened billy can, but no fire. The old man was sitting at the base of a tree, quite dead.

He made a lovely picture, iconic. Hans Heysen would have loved him.

Becker called the police, who called an ambulance. The old man was taken away. Becker never heard who he was or where he'd come from or where he was going. On his bad days, Becker felt like that old man. He too would be carted away, removed from the landscape and no-one would know he'd ever existed. He did not know why he thought of that old man. Maybe it was one of those pictures in which nothing happens. And yet they seem to be overwhelmingly significant. Significant of what? He did not know. But one thing was clear. One minute you can be alive and the next minute you can be dead. And it doesn't take a bullet to do it.

'Yeah?' he said.

'Bingo!' she said. It was Chook. She sounded happy.

'Bingo?'

'Everything went like clockwork.'

'And Angelina?'

'She's flying first-class with a female officer beside her.'

'Where?'

'Ah-ha!'

'So what about the bust?'

'Like clockwork, too. Last time I saw your little cousin, he was rolled up on the floor of an interview room, crying his heart out.'

'On the floor?'

'In foetal position, sayin' he couldn't help it. It wasn't his fault. His fuckin' Dago wife had got him into it. Just to pay off a few bills. And have a good time. Be somebody.'

Becker remembered a scene.

Many years ago, when he was ten or eleven, he was walking along Fitzmaurice street and heard someone crying. The sound was coming from a garage. It wasn't much of a garage, just three pumps, Super, Special and Diesel, all Mobil. A dark little workshop, only one dim and yellow and spotty light hanging over a utility truck, its bonnet up. Barry Barnes was crouched against a bench, crying. His father towering over him, saying, I told you to hand me a fuckin' plug brace, didn't I? And what d'you hand me? A fuckin' monkey wrench! A monkey wrench for a spark plug? What've y'got t'say f'y'self, eh?' And he was kicking the boy, curled up like a baby in the womb. If not kicking him with his greasy boot, then tapping him with the toe. 'Y'fucking useless little bastard!' And little Barry Barnes was saying over and over, 'I didn't mean to, Dad! I didn't mean to!'

'What's happened to him?'

'We let him go, as soon as we'd milked him dry.'

'What about his wife?'

'We nabbed her too, screaming her head off. This must have been shortly after twelve, when she turned up with the package in Wagga. But we let her go too, when we'd finished with her.'

'Denying everything?'

'She couldn't deny it. Angelina had given the package to her as soon as she left the motel. Maria drove home and gave it to Barnes. A few minutes later, we burst in.'

'You and the couple at the next table?'

'Ah, you noticed them?'

'Couldn't help it. She was winking at me.'

'Then you cottoned on? That was Laura.'

'Laura who?'

'Langley, she's from the CIA.'

'Really?'

Chook laughed. 'No, she's our woman in Wagga. Dave Hanson is her side-kick.'

'So that was the team?'

'No, we had three others flown in from Sydney. In case Cosco tried to stop her.'

'And Cosco himself?' Becker asked. 'Will he talk?'

'Never in a million years.'

'Who was the old man welcomed with open arms at the big table?'

'The big cheese out there in Griffith, Mario Pescii.'

'He's running things there? A derelict like him? He could hardly walk. And he grinned like a demented child.'

'They all respect him.'

'So I saw. And Melbourne? Who's the big cheese down there?'

'Laura doesn't know. But she said she thought it's a woman.'

'A woman? They'd never allow a woman to be the big boss. She must be wrong.'

'Maybe, maybe not.'

Becker felt both pleased and sorry. He was not dead. All was back to normal. But someone in Griffith would remember him, the guy with Angelina. The one she was with in his room the night she crossed over.

'She was brave,' he said. 'Angelina,' he added.

'Did you have a cuddle?'
'Just a kiss on the cheek.'
'I told her to give you kiss and a cuddle. A big cuddle. She must have been shy.'
'Why?'
'Why what?'
'Why a cuddle?'
'To put her scent on you. In case anyone sniffed you.'

CHAPTER 17

NUTTY WAS MAKING a hell a racket one day, barking at the other fence, the one on the right-hand side, the western side. A really furious bark, even growling. Much unlike him. So Becker went out, angry. He'd been talking to Chook on his mobile, getting the latest. The dog was at the fence, going at it so hard it was amazing he hadn't burst through it. Which would have been suicidal, if he had. On the other side was a big blue cattle dog, baring his teeth, hatefully. Not so much barking as snapping and snarling and walking around menacingly, as if thinking of jumping the fence and making a meal of Nutty. And beside the cattle dog was old Albert Henschke, standing there, hands in pockets, looking around, seemingly deaf to the racket. A strange look on his face too, indifferent. As if he did not care what the blue dog did, even killed his neighbour's dog. A good-for-nothing animal like that. A yappy young sheep dog.

Becker went over. 'What the hell is going on?'

Bert did not reply. Instead, he continued looking this way and that, sniffing like a man testing the air.

'Nutty! Come here!'

Nutty did not respond. He kept on barking at the blue dog, even when he dragged him away from the fence. 'Come on, get back there! Go to your kennel! No, no, no! Go back, go back!' Becker raised a hand. Nutty cringed, then thought he'd have another go at the intruder, then thought better of it. He circled back, panting, tongue hanging out. 'That's better,' Becker said, and went to the fence.

'Got a new dog, Bert?'

'Not exactly new, been 'round a bit.'

'Haven't seen that one before.'

'Son's dog.'

Becker knew Bert had a son, sometimes living with him, sometimes not. But he'd never seen the dog. The son was the kind who never talked, just nodded and walked on. A surly type with tattoos and a shaven head, like a truck driver or a shearer. He drove a beat-up utility and did some work each year, when the shearing was on. Otherwise, he didn't seem to have any visible means of support.

'Staying with you for a while, is he?'

'Could be.'

'Well, I'll try to keep Nutty on the other side of the house, while he's here.'

Bert did not respond, still looking around. He had an irritating habit of not looking directly at you, even when speaking to him. But anywhere else, as if he couldn't bear the sight of you. Impossible to have a real conversation with him. The really strange thing about Bert Henschke was that he did nothing with his property. Like Becker's place, it was one square mile. Worth at least 350,000 dollars. What he did to earn a living was not apparent. Possibly he was on an age pension. Becker could not see why a man who was sitting on that much money deserved to have a pension. He should sell it, support himself.

He didn't grow anything—no wheat, no corn, no meat or any sort of sustenance. The land was neglected, weedy, bracken here and there. Occasionally a fallen tree, or at least a fallen branch. It had no creek, but there was an old dam and an old windmill, plus a couple of rusted sheds behind the house. It was a small timber house, not much bigger than a hut. Probably only four rooms and a verandah and a red tin roof. Whether it was red with paint or rust was not clear. At a distance, the cottage looked picturesque, the kind that artists loved to paint. But close up, it was dying on its feet. Occasionally they heard him blasting away at something in the distance, probably rabbits or possums. Or kangaroos. Or crows.

'Nice to talk to you, Bert,' Becker said, with an edge of sarcasm, and began to retreat. He was not sarcastic by nature, but couldn't resist it. Old Bert was a pain in the arse. But, as Becker's mother used to say before she was admitted to Kirralee, it takes all types.

He'd not gone more than a few steps, when Bert spoke.

'That Bob Elliott, the other day, was it?'

'Bob Elliott?'

'Bloke on the verandah, talkin'?'

'A couple of weeks ago? Know him, do you?'

Bert did not answer at first, still looking around, the new dog at his heels, panting and staring at Nutty, himself standing behind Becker and panting.

'Yeah, I know 'im.'

'Where did you know Bob Elliott?'

'Where'd I know 'im?'

Old Bert always flung your question back at you.

'Out there,' he said. He might have been indicating some remote spot out west. But on the other hand, he might not.

'Wybilonga?' Becker asked.

Old Bert did not answer the question. 'Yeah,' he said again. 'Knew all about Bob Elliott, once.'

Next day Becker went to town. He always said he had to go to town to pay bills or see the bank or talk to old Tommy. Which was true, but he didn't always do that. Or didn't do all of it. He had to see Chook, whenever she had something best not to be said on a phone. So he met her and the two others at the Hovell. They were sitting in the front lounge with the wide windows, through which you can see the passing parade on Baylis Street, the four of them—he, Chook, Laura Langley and her side-kick, Dave Hanson. He and Hanson were both having a beer, Chook, her usual Jack Daniels and Laura was playing with a gin sling.

Laura gave him a rundown on Saturday night.

'We got Barnes to talk. He had to agree that Cosco had given him the coke. Otherwise, we'd charge him with receiving and that'd be the end of his career.'

'But Cosco didn't give him the coke.'

'That doesn't matter. He was caught in possession.'

'What'd Cosco have to say?' Becker asked.

'Nothing,' she said.

'Nothing?'

'Nothing at first. We said, "Quite clearly you ordered her death. And you made your son Silvana do it. That's what's in Angelina's statement. It's signed by her. Look, see here, her signature." We gave him a copy. He took a long time reading it, his eyes going as hard as a stone. He is a tough bastard. Never gives anything away. So, we said, "What's it going to be, Angelo? You tell us who's running the Mafia and everyone from him down, the whole structure. And who killed Evelyn Crowley and Polly Politis in Canberra. Or, do we show this statement of Angelina's to the press?" Remember, it was a signed statement. Everyone knew her signature. All her friends.'

'How did he take it?'

'He was astonished for a moment, wasn't he, Dave?'

'Yeah, right,' Dave said.

'As if he couldn't believe it. He was trapped. If he did talk, he wouldn't be charged with the murder of his daughter, Concetta Cosco. But, if he did talk, he'd be killed by the Mafia—way before he got to court. Of course, the agreement was to be between him and us. The state cops did not know a thing about it. But if they got wind of it, if they charged him, that'd be too bad for him. Nothing we could do about it. If he did not agree, the whole world would know he'd killed his own daughter, Concetta, with acid.'

'So what happens now?' Becker asked.

Laura shrugged. 'We wait.'

'How long?'

'Two or three—'

There was a sudden scream, more like a shocked gasp.

They looked around. The young waitress was backing away from a group of men at a far table. A hand to her behind, insulted.

'What happened?' Becker asked.

'It looks like someone groped her,' Laura Langley said.

'I saw it,' Chook said.

Becker was going to intervene, but Chook got up. 'Stay there, mate.'

She went over and leaned on the smelly little bonehead, who'd groped the girl. Leaned on him heavily, full force on a shoulder and her fingers about his neck. The young lady was standing back, red-faced and trembling and ashamed. Such a thing happening to her in front of a whole room full of patrons. She being a decent sort of girl, well brought up and probably trying to earn a few dollars while she worked her way through college.

Chook bent down, spoke in an ear. 'You,' she said, 'get up.'

'What the fuck?' he said.

'Get up, or you'll be shitting teeth.'

'Eh?' he said.

'Are you deaf or something?'

'Ah,' he said, wriggling in his chair, trying to elbow her out of his life. He had no hope.

She lifted him out of his chair. Took him by the scruff of his neck, dug in her fingers so far the tips must have reached bones. He gasped, he began to go blue. Magically, like in one of those wizardry shows on TV, where you see bodies float slowly into the air at the wave of a wand, the slob rose slowly, squealing like a stuck pig. She got him to his feet, then turned his head around. So everyone could get a good look at him.

Becker was surprised. It was old Albert's son, or so-called son, the one who never said even good day, when you tried to be polite over the side fence. He was as bald as an egg and twice as yellow. His eyes were popping. His tongue was out. He looked as though he were going for the big spit.

'What's your name, sport?'

'Uh, uh, uh,' he was saying.

'Can't think of your name?'

He glared at her with eyes which refused to focus.

'Can't think of your name?'

The two young boozers with him were astonished. They sat there, beer in hands and a mouthful of frits and sauce, chewing.

'You're going over there and you're gonna apologise to the little lady.'

'Eh?'

'Walk, shithead!'

Chook was still speaking quietly, but you could guess what she was saying. A few inches from his gormless face. He had a few days' growth, but that did not make him look tidy or intelligent or worth knowing in any way.

'Eh?' he said again.

'Do it,' she whispered. 'Don't make me have to hit you.'

'Eh?'

'Go over to her and apologise.'

'What?' He was trying to claw her fingers away from his throat.

She whispered in an ear, 'Move, arsehole!'

He moved like a bloke with a broken neck.

'Ah, Christ,' he said.

'This way.'

The girl was still standing defensively, order book and pencil in one hand and the other hand still behind her behind. She was the pretty girl who'd served Becker and Chook on her first day at the Hovell. She backed off, alarmed.

'I don't hear anything,' Chook said.

'Who the hell are you?'

'You don't need to know.'

'Ah, Christ, I wasn't doin' nothin'.'

'Apologise or I'm gonna march you into the nearest cop shop and have you charged with assault.'

'Ah, Christ,' he said again.

'We're waiting. Everyone's waiting.'

'I'm sorry,' he said.

'What's your name, honey?' Chook said.

'Deloraine,' she said.

'Deloraine?'

Chook shook him. 'Say it again, I'm sorry, Deloraine.'

'Del—'

'I'm sorry, Deloraine!'

'I'm sorry, Deloraine.'

'That okay with you, honey?'

'Y-yes,' she whispered, and withdrew.

Chook put an arm around his shoulders. 'Come over here, mate.'

'What?'

'To meet my friends.'

'Why?'

'To have a little chat. What's your name?'

He wasn't going to give it, so Becker said, 'Ray, it's Ray. He's living next door to me with old Bert Henscke.'

'That your name, Henschke?'

'Yeah.'

'German name, is it?'

'I reckon.'

'What do you do?'

He wasn't going to give that either. So Becker said, 'Says he's a shearer.'

'A shearer, eh? How long does the shearing season last?'

'Ah, about—'

'Three months? At the most?'

'Yeah.'

'When does it start?'

'Ah, I dunno. In August, September.'

'It'd be finished now, wouldn't it? In April?'

'I reckon.'

'You've got to finish by October at the latest, haven't you? Cause the sheep start to shed their wool for summer, don't they?'

'Yeah.'

'So what've you been doing since October? For a crust?'

'Ah, a bit of work, here and there.'

'What sort of work?'

'Ah, I dunno.'

'You don't know? You know this lady here?' She was pointing at Laura Langley.

'Nah, never seen her b'fore.'

'Works for Social Security. She's an inspector. You on the dole, Ray?'

'Yeah, sometimes.'

'Laura has the power to cancel your dole.'

'Eh?'

'She goes after people who claim they can't get a job, but they have a lot of dough. Money they can't explain. Know what I'm talking about?'

He was too scared to answer.

'What's Bert living on?'

'Eh?'

'A bloke who lives on a big parcel of good farming land out there without producing an ear of corn or a pound of wool must have other means, eh?'

She shook him.

'You're not mixed up in anything, are you, Ray?'

'What d'y' mean?'

'You know what I mean—stuff you smoke.'

'Ah, I wouldn't touch that.'

'Yeah? You stink of it. Your clothes stink of it.'

'Ah, shit.'

'I've got a hunch you're not too smart, Ray. I mean, any bloke, who gropes a girl before a dozen witnesses, isn't too bright, is he?'

'I reckon.'

'Perhaps we might have a little chat sometime?'

'What about?'

'You know what about, your means of support.'

'You a cop?'

'What do you think?'

'Ah, shit.'

'Laura does the thinkin', I do the shootin'.'

'Ah, Christ, I ain't done nothin'.'

Becker was amused. They all were. Chook was an expert. You threaten to slam someone in the clink, then you pat him or her on the shoulder and have a heart to heart in full daylight, the whole world to see. It was an old trick, but it worked. That's what they had done to Angelo Cosco on a large scale. Make him an offer. Either you talk or your mug goes on the front page of the local rag. But, if you do talk, you're dead. So far, Angelo had not made a decision. He was still thinking. They'd given him three days. This was the last day.

'I'll be out to see you, Ray. At Bert's place.'

'I might not be there.'

'You'd better be, or I'll have you slammed up faster than you can take a piss on a cold night.'

'Jesus!'

'For indecent assault, that can get you six months.'

'Ah, Christ!'

'Jesus Christ ain't gonna help you, Ray. Get back there and finish your steak.'

She patted him on his way, then looked at the others. 'Time for lunch? Want to eat here?'

'I can't stand pub food,' Laura said and stood up. 'I'll get a sandwich and sit in the park.'

They followed her out. Dave didn't say anything. He was that kind of fellow.

Becker said: 'I'm going home, Chook—' Too late, he caught himself.

'Chuck,' she said.

'What?'

'It's Bab*chuck*, not Bab*chook*. It's fuckin' Ukrainian and we say *chuck*, not *chook*.'

'I'm sorry.'

'Ignorant dickheads!'

For a moment, they stood there, smiling at her. She sure had a way with her, even when angry. And a sense of humour, when you got to know her.

'Who started calling you Chook?' Becker asked. 'Was it Polly?'

'The bitch, the bitch,' she said. 'Why did she have to die?'

CHAPTER 18

WHEN HE ARRIVED home, he got a surprise. No-one was at home when he left. Which was not surprising, the two kids being at school, Wendy in Wagga and Terry still at the little bush school at the turn-off. Which had a name, Old Man Creek. Unsurprisingly, there was a creek of that name, quite a big one, which was not a creek at all, but an anabranch of the Murrumbidgee River. Which had several good fishing spots. From there on, out past Lockhart, past Boree Creek, past Wybilonga, there was nothing but plains, red plains, sandy plains. Plains which went on and on. Good for nothing but wheat and sheep. Then, no good for wheat, just sheep. Then, nothing but the endless saltbush plains and the mythical outback. Out in the back of beyond. The back country, as they called it out there. Beyond the rivers and beyond endurance. Frequently beyond hope. It was said of the back country that it was littered with the bones of little men who'd tried to get big.

The surprising thing was that Nutty was on the front verandah. Normally he was tied up out back, when no-one was at home. If not, he'd be at the side fence, barking himself hoarse at Blue. Then, as he drove in, Becker saw, sitting on the verandah, behind the old pepper tree, a woman and two children. They were patting Nutty, or trying to. He was excited, dancing this way and that on the verandah. He looked happy, as if he'd found new friends.

Becker got out of the BMW slowly, surprised.

'Addie?' he said.

'Yes, Harry,' she said. She looked a perfect picture of misery. Or what she thought or hoped was a perfect picture.

'What's happened?'

'We had to come,' she said.

'What has happened?'

She had been his wife. His first wife, before she'd kicked him out. After what he'd done good for her years before. Told him in the patrol car in Sydney that she was up the duff and did not know what to do. Told him while he was driving her home after a smash and grab in Hurstville. He wasn't the father. Just doing her a good turn, a woman in distress. She'd said her father would skin her when he found out. He would have found out pretty soon, she being three months gone and beginning to show. She'd burst into tears and said no-one'd marry her now. So, he, Harry Becker, stupid mug, had said, 'Don't worry, I'll marry you instead.'

'I hope you don't mind, Harry. We couldn't find anyone at home but your lovely doggie. So friendly he was, all chained up and wagging his tail. And begging us to let him off, so we did. And smiling at us, even though he had hurt in his eyes, the way doggies do, when everyone has gone and left them all alone. So affectionate, isn't he? We let him off and have been sitting here, haven't we, kids? Waiting with him and he's been so good to us, going to the gate now and then, looking up and down, then coming back and saying, No sign, no sign. With his eyes the way dogs do.'

'Jesus,' Becker said.

'I'm sorry, Harry, but you've got to help us.'

It was the word 'us' which made it sink in. The two girls were his.

'What about Cornelius?' he asked. Cornelius being the bun she'd had in the oven in the patrol car.

'He's with Mum,' she said.

He sighed. He'd always thought he'd never see her again, Adeline Atkins as she was before they'd married. Never see her again after paying her off with some of Evelyn's money. And setting her up with her live-in lover and a house all paid off, and worth a million dollars now, if what you read about house prices in Sydney, or at least in Maroubra by the sea, was true. And now, of all the rural paradises she could have walked into, she'd walked into his.

'Although,' she was saying, 'I shouldn't have, *she* being now in a shocking state with the lupins.'

'The what?'

'She means lupus,' one of the girls said.

'It's all over her body now, isn't it, kids?' They nodded. 'Her face too,' she added.

He sighed again, but perhaps unconsciously or perhaps prompted by some deep-seated compassion for even the worst of humans, he went up the steps and sat in a chair, and rubbed the ruff of the puffing and loving and always forgiving dog.

'What do you want, Addie?' he said.

Not really waiting for an answer, but looking at the two girls. The elder was ten and the other was eight. Or at least he thought so. He'd lost track of birthdays. He hadn't seen them for years, not since Kat's confirmation. Not in the Baptist church on Stoney Creek Road, Hurstville, where he and Addie had been married, but in an Anglican Church on Anzac Parade, Maroubra. Not because of any change of faith, but because her father, who'd done time for burglary, having said, 'They've got more money, and gold candle sticks, that's why.' Just joking, he was. But not necessarily. Her father was a man of grim humour. And a criminal mind.

'How are you, Ches?' he said to the older girl, she being Chesney.

'Starving,' she said.

'How are you, Kat?' he said to the younger. Not Katrina but Ekaterina. Adeline had seen a movie on the Czar and his wife and children, who had died at some remote place called Ekaterinburg, far out east on the Siberian railway. She too had died when they were all shot. In the freezing snow. Next day, Addie had given birth to the second daughter. And that's how she got the name, Ekaterina. Which, of course, in Russian means Katherine.

'We haven't had anything since we left home,' she said.

'Long trip?'

'Twelve hours.'

'Twelve hours? From Sydney?'

'It went via Canberra,' she said, as though that explained everything.

'And they let you off here?'

That was a stupid question, he knew. If they'd not been let down at his place, they would still be on the bus. Which he wished they were. He did not want them. They were intruding. They did not go with Robyn and the farm and the new life. He didn't like Chesney. She had an insolent manner and was argumentative for the sake of being argumentative. The young girl was better, not so smart or insolent or scruffy. She wasn't chewing gum. He'd always thought she was bright. There was some hope for her. He should do something about her, send her to a good school. Get her away from Addie. Her mother was a disaster, always had been. He should never have married her. She, Adeline, was predatory, like some large, iridescent insect which devoured everything it touched. Even its own mate.

'He wasn't going to, Harry, it not being a recognised stop. All the way to Adelaide, the sign on the front said.'

'What did you do? If he wouldn't let you down?'

'Well, we argued and argued all the way out from Wagga. He was not going to stop, the frog-necked old b—that he was.'

'How did you know he had a frog neck?'

'Oh, Harry, I was standing behind and hanging onto the back of his seat.'

'And?'

'Finally, desperate and seeing the sign coming up, I said: 'If I give you a look—' 'Yeah?' he said. He took a look, trying to keep one eye on the road. That sign was coming up fast. I was scared we'd go right past.'

'This is not another of your sob stories, is it?'

'Harry, as Dad used to say, by all that's holy and not nailed down, I had to do it.'

Becker almost laughed. It wouldn't have been fair. Adeline was naturally pretty, but dim-witted. She was born that way. Born into a family of incorrigible thieves, liars, conmen and women and shonky dealers and shifty shysters. For which she was not to blame. She couldn't help being stupid. A real ditsy, if ever you saw one. She saw the world as an emporium of lollipops, into which she had to get her sticky fingers.

'So, what happened?'

'I did it,' she said. 'Slowly at first, I lifted my—' She did not say it, but slowly lifted her skirt, showing an inch or two of stocking. 'He took a quick look, saying, *Strooth*! But it was too late, wasn't it, girls?'

'What was too late?'

'We were running off the road!'

They said nothing. One was holding her belly and grimacing. They were really ugly children. Perhaps they were not his at all. Perhaps she'd deceived him all along. Shagging one footballer after another. And only eighteen when he'd met her.

'Off the road?'

'It's true, isn't it, girls? He tried to get it back up, but too late.'

'Mum, I'm gonna be sick.'

'You crashed?'

'Yes and no. Ches says it was a crash and Kat says it wasn't.'

'Well, what was it?'

'A smash,' the elder said.

'A run over,' the younger said.

'What's the difference, smartie?'

'There is a difference, if you think about it, Miss Ignoramus.'

'Girls, girls,' Adeline said.

'So, what was it?'

'The bus ran over the sign.'

'There!' the younger sneered.

Becker was surprised. He'd not noticed as he had returned from Wagga that the sign was not there, fifty yards before the bridge. But had sensed that something had changed about the environment, about the world. The sign that had been there for-ever: Kettles Creek. Without an apostrophe. He'd never noticed the missing apos-trophe. It was strange how you could see something every day of your life and not notice it.

'Kat, you may be the genius in the family, always getting top marks. But there is a limit to what Mummy can take on a hot and lonely and possibly fatal expedition to plead and bespeak from your father both of you some sort of—'

Becker was fed up. 'For Christ's sake, Addie, get to the point!'

'The bus stopped suddenly. I was thrown forward, there not being seat belts on buses, when there should be, shouldn't there? I could have been killed. And me with no panties.'

'No panties?'

'They were all in the wash.'

'So the bus stopped? And you got out? One hundred yards from my gate?'

'Yes,' she said.

Becker was bemused. He did not know what to do. He looked at the gate, but no sign of the Nissan. 'Addie, what do you want?'

'Sucker, Harry, sucker—'

'You mean succour, Mum.'

'Hush, darling. Not so much for myself, but for *your* children. For *our* children. Aren't they lovely?'

He took another quick look. They weren't lovely at all. They had the snub-nose and the pussy-cat eyes of their mother, plus a few freckles.

'We're done for, Harry, done for.'

'In other words, stuffed,' the elder said.

'Broke,' the younger said.

'Stuffed!'

'Broke is the right word.'

'Girls, girls, please stop it. Daddy's thinking.'

Becker did not know what to think. He had to get rid of them, but he didn't know how. Adeline tended to stick like a leach. She was the whining kind. She rose, hands clenched and pressed down almost into her groin, and weaved and wove before him, begging, even supplicating.

'Harry, to put it frankly, we are your wife and—'

'I have a wife.'

'Your first wife—'

'What do you want, Addie?'

'A home for *our* children.'

'And food, I suppose?'

'Oh, only what you can spare.'

'Dog food, I bet,' said Ches.

He got up, exhausted. Put a hand on a verandah post. Stood looking at the gate, and listening for sound. Robyn would return any minute. The Nissan did not make a sound, not when it was slowing down for the gate. He was stumped, he knew. He had an obligation to his children, if they really were. But he would never accept his former wife. She was a thief and liar, who'd taken him for all she could get. And so sweet and innocent with it. Last thing he'd heard she was living with a heavyweight boxer. But that was months ago.

'What happened to the boxer?' he asked.

'You mean Boris? Oh, Harry, he's dead.'

'What happened to him?'

'Knocked out in the ninth, the coroner said.'

'The tenth,' Ches said.

'If you say so, darling, the tenth—only eighteen seconds from the final bell. He would have won if he'd gone the distance.'

Becker was surprised. 'The coroner said that, if he'd gone the distance?'

'He was there, Harry.'

'Who, the coroner?'

'Yes, he was the doctor.'

'What doctor?'

'They always have a doctor. It's the law.'

He was going to argue, but gave up. It was hopeless, he knew. You could never get any sense out of Adeline, she being she.

'Where's your luggage?'

'Oh, Harry, we don't have any, do we, girls? We had to leave in such a hurry. The bailiffs were coming. We owing six months and several eviction notices. We hadn't even done the washing. Had to leave it all soaking in Vanish.'

Becker realised something. 'Just a minute. You had a house, debt-free house, which I paid for. It was not fun. I had to work twelve hours a day to do that for you.'

'Oh, Harry, I'm sorry, but it was all Eddie's fault.'

'Who is Eddie?'

'Eddie Sweetwater, he was in real estate.'

'Don't tell me!'

'He was standing outside a butcher's shop in Fitzgerald Avenue one day, when he offered me a piece of fried sausage with herbs. It was a Saturday morning. They always do that on Saturday morning. Giving it away. To get the trade, you know. It was delicious. I told him, and he said, 'So are you, darling,' and gave me a wink. So I winked him back, and somehow he ended up at my place that afternoon, the girls being at the beach. Well, we were lying on my bed after you know what, and he said, looking around, How much would this place be worth? I don't know, I said, but it's all mine. Yeah? he said. I reckon I could get you a good price for this. At least twice what you paid for it. You could, I said? Yeah, I've got a mate in real estate. Benny would be interested in this. So, I said, Oh, do you really think twice as much? Yeah, he said. Got the papers? Yes, I said, somewhere in a drawer. Show 'em to me, he said, taking a thoughtful drag on his Phillip Morris, and I'll see what I can do for you—'

'You're a moron, Addie.'

She was panting, a hand to her breast. She was great at gestures, theatrical gestures. Adeline was a well-read idiot. Loved romances, especially those in which the girl always got the boy, especially by the balls.

'Please don't say that, Harry. I did not see him again. I had no idea what had happened until one day a furniture van pulled up. And a car. Someone got out of the car and walked straight in, a man. He had a key and the papers. It was my title, but all the names had been changed. At the Titles Office, they said. They had a certificate of registration, they said. And showed me something. It looked more like a receipt for dressed timber than a title. But, how could I argue? These people are experts.'

'Experts?'

'At conning people. Poor innocent women, like me.'

For some reason Becker began to sing to himself. It went like this: 'Have you ever had your balls caught in a rat trap? In a rat trap?' Apparently, it was a soldiers' song. His father used to sing it before he went off to Vietnam. In the shower.

Addie was close to tears.

'We had to move out, Harry. I found a little stone cottage in Botany Road, near the university, for rent, where, at wits' end, I had to turn to doing you know what. Although it wasn't all that bad, Chinese students looking for a quick one between lectures and the occasional professor between conferences. Some of them very well educated. That's where I picked up *bespeak*.'

'You're lucky you didn't pick up something else.'

She stopped, panting. 'I'm so sorry, Harry.'

He did not know what to say except the obvious.

'And so you turned up here?'

'Well, yes, hoping—'

'Get in the car,' he said.

'Mum, I'm gonna be sick,' Kat said.

'You're not going to drive us back, are you, Harry? All the way to Sydney?'

'Into Wagga to put you up in a motel.'

'A motel? Oh, I hope it's not one of those awful three-star places, where they never wash the sheets and the soap keeps falling out of the holder in the shower.'

'They'd better have pool,' Ches said. 'Or I'm not stayin' there.'

'Darling, it's winter. They don't have pools in winter, do they, Harry?'

'Addie! Please shut up and get in the car.'

But it was too late.

The Nissan was as at the gate. Becker went up and opened it for her.

'Visitors?' she said as she drove past him.

'Yeah.'

'Oh, how lovely,' she said. 'Going to hop in?'

'No, you go.'

He closed the gate and followed the big four-wheel drive, trudging, head down. He was beaten, he knew. He was not the brightest bloke or the best at conversation, but he did try. Even if it were only to stay alive. In the faint hope that one day, things would turn out better. He had no other aspiration. He thought he'd found it at last—a good wife and a good home and good dog and good prospects. Suddenly, everything had gone wrong. The past had come back and bitten him.

When he reached them, Robyn was alighting, showing one pretty leg, the Nissan being so high. And saying in her own kind Christian way: 'So, you are Harry's family? Oh, this is a surprise! Oh, how nice. Oh, what lovely girls. And you must be—'

CHAPTER 19

HE WAS WAKENED two days later by a phone call. He felt like hell, not because he'd been drunk or sick or had eaten something bad or overeaten something good. But because of the noise. His good but overly good wife had pounced upon the tribe from Sydney. When she'd heard Becker was going to take them to Wagga and set them up in a motel she'd said: 'Oh, no, no, they wouldn't want to stay in a smelly old motel, when we have all this room here? Would you?' She'd looked at Becker, who'd tried to argue. He could not endure one more minute with this kleptomaniacal bimbo, Adeline Atkins who once was, then Addie Becker, then Mrs Boris Kalash and was now a wandering and stateless and boring pain in the arse, who wouldn't bloody well shut up. Going on and on in her little whining little-girl voice, hour after hour. About her struggles to keep body and soul and family and fortune together.

Thanking Robyn for being so kind and understanding, her girls being delighted, chasing cows and climbing trees and ducking each other in the creek now running free, it having rained. It, she said, was lovely to be in a good, quite clean home. It was a joy, the fresh air, and the home cooking and such lovely things you have, Robyn.

On top of which, the kids talking all night. Normally Wendy and Terry weren't noisy at all, not at night anyway, but their juvenile visitors from Sydney wouldn't stop arguing and hitting each other with pillows, which set off everyone laughing, including Nutty.

For Becker it was a night—no, *two* nights—of hell. They had moved in. When he'd protested to Robyn that they had only three bedrooms, she'd said: Oh, we could rearrange things, couldn't we, dear? Now, you and I in one room, Addie and Chesney in another, and Wendy and Kat in the third. When Becker had pointed out that would leave Terry without a bed, she'd said: Oh, that's not a problem, dear. He can sleep on the verandah, in a sleeping bag, can't you, darling boy? He wants to be a boy scout and go camping, don't you, Terry? To which the stupid kid had said, his eyes lighting up, 'Yes!' He was all for sleeping out, so he could go hunting possums in the dark with a torch and a ging—*ging* being country boys' lingo for a catapult.

The racket, the arguing, the banging of doors, the flushing of toilets—there being only one, but it sounded like a dozen, the fights and demands for refreshments at all hours, banging of the refrigerator door and switching lights on or off, or not switching them off at all and wasting all that electricity. And then, in the middle of the night switching on the television. Two nights and two days of it. He felt like shooting someone.

Becker picked up the mobile from a bedside table.

'Yeah?'

'Am I too early, dear boy?'

'Early? For what?'

'News.'

'What kind of news?'

'Ah ha! Not on the airwaves. I'll come out. What time's breakfast?'

'I think they've all had it, judging by the noise. Most likely there's nothing left.'

'You have visitors?'

'Yeah, the relatives from hell.'

Chook laughed. 'I'll be out in twenty.'

'Ah, Christ,' he said.

'What was that?'

'Where are you staying?'

'At the Hovell.'

'You can sleep in that joint?'

'It quietens down after midnight.'

'I wish this place did.'

Chook had hung up. Becker tried to go back to sleep for a few more minutes, but he could not. So he struggled out, grumpy and not his usual cheerful self. Or, if not cheerful, his usual polite and restrained self. At one time during the night, he'd dreamed he was in bed with a woman, who he thought was Robyn. And he'd rolled over and put an arm about her, and she'd stirred and smiled and said something. He couldn't see the smile, but she was one of those gifted women who could smile with her voice.

She'd yawned shortly and apologetically, a hand over her mouth, then breathed in, in a half awake and going off again sleep. Himself half-wondering: Why aren't they screaming and shouting and turning on the TV and making one great bloody disturbance, when: Hullo, Harry? she'd said. Who is that? he'd asked. Forgotten me already, have you? Evelyn? Yes, darling. She'd never called him darling. Not such a woman, very reserved, careful, never giving an emotion away.

Except when she'd broken down and cried in the living room at her place that second last night and said, "They are going to kill me, aren't they?" Or words to that effect. On thinking about it, he was not now sure exactly what she'd said. But one thing was certain. They'd had to get out of Canberra, or someone was going to kill her. And if he, Harry Becker, got in the way, too bad for him.

When he entered the kitchen, they'd all finished, thank God. And cleared out, yelling and screaming down by the creek, Nutty the worst of them, barking his lungs out with delight. Becker was surprised. Sitting at the breakfast table, long-legged and off-handedly yarning with her hostess, was Chook. Drinking coffee.

'Your friend thinks we have a lovely place, Harry.'

'Any coffee left?'

'Coffee and toast and bacon and eggs and cereals if you want, also chopped bananas and orange juice freshly squeezed, and prunes if you feel you must. Coffee fresh coming up, as they say in the films. In America anyway.' She never said movie, being an old-fashioned sort of woman, like her father. And her grandfather, the Anglican vicar. Who'd had a way with words, he having been an Oxford man. But that was long ago.

He sat. 'How long have you been here?'

'No more than five.'

'Sorry, I couldn't get going.'

He yawned, shaking his head. Chook was laughing. 'What it is to be a father.'

Robyn placed a cup before him, steaming. 'There's runny cream, if you'd like it, dear.'

He did not reply.

'What would you like to eat, dear?'

'Is anything left?'

'Oh, yes, lots of eggs. No bacon, however.'

He thought about it. 'We've got to get rid of them, Rob.'

'You've had a bad night, haven't you?"

'I'll drive the whole lot of them to town this morning and force them, kicking and screaming if need be, into a motel, a five-star if there is one. I can't take any more of that f—'

Chook kicked him under the table. He felt guilty, never having used such a word before or to Robyn. But he was too fractured to refrain.

'That birdbrain of a woman any longer. Her little-girl voice and the dim-witted innocence—'

'Harry, please, the children are having such fun. They've not yet had anyone for a sleepover.'

'They don't go to sleep. They talk all night.'

'It's so exciting for them. Addie was telling me she's never had a place of her own—'

'That's a barefaced lie!'

'That's lasted more than a few weeks.'

'She lost the house I slaved my guts out to pay off for her. Twelve hours a day at night. To get the money. It was part of the settlement.'

'Poor, darling,' she said. 'I've burdened you with so much, haven't I?'

Afterwards, he and Chook strolled up the creek, past the kids running around, saying *boo*! and *moo*! to the cows and running away. Or saying, Gotcha! Gotcha back again! Gotcha you too! And throwing stones at birds in the trees, making cockatoos fluster and fly away in a great wheeling arc across the face of the morning sun. So you had to squint and blink and show your teeth, fresh in the morning air as you watched, the steam rising like a hovering host from the wet and warming fields, the cattle lowing. And swishing their long black and highly swishable tails.

'What now, Chook. Sorry, I mean, *Chuck*.'

'I prefer to be called Stacey.'

'Stacey? Yeah, I know. I'll remember.'

'I'd really prefer to be called Anna, but I can't for obvious reasons.'

'What reasons?'

'Polly's name was Anna Polites.'

'So it was.' Polly had explained all that while they were driving him to the safe house, back in Canberra. The unsafe house, as it had turned out.

She kicked at a stone. 'Memories are hard to lose, aren't they?'

He almost said, Memories are driving me mad. But he didn't.

They walked on a few steps and stopped. Watching the rippling and chattering water bubbling over the stones, bringing down the leaves flattened in the midnight rain. On a branch by the creek, a kookaburra sat, thinking. The kookaburra always seems to be thinking, such quiet birds. Not real fishers at all, but big brown and creamy and dirty white birds, with huge beaks. Watching the ground for anything that moved, anything edible. Grab it in its big beak and fly back up to the branch and bash the critter to death. Then tear its catch apart, strip by strip. A very patient animal is the kookaburra. And not a sound out of it, except that maniacal laugh. Suddenly, earsplittingly.

'Cosco has decided to talk,' Chook said.

'What! Did you have to break an arm?'

'He saw reason, thinking about our offer. Either co-operate or we give the story to the press—the biggest story to hit the bush since they got Ned Kelly at Glenrowan.'

'Why?'

'We, in a sense, give him immunity. Not official, you see. He tells us who killed Polly and Evelyn—not held the gun but gave the nod—or he gets the big exposure, front page in *The Area* News. Also the Wagga *Bulletin*. The wire services will pick it up. Maybe front page of the Sydney *Herald*. The State cops would have to arrest him. On suspicion, at least.'

'You mean you prefer to do a deal with Cosco? Piece of shit like that?'

'How are we going to get a name otherwise?'

Becker was angry. 'He killed his own daughter!'

'Yeah, yeah, I know.'

'You should arrest him. Stick him in to jail! If I could, I'd kill him myself.'

'Yeah, I know. But that's what's going to happen to him anyway.'

'What do you mean?'

Chook was leaning against a tree. She had one hand on the trunk, on the fresh grey bark among the bits a pieces of brown bark hanging off its sides. Like apologies for bark, droopy, sad. Unwilling to die, but die it must. Good bark. To fall and rot and return and be forgotten. But once beautiful. Hanging off a coolabah.

'Let me spell it out, Harry. We can't arrest him.'

'Why not?'

'He'd go to trial.'

'So, he should.'

'But he wouldn't get that far.'

'You mean someone'd kill him?'

She shrugged. 'Why not?'

'They'd kill a big man like that?'

'Why not? Everyone's expendable in the Mafia.'

He thought about it. Angelina had said as much. If he talked, they'd kill him. That's exactly what she had wanted. Her father to talk, so that they would kill him. A daughter contriving in her father's murder. It sounded like some old-fashioned play by Shakespeare or something contrived by Mickie Spillane. Kill or be killed.

'They don't love each other,' Chook said gently, as if speaking to a child. 'There's no love between 'em. The Mafia is like a corporation of crocodiles. As long as there's something else to eat, they're friends. If not, they eat each other.'

Becker said nothing. He was thinking about the world. It was a dog eat world. He'd never eat dog, he was sure. But if he were starving, he'd eat dog, he was sure. But he would eat a dog he knew. Not Nutty. Or, he would eat him, but leave him to last.

'And another thing,' Chook said.

'Yeah?'

'If Cosco did go to trial, we'd have to produce Angelina.'

'Why?'

'To be cross-examined. The defence has that right. And if she did appear, she might be next. Do you want that?'

'Ah, shit, no, no,'

'That's why we're doing it this in a roundabout way, Harry. To keep her out of it. So, no-one can touch her.'

'Yeah, yeah, I see. What'd Cosco say to all this?'

'What'd Cosco say to all this?'

'He stared at us for a long time. These peasants from down south are very slow thinkers. Afraid of anything that makes them look idiots in the eyes of their families. Big fellas like that. They can't take it. Well, Cosco finally said something. Our ears pricked up. 'Medich,' he said. 'Medich?' we said. 'The kid, he was Marko Medich,' he said. 'Some *anale difetosso* from Serbia.' Which means anal defective, so I'm told. Which he was, as you may remember.

'We know that already,' we said. We already had his bike and its number and his name, thanks to your little cousin, Barry Barnes, who'd found the bike. 'Come on Angelo,' we said, 'we know that. Who was the fat man?'

'What fat man?' he asked. 'The one there at the lake with Adams. In Canberra.' 'I don't know nothin' about nobody called Adams. Don't know nothin' about no lake in Canberra.' 'Well,' we said, 'you can find out, can't you? A man in your position. Being a big fella here in Griffith.' He stared for a long time, considering his options.'

'Wouldn't Adams talk?'

'No, he was scared shitless. I don't think he'll ever talk, or he might in a note he might or might not leave beside his body, if he can find something in jail with which to top himself.'

'He's still there?'

'In Goulburn supermax. Well, we waited a long time, some looking at their watches, some whistling *Dixie* silently and others waiting for him to jump at us, so we had our hands close to our pieces. We had Angelo Cosco holed up in a room in the *Capriano* in Griffith, the one where you did the deal with Angelina.

'We even had room service, beer for me and Dave and a gin-sling for Laura, it being touch and go. We suggested a Campari on ice for Angelo, seeing he looked a bit dry and yet sweaty at the same time. But he refused, possibly fearing it'd be doped with some truth drug—which we should have used to save time, if we'd thought of it.'

'Did he give you a name? For the fat man?'

'Yeah, Guido Caselli.'

'Who's he?'

'An importer, down in Melbourne.'

'What's he import?'

'Fish, from Italy.'

'Do we import much fish from Italy?'

'Nope.'

'So it's just a front?'

'Seems like it.'

'What's the connection?'

'Remember the old geezer in the shop in Melbourne? The bras and girdles shop in Chapel Street? He's in it too.'

'Importing fish?'

'Yeah, they're joint owners.'

'That guy's name was Terracini.'

'Yeah, and the Terracinis in Griffith are connected with the Cosco family.'

'It all ties up, then?'

'Looks like it.'

'So, Caselli is the big boss?'

'Maybe, maybe not.'

'As it happens, our people in Melbourne have come up with this.'

Chook pulled out a photo from inside her jacket. Becker took it, turned it to the best light. It was taken in a busy street, maybe in Carlton. Outside a restaurant, apparently through the front window of a car. Probably a police car. It could have been Gianelli's where the kid had popped Ritzi Carbone. And ridden off singing, 'Hi ho, Silver! Again, he was side on. Talking to a man with a long, hawkish face. Who was smoking a desperate cigarette, eyes closed, squinting. And thinking about things. It was Alfredo Scarafini. It must have been last year. Possibly just before Alfredo realised he had to get out of town.

'Is this the fat man?'

'The fat man?'

'The one who killed Vincent Torrence by the lake?'

'What do you think?'

'I didn't see him.'

'You saw a fat man sitting by you and Evelyn in Manuka. Having coffee.'

'I don't know,' Becker turned the photo this way and that, trying to catch the light. The man in the photo didn't look any better, no matter which way you turned him. He was only a fat man pointing a finger at Alfredo. Telling him something. Maybe he was saying: Be careful. Be careful about what? Maybe the people you talk to. Or else.

'What are you going to do about him?'

'Kill him.'

'Kill him?' Becker was shocked. 'You are mad, Chook.'

She was laughing, or half-laughing. Her eyes crinkly with mirth. She put an arm about his shoulders. He thought she was going to shake him. Or punch him. Or beat him up, just being friendly. But she did not.

'Don't worry, Harry. You worry too much.'

'I've got a wife and kids.'

'I envy you.'

'Yeah, well, you will be caught one day,' he said.

'No, I won't. It's quite easy, when you know how.'

'Know what?'

'We'll set a bait.'

'What kind of bait?'

'Human bait.'

'Human?'

'Caselli will hear that Cosco has fingered him. So what does he do? He kills Cosco, or tries to. That's when we grab him.'

'How is he going to hear?'

'We'll tell him.'

Becker was going to ask: How are you going to do that? But he did not. The Feds probably had a mole planted close to Caselli.

'What about Cosco? Why would he co-operate?'

'He has to. If he doesn't, we'll give the papers a copy of Angelina's statement.'

'Jesus.'

'Neat, isn't it?'

'You've got people watching him?'

'Cosco? Yeah, a lot of them.'

Becker did not like the sound of it.

'What if this guy, Caselli, is innocent?'

'No-one in the Mafia is innocent.'

The kingfisher swooped. It grabbed something with its beak, a wriggling thing, some sort of lizard, too slow and too innocent. Too late to complain to Mother Nature.

They watched for a while. Then Chook said: 'Hey, we have a surprise for you.'

'A surprise?'

'Someone you know.'

'Who is it?'

'It wouldn't be a surprise if I told you, would it?'

CHAPTER 20

HE SAT ON a seat in the sun in Memorial Park, listening to ducks quacking on the lagoon. Dreamily awake, or half awake, floating in a sort of half-way world, where you are mildly and sensuously aware there is a world around you. People passing and looking and nudging each other, one saying or whispering: Doesn't he look good, sound asleep in the July sun? And the other saying or whispering: 'I'm going to get a snap of him.' He didn't open his eyes. Didn't care who was snapping him. He was thinking in a warm sort of doze. Thinking with some sense of relief, he'd got rid of the mad little bitch at last.

At daybreak, which was not until a few minutes before seven, they'd refused to get out of bed, determined not to move without a fabulous incentive—such as a mountain bike each or at least a pony to ride and new shoes. Doc Martens, if they had them in Wagga. And complaining it was much too cold to get up yet. Robyn had reported frost upon the paddocks.

So she, in her own tolerant way, had to nudge and edge them out with the threat of no breakfast if they didn't make the effort. Had got them to get some clothes on. New clothes she bought for them at Grace Brothers the day before, without which they would not have had a stitch. Except of course, the smelly and rumpled and in places, spotty and torn gear, in which they had arrived two days ago.

After all the excuses in the world, Adeline dug her heels in unless there was an irresistible incentive. Such as a four-star motel, to which they might retreat and loaf and laze and jump in the pool, which was sure to be closed for the winter. But that would not deter the girls, who would whinge and cry and bemoan, until the pool *was* opened.

Becker had brought them to town, got them registered at a reasonable-looking four-star place on Sturt Highway, just not far from Baylis, given them one-hundred dollars to get something for lunch. And had departed, leaving at the reception desk a credit of one-thousand dollars to cover a few days' accommodation until he could, somehow, send them to back to Sydney. Against which, he knew, they would fight, kicking and screaming. He feared he was stuck with them. Possibly for ever. He was exhausted.

'G'day, mate' someone said, 'how are you going now?'

And sat beside him.

It was the 'now' that alerted him. The implication that the speaker knew him from somewhere. And a hint that he was going to touch him for a loan. Which of course would never be repaid.

Becker opened his eyes. He was not wearing sunglasses and had to squint against the July sun.

'Thought it was you,' the newcomer said.

Becker blinked, sat up, tried to get the figure into focus. A long and listless figure of possibly fifty years dressed in what appeared to be cast-off clothes. His shoes were old and cracked but clean. Becker unwound and sat up. He'd been waiting for Robyn.

'Ah? Sorry, I was half-asleep.'

'Good in the sun, eh? Good in winter. Good place to sit and think, eh?'

'Yeah, well, I—' He looked around. No sign of Robyn. 'I'm waiting for someone, then off back home—'

'Don't remember me, do you?'

Becker looked closer, his eyes having adjusted. The figure looked familiar.

But too well-dressed and too well-spoken to be—what was his name? In Canberra, sitting on the seat in Garema Place? A deadbeat who used to turn up from nowhere. Try to touch him for a dollar, two dollars, in fact.

'Buster?'

'Yeah, mate. They said you might be down here.'

'They?'

'Friends of yours.'

'What friends?'

'This bloke that reckons he's a sheila and says he can prove it. And this lady with the blond hair over one eye, as if she's trying to be like some girl used to be in the old black and whites.'

'Laura Langley?'

'No, no, Veronica somebody. Jesus, my memory's still shot. But it's comin' back.'

'What are you doing here in Wagga?'

'What am I doing? I was born here.'

'In Wagga?'

'Yeah.'

So, this was the surprise Chook had mentioned? This was the someone he'd once known? Buster Keaton himself. One-time schoolteacher and long-time wreck, kicked out for doing something at some school out in the bush, possibly to a young girl. It had not been clear. But caught and dismissed, never to return to teaching and never to make a go of anything else. Disgraced, no-one wanting to see him again. A man like that, touching up girls or the like.

He shuddered. He had two girls of his own, plus Wendy, not a bad kid at all, not brightly gifted but making a go of it. First-year high school here in Wagga Wagga. A steady plodder, as quiet as a mouse. Never gave anyone any trouble. Did her homework with almost religious fervour. And helping her grandmother in the house. Staying with Bob and Muriel now. A responsible sort of girl. The bus trip in and out too much even for an indefatigable girl like her. And a waste of homework time.

'I thought you were dead,' Becker said.

'Ah, yeah, pretty close to dead. They fixed me up pretty good. Stuffed me full of vitamins, too. Good tucker every day.'

'You were run over, by some creeps one night.'

'Yeah, I was.'

'Deliberately?'

'Yeah, deliberately. They were gonna come back and make a meal of me, but this cop's car came up, two ladies in it. One gettin' out and shouting, Stop! Had this bloomin' revolver out. Could see her wavin' it in the lights from her own car. Silhouetted, you know, like on the pictures.'

'But they got away? The people trying to kill you?'

'Yeah, but these young ladies came back, called in on their phones and got an ambulance real quick. And raced me off to Canberra.'

'Hospital?'

'Yeah, I was in for six or seven weeks.'

'And now?'

'Are yeah, well enough. They cut it off, what was left of it.' He lifted his left leg. 'Enough of a stump left though to attach an orthopaedic.'

'Limb?'

'Yeah.'

'What about the other leg?'

'Broke it too, but not so bad. Managed to patch it up. The docs worked on me for weeks. Feelin' good now. Bit of pain now and then, but they gave me pills. Celebrex and Osteo, they call 'em. Still have physio now and then, when it gets real bad.' He paused, then corrected himself. 'Really bad.'

Becker was impressed. Buster was a different man. Or, to put it another way, the same man, but more like the man he was years ago. When he was starting out, an educated man. Like Becker himself, trying to make something of himself. Had tried and failed.

'Is the left leg heavy? To walk, I mean?'

'Ah, it's not so bad. Clunks a bit, though. Thought I might've waked you when I came up.'

Becker glanced around. Still no sign of Robyn. Buster had changed, he realised. A lot healthier, his speech better and he was clean shaven.

'They were after that card?' Becker said. 'Those who hit you?'

'Yeah, but I'd given it to you, hadn't I?'

'You got twenty dollars out of me.' Becker yawned a little. He hadn't slept too well last night, the television going full-blast once again. 'So what's the deal with Chook and Laura?'

'Who?'

'Stacey, the tall blond?'

'Lake,' Buster said. 'That's the one, Veronica Lake.'

'The actress?' He recalled the name, the face. Yes, Laura did look like Veronica Lake. He'd seen her in a movie with Alan Ladd not long ago in Canberra. It was a very old movie, but he couldn't recall its name. 'No, no, let's concentrate for a minute. Where did you meet up with Stacey?'

'Ah, she saw me in the street.'

'She remembered you from Canberra?'

'Yeah, she used to come and see me in hospital, day after day, trying to get some information out of me. Thought she was a man at first. Bendin' over me in bed, a six-shooter on her hip.'

'I see.'

Yes, he could see. Buster had been a witness to murder, and his memory was improving. If they ever caught the fat man, Buster would be very useful.

On the other hand, if they did *not* catch the fat man, Buster would be dead.

'Where are you staying?'

'Me? Ah, at the Salvos.'

'How are you managing? What are you living on?'

'Ah, well, they gave me a pension, permanently disabled. And gave me a card, lets me travel anywhere. Only twenty dollars to get to Wagga. So I thought I'd come back and see the old town again.'

'How long since you were last here?'

'Must be more'n twenty years.'

'Must have changed a lot?'

'Ah, yeah. Started off teachin' here. Then they sent me out in the bush.'

'Out west?'

'Yeah. Can't think of the name of the place. Had a lot of silos.'

'A wheat town?'

'Yeah. Real small place, at the end of a line. Nothing ever happening, except during the harvest.'

'Wybilonga?'

'Yeah, that's it.'

Becker was looking around. He had an uneasy feeling. He could smell cigarette smoke. It was distinctive, rich, aromatic, strong. He thought of Alfredo in the cemetery back in Canberra. He'd been smoking a *Sobranie*. But it was not quite like that. It was heavier, more like smouldering camel dung. More like the stuff the fat man at the next table outside the bookshop in Canberra had been smoking—heavy, stifling, repugnant. When he'd been talking to Evelyn. Talking about her husband and what he was doing at the bank. A big bank. He'd been sure that the fat man at the next table had been listening. A big bank.

Becker looked back. Behind them, two men were talking. It sounded like Italian, but he could have been wrong. One had his back to them. Talking fast and noisily, not caring who overheard. And smoking a cigarette. He'd put it to his mouth, suck hard and blow hard. At the same time drop his hand in some sort of rhetorical gesture, up and down. Up and down.

The breeze was coming from that direction.

The other man was looking over his shoulder, looking at Becker and Buster. It could have been quite innocent, but he was holding a camera. He was listening to the fast talker, or not listening. It was hard to tell. The fast talker was a fat man with a grey moustache. No doubt there was nothing to it. Anyone could look dangerous. But Becker was worried.

'Look, Buster, you've got to get out of here.'

'Eh?'

Becker nudged him. 'Come on, let's go!'

'Eh?'

'Come on, get up!'

'Hullo,' someone said.

Robyn was standing by them. Becker had not seen her approaching.

'Oh, hi, Rob, I was chatting to my friend here.'

'Oh?'

She moved around the better to see. Hugging her bag and something from Grace Brothers. And peering, her smile slowly fading.

'Oh,' she said again.

'Just in time, Rob. Come on, mate.'

'Harry, what is it?'

'He's a bloke I knew in Canberra.'

Robyn was peering closer and closer, astonished.

'Mr Keaton? Is that you?'

CHAPTER 21

HE WALKED BOTH of them, almost stiff-armed, to the Nissan, parked down the road past the lagoon, and pushed them into it. Robyn was alarmed, not so much by his action but by the presence of Buster. But, firmly believing that her husband knows what he is doing, especially an ex-policeman, she had immediately complied. Had got in up front with Becker after he'd pushed Buster into the back. Not having paused for a moment to ask her why she'd asked: 'Mr Keaton? Is that you?' He'd swung the Nissan around and gone back up Baylis street to the Highway and swung right, then pulled over and said to her: 'You drive.' And she'd said: 'Harry, what is it?'

'Take him home. Get him out of here.'

'But why, dear? Please tell me *what* is the matter!'

He'd leaned closer, kissed her quickly. 'Go, I'll see you later.'

'You want me to come back for you?'

'No, no, I'll be right. Go on, Robbie!'

She went, hoping by the grace of God that Mr Keaton did not recognise her.

Becker walked back to the office in Thompson Street. When he reached it, he was angry. He paused outside a door marked: Private. Then plunged in without knocking. Laura Langley was sitting at a desk, staring at a computer. Chook was leaning in the way only Chook could lean—against a filing cabinet with both arms and legs crossed. Neither was surprised to see him.

'What the hell?' he said.

'What the hell, what?' Laura said. She looked too perplexed to be startled. Chook did not stir. In a corner sat Dave, by a phone. In fact, his hand was resting on it, as if reluctant to let go. Or, he had to make a call he did not want to make.

'Buster's here in town.'

'Yes, we know.'

'Why is he here?'

'He was born here. He wanted to see the old town.'

'You should have kept him out of this area. It's dangerous for him.'

Laura glanced at the other two. 'Someone in Canberra thought it would be a good idea.'

'Why?'

She did not answer. Chook smirked. 'Some dickhead in an Armani suit,' she said.

Laura was about to chastise her, but Becker got in first.

'Did you know the fat man is here?'

That really startled her. 'What fat man?'

'The one who killed Torrence. And later tried to kill Buster.'

'Are you sure? How do you know?'

'I saw him, in Memorial Park. He was there with another guy, who was looking at me. And Buster. Buster saw him kill Torrence.'

Laura sighed, pushed back her hair. She really did look like Veronica Lake. At last he recalled the name of the film: *This Gun for Hire*. About a man hired to do a job. He does the job, but finds afterward that he has been paid off in marked bills. Now *he* is the target.

'Did you get a good look at him? This fat man?'

'No, but—'

'How do you know it's the same man?'

'Well, I don't, I suppose.'

'Dave, hand me that dossier. On Caselli.'

She snapped fingers at him. He did so. She flipped it open, extracted a print. 'Is that the man you saw? In the park?'

It was a fat man, no doubt about it. But not the one Chook had already shown him. This was taken at a distance, and the man was walking by. And quickly too, not looking at the camera this time. Becker had not seen the man in the memorial park full face and he'd not seen the man at the table in Canberra full face. The moustache looked the same, what he could see of it. Laura showed him others, yet he couldn't be sure. Becker felt stupid. He must have made a mistake. It could have been anybody. Perhaps an excitable local Italian shopkeeper or grower or driver for the big wineries, anyone really. Talking to an unexcitable photographer he knew. Becker calmed down. He felt ashamed. He'd overreacted, jumped to conclusions. Yet the old apprehension he'd known in Canberra—that he could be hit at any moment—had not left him. That the job Whitford had begun in Sydney four years ago would be finished one day. Any day, he could be whacked. Killed. Rubbed out.

'I'm not sure,' he said.

'The one you saw today could have been any fat man. On the other hand,' she said, 'you may be right.'

'Yeah?'

'We've heard that *someone* is in the area. No description given, but a man important to the local Mafia. A man to be feared, a man who solves problems for a price. Apparently he is very expensive—at least one-hundred-thousand dollars a hit.'

'A description?'

'No name, no description. Where's Buster now?'

'I sent him home with Robyn.'

'To hide him?'

'Yeah.'

'You'd better bring him back, Harry. We'll show him these photos of Caselli. That might help, depending upon whether he recognises the guy or not. If he does, we'll move him out of town. Put him into protective custody.'

'Buster saw those guys at night.'

'Under a street light, I believe?'

'Yeah, but he did not clearly see the faces. He can only describe them as the fat man, the skinny man and the short guy. Just shapes, not much more.'

'The Mafia is not to know that.'

'You think they're gonna kill Buster?'

'Not necessarily Buster.'

'Then who?'

She did not answer. In fact, she changed the subject. Quite abruptly, Becker thought.

'We've had a message. About half an hour ago.'

'What message?'

'Tell him, Dave.'

Her sidekick picked up some notes on his desk. 'At approximately 12 hours 16 minutes today, I took a call—'

'Spare us the details, Dave. Just the facts, please.'

'Angelo Cosco is dead.'

'Dead?'

'No doubt about it. Shot many times. They're still counting the number of holes.'

'Cosco, the father?'

'Check.'

'Where? When?'

'At his house, apparently,' Laura said. 'There was a lot of gunfire. Even though his house is at least one-hundred yards from the nearest neighbour, people heard it. Screaming too. They called the Griffith cops, who went in and—You finish it, Dave.'

'They went in and saw it,' Dave said.

'Saw what?'

'A bloodbath,' Laura said.

'Right,' Dave said. 'So the first guy in said, 'What the hell? Who did this?' A young guy was sitting in a corner, not actually sitting, but squatting on his heels and crying. One hand to his head—' Dave looked around. 'The other holding a Tanfolio16 pistol.' He paused again, glancing at Becker. 'You familiar with the Tanfoglio, Harry?' he said. Becker was too surprised to reply. 'Holds sixteen rounds.'

'Sixteen?'

'Check. It seems the kid—I'm quoting Sergeant Jackson here in Wagga. You know the son, Harry?'

'Can't say I do.'

'Sergeant Jackson had a call from the police in Griffith. The kid emptied the whole magazine into his father. Must have followed him from room to room. Afterward, he must have kneeled down and nursed the old man, most likely his head. As a consequence, the boy was covered with blood. It was everywhere, the sergeant said. He'd been out there to see for himself. It was like a horror movie, he said.'

Dave, who never spoke much, loved an audience.

'Get on with it, Dave, so we can all go and have a stiff drink.'

Dave cleared his throat. 'It would appear, the contact in Griffith said, he'd nursed his father's head or took him in his arms, kissing him. It was all over his own face and hands and chest and even on his legs. And saying over and over, I'm sorry! Or something like that in Italian. The sergeant—the sergeant in Griffith, that is—knew a few words, although he wasn't Italian himself. He said the boy was saying, *Forgive me, Papà, forgive me! I don't know why I did it!* Or something like that. Then he started crying, and I quote again here: '*Papà! Papà!* Please come back, *Papà!*' Or words to that effect. End of notes.'

Becker knew why he'd done it. It was Silvano. The son who'd been forced to kill his big sister with hydrochloric acid, on instructions. To save the family's honour. And to make a man of him—a hard man, who'd do whatever he was told to do.

'Jesus, the poor bastard!'

'Which one, Harry?'

'All of them, I suppose. What a way to live.'

Laura stood up. 'So, Harry, we now have no *Signore* Cosco to lead us, step by step, to the don.'

'The don?'

'The big man in Melbourne, the one who ordered the hit on Evelyn.'

'You think he knew?'

'Cosco? He was the real *capo* in Griffith, by all accounts. Not that doddering old dodo we saw at the *Capriano*. If anyone around these parts knew, Cosco had to be the one.' She picked up her bag. 'I need a stiff drink. Anyone else?'

They walked up Baylis Street to the Hovell and ordered Jack Daniels all around. She insisted on paying. They were sitting at a table by a window when the girl came over with the drinks on a tray. Respectful and eager to please, and excited too, glancing almost shyly at Chook.

'How are you, pretty one?' Chook said.

She blushed, not spilling a drop.

'Oh, gosh, I was hoping you'd come in today, sir.'

'Were you?'

'Oh, yes, I was—I was hoping to speak to you.'

'What about, honey?'

'Oh, I don't know whether you would be allowed—' She glanced nervously at the others, then at the barman, who was eyeing her. As long as she kept the boozers drinking, a quick chat with a customer was not forbidden.

'What did you say your name was?'

'Deloraine.'

'I recall.'

'From Sir Walter Scott, *The Lay of the Last Minstrel.*'

'You want to talk about Sir Walter Scott?'

'Oh, no, you see—' She glanced around quickly, almost furtively. 'I'm at Charles Sturt.'

'What the hell is that?'

'The university.'

'You have a university, right here in Wagga Wagga?' Chook was playing dumb. She knew all about Charles Sturt. They were watching some kids out there peddling dope in the toilets. And the Library too, under the desk. Dave Hanson was doing something out there, part-time. He would sit at a desk wearing large horn-rimmed glasses and thumbing his way through Keynes and trying to look like a nerd. And gradually going blind. Not because of Keynes, but because of the glasses. They were of the wrong focal length.

'Yes and I'm doing journalism. We have to do an assignment. As if we are on the job already, and reporting and—'

'You want to interview me?'

'Oh, could I?'

'About my manly figure? People are always asking about that. Asking me if I'm a bloke dressed up as a girl.'

'Really?'

'Whereas I'm a girl dressed up as a bloke.'

'You're a girl?'

'I was last time I looked.'

'Oh, gosh, I thought you were very strong for a girl.'

'You want to feel my biceps?'

'What?' She jumped, laughing. 'Are you a policeman?'

'A policeman? What would make you think that?'

'You showed him a pass.'

'Oh, that was to show I work for the Commonwealth.'

'For the government? Here in Wagga? And what do you do?'

'I work with Laura here, at Centrelink.'

'But, what do you do?'

'I'm a sort of collector.'

'A collector?'

'A debt collector. I call on people, who like to cheat the taxpayers.'

'Oh, really?'

'The sort who claim pensions they're not entitled to. Or claim more children than they have. Or, claim to be a dozen other people. So that they can get a dozen pensions. And have a good time. Pacific cruises, a Mercedes in the garage, popping down to Melbourne for the Cup, that sort of thing. I call on them, shake them up a bit.'

'Oh, my gosh. Do you carry a gun?'

'You've noticed? Sadly, yes. You never know who you might meet. Our staff have been sworn at, punched and spat on, reduced to tears and, in a few cases, threatened with castration. As a result, the department now provides an armed escort. Twice I've knocked and someone with a double-barrelled shotgun has opened the door.'

'Oh, you must be very brave.'

'Another time, the door opened and a couple of doberman pinschers flew out at me. In no time one had me by a leg and the other by the throat.'

'My goodness, what did you do?'

'Shot the lady, who'd opened the door.'

'You did? Oh, my gosh!'

'That was the only way I could get them off me.'

'Oh, they rushed to help her instead?'

'No, they started eating her.'

'Good heavens, what did you do?'

'Ran for my life.'

'Oh, my gosh!'

'She was the meanest old bitch, wouldn't even buy dogfood.'

'Oh, my gosh!'

'You're not one of these girls who say, Oh, my God! all the time?'

'Oh, no, Mummy told me to say Gosh.'

'So, Deloraine, you still want to interview me?'

'Oh, yes, please!'

'I'll have to ask my boss first.'

The other three were nearly pissing themselves. Chook looked at Laura, who nodded.

'Okay, honey, what time do you knock off?'

'At one, but I have a lecture at two. And I'm there until five.'

'I tell you what, Deloraine, why don't we meet this evening somewhere nice and cosy? How about cocktails for two?'

'Oh, we have a cocktail bar right here!'

'You do?'

'Upstairs!'

'What time could you make it?'

'Today? Oh—'

'By six?'

'Yes, after I rushed home and changed into something—'

'Slinky?'

'Slinky?'

'Short and slinky. Otherwise all the cats in the place would be asking, Who's this kid in the school uniform?'

'Uniform? Oh, I would never do that!'

'You have gorgeous legs, you know.'

'Have I? Oh, thank you.'

'Cocktails at six, then?'

'Yes. Oh, what's your name, please?'

'Anastacia.'

'Anastacia? That's a lovely name for a girl.'

'So is Deloraine.'

'Oh, thank you, thank you.'

She made to go, but Laura called her back.

'Honey, your boss is looking daggers at you.'

'Oh, gosh.'

'You'd better go back with a big order.'

'Oh, yes, what will you have?'

'Four Jacks again, please.'

'Jack Daniels? Oh, thank you, thank you!'

They watched her skip away.

'Oh,' said Laura, 'to be young and beautiful again.'

'Just once would be enough,' Chook said.

Walking out later, Laura said: 'What the hell do we do now?'

No-one had any ideas. They might never find Evelyn's killer—and Polly's. It later turned out that the guy, Caselli from the Gulf of Tarantino, was relatively clean. There had been a misunderstanding. He was an honest businessman. Maybe he had to grease a few palms now and then to fix a deal. But that happens the world over.

So, why had Angelo Cosco named Caselli? Perhaps he wanted to steer the police away from the real killer. Or he might have wanted to get rid of Caselli. Maybe Caselli was a *Carabinieri* agent, checking up on a few people in Australia. After all, he'd been seen riding around in an embassy car. A simple fish merchant would not normally get such treatment.

And who was the fat man Becker had seen in the gardens? Perhaps some vociferous greengrocer trying to help a tourist. No-one had seen the real fat man, except Buster. But Buster's memory, as bad as it was, was coming back, slowly but surely. After all, he had remembered Veronica Lake, and that was a long time ago.

CHAPTER 22

HE HAD FORGOTTEN all about Robyn. Or, to put it another way, he'd had it in mind that he'd sent her home expeditiously with Buster, whom she'd called Mr Keaton. And had been fully conscious in an unconscious way he should have got off earlier and attended to what seemed to be some sort of fear of the man. But Buster seemed to be a harmless old codger, not all that old, perhaps down and out and next to unsaveable when he'd known him in Canberra, popping up now and then, bludging for a handout. He'd been a harmless sort of deadbeat, who, miraculously, had had a lucky day or night, being knocked down by two Mafia thugs, after picking up something dropped at a murder scene. Namely, a credit card with a name on it, Italian. But the cops had come along in the nick of time, two lady cops, in fact. Who'd jumped out and tried to catch the critters, who'd raced off, not wanting to be identified. One of whom, it now turned out, had been Chook. The other had been Polly.

Becker grabbed a taxi and got back to *Nil Desperandum*, where he found Robyn not anxious or frightened, but sitting with Buster on the west side verandah, trying to catch a bit of sun, lovely for July.

They were chatting and enjoying a late lunch, thrown together. Having given up waiting for him. Veal and mushroom pie, fresh but not just out of the oven. She'd baked it two days ago and set it aside *in case* anyone should unexpectedly drop in. Handing him the salad bowl, he'd tried to take a serve, but had dropped, so she'd had to do it for him. Like a good carer of the aged and infirmed. Which he was, although, if you thought about it, being only fifteen years older than she, he must have been little more than fifty, Robyn now being thirty-six and seven months gone. He looked a lot older than that, at least sixty, a bad sixty, worn out despite his attenuated recovery.

'Sorry, Rob, I had to stay and sort something out.'

She looked up and smiled. 'No worries at all, Harry. We are having a good time, weren't we? He was telling me about his early days out this way. Do you know, dear, he was at Wybilonga?'

'Got any more of that pie?'

She got up slowly and awkwardly. It hurt, but she did not mind. Insisted on carrying on as normal. She'd had an easy pregnancy so far. They said that having had two already made it easy. As easy as shelling peas, one of her friends had said. Nothing to worry about. It being a matter of pride for her, that she could carry on. Being a farm girl helped too, she thought, or liked to believe. They were tough, took the bad with the good. Never complained. God did not like complainers. Her mother had said that. Which is why Muriel was a stoic. Yes, everything was sweet. Even seeing this man again after all these years was strangely sweet. It was like seeing a snake and screaming your head off, then seeing the same sort of snake twenty years later and not feeling anything at all. Just curiosity. And wondering why on earth what all the fuss had been about.

'I kept a big slice for you, dear. I'll pop it in the microwave again.'

She went to the kitchen door. 'You want a beer with it?'

'How about you, Mr Keaton?'

'What's that? A beer? You havin' a beer, mate?'

'I've just had two whiskeys, but you have one.'

'You're sure?'

'Yes, go ahead.'

'Better not, tend to nod off.'

Becker himself was feeling a bit woozy. It was not the whiskey, but the sudden panic in the park. He'd jumped to conclusions. There was no reason why the fat man should be in Wagga. On the other hand, the real fat man, wherever he was, had a good reason to get rid of Buster. Two men had shot Vincent Torrence, who'd become a problem, demanding money for a job he'd not done. He'd wanted five-thousand dollars, but they'd given him five dollars and then had shot him, *Bang! Bang!* And Buster had seen all this, from behind a bush in Commonwealth Park, late at night.

Robyn came out with the hot pie. And a pot of cold beer.

'There you are, dear. There's chutney too,' she added. Standing with hand on hips and watching Becker. Bursting to tell him something. But knowing she'd be sick in the telling, if she did.

'Would you like coffee, Harry?'

'Yeah, sure,' he replied, munching.

'And you, Mr Keaton?'

'What's that, love?'

'Coffee or tea?'

'Tea if you've got it, yeah tea.'

'Strong or weak?'

'As it comes out of the pot.'

'Out of a bag these days, I'm afraid.'

She went off again, heels hard on the boards.

While both men sat there, looking cross at the clouds and the fields stretching away to and beyond Wagga to the distant hills beyond, where and whence good things came, the Western Slopes. Water, for instance, and tourists and people trying to get back to the beautiful countryside of Australia. Hoping to relive what they had never really known, but had heard of or seen in pictures, real moving pictures of the old farms and broken stables and sheep runs and the sheds, the golden fleece being peeled off the backs of discontented sheep. And the agonies. The district only now recovering from the drought of the early nineties. Things were looking good.

'Beautiful spot here,' Buster said.

'Beautiful,' Becker said, polishing off the pie and nutty salad with avocado and radishes, also from Robyn's garden.

At which she was often to be seen on hands and knees, working with trowel or hand fork, digging and working in the mulch and manure and chemical fertiliser in her rough and dirty gloves, a bandana around her hair and brushing with the back of a hand or glove, as the case may have been, flies away from her face, this being sheep country too, although not so many.

The big spreads having gone, long ago. And looking up and smiling and saying with a flush, not always the flush of exertion, of which there was a few indeed, her shoulders and elbows hurt. Her hands too, in the rough and ready gloves. But looking up and saying, 'Hullo, darling, did you have a good day at school?'

When Becker had finished his coffee, he realised Buster had not drunk his tea.

He was asleep in the easy chair, cane backing. Not deeply, he was not snoring, but his chest was heaving a little, and his head had lolloped, as if it were against or in the breast of a tender someone or something. He was not so old-looking now, freshly shaved by himself with the Braun electric the Social Services people in Canberra had given him and which he'd packed with some pride in his overnight, riding along as free as the breeze with Chook at the wheel.

She'd been back in Canberra, not so much to pick him up, but to see some people in Federal Police headquarters and report on what was or was not happening in Wagga. In which someone at a table had suggested, with the lopsided weariness of anyone who thinks too much, that she take Mr Keaton back to Wagga to see what the reaction, if any, might or might not be. She'd not been happy about this idea, warning there might be unforeseen consequences.

Becker picked up his dish and went into the kitchen.

'How is he?' Robyn asked.

'Pretty well out to it. Contented, I'd say.'

She was dying to ask, he could see.

'That business in the park,' he said. 'I overreacted. I'd seen some bastards, young blokes probably still at school, going around and whacking old people—' This was a lie, but he'd had to think of something. 'Just sitting in the sun, and I saw them coming, and felt sure they'd spot Buster.'

'Buster?'

'Yeah, well, that's what I'd known him by in Canberra.'

'You knew him in Canberra?'

'I used to sit in Garema Pace and have a late lunch. He'd come and chat and try to get two dollars out of me.'

'You are very kind, Harry.'

'Ah, he's a bloke, who's got nobody now and likes to talk.'

'Yes,' she said. Thinking.

'I'll take him back, when he wakes up.'

'Oh—' she said, and put the last of the pie back in the refrigerator. And turned and said: 'Harry, I knew him.'

'You knew him?'

'A long time ago—'

'Yeah?'

'In Wybilonga.'

'Yeah?'

'When I was at school there.'

'How old were you then?'

'Ten,' she said. 'Almost eleven. He was such a nice man, young, new to teaching. I think Wybilonga was his first posting, or perhaps the second. They send them out into the bush, don't they? The new teachers. If they are single,' she added.

'Something happen, Rob?'

'There were only two classrooms, and two teachers. Thelma Danby was the head. She was a cranky old lady, most probably because some of the kids used to muck up. And most probably she saw and had long realised she would never get out of a such a position. Always on the outer. A spinster, she was. With horn-rimmed glasses and a mole on her chin. Hairy in some lights.'

'So?'

'No-one liked her, but everyone liked Mr Keaton. He was young and enthusiastic and had everything to look forward to. Good at sports and always a sharp retort if you tried to be cheeky with him. Or, make everyone laugh. And always addressing us by our first names instead of the last, not crabbily as did Miss Danby, glaring at us over her glasses, if we said or did anything out of place.'

She paused, thought about her next words.

'One day I had to stay back, write out fifty times: Procrastination is the thief of time. I hadn't done my homework for Miss Danby. Twice I'd failed to meet the deadline. I was sitting there when he looked in and said: 'How's it going, Robbie?' 'Good,' I said. 'I've done twenty-eight.' 'Don't let me interrupt you,' he said. 'I've been instructed by Her Majesty to see you pay your penalty.' 'Excuse me, sir, what's happened to Miss Danby?' I asked, looking up and at the same time still writing. 'She's gone to Wagga', he said. 'Had to see a doctor.' So I pressed on, thirty-three, thirty-four times.'

'And?'

Robyn was leaning against the refrigerator, arms folded and looking down, penitently. He waited, leaning on the bench, legs crossed, in effect standing on one foot. And watching her. Something was wrong, he knew.

'He was softly whistling a tune and looking out a window. It was that lovely one: '*Singing in the Rain* with Gene Kelly and Donald O'Conner and Debby—'

'Reynolds,' Becker said. He used to watch a lot of TV with the Indians with whom he had lived in Canberra. No-one said a word, while they watched. The Indians couldn't understand a word of it. They didn't laugh, even when O'Connor did his famous dance on the furniture and the walls. Trying to make them laugh.

'He went on like that, his feet starting to move. I was watching with one eye and at the same time pressing on, thirty-seven. And trying not to chuckle. Then he began to dance.'

'He danced, while you were trying to write out fifty times?'

'Quite good too. I heard later he'd been on stage before he got the teaching diploma. Amateur stuff, town halls and such. Well, suddenly he went the whole way, singing and dancing in the rain. Even taking off an imaginary hat and bowing to me. I was so delighted I jumped up and ran to him.

'He grabbed me and we danced, back and forth across the room, it being one of those old-time demountables, an iron-pot stove in the corner for winter. Which I think it was. We danced, and danced, chuckling and laughing like mad. Delighted, I was.

'We stopped. He stood still, looking at me—admiring me, I know. And thinking about me. I was still laughing, it being so wonderful, a teacher doing such a thing, quite out of the blue. Then he kissed me.'

'He kissed you?'

'Yes, full on the forehead. I was startled, I pulled away, but he enfolded me in his arms and kissed my neck and—and—'

'He did something?'

'He held me. I could feel his hand running over my back. I started to struggle. He was saying, "I love you, Robinski—" He used to come out with funny names like that. "You are quite the most beautiful girl, I've ever seen." I was becoming panicky. I didn't know what to do, I began to cry. I tried to back away, my bottom stuck out, trying to get away. I thought he was going to touch it.'

'He touched you?'

'No, well, not quite.'

'Jesus,' Becker said.

'He stood back. Must have realised he'd gone too far. Had not been able to control himself. He looked shocked, genuinely shocked, as shocked as I.

'He let me go and said, "Oh, oh—" He looked horrified, no doubt of the possible implications. I was only a girl, aged eleven, tall for my age, and pretty to some extent, I suppose. I started to cry, itchy tingles coming to my lids. I blinked. "I'm sorry," he said. "Please believe me, Robyn, I did not mean to touch you. I didn't mean it," he said again.

'Then he walked away backwards, to the door. And said there was no need to finish the fifty. I could finish them at home. He would swear I'd done them all at school. I stood there, hurt and crying, somehow blindly gathering up my books and pen and started for the door. My head was down, afraid I'd cry like a baby. I did manage to hang onto some measure of control.

'I passed within inches of him at the door. And walked out and ran all the way home, my school bag rattling, both crying and not crying, ashamed of what had happened. And what I had done.'

'What *you* had done?'

'Yes, that's how I felt. I had done something bad. I knew. I had led him on, dancing with him and laughing with him and dancing with him. And being happy with him for the first moment in my life. You see, Harry, I was in love with him. I'd dreamed of dancing with him, cuddling with him, kissing him. He was quite good looking then.'

'These things happen,' Becker said. 'Did you tell anyone?'

'Not at first, not that night, nor the next day. But on the next weekend I was so guilt-stricken Mother noticed and said, "Whatever is ailing you, child?" I thought about it for some minutes, eating an apple which was not ripe and bitter and uneatable, but I deliberately ate it. I suppose I wanted to make myself sick.'

'What did you say? To Muriel?'

'I told her. She was horrified. I tried desperately *not* to make it sound worse than it was. But I'm not a good liar, Harry. She sat me down and squatted in front of me and looked deeply into my eyes, her fingers tight on my arms and asked. I could not get out of it then. I told the truth, essentially. Suddenly, she was holding me in a crushing embrace, stroking my face and expecting me to burst into tears. But I could not, not really—'

He moved in and held her, an arm about her shoulders. She was close to crying.

'You don't have to say anything, Robbie.'

'Yes, I do.'

'No, you don't. It's all over now.'

'No, no—' She was gasping against his chest. 'I have to tell him.'

'Tell him what? That old derelict? What the hell have you got to tell him? Now? After what is it? Twenty-five years? What can you tell him?'

'Who I am.'

He held her back, looking in her eyes.

'Are you crazy?'

'No,' she said, rubbing her nose, searching for a tissue. He picked up from a box on the bench. And waited until she had picked up a little.

'I told my mother, who told Miss Danby, who told my father, who wrote to the District Inspector in Wagga, who called my teacher to come and see him. And fired him on the spot, so we heard when a new teacher came, Miss Prince. Not more than eighteen, her first job. Much to our relief, she turned up after a few days of having to put up with Miss Danby doing both classes—chaos breaking out in whatever room she was not.

'The poor man, we heard, when I was a lot older and was at Wagga High, had escaped a day in court, and perhaps a term in jail. The Inspector had hushed it up the best he could. But that man never worked again as a teacher.'

'Cut out, you mean?'

'The last we heard of him, he was clerking in woolsheds out west. During the season,' she added. 'God knows what he did during the rest of the year.'

'Ah, Jesus, Rob, Rob, Robbie.' He kissed her on her head. 'It's not your fault. These things happen.'

'It *is* my fault. I should have kept quiet about it. I'm sure he would never have done it again. He did not assault me. He cuddled me. I was embarrassed and tried to push him away. I'm sure his action was quite spontaneous. He apologised immediately.'

'Oh, you never know. That type of bloke—'

She sighed.

'No, Harry. You are an outraged husband, hearing this. My father was an outraged father. But I have always felt guilty about it. Here, now, I have everything, and that poor man has nothing. And another thing, when Mother asked me if he had *touched* me, I thought she meant anywhere at all, so I said Yes. He *had* touched me. We were dancing, but that was not what she *meant*, was it? He did not touch me *there*. Which was what she meant, wasn't it?'

He patted her. 'Come on, Rob, forget it.'

'No, no, I did a bad thing. I ruined him. I'm going to speak to him. And apologise.'

Becker jumped back. 'Apologise for what? No, don't! He probably doesn't remember a thing. His memory's gone now, lost to booze and bad food. They've tried to help him in Canberra, fixing him up, feeding him, giving him a new leg, pumping vitamins into him, trying to bring back something of the man that was—'

'Is he still asleep, I wonder?'

She had moved to the door.

'Rob, I'll take him back now.'

'I'll have one word.'

He tried to stop her, but she would not be restrained.

Buster was sitting up, trying to get out of the easy chair, outdoors style, thick cushions tied on. At the same time stretching.

'Mind, I'll help you,' she said, a hand out. 'Had a good sleep, have you? Harry's going to drive you back now, but before you go—'

He stretched, holding onto her hand.

'By gee, that was a funny sleep. Not the usual jumble you can't make head or tale of, but quite clear. Thinking about times long ago. Think I was a teacher then. Don't know what happened to that, but moved about. Saw the country. The beautiful country. You have a lovely place here, Mrs Becker. Nice to think about what has been, ain't it? Yeah—'

He stretched some more, moved a foot heavily.

'Mr Keaton,' she said tentatively, 'you were a teacher at Wybilonga school, twenty years ago, weren't you? Do you remember? Wybilonga? Out past Lockhart, a small place with tall concrete solos and the old bush pub?'

'Wybilonga?'

'It was a two-room primary school. I was one of your pupils.'

'Were you?'

'Robyn Elliot. Do you remember?'

Becker was whispering: 'Leave it, Rob. He *does not* remember.'

'And we danced one day? *Singing in the Rain*? And you were Gene Kelly? Do you remember that?'

'He doesn't remember, Rob.'

'*Singing in the Rain*? By gee, that was an old one.'

'Do you remember?'

He hesitated, thinking. Or trying to think. 'Could have. Used to like dancing. Ah, well,' he said, looking around again. 'You've done me a power of good, both of you. It must be that pie of yours, Mrs—'

'Becker, but I was Robyn Elliott. You remember at all?'

'Can't say I do.'

'Okay, mate, let's get going.'

So they went.

They'd just passed through Yarragrundry, which is not a town but a spot on the map with a few farms among desultory gums, when a four-wheel drive came up behind. But instead of passing on the right, it shot up on the left. Gravel and dust flying. Too late, Becker realised why it was coming up fast on the left. Buster was sitting on the left.

'Look out!' He tried to push Buster down. Buster did not react. He was not old in years, just faded and, for once in a long time, happy.

Suddenly, one shot, straight through the left-hand window. Through Buster's head, past Becker's nose and out the right-hand window. Glass flew everywhere, both side windows smashed. Something wet hit Becker's face. Blood, he thought, Buster's blood.

He jammed on the brakes.

The four-wheel did not stop. It skidded back onto the bitumen, stones flying, one or two hitting the BMW. Then accelerating hard along the bitumen toward, but not necessarily to, Wagga.

Becker grabbed the Smith and Wesson under the seat, jumped out, sighted up, knelt down and, with both hands, fired, hitting something, he was pretty sure, doing some damage, which might help to identify the vehicle—if they ever found it. At the same time, trying to make out the number. He got off three or four shots and gave up. The big vehicle was out of range, and pretty soon around a bend and out of sight.

Becker pulled out his mobile and called triple zero. It was not much use. The vehicle, a big, fat Toyota Land Cruiser, he thought, would not have gone into Wagga, where the police, having picked up his call, might have been waiting. It would have dodged into some back road, and found its way back to Griffith or wherever it had come from.

He looked in at Buster. It had been a quick death, straight through the left temple. Apart from a dribble, there was little blood. Buster looked at peace. As if suddenly, after a contented day, he had nodded off.

Becker stood by the BMW, leaning on it in fact, holding and wiping the left side of his face, where it had been hit by shattered glass, but only skin-deep. And holding the Smith and Wesson. He did not bother to hide it from the gaze of those who slowed to have a look. Nor did he move when he heard the first siren. But he did reach in and flash the lights of the BMW as the first patrol car slowed to a stop.

The driver looked across at Becker, swung around and stopped. A door opened and Barnes got out, adjusting his cap and his belt, dangling with the usual gear that a uniformed cop has to carry—handgun, taser, baton, pepper spray, handcuffs, gloves, torch, two-way radio—and walked up like the little schoolyard bully he was. Swinging his arms importantly, his head down. He always walked with his head down, never up. As if he were going to charge you like a bull. A come in fighting sort of approach.

'So you got him?' Becker said.

CHAPTER 23

AT FIRST BARNES just stood there, gaping. Then something must have clicked in his brain. By this time, it must have been in pretty bad shape, things having gone wrong day after day.

'What?' he said.

'I said, You got him.'

'Got who?'

'Got the old guy.'

'What old guy?'

'The one with the hole in his head.'

'What the hell are you talkin' about?'

'The one in this car. Leaning against the window, shattered.'

'This window?'

'No, the other. Take a look.'

Barnes didn't move. Maybe he didn't like being told what to do, not by Becker, anyway. He stood there, gaping at him.

'The bullet went in that side and came out this,' Becker said. 'I ducked back when I saw what was going to happen, but he ducked forward. And copped it.'

At last Barnes went around. 'Jesus,' he said. 'Who done this?'

'I thought you'd know,' Becker said.

'Me? Why'd I know?'

'You seem to have some nasty friends,' Becker said.

'You tryin' to give me more shit?'

'Nothing compared with what you're going to get,' Becker said. 'We have company.'

Another siren and then yet another. A patrol car came around the bend, followed by an ambulance.

'Anyway,' Becker said, 'why aren't you in jail?'

'What?' Barnes had come back to the driver's side.

'For receiving a packet of coke.'

'Me, coke? What are you talking about?'

'I hear that the Feds found half a kilo on you.'

'What? Eh?' Barnes went white and then red and finally grey. As if his heart had stopped. His pokey little eyes seemed to jump out of his head. A hand went to his sidearm, then changed its mind. He both gaped and gasped.

'By Christ, you bastard, you set me up. They told me that bitch got it from you.'

'Angelina?'

'Yeah, that bitch gave it to Maria and she gave it to me. I'm standin' there lookin' at it in me flamin' hand and she's tellin' me we're goin' to be rich beyond our wildest dreams, when the door bursts open and in come these Federal cops. I'm caught red-handed, they reckoned. I didn't know anythin' about any fuckin' coke. Ah, Jesus—' He stamped a foot. The emergency vehicles were almost upon them. 'You want to get rid of me, don't you?'

'You didn't have to accept the coke.'

'Eh? What'd you do if y'wife suddenly gave you a bag full of stuff. You wouldn't know people were hiding out, watching. Ready to pounce as soon as y'touched it. It was a whole fuckin' set up.'

'You didn't answer the question.'

'What fuckin' question?'

'Why aren't you in jail?'

'Why am I? Why am I? No-one's said anything to me at work. They know it was a set up. Fuckin' Federal cops, never do anything useful for the community. Just set up traps and secretly record people havin' private conversations and tyin' 'em in with geezers you've only met once or twice for a drink. But who, it turns out, are wanted for grand larceny or drugs or terrorism and every other fuckin' sensational scandal in the whole world. I'm fuckin' sick of it. I've just about had it. I mean—'

He didn't seem to know what he meant. Barnes was at the end of his tether.

The first vehicle, the patrol car, was slowing right down, the siren dying.

'Anyway,' Becker said, 'you can explain all this to your colleagues.'

'Explain what?'

Becker ignored him, waiting for the first man to emerge, a sergeant.

'Harry Becker,' he said, shifting the Smith and Wesson to his left hand, ready to shake with the right if necessary. The sergeant did not bother.

'Jackson,' he said. 'What's going on?'

'There's a dead guy in my car.'

'Is that a bullet hole?'

'Yeah, same on the other side.'

'What the hell?'

The ambulance was pulling in now, backing up in front of Becker's car. Jackson opened the door of the BMW, had a look. 'Who did this?'

'Ask him.'

'Who? Constable Barnes? Why are you holding a pistol?'

'I shot off three or four rounds,' Becker said.

'At another vehicle?'

'Yeah, a big Toyota Land Cruiser. There may be a hole or two in the back.'

'You get a number?'

'I don't think there was a number. No plate on the back, anyway.'

'Max, get on the blower. A Land Cruiser, there may be a hole or two in the back. Search everywhere. No number plates. May have put 'em back on by now.'

'A big white vehicle,' Becker said again.

'We got all that.' He came back to Becker. 'Is that a Smith and Wesson?'

'I bought it on the market.'

'Around here?'

'In Sydney, years ago.'

'Why did you buy an ex-police pistol?'

'I'm an ex-police officer.'

Jackson said, 'Mmmm. Let's see your licence?'

Becker got it out. 'He was going to have a go at me,' he said.

'Barnes? He was going to have a go at you?'

'He came up to me with a hand on his piece.'

Barnes cut in: 'He was holdin' a weapon.'

'I'd just then shot at a vehicle.'

Jackson said 'Hmmm' again. 'You can put that thing away.'

'Not till you've taken him away.'

'Why would I do that?'

'Ask him,' Becker said.

'Something between you two?'

'We're cousins.'

'A family feud?'

'Not exactly.'

'Who was the old guy?' Jackson asked Becker.

'A witness to a killing in Canberra, last year.'

'And someone shot him?'

'Yeah, from the left side.'

'The bullet went through your window, too. How come you're not hit?'

'I leaned back, Buster leaned forward.'

'Buster?'

'Yeah.'

'Why would someone do that?'

'They didn't want him to go to court.'

'Ah, Jesus.'

Barnes had been standing, hand on weapon, fuming. And listening, as far as the pounding pulse in his ears would allow. Both happy to see someone standing up to that bastard, Harry Becker, and yet frightened something awful might happen. He'd had enough. He couldn't take it any more from that fucking bastard, who had everything, a million dollars they reckon, given him by some Mafia boss's wife in Canberra, who was gonna split and run with him. To live it up on the Riviera or some flash dump like that. But they got her, shot her in bed. So he'd heard, anyway.

Now his fucking smart-arse cousin who wasn't a real cousin at all, Harry fucking Becker, was standing there in front of him, telling a pack of fucking lies to that bastard of a boss, Jack Jackson, who'd never liked him, never given him a break, knocked him back every fucking time he'd applied for promotion. If he could have been made senior constable after all this time, ten fucking years, he would have been someone. Maybe with prospects of retiring as a sergeant one day. It had all gone wrong. Just because that bitch of a wife of his had told him that something was gonna happen. And he'd better be ready to verify that it had happened. Or else someone down in Melbourne would not be too pleased. Now, he was on a road to nowhere. Stuffed this time, really stuffed…

All of this was going through his head at a million miles an hour.

'Check the times,' Becker was saying.

'Why?' Jackson asked.

'Check what time you sent out the call to him.'

'What are you getting at?'

'I think you'll find he received a call on his personal phone before that.'

'Who from?'

'Someone to say the hit had been made. But he should go and see if the old man was dead, really dead. And another thing, who would drive along a highway without plates? Someone who had no need

Someone who had no need to worry about being picked up by a patrol car, eh?'

Jackson looked bad. Looked as though he was going to bite off his bottom lip. His young offsider had finished his phoning. Now standing back behind Barnes, a hand on his sidearm. Just habit, or a creepy feeling that something bad might happen. Very suddenly.

'Constable Barnes, what do you say?'

Barnes was going deaf. He couldn't hear properly. His neck had gone as stiff as steel, or as hard and cold as ice. Hard to say which.

'Barnes? Did you receive a call about this incident *before* we called you?'

'What?' His heart was pounding. Something was going to break, he knew.

'We can check, you know.'

'What?'

'Can you hear me?'

'What?'

Barnes began to fold up, cringing.

'Constable? Do you know anything about this incident?'

'Ah, shit,' he said. 'Ah, shit—'

He began to cry out, cry for help. He couldn't take it any fucking more.

'What's the matter with you?'

He hit the ground before they could catch him.

CHAPTER 24

BECKER WENT HOME and told Robyn. There was no point in trying to hide it from her. It would be all over the TV news that night and all over the local paper next morning. She was pretty upset when he did. Shocked to hear what had been done to poor old Buster, who once upon a time had been the respected young Mr Keaton at her little school in Wybilonga twenty-five years ago. Now he was dead. Why? What harm could a decent old man do to anyone? Not really old, not much more than fifty. For no reason other than he'd witnessed a murder in Canberra a year ago.

Becker held her for a while, as she wept. She was like that. She took the misfortunes of others to heart. If only I could have done something to atone, she said. It's not your fault, he'd said, patting her back. The kids were standing in the doorway.

'What's happened, Mum?' Wendy said.

'I caught another yabbie today,' Terry said.

They'd stood like that until all had dried out. Saying nothing for about a minute, which had helped.

Then Robyn blew her nose and said: 'She called today.'

'Who called?'

'Adeline.'

'She's still here?'

'You put her in at the Pioneer, dear. And told her you'd do something for her.'

'I told her to go back to Sydney. What did she want?'

'She said she'd run out of money.'

'Run out of money? I left a thousand dollars on her account at the motel.'

'She said she'd had expenses.'

'What expenses?'

'She said they'd had to make a lot of phone calls to Sydney.'

'Why?'

'She had to tell all her friends what a wonderful man you had been. Also, she had to get her father out of jail.'

'How is she going to do that?'

'She's hired a lawyer.'

'She's hired a lawyer? Who has she hired?'

'Someone named Waterford. Apparently he's famous.'

'What for?'

'Taking on impossible cases and winning.'

'Is he any good?'

'Apparently his family make crystal.'

'She said his family makes crystal?'

'That's what she said, dear.'

'So that impressed her? His family makes crystal? How does that make him a good lawyer?'

'Harry, I don't know. That's the way she talks.'

'She's totally irrational.'

'She's such a sad woman,' Robyn said.

'She's a conniving little bitch.'

'Oh, she can't be that bad.'

'She was born that way. She has a small reptilian brain, the kind that has to snap at anything that moves.'

'Oh, please don't say that. I've never heard you say such a thing about any woman.'

She was pouring him a whiskey. He was exhausted, could not take much more of this. She brought it to him with a coaster, placing it on the small table at his elbow. It was perfect blackwood, Tasmanian. Highly polished. She always polished everything at least once a week. It smelled wonderfully of polish, Sheraton.

She'd picked up the table at a place down a back lane in Wagga, where you could always find some wonderful old stuff. If you knew where to look. Although she found it a bit difficult to get around. Hardly get behind the wheel of the Nissan, now being seven months gone. She tended to waddle a bit and to lean back for balance. But it was a joy, being pregnant again. And smilingly proud.

Everyone saying she looked marvellous and asking who was her doctor. She had regular check-ups, and, against her better judgement, had had a scan. It was a girl.

She did not, however, tell Becker. He probably wished for a boy, not having one of his own. And she not wanting to disappoint him at this stage.

'So,' she said, sitting beside him with her bitter lemon. She was off alcohol completely and had been since she'd first heard. 'What are you going to do?'

'Do you mean to tell me she's gone through a thousand dollars in a day?'

'She said she's been buying things at Grace Brothers.'

'On tick?'

'No, she said she'd come to an arrangement with the manager at the Pioneer. She assigned the whole one-thousand dollars to the motel, which promised to pay for her purchases up to a limit of seven-hundred dollars.'

'What happens to the other three hundred?'

'Apparently the motel keeps it as a service fee.'

'Thirty per cent service fee? They are worse than the banks.' He was fed up. He had an obligation, he knew. Not to Adeline, but his children. If they were his children, the two girls. Sometimes he doubted it. He sighed. 'Oh, God, Rob, how can I get rid of her?

At that moment, there was a knock on the front door, a *ratatatat*! knock. Quite determined, but not unfriendly.

'Oh, hell, who is that?'

'Shall I go, dear?'

'No, I will.' Wearily he went to the door, opened it. Chook marched in.

'Thought I'd drop in,' she said. 'With some news.'

'God, no, what now?'

'Heard about old Buster, of course, and the collapse of your unlovely cousin. I was in the area doing some business. Thought I'd see how you're holding up.'

'What's happened to Buster?'

'At the morgue. The local cops are trying to trace any relatives.'

'What happens if you can't find any?'

'We'll take care of him. After all, he was our star witness.'

'Poor Buster, he may be the only one at his own funeral.'

'I'll go,' Robyn said.

'You don't have to go, Rob.'

'I'd like to go,' she said.

'We'll both go.'

'We'll all go,' Chook said

'Thank you, both of you.'

'We don't have any Jack Daniels,' Becker said to Chook.

'But we *do* have some Jameson,' Robyn said. 'Would that do instead?'

'Ah, the smell of the peat.'

Robyn began to heave herself up, but Chook had already pounced on the bottle on a sideboard and was helping herself to Jameson and water. Unusual for her—the water, that is. But she had a reason.

'What happened to Barnes?' Becker said.

'In hospital, suspected heart attack.'

Becker did not respond. He didn't care about Barnes, although he felt he should. He was one of the family. It was an ill-fated family. Nothing ever went right. No matter what you did, it always came out wrong.

'How are you both?' Chook asked.

'Depressed, my ex-wife is going through money at a fast rate. Of knots.'

'Expecting too much, is she?'

'*Too much* is beyond her comprehension. Now she wants me to help get her old man out of jail.'

'Why is he in jail?'

'Passing valueless cheques.'

'How much would it cost?'

'Fifty grand.'

'Fifty grand? Are you going to pay up?'

'Never, but I have to get rid of her somehow.'

'What most attracts her?'

'The smell of money.'

'The smell of money?' Chook thought about it. 'Did you tell me her last husband was a boxer?'

'Yeah.'

'Boris Kalash?'

'Yeah, it was.'

'As I recall, Boris was knocked out just before the bell in the tenth?'

'Yeah, he was.'

'And he got nothing but ten-thousand?'

'Quite right.'

'And Rocky Rostrum got what?'

'I have no idea.'

'It might have been quite a bit, for the State title. Fifty grand, do you think?'

'I'm not into boxing.'

'I am, or was. I used to fight at Macka Doolan's gym in Footscray—other girls, of course. We were lucky if we got five-hundred for a fight, even though the girls got a bigger or at least a more enthusiastic crowd, screaming at us, "Kill her! Kill her! Kill her!"

'Blood-thirsty bastards.'

'It was the women. They wanted to see blood.'

'God, what a world we live in.'

'I've got it,' said Chook.

'Got what?'

'You want to get rid of her. I think I know the trick.'

'You're not thinking of terminating her?'

'I wouldn't do that to the mother of your children.'

Robyn rose, smiling. 'I think the pork is done. Will you stay for dinner, Stacey?'

'Thank you, but no thank you. I have a date.'

'Oh, really?'

Becker asked: 'Anyone we know?'

Ah hah!'

'Not that pretty girl in the Hovell?'

'Her mother's asked me to dinner.'

'What?'

'I'm telling her all about the Siege of Odessa. How we fought on for two months until the Germans beat us to a pulp. Then the Rumanians came in.'

'What did they do?'

'Stood us up against a wall and shot us.'

'Jesus.'

'Oh, it could have been worse.'

'How?'

Chook did not reply, finishing her drink. 'I must fly. Bye, Robbie!'

'You must come to dinner soon, Stacey.'

'I will.'

Becker followed her to the door. 'Why are you in this neighbourhood, mate?'

'Chatting to my business associates next door.'

'You mean Albert and his mangy son?'

They walked out onto the verandah. It was a cool to cold night. But the moon was high and a cloudy cuckoo was trilling up the birdie scale of trills, enchantingly. Echoing in the stillness of the night. No bird answered. It went on and on, which showed that even birds longed for love, or if not love, then a little tender consideration.

'I've got a deal going. They supply me with dope of the informational kind and I leave them to get on with supplying the stupefying kind.'

'Is it working?'

'You'd be surprised.'

'Isn't that illegal? A cop turning a blind eye?'

'Not if it's approved up top.'

'You mean in Canberra?'

'I mean right here by Laura. We have a lot of leeway. Allowed to use our initiative. We can do anything that gets results, as long as it's legal, of course. A roving commission, you might say.'

'Are you smoking the stuff?'

'You don't approve?'

'I could smell it when you came in.'

'I'm sorry. I won't do it again.'

'Not near Robyn, that's all.'

'Understood.'

'You reckon you can control it? Smoking hash?'

'That's all I touch.'

'Okay, okay.'

'When I say that's all, I mean it.'

'Yeah, sorry, mate. Getting good information?'

'Good enough. Ray knows some people in Griffith. Given me a few names. Pretty sure one of them knows who the Lady is.'

'And who is she?'

'Ray doesn't know yet, but he's working on it. That's why I've got to be nice to him. Give him some cover.'

'You mean, let him trade?'

Chook nodded. 'Yeah.'

'Protection?'

'You could call it that.'

Becker was not impressed. He wasn't too sure he liked the way these Federal agents did things. They never seemed to do anything by the book. Maybe there wasn't any book. Maybe they made up the rules as they went along. Act first and get the okay later. That caper with Cosco. It had gone wrong. It was a bad move, making a deal with him like that: You give us a name and we won't give the press Angelina's statement. Now they didn't have any way to the top. They might never get to know who killed Evelyn. Who killed Polly.

And the fat man was still around. He'd killed Buster. Or had not personally killed Buster. He'd got someone else to do it. Someone local.

'Is that your bike there, black under the silvery moon?'

'It is.'

'I didn't hear you.'

'Nor you should.'

'I thought all Harleys were ear-splitters.'

'Not this one, it's water-cooled. I like to creep up on people. Say *boo*! to them. *Boo* or *bang*!'

'Have a nice evening, Chook.'

'I hope so.'

'*Adios, amigo*!' She was about to move off when she said, 'Hey, guess what I heard next door!'

'I'm sure you're going to tell me.'

'I asked Ray why is Bert giving you a hard time, staring at your place all the time? He thought for a long time. You know Ray, it takes a lot to get him to open his mouth, except when he has a bong stuck in it. He said it's all about a girl named Caitlin.'

'Caitlin?'

'Don't ask me who she is. I asked him and he went blank, the way he does when he's high.'

'Did you ask Bert?'

'I never ask Bert anything. He just stares at me then walks away, very slowly, as though he's lost something in the grass and weeds and bits and pieces of a leftover life scattered about that place. Might be worth following up, though.'

With that she was up and away, swiftly and silently like a swooping magpie, which has got behind you in the nesting season.

He went back inside. Robyn was making a salad.

'What's the matter?' she asked.

He was going to deny it, but it must have shown all over his face and hands and body and even his hair, which was untidy enough most times. It always seemed to bristle when he was angry or worried or sceptical or edgy.

'That bloke,' he said.

'What bloke? Old Bert?'

'I don't trust him.'

She took her hands out of the bowl. She always used her hands when tossing salad. Something a good chef did, she said.

And wiped them.

'Why, dear?'

'His silence.'

'He's an old man. I get along okay with him.'

'He stands and looks.'

'Looks?'

'At this house. At us.'

'He doesn't seem to have much else to do, dear. I mean, that place of his is all weeds. It's that or stare at the traffic on the road. Or, the occasional bird in the sky, going home to the river for the night.'

'He looks as if he's thinking things.'

'What do you mean? Thinking what, Harry?'

'I'm not sure.'

'Oh, come on—' She went to put her arms about her neck, careful not to touch. Still smelly with dressing.

'He looks as if he's gonna do something.'

'Do what?' She jerked. 'Harry? Do what?'

'I don't know.'

'Harry? What? Why would he hurt us?'

'I don't know.'

'Then, why do you think he will?'

'I'm not saying he will.'

'But, you think he's thinking?'

He edged away. Went to wash his hands for dinner.

She followed. 'Harry? Harry? Did Stacey say something?'

He paused at the bathroom door. 'Ray says it's all about someone called Caitlin.'

'Caitlin? Caitlin? What about her?'

'I don't know. Ray didn't say anything else.'

'But, dear, Caitlin was Dad's mother.'

'Yeah, I think that's the whole point.'

Becker sat at the table, eating a large pork chop slowly cooked with sliced onion, lemon and tomato and a sprinkle of caraway seed. He didn't say anything more about Caitlin. He wanted to go on with it, but she did not. He didn't want to talk about some girl who had died long ago. So, that was that.

'There is salad and sliced potato,' she said. She often did sliced potato with butter dripping hot. Reminding her of the night when he'd taken her to Romano's Hotel, sat her down and told her he was going to buy a farm and asked whether she'd like to see it. And she had said, clutching her throat: Oh, gosh, wow, do you mean it?

All of which she knew he would have forgotten long ago, but *she* never would. She often served up what she thought was as good scalloped potatoes. But knew she never would recreate what had been so wonderfully *there* on that night. He had, in effect, asked her to marry him. And he was a policeman, or had been a policeman. He looked as though he could handle men like Martie. And he had handled Martie like an expert. Saved them all from murder. So, she had gone to bed with him that night. She'd never done such a thing, not so quickly. But she wanted to be with him, live with him. So that no-one would hurt her again. And had surprised all her friends. Who'd said, surprised, 'You've known him only a few weeks or so, and he's asked you to marry him. And you've said, yes. Do you really know this man, Robbie?' 'Yes,' she had said, 'Yes I do.'

'Harry? Have you remembered what night it is?'

'Huh? Oh, someone's birthday?'

'No, dear, it is exactly a year since you took me to Romano's.'

'Is it? Oh, yeah, sure. We must go there again.'

'That would be nice, wouldn't it? Candle light and the music, not too loud and a woman singing, *Besame*—'

'*Besame?*'

'*Mucho,*' she said.

She began singing to herself, with a mouth full of food, humming. And looking to one side as if there again. Eating with him by candlelight. And a woman in the background, singing, recorded. So that, at the thought of it, she began to sway. To the rhythm and her own thoughts. Robyn was one of those women who could dance while seated. Her feet going.

Becker did not notice. He was eating thoughtfully. He loved pork chops, slow-cooked. The lemon was great.

'*Besame mucho?*'

'Kiss me a lot.'

'Yeah?'

She stopped dancing. There was something on his mind, she sensed. Something else, not her grandmother, Caitlin Elliott. So she let it pass. There was always something on his mind. Possibly what had happened to his cousin that afternoon. Arrested, taken to Wagga Base Hospital, for examination. The poor man, he'd fallen down, raving. Even crying, Harry had said. They didn't know what to do with him. Her husband was eating too fast. It was not good for him, she knew. He was starting to put on weight, even with all the work he did on the farm, feeding the cows with oats and barley every day now. It being so dry. They were going into another drought. Everyone said so.

CHAPTER 25

HE CHANGED THE subject. He asked her what he'd been thinking of asking ever since old Bob had said there had been something strange about the truck crash. 'What happened to Arnold?' She'd frozen, had stared at him for several seconds, then had said, 'I don't wish to talk about it.' You could not have shocked her more stingingly. She'd known that one day the question would come up. But if it did, he would not understand, or if he did, would not see the significance. 'All I am asking is what happened to him,' he'd said. 'Arnold?' she'd said, distantly. 'I only know his truck ran off the road, not far north of Tarcutta,' he'd said. 'It seems he'd gone to sleep at the wheel. And the truck had burst into flames, after hitting a tree?' 'Yes,' she'd said. 'As simple as that?' he'd asked. 'Yes,' she'd said, 'as simple as that.' She was getting up, taking the dishes and walking out. 'But,' he said. 'why did Bob say: Who'd want to leave a lovely girl like that?' She' d stopped at the door, stock still for a moment. 'Why not?' she had said.

Then she was gone, into the kitchen. That had been that. Nothing more had been said on the matter until they'd gone to bed, the lights out except one in the hall, illumination enough to undress by and to get to sleep in. She slept on the right-hand side, near the door lest one of the kids cried or called in the night. So that, if you looked at her from his side, she was outlined against the dim and yet pellucid glow, lying on her back, wide awake and fiddling with her fingers. 'Harry?' she said. 'Are you awake?'

He was nodding off. 'Yeah?'

'I'm sorry, I can't sleep.'

'Come here,' he said. She rolled toward him. 'What is it?'

She sighed. It was a long sigh, having made a decision but not sure of the words.

She lay in his arms for a long time, apparently thinking, one hand to her lips, the thumb not in her mouth so much as a thumbnail to her teeth. And thinking.

'He *did* leave me,' she said at last.

'Why?'

'To kill himself.'

'Yeah?'

'It is true, he did it deliberately.'

'Deliberately ran off the road?'

She nodded, the thumbnail still under her top teeth. 'Yes.'

'Did he say he was going to do it?'

'No, not to me.'

'To someone else?'

'I don't know. Possibly.'

'Why wouldn't he tell you?'

'Because I was his wife.'

'Was it money?'

'No, he had enough. We had enough.'

'No threats of foreclosure, nothing like that?'

'No.'

'Why do you *think* he did it?'

She did not answer at first. Then she said: 'The shame, I suppose.'

'You mean he'd *done* something bad?'

'Yes.'

'A crime of some kind?'

'No, not really, not now.'

'Not fiddling the books, something like that?'

'No, not at all.'

'It was something, not much of a crime but shameful?'

'Yes, I suppose that was it.'

'Another woman?'

'No.'

'He was a bigamist?'

'No, not at all.'

'I give up.'

She sighed again. The time had to come. Harry was sure to hear something or other. Thank goodness her parents did not know. Although her mother might have sensed. She waited, trying to put it off, but inevitability is hard to resist.

'He *was* gay,' she said.

'Gay? You mean—'

'Yes, he did it with men.'

'In Wagga?'

'No, in Melbourne. He used to go down there with a truck load of stuff, two or three times a week.'

'Did you know about this?'

'I had no idea.'

'Did you know he was gay, when you married?'

'I don't think he was gay then. Perhaps he'd done something when young, just fooling around. I don't know.'

'When did you find out?'

'When he was arrested.'

'The police came to your house?'

'Oh, no, it happened in Victoria. He used to go down one day and back the next. Sometimes he'd work six days. He always had Sunday off.'

'He had friends in Melbourne?'

'Yes.'

'Were they caught?'

'Only one other.'

'How did you find out?'

'It was in a paper, a clipping.'

'The local paper?'

'No, the Melbourne *Sun*.'

'You read it in the *Sun*?'

'In a list of court appearances. The name Sheldrake jumped out at me.'

'What did it say?'

'He was charged with committing an indecent act in a public place.'

'In Melbourne?'

'Yes.'

He didn't know how to put the next question. But he tried: 'An indecent act? With another man?'

'Yes.'

'Who sent the clipping to you?'

'They did not say.'

'They must have said something.'

'Only a few written words: *Do you know about this?*'

'No clue whatever?'

'Nothing.'

'What about the handwriting?'

'I did not recognise it.'

'How did you know it was in the *Sun*?'

'It was cut out too. The name of the paper and the date. They print it at the top of each page.'

'So they do.' He looked away, his arm still around. 'Who do you *think* sent it?'

'I've wracked my brains, trying.'

'You didn't suspect anyone? Not a friend? Not an enemy?'

'No-one I could think.'

'What friend would do that?

'I dread to think, Harry.'

He thought about it. 'So he could not face you, after you told him?'

'I didn't tell him. I showed him the clipping.'

'And what did he say?'

'Nothing.'

'Nothing at all?'

'He just got dressed as he always did before making a run.'

'Did he say goodbye?'

'He mumbled something as he went out. It could have been goodbye. Or, I'm sorry. But he did not kiss me. He always kissed me, when he went off to work.'

'He just left? In the truck?'

'Not in the truck. He always walked to the depot, where he'd pick up the truck, already fully loaded.'

'Then he drove off, down the Hume, as per normal?'

'It seems so.'

'Until he reached Tarcutta?'

'Just before Tarcutta, a mile or two.'

'And suddenly turned off, plunged off?'

'It seems so.'

'He wouldn't have fallen asleep after such a short trip?'

'No, not at all. He was quite bright and cheery before I showed him the cutting. He had slept well, as if happy with life. He always went off happily, happy to be on the road again.'

'Such a terrible shock, Rob.'

'Yes, it was.'

'Finding that out, then hearing from the police, about the crash, I mean.'

'Yes.'

'A terrible way to die,' he said.

'Yes, terrible.'

'So what did you do, then?'

'Gathered the kids after school and went up to Dad and Mum in Railway Street.'

'Did you tell them?'

'I just said Arnold had run off the road near Tarcutta and crashed. I didn't say he was burned to death.'

'They would have soon found out.'

'Yes, in *The Bulletin*, next day.'

'So how long did you stay with them?'

'Until after the funeral.'

'How did you feel about all this?'

'Oh, very bad. The looks and stares I was getting, people talking about me.'

'Because of the crash?'

'The press item, I think.'

'So, you decided to leave, get out of Wagga?'

'That's when I met Martin.'

'The Vietnam vet?'

'I was walking through Memorial Park one Sunday with the kids, looking for a seat, when a man said, 'There's a spot here.' He was a red-haired man with a beard, or he had been red-headed but going grey, quite well trimmed, I thought. So I told the kids to go and throw biscuit bits to the ducks and sat there with him. Not actually *with* him, but beside him. And we got talking. He said he was from Canberra, just down to look around. I said I was a local, but thinking I was going to move off somewhere. He said, 'Come to Canberra,' and a few weeks later I did.'

'Where he drove a taxi?'

'Yes.'

'And you got involved with him?'

'He was quite reasonable then, quite personable, as they have to be, driving a taxi.'

'Did he own the taxi?'

'No, but he was always very polite and looked after me, showing me around, in Canberra I mean, and the kids. I thought I'd marry him; he wanted me to marry him. He didn't put any pressure on me at all. I was quite happy with him. But if I mentioned anyone else, even a female friend, he'd wanted to know everything about him or her. He'd drill me, as if I were a spy. He became quite obsessive and—'

'Possessive?'

'Yes, he seemed to think I belonged to him. I mean, once we'd gone together.'

'And that's where I came in?'

'Yes, we got chatting at the checkout that day, and you asked me to have coffee with you—and, quite spontaneously, I said I would. I thought I'd be safe enough, if he didn't find out.' She was now huddled against him, her arms together against his chest, hands before her lips, as if praying. 'And I'm glad I did,' she said.

'Thank you for telling me.'

They lay there, both thinking and not thinking. Listening to the traffic passing by, especially the big interstate transports. Gradually aware the moon, which had been full on her face, had finally passed out of sight and was going wherever the moon went, when it went down. Until he decided he had to tell *his* story. It being only fair to her now.

Which he did, leaving out his own involvement in the scams and deals and benefits and bashings in the name of the law at King's Cross. He said he'd decided to go to the top and report what Whitford was doing, but until one night as he was taking out the garbage bin, and was shot.

He'd been kept in hospital for weeks, at the end of which he'd been dismissed without a pension, only his contributions over the years with interest. Which had gone to his pretty but pretty mendacious wife, as soon as she had an excuse for divorcing him, getting most of his payout as well as fortnightly support. Quitting Sydney in disgust, going to Canberra, ending up doing night rounds for a security company called Stanton.

Then, one lunchtime, picking up a handbag in a litter bin, inside of which was a letter addressed to Evelyn Crowley, who lived in a posh suburb. Who turned out to be a posh but very private sort of woman, who'd asked him if he did private jobs.

'What did she want you to do, Harry?'

'Locate the daughter she'd had seventeen years ago, which I did. She, Mrs Crowley, was quite pleased and asked me to find out who was blackmailing her—'

'Oh, my goodness! What did you do?'

'Well, I did that too, or I thought I did, but it was not what I'd thought it was.'

'Oh, dear, she wasn't one of those dreadful women you read about, was she?'

'What kind is that?'

'A *femme fatale*.'

'I guess she was, but not all bad as it turned out.'

He told her the rest of the story, how he'd tried to get Evelyn out of Canberra, but had failed. She being shot dead in the bed beside him, he being fast asleep at the time.

'Oh, Harry, how awful for you.'

'It was worse for her.'

'Of course, of course. What happened next?'

'I hung around in Canberra after I heard Evelyn had left me half her money.'

'For just one night with her?'

'There was more to it than that. I'd known her for six weeks.'

'Yes, of course. You ended back up in Wagga?'

'On a farm with a nice, kind…'

His voice trailed off. He'd thought the story through many times, wondering who the hell Evelyn really was? A bit of a mystery woman, a mystery woven by herself, trapped in a marriage she could have got out of if she'd really wanted. But she'd remained for the lifestyle, the clothes, the expensive look, the desirable look. In effect, trapped in a trap of her own making. And not really a nice person about it.

'What an amazing thing,' she said. 'I'm very proud of you, dear Harry.'

They lay together, the moonlight fading, the night passing, their thoughts fluttering like moths, her running a finger along the line of his jaw. 'You know, Harry, if I'd read all that in a book, I wouldn't believe it, would you?'

He did not answer, dozing off again.

'Harry, just one more thing.'

'Robbie, what is it now?'

She held it back with the most pregnant of pauses. Until she could hold it no longer.

'It's a girl,' she said.

CHAPTER 26

AFTER SOME DISCUSSION, they decided to call her Roberta. He'd wanted to call her Robyn, but Robyn herself was not in favour of that, despite it being an honour. She appreciated the gesture. Now, she was sure, her husband truly loved her. She need not have to worry about that woman in Canberra, Evelyn. It did not matter how much he remembered or felt for her, a woman who'd had everything, including the most expensive clothes and a flash car, which she had left to Becker, or at least he had somehow acquired it. And a lot of money, it would seem.

It did not matter if the farm did not make a profit. It was a hobby and an interest. Although, now that she was so well advanced, she did not like the thought of sending any of the cattle off to the saleyards. Even hoped none of them sold, so they would be brought back home, to chew contentedly. For the rest of their natural lives. Such beautiful animals, staring at you when you approached, wary at first, but then relaxing, prepared to trust you. Especially if you had a pat and a friendly word. But, she knew, the matter was out of her control. Whatever Harry decided, Harry would get. She saw to that. He'd had a bad time. He deserved to get his way. Have relaxed time. Nothing to worry about.

Three days later, he was on the eastern verandah, polishing his best boots.

'Harry,' she said, 'would you like a party?'

'A party?'

'It's your birthday next month. You'll be forty.'

'Oh, I don't want a party. I'm not very sociable. But we'll have a party, when she arrives. We'll celebrate that.'

'I want to do something for you. All your friends—'

'You won't be fit enough. You have only five weeks to go.'

'Oh, I'll be fine. Mum will help me, so will Anika. She said she would.'

'You've discussed it with her?'

'Yes, she was quite excited. Wanted to do the catering.'

He stood up, having finished polishing. She really wanted to do something for him. Women were like that. Birthdays seemed to be important. There was a time a year ago, when he did not care if he never had another birthday, things had looked so bad. Until he'd met Evelyn Crowley. But they were much better now, thanks to Evelyn and her money. Perhaps he was being selfish. Women loved parties. The bigger the better.

'We'll have it catered,' he said.

'Catered? You mean it?'

'You make the arrangements.'

'Oh, thank you, dear—I mean darling.' She'd been calling him 'darling' since first light. And kissing him whenever she got the chance. She was big now. And had to lean in toward him or beg him to lean intoward her. Or come up beside him and put an arm about him and snuggle. She was a snuggly sort of woman.

He drove into town a little apprehensively. This was the day. This was to be the end for his blasted first wife. No more money. He'd had to pay another thousand toward her bills two days ago. He would not pay one more dollar. The management would have to throw her out if they did not wish to be stuck with her. She was like a leech. Once she got her teeth into you, she would not let go. But, on the other hand, if she were thrown out of the motel, she'd simply move back to *Nil Desperandum*. The noise, the squabbling.

And Robyn so far gone. She did not deserve another invasion.

But when he reached the motel, full of fire and fury, he was astonished. Adeline had departed. So had the girls.

'Gone?' he said.

'Gone,' said the manager, her nose in the air. She had thick black hair and butterfly glasses. Much like Dame Edna Everidge's spectacles, but without the sparkles.

'Gone where?'

'Back to Sydney, on the first flight this morning. First class, she said.'

'First class?'

'So she said.'

'Who paid for that?'

'The World Boxing Commission, so she said. She'd had a letter, which I handed to her not long after five yesterday. She'd only then returned from the races.'

'The races? Horse races? On a Wednesday?'

'We do now and then have them mid-week.'

'Did she say what was in the letter?'

'Apparently, the Sports Doping Agency had been checking again samples taken from boxers at recent matches. Tests had now shown her previous husband's opponent in the State titles bout early this year had been on steroids. As a result, he had been disqualified. Her previous husband was now the declared winner. The purse, some fifty-thousand dollars, would go to him.'

'But her husband's dead.'

'I thought you were her new husband?'

'No, no, her first husband. She divorced me years ago.'

'Oh, she said you'd look after everything.'

'Everything?'

'Including the bill.'

He was stunned. She had gone, really gone? He could not believe it, but the invoice stated quite clearly Ms Adeline Becker and family had departed the motel at 07.13 that morning. He paid the bill and went back to the Nissan, replacement windows for the BMW not yet having arrived. And sat, feeling there was something fishy about the whole matter. He was about to head for Railway Street, when his mobile went off.

'Are you fresh his morning?' a voice asked.

'Chook?'

'How are you, dear boy?'

'Why are you speaking in a funny voice?'

'I've been listening to the BBC.'

'Where are you?'

'In Sydney—'

'Sydney?'

'Supervising things.'

'What things?'

'The arrest of your kleptomaniacal wife.'

'What the hell do you mean?'

'Caught at Sydney airport this morning with a bag of weed in her bag.'

'Oh, hell, where is she now?'

'Under police guard at the airport, being interviewed.'

'What'll happen to her?'

'She could get two or three.'

'Years?'

'Yep.'

'For a bag of weed?'

'With her record, definitely.'

'What record?'

'Lifting stuff that isn't hers. Petty theft, passing valueless cheques, soliciting in a public place.'

'Oh, God, what about the kids?'

'Right now they're trying to bring down aircraft with lazars.'

'Oh, hell, Chook. How do you know all this?'

'I know Ray Henschke and Ray knows a few people.'

'Did you arrange this?'

'Don't worry, she was going to take you for every dollar you have.'

'What's going to happen to her?'

'She'll come up in a bail court tomorrow, I imagine.'

'Bail? Who's gonna pay that?'

'You can expect a call.'

'Me? Never.'

'Then she'll be in custody for a maybe a year, awaiting trial.'

'Oh, God. What about the kids?'

'That's your baby, baby. Must run. *Ciao*.'

He listened to the phone purring for a while. It had a sweet, happy sound.

When he called at the small house near the station, Bob Elliott was not at home.

'I thought he'd still be reading the morning papers,' he said.

'He's at the station,' Muriel said. 'He likes to look at trains.'

Muriel Elliott was a tall and gentle woman, the daughter of an Anglican vicar many years ago, when a man, already hat in hand—she obviously being a lady—had walked through the lichgate and asked politely: 'Is the vicar in, by any chance?'

She had smiled, amused.

'Quite often he is and quite often he is not, even when he is,' she had said.

This was soon after the war. Robert Elliott had been back only a month or so. Something to do with the Occupation in Japan and war criminals. Captain, Ninth Division, he was. She had been picking roses at the time, or snipping them. In one slim, to the point of being bony, hand was a pair of secateurs and in the other a single rose, a damask. It went with her complexion. It was quite warm, even pleasantly hot, and she wore a floppy straw hat with a ribbon. Which hung down indolently. And gloves, gardening gloves. And something shimmery over a satin slip. He could not actually see a slip, but the muslin dress was so thin there had to be a slip.

'Oh?' he'd said.

'If he's reading, he is not in.'

'I see.'

She'd smiled in the reserved and yet welcoming way that you'd expect of a vicar's daughter. Doing it with her eyes rather than her pretty pink lips. Not red lips, mind you. She never wore lipstick.

'If you'll just wait a moment,' she had said, 'I'll just look. What name shall I say?'

'Elliott,' he'd said, 'Robert Elliott.'

'Of course, I'll just see.'

Miss Maplethorpe lightly tripped to an open door and called: 'Hullo? Father? Are you *there*?'

Distantly came back a voice: 'Yes? Yes? I *am* here.'

'Oh, good, there is a Mr Elliott.'

The ecclesiastical gentleman appeared.

'Ah, yes, Robert, isn't it?'

'I've just returned,' he said.

'Yes, of course, someone did say. Please do come in.'

He was a tall, painfully thin and perfectly clean Englishman with an Oxford accent. 'You have met my charming daughter, I see.'

Elliott nodded.

'It's about my father,' he said.

'Oh, yes, of course. I did hear, only this morning. I am so sorry. My dear fellow, won't you please come in?' Elliott had followed, still holding his hat. The reverend gentleman had called back: 'Muriel, dearest, is there any chance of tea?'

'Of course, Father.'

Like the swan in the evening, she moved through the door.

Becker followed her in. Muriel was still tall and thin, almost skinny now in a tragically diminishing way. She had a stilted, school-mistressy sort of walk. Not quite lifting her feet. Nor her voice.

'I wish he wouldn't.' She dared for a moment to add: 'He's been watching them since we came here,' she said. 'Trains don't change much, do they? Over the years, I mean.'

'I suppose not.'

'Could I get you tea or coffee, Harry?'

'Oh, no, I had a good breakfast. I don't drink a lot of coffee now. I never liked tea.' It was always cool in the small timber house—not the coolness of a low temperature, but of good manners. 'You know about the party?' he said.

'Yes, Robbie rang. She's quite thrilled. A catered party too? That's very thoughtful of you, Harry. She being in her condition. She won't have to do anything, will she? Just sit there and be a lady, she said. She's very lucky,' Muriel added, 'that she's got you.'

'I'm lucky too.'

He began to edge to the door. 'Was there something?' he asked. She seemed to be in two minds, as if wanting to talk to him about something important, but not sure.

'Oh—' She was clenching her hands, now painfully thin. Muriel was in her late sixties, well brought up. Devoted to the church. And to seeing that guests were treated with the respect they deserved.

'She said she'd told you, last night,' she said.

'About the baby? We're going to call her Roberta.'

'Yes, isn't it wonderful? Robert is so pleased. I think he was about to cry.' She was having difficulty with her hands. Difficulty looking directly at him. She was going to tell him something, he knew.

'I'll find him up there.'

She stepped forward, as if to touch him, even clasp him. 'Oh, Harry, Robyn has told you about her husband, Arnold? And what had happened?'

'I already knew about the crash.'

'And about the press clipping?'

He was surprised. 'That too.'

'It was a dreadful shock for her.'

'I can imagine. Any idea who sent it?'

She faltered and fiddled. 'I did.'

'You, her mother?'

'Yes, she had to know. I was in the library, filling in time, flipping through *The Sun News-Pictorial*, when I saw it. First, I saw 'Wagga', then it jumped out at me. The name, I mean. I was shocked. I had to tell her, but I could not. I would have been so embarrassed, not so much for myself as for her. The dear, sweet girl. Such an awful thing to know. But I could not tell her to her face, could I? You understand? I would not have been able to face her. So I made a copy. They have a machine. At the top of the page was the name of the paper and the date. So, I included that too. I took it home and folded it and put it in an envelope and addressed it to her, printing with my left hand. It looked awful, such an ugly scrawl. I felt ugly, doing such a thing. And awful posting it, but I could not tell her face to face. I could not. Such a terrible thing—'

'Does she know *now* that you sent it?'

'No, no, I have been trying to tell her for some time, months, a year, but cannot bring myself. I feel so ashamed.'

He put a hand on her shoulder. It was a thin, bony shoulder, which flinched at this touch, but soon relaxed.

'I think you should tell her. But after the baby.'

'Do you think?'

'Yes.'

He found Bob Elliott at the station, sitting on a long, hard bench, saying: Wagga Wagga in white on blue. Bob was surprised to see him. He had the expression of a man quite contented with his life, but worried he might die soon and miss out on something, although he could not think what it was.

'Hullo, Harry. Looking for me?'

'Muriel said you would be here. I was wondering,' he said as he sat, 'whether you can tell me why my grumpy old bastard of a neighbour is so interested in us?'

'Which neighbour is that?'

'The one on the western side, Albert Henschke.'

'Henschke?'

'He says he knows you.'

'From where, I wonder?'

'No idea. But his son says it's all about a girl named Caitlin.'

'Caitlin?' Bob twitched a little, at least his hands and feet did.

'You told us about Caitlin, the Irish girl who worked for the Mountford family in Victoria—'

'So I did, at that pleasant lunch at your place. I went on a bit, didn't I? Yes, Caitlin was my mother.'

'And she married Walter Elliott, who worked on the Mountford property?'

'Yes, he was the groom.'

'What about the Mountford family?'

'The family?'

'Did they have children?

'Children? Yes, I believe there were two sons.'

'What were their names?'

'Their names? Oh, I don't know—. There was one named Roderick. Not a decent sort of chap at all.'

'Why?'

'Oh, I don't know. I think he was a cruel sort of fellow. Got into some sort of trouble, with a girl, I think.'

'A girl named Caitlin?'

'Oh, no, no, no. My mother was a girl of unquestionable virtue. No, some other girl.'

Becker hesitated. Robert Elliott seemed to be disturbed. He'd put a hand to his head and bowed it, as if in thought. But his eyes were squeezed shut. Not a thinking sort of gesture, but a hurting.

A goods train came in slowly. When it reached the station, a wall of air hit them. Bob Elliott had a hat. He always had a hat outdoors. Wouldn't be seen dead in the street without it. He was sitting in shade and held the hat on his lap. It was an old hat, but a good hat, the kind which is the mark of a man. A retired man, a prosperous man. Or, at least, a once-prosperous man. It was a long train, truck after truck, going south. They waited until it had gone.

'What about him?' Becker said.

'Who? Oh, Roderick? Oh, he was kicked out. Cut out of his father's will.'

'You said he'd become a wreck.'

'Did I?'

'At the party.'

'Oh, yes, well—' He sat up, watching the last of the freight trucks disappearing down the line.

'So he did.'

'Did he ever marry?'

'Roderick? I think he did later, much later. Or, perhaps he only lived with her. Or, even met her only once or twice. She was a shopkeeper's daughter in Ballarat, I think. He may have worked for her father at one stage, but not for long, I'm sure. Not the kind to stick at a job. Always moving on, or being forced to move on. Or getting the sack, being so unpleasant to everyone. I heard he was always complaining that he'd been robbed. That he was going to the Supreme Court to get justice. Whether he ever did, I don't know. Probably all talk. He was all talk, that fellow. A thorough brute, if you ask me.'

'Did she have a child?'

'The grocer's daughter? I believe she did, out of wedlock.'

'What was *her* name?'

'Oh, I don't know.'

'Was it Henschke?'

'Henschke? Oh, I don't—' He rubbed his head. 'It's such a long time since I heard that name.'

'You've heard that name?'

'Yes, yes, I think it was Henschke'.

'And the child's name?'

'I have no idea.'

'Albert Henschke?'

'It could have been.'

'Why not Mountford?'

'Mountford?'

'His father's name.'

'I don't know. Maybe he'd left her by then. This was during the depression, the thirties. Lots of men on the roads then. It was awful, the depression, the Great Depression. I know, I lived through it. It was awful, being on the land,' he added. 'We still had something to eat, even if it was only bread and butter and sugar. And we didn't have to beg. That must have been the worst part of it, going up to a back door, cap in hand, and asking for something, anything, even a few crusts. To eat.' Old Bob gazed away across the rail lines and the roofs of suburban Wagga Wagga. 'I still have the letter, you know,' he said.

'What letter?'

'The one Christopher wrote to Caitlin. Would you like to see it?'

'Who was Christopher?'

'The other Mountford son. He was in love with Caitlin.'

'In love with your mother?'

'Oh, no, she wasn't married then. Would you like to see it?'

'Yes, I would.'

'It's all about the other girl, you know.'

They went back to the house in Railway Street. Bob had it preserved in a plastic cover in a folder marked Personal. He handed it to Becker. 'It makes for ugly reading,' he said. 'I've never shown it to Robbie, but seeing that you are a member of the family—'

Becker read it out front, seated in a chair aged by rain and shine. Bob sat in another, its cane backing beginning to break. It would soon need repairing, if it were not to collapse. The writing was scrawly, the kind you might dash off in a hurry and possibly in very poor light. And possibly in a highly emotional state. It was crumpled and worn, even yellowed with age. But it was legible enough.

'I have thought about it for a long time,' he read, 'I can no longer assuage my guilt. I was there when my brother, Roderick, murdered that girl. We were out walking, now and then taking a pot shot at a rabbit. At least Roddy was. We were taking turns with the one rifle. I was having the occasional shot but deliberately missing, when we came to this hut or cabin, behind the Elephant, smoke coming out of the riveted sheet-iron chimney.

'It was the Colley place, such poor people, but decent. You probably know them, my dear. Roderick went up to the door and knocked, loudly and even shouting, 'Open up, Colley! I know you're at home. I can see the smoke!' There was a pause before the door opened. It was not Mr Colley, but I think the girl herself, Miss Kiera Colley, sixteen or seventeen. Roddie said, Is your fairther at home?' Trying to be funny and sound like an Irishman. 'No, sir,' she said, shaking her head. 'Ah,' he said, 'in such case, are *you* at home, my darling?' 'Yes, yes, sir,' she replied, very courteous. She knew who he was, so she invited us in, and gave us tea and toast, black tea it was. All the time, Roderick was eyeing her and saying what a lovely colleen she was. And asking if she'd ever been kissed. 'Yes, of course,' she said, 'once or twice.' 'Have you ever been—?' he then asked. At which point she leapt away, but he went after her.

'I was horrified. I tried to stop him, saying, 'Don't, don't, don't! Leave her be, Roddie!' But he pushed me out, even pointed the rifle at me and said: "Get out, get out, if you don't want to be in it!" I was quite shocked that my own brother, up to whom I had always looked, would wish to do such a thing to such a fair young girl, she fighting back at him. I went outside, crying to myself, horrified. And frightened. I walked around and around, hearing her screams. Then the silence.

'I was sitting on an old bench under an old pear tree, my head in my hands, when he came out. This must have been some fifteen minutes later, stuffing in his shirt and buttoning up his breeches. Holding the rifle, leery.

"You want to have a go?" he asked. '

"No, no, no!" I said. "How could you do such a thing to a girl?"

"Ah, go and—her," he said. His language was disgusting. "It'll make a man of you," he said.

"What?" I said.

"No?" he said. "No? No? I always thought you were a spineless little—No spunk in you, no spunk at all! All right," he said, "if that's the way you feel."

'He went back inside and nothing happened at first, although I thought I could hear her weeping. One short cry after another, like the cry a baby makes before it finally goes to sleep. I could hear him speaking to her, short words, silences between. As if he were asking her something and she being not able to reply.

'Then an explosion.

'I couldn't believe my ears. He had shot her.

'He came out, holding the rifle in one hand, closing the door with the other. And looking around, quickly. "All right" he said. "Let's—off." Like a faithful dog, which can forgive its master anything, I followed him home, stumbling. I could not see, so I followed his legs and boots. Forgive me for writing such loathsome words to you, my dear. But I must tell someone, someone who has my heart and admiration and of whom I am so unworthy.'

At this point, the writing was difficult to read. Christopher seemed to be saying, or at least trying to say, to Caitlin that he loved her. He adored her. He used to watch her as she went about her duties. His heart leaping at the sight of her. And had hoped (this is especially obscure) that one day they would stroll together through the almond orchard in bloom. She with her hand on his arm and he with his heart in heaven, as his wife. There were many crossings and scribbles and a last few unintelligible words, which had plunged over the bottom of the page. It was signed, however, sideways on the right-hand border and dated. Although he seemed to have forgotten the year. Not that it mattered in the circumstances. The gist of the last rambling paragraphs, however, was that Caitlin would inherit the lot.

'I think he then took the poison,' Bob said. 'Lysol, as it turned out.'

'Lysol?'

'Pretty common back in those days. Often used by suicides.'

Becker put it back in its plastic folder and handed it to Bob.

'The lot? She got the lot of a big estate?'

'Well,' he said, 'it seems Christopher would have married her if possible. His father, old Sir Ralph, would never have agreed. The boy wanted to give her what he could not now keep, it being on his conscience so badly. But he never confessed. Never told a soul, until he wrote that letter, which now lay upon the kitchen table. For all to see.'

Another train came in, slowly this time. Also, southbound. You'd think the express, being an express, would soon catch up with the freight train, but it would have to stop at several main stations, such as Albury and Wangaratta and so on. The freight would not stop. It would roll on and on and on like old Father Time until it reached Melbourne. Inexorably.

They sat there, watching passengers getting off and on. The guard hung out of a door at the back, watching up and down. He pressed a buzzer and the brakes went off. The express began to move, two big diesels straining. Slowly at first, then faster, it moved on and away, out of sight, leaving the two men sitting and looking at nothing in particular.

It was that kind of day, when it was good to look at nothing in particular.

'Could I have a copy?' Becker said. 'Of the letter?'

Bob Elliot was surprised. 'The letter?'

'I want to show it to someone.'

CHAPTER 27

LATE THAT DAY, Becker went to see old Bert again. It was a good walk. About two-hundred yards to the boundary fence, then another three-hundred to Bert's house. Nothing but weeds all the way from the boundary to his door. There had been fences each side of the driveway from the front gate to the house, but they had deteriorated over the years. There still some Cyclone wire on metal stakes around the house, but they did not stop the weeds—dandelions and skeleton weed and rye grass and thistles, not to mention the bindi-eyes and Bathurst burrs. All the noxious weeds you could think of. Why the local council had not forced Bert to get rid of them years ago, Becker did not know. Perhaps it had tried and given up? How do you force an old reprobate like Bert to do anything? You could fine him, but he had no money. You could perhaps stick him in jail, but the weeds would get worse. You could take away his title, but it was freehold land—not leasehold. He could fight you in the courts for years. And if you won, who would buy it? It would take years to get rid of the weeds.

Becker knocked on the door. It took some time for Bert to get to the door. Blue came out first and sniffed him, then went back inside. At last, Bert's head appeared. Becker tried to hand over a copy he'd made at a shop in town.

'You should read this, Bert.'

'What the 'ell is that?'

'A copy of a letter. It explains everything.'

'Who writ it?'

'Christopher, before he died.'

'Christopher?'

'Christopher Mountford.'

'Mountford?' He spoke as if he'd never heard the name.

'He inherited the property.'

'Who?'

'Christopher did, then he killed himself. It's all in the letter. It's his last will and testament, in effect. I took a couple of copies. You can keep this one.'

Becker tried to force it upon him, but Bert pushed it back.

'Christopher fuckin' Mountford?'

He was not looking at Becker. Anywhere but at him, mostly over his head. Didn't seem able to see. His mind full of failed expectations. And a glassy sort of hate.

'Git the hell out of 'ere—'

'He left everything to Caitlin. Your father was not entitled to anything.'

'Git out or I'll set the dog onto yer!'

'Bob Elliott is not responsible for the fact that everything went his mother's way. It's just how it was. No-one is responsible for what happened to your father, except himself. Can't you get that in to your stupid head?'

Old Bert leaned against the door jamb. He seemed to slide down, not against the jamb but inside himself. As if some ancient dream had come to nothing. Or, that had come to something that could never be put into words. It was the hopelessness of hoping.

'Bob Elliot's mother had four wheat blocks once. They were sittin' pretty. Then the banks took three off them. That left them with one back in the bad times. But they battled on. They stuck it out. They won through. You've got one block. You could be growin' wheat, but you do nothing, nothing at all! You let this fucking place run wild. It's a disgrace. It's full of weeds and rabbits and snakes and neglect and despair. It's a fuckin' eyesore, Bert. You should be bloody well ashamed of yourself!'

Becker was angry, stamping around, startling Blue. Who was sniffing and snorting, his rheumy little eyes going this way and that like two frantic flies in a bottle. He caught his breath.

'Why don't you sell up, Bert? This place'd sell if it wasn't such a dump.'

Bert said nothing. His arms were folded and his eyes lowered, perhaps closed. He had slipped right down inside himself. So that his soul, if he had one, was down in his laceless boots.

'Y'd take me place?' he said, as if to himself.

'I'll make you an offer. I'll give you three-hundred for it.'

'Three hundred?'

'Thousand.'

Bert said nothing.

'I'd clean up this place and do something with it. Plant some sorghum or canola or—' He was so angry he couldn't think straight.

'Y'd take me place?' Still not looking up.

'It'd be good riddance. This place is an eyesore. A blot on the landscape.'

'I ain't sellin'.'

'Have you got a pension, Bert?'

No reply.

'Is that how you support yourself? You get a pension when you're sitting on three-hundred thousand?'

No answer.

'You're a cheat, Bert. Bludging off the taxpayers, aren't you?'

'Got a pension,' Bert said, not loud. More like a hurt undertone.

'You've got a pension? What kind of pension?'

'For me war effort.'

'You mean a veteran's pension?'

'For me service. For the compensation.'

'You mean you've got a disability?'

Bert didn't nod or shake or say anything. Becker was stumped. It should have been obvious from the start.

'You were in New Guinea?'

No answer.

'All right, I'm sorry.' Becker looked around, calming gown.

'Shaggy Ridge.'

'What's that?'

'Shaggy Ridge.'

'What?'

Bert was still not looking up.

'Me and me mates, we went up Shaggy Ridge.'

'You went up Shaggy Ridge?'

Becker had heard of it. His father used to tell how his own father had fought the Japs in New Guinea, but that was long ago. Back in '43.

'They was firin' down on us. Men fallin' off the mountain, screamin'. Bert took a deep breath, remembering. 'Was one of the first to the top.'

'You got to the top?'

'To the Pimple, they called it.'

'What happened?'

'A Jap was standin' there, lookin' at's. Holdin' a rifle.'

'What happened?'

'Knew I was a gonna. Then a shell hit's.'

'Hit you?'

'Hit's both.'

'From down below? One of your own?'

'Tryin' to support us. They was fallin' short. Because of the angle, straight up almost.'

'What happened to the Jap?'

'Cut to bits.'

'Jesus.'

'Standin' there with his guts hangin' out. Bit of shrapnel, y' know.'

'Yeah?'

'Then 'e fell on top of us.'

'On top of you?'

'Yeah, guts an' all. Didn't say a word. Still alive and lookin' at's. Then 'e closed his eyes an' died.'

'And you?'

'Got's too.'

'Yeah?'

'In the shoulder an' arm an' the 'ead.'

'In the head?'

'Yeah.' He touched his above the right ear. There was a scar now that you looked. 'Couldn't get that bit out, not in the bush. So they flew's right back to Australia. In one of them DC3 things. First time I ever flewed. They dug in and got it out. Townsville, that was.'

'But you took the mountain?'

'Yeah, we took it.'

'How did you feel about that?'

'Didn't care if I fuckin' lived or died. Not with a bit of metal in me 'ead. Didn't know much about it, anyway. Couldn't flamin' well think or anythin'.'

Becker gathered himself. The sun had gone down, but the sky was still alight. Like a great big bushfire somewhere out of sight in the west.

'I apologise, Bert.'

'Ah—' He still hadn't looked up, as if he felt rotten about his life and the whole rotten struggle to make something of it.

Blue had settled down, head on crossed paws.

Becker stepped off the verandah.

'If you ever want to sell, Bert—'

The old man did not reply, but he did take a deep breath and shifted his weight and stood up a bit for himself.

'I ain't sellin',' he said.

'Good night, then.'

Becker had gone only a few yards, when Bert said again, as if to himself: 'Gonna die 'ere. In me own 'ome.'

The sooner the better, Becker thought. And walked on home.

CHAPTER 28

EVERYTHING WAS GOING swimmingly. In a few days, all had been arranged. Robyn hadn't had to do a thing. Anika was very bossy. She saw that the caterers knew exactly what to do and when. She was a good neighbour. They had known each other for a year now. Took to each other like ducks to water, although Anika was so much older. Amiable, affectionate, generous and always willing to give a helping hand. Robyn was excited by the thought of having a big party and being the lady of the house with nothing to do—happily and wondrously sitting back, indicating to the hired help. Empty glasses here, more nibbles there. Quite worn out by thinking rather than by doing. Went to sleep each night with a smile on her face. Then she'd think of someone else who should be invited. The list of invitees grew and grew almost daily, so when the big day came, there were more than fifteen.

On Friday, the day before the party, Becker thought he'd try to get Bob and Albert Henschke together. Get them sorted out. Try to patch up things with Bert. He was a difficult old bastard, but a good man. Any man who had fought his way up Shaggy Ridge had to be a good man.

He went across and knocked at Bert's front door. Heard movement in the house, knocks and shuffles and screaks, possibly furniture being moved, a movement at a curtain. Old curtains, frayed. Holes here and there. They looked brown with age, like newspaper which has been lying out in the sun for days. Becker did not catch a face or even an eye. But he'd been inspected, he knew. Knew he was being brave, confronting an old bastard who had a shotgun, an old Hollis. The stock hand-carved in London. A collector's piece, in fact.

The door opened an inch or two.

An eye appeared.

'Good day, Bert.'

No reply, Becker thought the eye was going to disappear and the door to close. Instead, it opened and Bert Henschke stood there. Holding the Hollis, sure enough.

'There's no need for that, Bert.'

His face was screwed up like an old dishcloth. Wrung out.

'You got that fuckin' letter again?'

'It's nothing like that.'

'Don't read no letters, not from the taxation people or the local council or the Lands Board or the noxious weeds people. Only from the Veterans. They look after me, all the doctorin' and medicine and dentists an' everythin' I need. Which ain't often.'

'It's nothing like that.'

'What's it got to do with you, anyway?'

Becker avoided the point.

'I had a talk with Bob Elliott.'

'Had a talk? With this bloke that got it all?'

'No, he didn't get a cent. His mother did.'

'His mother?'

'She was Caitlin. Remember Caitlin?'

'One who poisoned him?'

'No, no, she didn't poison anyone. It's all in that letter. Anyway, I came to ask you if you'd like to meet Bob Elliott? Have a chat about the old days?'

'With that bloke, Bob Elliott?'

'Yeah, you see his father knew your father, Roderick.'

'Roderick Mountford, y'mean?'

'Yeah, Bob's father was Walter Elliott, the groom at the Mountford place. At Mount Elephant.'

'Mount Elephant?'

'That's right. Did you know your father? I mean, well?'

'Did I know 'im?' The door opened and Blue walked out, his nails tapping and scraping on the old boards.

'Did I know 'im?'

'I thought you lived with your mother. In Ballarat?'

'Mother? What mother? I never 'ad no flamin' mother. Might of been with 'er early on. When I was little. Might of looked after me. Don't remember that far back, do I?'

'How did you meet up with your father?'

'Dunno. Must of come and got me. From 'er. Was with 'im f'years. Walked miles, 'im an' me. On and on across the plains up in New South. Gettin' hitches 'ere an' there. We was all over the place.'

'Around here?'

'Around 'ere, out at Hay. Then Balranald one time. Went to school there for a bit. Swan Hill too. Echuca, all them places along the river. Plenty of fishin'.'

'With your father?'

'Always together. Until 'e died. Ruined, by a bitch of a woman that told all them lies about 'im. Said 'e done somethin' bad—'

'You mean Caitlin?'

Bert stepped out. Or, not stepped out exactly, but standing in the doorway, half in and half out. He'd put the shotgun in a corner. Blue was still walking around, sniffing. His nails scratching.

'It wasn't Caitlin, Bert.'

'And that bastard of a son, the young one—'

'Christopher?'

'Backed 'er up.'

'That's all wrong, Bert.'

'Know what 'e told's. Was with 'im when 'e died.'

'He died?'

'On the way to flamin' Ballarat. Told's the whole story, walkin' along. Tryin' t' go back, 'e was.'

'Back where?'

'To the place, the big place by the Elephant. Canley Vale, it was called. Said it was 'is by right and it'd be mine one day.'

'Mount Elephant is a long way south of Ballarat, especially if you're walking.'

'Yeah, 'e was always talkin' about it. He owned it. He was the rightful owner.'

'Why was he going back, Bert?'

'Said 'e was gonna get a lawyer and make 'is claim. On a statutary deck.'

'Declaration? What was he going to declare?'

'It was all a pack of lies, what they writ.'

'Who writ?'

'That young sheila, Caitlin they called 'er. And that bloke, the groom. They was in it together, Dad said. An' 'e c'd prove it.'

'When was this?'

'When was this? Back in the old days, when I was a kid. When everyone was out of work.'

'Back in the depression?'

'The thirties,' Bert said.

'What happened?'

'What happened to what?'

'To your dad?'

'To me dad?' Bert scratched his head again. He did a lot of that. He was worse than old Blue. It was the only way he could think. Get his ideas and memories and words together, in some sort of logical order. Or, if not logical, then narrative order. Not so much for to tell, but to put his whole life together, while he still had some. Life, that is.

They were walking on, cadging lifts now and then, gradually getting closer to Ballarat. Following some sort of river all the way down from Echuca. Except that the river was going northward to the Mighty Murray, as they called it. Which is only a tiddler compared with the Nile and the Amazon and the Mississippi. Whereas, they were going southward toward the bold and yet listless granite hills of the residual Great Divide at Ballarat. And then the Grampians. And then Mount Arapiles. And then nothing. Merely flat land, the limestone deeps and wells and sinks and vineyards and on to the never ending and always cold grey and unwelcoming sea. White caps flying.

'There was a lake, I think, or a dam. And there was all these dead trees, standin' 'round in the water with their arms up, like dead men. An' Dad was startin' t' complain.'

'What about?'

'Holdin' 'is side and sayin' Ow and Ah and God give me strength, an' all those things people say when they're in pain. And frightened,' Bert added.

'Frightened?'

'Yeah, looked real worried. Short o' breath. Said 'is 'eart was goin' mad. We'd just passed all this water with the dead men, when 'e went down.'

'He fell?'

'Nah, just went down slow on 'is knees, but screamin'. Never 'eard a man screamin' before.'

'What'd you do?'

'Ran to 'im. Dad, Dad, I said, what's the matter? He keeled over, 'oldin' is side, then 'is chest. Thought it must be the colic, which 'e'd 'ad a few times. But which usually went away. After 'e drunk a lot of water. But said 'e 'ad terrible pain in his left arm an' in 'is froat. So 'e couldn't swallow.'

'What'd you do?'

'Nothin', I didn't know what t' do. Kept lookin' for a car to come along, but—'

'But what?'

'Bloke come out of the bush. Must've come from the water. Had a gun in one 'and an' a brace o' ducks in the other.'

'What'd he do?'

'Said Dad looked crook. I said, Is 'e dyin'?'

'Don't look too good at all, the man said. Said to stay right there and 'e'd get someone. Went home t' phone. After about twenty minutes 'e come along with this old International utility an' said 'e couldn't get none. Think 'e meant the ambulance or the police or somethin' like that. They was all too busy.'

'So, what did you do?'

'Lifted Dad up and put 'im on the tray.'

'The back of the utility?'

'Yeah, the man told's to 'old his 'ead. To save it bangin' on the boards. Then off we went. Makin' poor time, because the road was just a dirt track and the pot 'oles and the gibbers was bad. But we got him to Ballarat and found the 'ospital and they took 'im in, the nurses. And told's to wait out there by the door. Waited an' waited, I did. Then this doctor come out and said we was too late. It was a 'eart attack.'

'Gee, eh?'

'Nothin' they could do for 'im. Massive, the doctor said.'

'So you were left alone? No-one to look after you?'

'Ah, they got the police and the police asked where I come from. I said, Ballarat. Which was not a lie at all. I was born there. Knew that much. The policeman said, You're in Ballarat, son. Have you got and any relatives 'ere? I said, Yes, Mum.

'Your mother lives here? he said. Yeah, I said, in a shop. What's 'er name? he said. I dunno, I said. What's your name? he said. Mountford, I said, Albert Mountford. What shop does she live in? 'e said. Dunno, I said. But you can get bread an' milk and all that stuff to eat there, Dad said. A grocery, you mean? 'e said. Yeah, I think that's what you call it. I didn't 'ave much education then, bein' on the road with Dad all them years. So the police asked 'round. It took hours. Just waited there at the 'ospital, feeling that 'ungry. We 'adn't eaten proper for several days. One of the nurses brought some sandwiches she made special. Then Mum turned up. Hadn't seen 'er for seven or eight years, so I didn't recognise 'er. But she said she was my mother by the sound of it. So, she took me 'ome to 'er place at the back of the shop, which was owned by 'er father, who was a German bloke with a pink face and a curly white beard. An' black glasses. So big they made his eyes look like two little dots in the middle of all that pink face and all them square teeth. Mum said that was because 'e was German.'

'You told me you never had a mother.'

'I 'ad a mother like everyone 'as a mother, but I never lived with 'er until I was eleven or twelve.'

'Then you stayed there with her?'

'Yeah, for years, except when I worked on a farm with Grandpa's brother and 'is wife and kids and got along with 'em. Mum said I was a Henschke now. And showed me the papers to prove it.'

'Did you go to school?'

'Yeah, on and off 'til I was fourteen. Then I left, which you could do then at fourteen. And got a job on the roads with the council. And 'elped Mum and Grandpa in the shop an'...'

Bert's voice trailed off. He had been scratching his head as if lifting his hat, which he was not wearing. It was a habit. And looking anywhere but at Becker. Although, often studying Blue lying on the verandah, scratching himself with one back leg. Thoughtfully, Becker thought. It was getting dark. Night was striding across the plains, chasing the sun. The long black shadows first, then the stars in the east. Something flew overhead, whirringly. Three or four black and winged shapes heading north. Probably ducks, but not quite. They didn't make a ducky sound. Not the same whirring.

'So, you stayed there in Ballarat?'

'Until I was eighteen, then joined the Army, an'...'

There was not much else to say. Somehow Bert Henschke had said everything you needed to know about him. About loss and poverty and obsession and death and survival and trying to make something out of yourself, despite everything. Becker looked at his watch. Had to hold it up to get enough light.

'Hey, I'd better go. It must be dinner time.'

'Yeah,' Bert said.

Blue sat up, expectantly. A decision had been made. It did not matter what. He was a dog and every little change was news worth having.

'Thanks for telling me, Bert.'

'Ah, well—'

Becker stepped off the verandah, then remembered.

'Hey, Bob Elliott will be here again next Saturday,' he said. 'That's what I came to tell you.'

'Bob Elliott?'

'Yeah. You might like to come over, have a chat. Have a beer, meet some people.'

'Wants to 'ave a chat, does 'e?'

'If you feel like it.'

'This a invite, is it?'

'Seeing we're neighbours. Any time after twelve thirty. For one,' Becker added.

'One what?'

'O'clock. That's when they'll start serving.'

'Food y'mean?'

Becker felt he'd done his best.

'Think about it, Bert.'

Bert Henschke looked around, twisting his neck, using a hand to rub it, screw it, loosen it. He had a problem there. Needed to get treatment. But he never would.

'Might,' Bert said. 'Then I mightn't.'

Becker walked back, thinking about Bert. He was a bastard, but he was a regular sort of bastard. The kind you could understand. More or less human being. Full of bitterness and deprivation and being treated like dirt most of his life. But a brave man. He'd been brave in New Guinea. They should have given him a medal. Maybe they did, but Bert would have been too proud to wear it or even mention it. Before he reached his house, he received a phone call. It was Chook.

'Yeah?'

'Want to hear some news?'

'What?'

'She couldn't raise bail, so she's in custody until her trial comes up.'

'Addie? When is it likely to be?'

'Six months at least, maybe nine.'

'And the kids?'

'They are your responsibility, unless—'

'Unless what?'

'You can prove they're not yours.'

'How am I going to do that?'

'DNA, mate, DNA. Not sure I can get a private job like that through our system, though.'

'I know someone in Canberra,' Becker said.

'Yeah?'

He felt rotten. He didn't want the results to show Adeline had been a liar from the start. But the whole family was, he knew. Her father had done time for opening safes without permission of the owners. He'd been a locksmith. Her mother had been running a charity for homeless girls. But the girls had never got anything. Charity, they say, begins at home.

'Ah, God, Chook, you shouldn't have planted that stuff on her. That's criminal.'

'I didn't plant any stuff on her.'

'Your friend at the airport?'

'That was Amos, a friend of Ray's. She already had it.'

'I don't believe you.'

'Yeah? Well, Amos noticed a small dog sniffing her bag, when she came in. When she'd checked in her luggage, he thought he'd have a peep. She had a big parcel of it, wrapped in plastic. Good quality weed.'

'Oh, God, no.'

'Amos asked me what to do about it. I said leave it there. Then I rang someone at Sydney airport.'

'How the hell would she get a parcel of weed?'

'She was at the races yesterday.'

'You mean she could have picked it up there?'

'Racing is not all about racing.'

'How much would it have been worth?'

'Amos thought, at a rough guess, ten grand wholesale.'

'Ten grand? Where would she get that?'

'You gave her your credit card number.'

'I gave it to the manager at the motel.'

'So?'

'Oh, shit.'

Chook was laughing.

'Have you looked at your bank account lately?'

CHAPTER 29

SATURDAYS COME AND Saturdays go, but this was a bad one. First to arrive were Hank and his grandchildren, two boys. Anika having been there for an hour to supervise the hired hands, whom she had recommended and for whom she felt responsible, working in the kitchen, loading the oven with all sorts of exotic dishes. And sticking bottles in the refrigerator, which was full up to dolly's wax as it was. Then came two teachers, who were known to be an item, from the local school. Plus the headmistress, who would have been snaky about it if she'd not been asked. Bearing gifts of course for the birthday boy, who was embarrassed, not having had a birthday gift since he first set eyes upon Adeline Atkins eleven years ago. She and her children being of the kind unable to resist opening any package, which looked as though it might contain something either edible or which you could return for the money.

Then Bob and Muriel, she being self-conscious since she'd made her shameful confession to Becker about the press clipping. And now unsure whether he had told Robyn and too scared to ask. Then the couple from across the road. Followed by the couple from up the side lane. Then Laura Langley and finally, almost late, Chook and Dell, she having had to wash her hair. Chook was riding her big black Harley, the girl up behind, hanging on for dear life. Smiling and giggling and saying, as she got off, 'Oh, my gosh, that was like wow!'

Taking off her helmet and shaking out her hair. Everybody staring at such a lovely piece of work, her mother being very clever. Getting off and walking up to Harry Becker in her skin-tight jeans and saying, 'Hi there, Harry!' and giving him a big birthday kiss on a cheek. 'You haven't met Robyn, have you, Dell?' 'Robin? As in a bird?' 'No, Robyn with a why.' Dell laughed. She had the prettiest of laughs. 'My, you are big, Robyn with a why. But it's perfectly obvious why, isn't it? When are you due?' 'Oh, in three weeks.' 'Three weeks?' 'Wow, that soon?' They laughed. Everyone was laughing. Happy, to say the least.

'Come in, Dell, and meet some people,' Becker said. He showed her around and everyone said, 'How nice to meet you, Deloraine.'

'Oh, please call me Dell, everyone does.'

'Dell?'

'Yes, Dell, but my brother calls me Delly and sometimes Dilly and, when he's really trying to be clever, Ding Dong.'

'Ding Dong?' Muriel asked.

'As in ding, dong, dell!'

'Really?'

'Yes, isn't that awful?'

'Oh,' Muriel said, 'this is my husband, Robert.'

'How nice to meet you, Robert—'

'Elliott,' Muriel added.

'Oh, yes, I was thinking, Robert, Roberta—'

'Yes, dear, for the baby.'

'Oh, isn't that lovely?'

Old Bob shook a bit. 'They're naming her after *me*.'

'Bob, I just said that to the young lady.'

He did not seem to hear her. 'Used to know a fellow named Duffy down in Victoria—'

'Excuse me, Dell,' Becker said, interrupting. 'I hear you always start with a soda, lime and bitters.'

'Oh, thank you, thank you!'

'You've met everyone?' Muriel asked.

'Not yet.'

'How's the assignment going?'

'Oh, it's *gone*.'

'Gone?'

'Yes, I handed it in a week ago and—'

'And?'

'My tutor said, 'The limit was two and half thousand words, Miss Duffy. This looks more like five-thousand!' 'Yes,' I said, 'I know, but she has such an amazing story to tell, hasn't she, Harry?'

'She?'

'Yes, Stacey gave me an interview.'

'She did?'

'Told me how her parents escaped from Odessa and all the terrible things which had happened there during the war and—'

'In Odessa?'

'Excuse me, Dell. Here's your soda and bitters.'

'Oh, thank you, Harry! Yes, Stacey told me about the siege of Odessa. It went on for two months until the Germans had flattened the city. Then they moved on, leaving the Rumanians to occupy Odessa, but the Rumanians went mad.'

Muriel could not quite hear. 'Mad, dear?'

'They did the most horrible things.'

'Horrible?'

'They slaughtered all the Jews and the Communists and Gypsies and anyone who was anti-fascist and—'

'Oh, how awful,' Muriel said. 'Did you hear that, Bob? How old was her father then?'

'Eleven.'

'Only eleven?'

'Yes, and he witnessed the horror, what the Rumanians did. People shot in the street, some strung up on poles as warnings, the poverty and despair and humiliation—'

'Excuse me, Dell,' Robyn said. 'Mum and Dad, would you like to come to the table, get something. You'll have to come back here with a plate. Or, shall I select something for you? We have turkey and ham and—'

And so it went. They had fifteen adult guests, two caterers and four children. It took a while to get everyone served, the table being overladen with all the food you could ever want, and then some. Everyone happy and chatting like mad. It was a lovely day at the end of August, a freshness in the sun. People taking plates outside to sit on the west-side verandah, the sun having come around. All chatting and sparkling.

Bob had been introduced to a teacher who knew Derrinallum. And Mount Elephant, and some of the story of Christopher Mountford, who shot himself and left the whole estate to this girl, Caitlin somebody. 'Caitlin Maguire!' Bob said excitedly. 'She was my mother!' So excited to have someone else to hear the story of. Muriel had to hold his plate, to stop the turkey falling off. He was getting carried away, something he should not do, a man with his heart.

There had been no sign of old Albert of next door. Twice Becker tried to spot him coming through the peppers, but not a movement.

Chook and Dell were on the verandah, leaning on a rail, eating from their plates and admiring the scenery. At least Dell was, but Chook was admiring her. You could see Chook was in love, nervously in love. A tough, mannish woman like her. It was both good and sad to see. She didn't have a hope. Anyone could see that. Dell was a happy-go-lucky girl, who loved to be alive. Loved to meet people. Loved to have fun. Loved to be the focus of all eyes.

'Excuse me,' she said, hushed. 'Where's the loo?'

'I'll show you'.

'Oh, just point me.'

'Back through the kitchen, turn left and then left again. There's a small doll on the handle, saying, This is it.'

'Really? What's the doll's name?'

'Lulu.'

'Lulu? A loo called Lulu? How clever!' She exited, laughing.

Laura Langley came up. 'My God, Stacey, you are outrageous.'

'I'm outrageous?'

'Everyone can see what you are doing. How do you propose to proceed from here?'

'On the way out, she said she'd like to ride for miles with her hair blowing in the wind.'

'Did she? And I suppose in her *naïvité* she thought she'd be safe in the hands of another woman?'

'I thought I'd take her down to The Rock.'

'What on earth is that?'

'About thirty 'k's' south. A great slab of the earth's crust sticking up out of the plains. One thousand feet up. Great view from the top too.'

'You've been there?'

'Yep, thought we'd climb it together.'

'In single file? With her going first, no doubt? In those tight pants?'

'Oh, to have a figure like that.'

'I suppose you hope to shag her one-thousand feet up?'

'She's too virginal to be shagged by anyone.'

'Really? Where is she?'

'Must have run into someone.'

Becker had put on one of his old favourites. Ray Charles and friends were singing: 'I can't stop loving you, I've made up my mind...'

Robyn came out, still picking at her salad. 'Hullo, you two.'

'Where's Dell?' Chook asked.

'Dancing,' she said, 'with Harry.'

'With Harry?'

'Uh hum, with her arms about his neck.'

'My God, he's trying to steal her from me!'

'Why not? He's the birthday boy.'

'How's everything going?' Laura said.

'Marvellously, isn't it, darling?' She patted her belly. 'A bit cramped in there, isn't it?' She finished chewing. 'Never mind, you'll soon be out. Out into the great big world.'

She walked to the edge of the verandah, above the steps. Stood looking away across the paddocks, taking in the world, complete in its fecundity. She complete in hers.

'Isn't this the most heavenly—? Aren't we the luckiest—'

At that very moment, twenty-eight minutes past one on a perfect day at the end of August 1996, the house blew up, *bang*! Short, sharp and terrible.

CHAPTER 30

LATE THAT DAY, Becker woke up in Wagga Wagga Base Hospital. He woke up slowly, fearfully. Had to blink and look hard to get his eyes open, to focus. His head was bandaged and something heavy was on his left leg, low down. His back felt broken. His guts felt awful, like he was going to vomit. He tried to look around, but his head barely moved, so he had to strain with his eyes. Something blurry was sitting beside him. Male or female? It was not clear. A senior nurse came with a dish. 'Ah, so you are awake, Mr Becker?' He didn't hear her say that, but he guessed that's what she'd said. She said something else, bending to give him jab. 'What's that?' he tried to say, but couldn't hear his own words. 'Metoclopramide,' she said. 'You've been vomiting.' He didn't understand; it was like trying to hear when your ears are full of water. So he watched as the needle went into a thigh muscle. 'You've had surgery,' she said. 'Your left leg is in a splint. Your back is badly cut. You have two fractured ribs, and you're deaf.'

'What?' he said.

'You, are, deaf,' she said. 'You've, been, blown, up!'

Still didn't understand, but could guess. It was coming back. He'd been blown up again, first in a car Canberra and now on a farm. He had to think. Where was the farm? It came back slowly. At least he had memory of some sort. It had been fun, he'd been dancing. There had been a pretty girl. Then chaos. Something had fallen on him, flopping him down. He'd fallen on something human, hard to say exactly what. Then something else had smashed his left foot, or his left leg, low down. Not sure, actually.

'A doctor will be with you soon, now that you're awake.'

What? he said. He wasn't sure that he had said anything. But the nurse seemed to understand.

'He will check your hearing.'

He thought she said something about hearing. He could not hear on the left side, but he seemed to have some hearing on the right.

'Can't hear me? He will stick something in your ears, to check them out.'

Out?

'Check your ears, in case of damage.'

Injury?

The nurse withdrew the needle, affixed a small plaster and picked up the dish. 'I'll be back to see you later,' she said. 'Doctor will be along soon. In the meantime, your friend here will explain what happened.' He couldn't understand. She saw that he couldn't understand and pointed, jabbing a finger to his left. With which she walked off briskly, the way nurses do, straight and true. He looked to the left. His neck hurt, but he managed to get his eyes to move far enough that way. Gradually he made out something, sitting or slouching or huddled or hunched on his left. Did she say, Friend? What friend? He didn't have any friends. Now.

'What happened?' His own voice was only a blurry thought.

'It blew up,' someone said.

'What?'

'Your house, it blew up.'

Still, he could not understand. The figure beside him rose and stood and turned around and came into view. It looked like a tall man with long blond hair.

'Chook?'

'That's me.' She leaned over, spoke slowly and carefully. 'Your house blew up.'

He got that. His house blew up. He couldn't quite hear it, could not quite read the lips, but he could guess.

'The house?'

He ached. He wanted to go back to sleep, but didn't. He didn't want to know, but he had to know. Before he gave up.

'Anyone—?'

'Injured? Almost everyone.'

'Everyone?'

'Some kids, outside playing, were uninjured. But Robyn—'

Robin? He did not know anyone named Robin.

'Robyn, she was standing on the edge, when the blast hit her. Of the verandah, I mean.'

'Who?'

'She was blown off, hit the grass. Head first.'

At last, it came to him. 'Robyn?'

'Yeah, your wife. She didn't make it, mate.'

'Robyn? Dead?'

'I'm sorry. They got her here to hospital. Still alive then. They tried, but they couldn't save her. Broken neck, mate.'

'Robyn,' he said again, whispering now. He was giving up. He couldn't think properly. His head hurt, a bad headache. His ear drums must be split.

'Brain damage too, they think. They managed to save the baby.'

He began to cry, not with his voice or with his mouth, but with his brain. It was too much. He couldn't come back. Someone was dead, then something about a baby. He wanted to get out.

'I'm sorry,' Chook said.

He sank down, eyes closing. 'No,' he said.

Chook leaned right down, a few inches from his face. Put a hand on his shoulder. 'I'm sorry, Harry.'

'No,' he said again. Then he sank right down. Glad to be escaping. Didn't want to come back. Not to a world where there never seemed to be an end to it. They'd tried again to kill him. Failed in Canberra, but they'd got Evelyn. Now they'd killed Robyn. He was a failure. He'd failed to protect her, a woman like that. Who wouldn't hurt a fly. A lovely woman, affectionate, grateful. True, a true friend. He wanted to cry. The failure and the misery and the loss—too much, too much. Life was an endless song of loss and longing, that's all there was to it. It had been a mistake, being born.

A man came and stuck something in his ears. Got down close to his face, breathing and grunting. Twisting the thing in his ear. And saying, Mmmm, to himself. Then did the same thing to the other ear. Then he said, 'The, drum, in, the, left, ear is split. Not, too, bad, in the right. No, damage, there.'

'Ear?' He managed to hear himself say that.

'Yes, the left eardrum, it, is, split. There may be damage to the cilia.'

'What?'

'The small, hairs, in the canals. It could become permanent if we don't act quickly. You need steroid treatment immediately.'

'What?'

'Steroid. The nurse will bring you some cortisone tablets in a minute. You must take them, if you want to save hearing in that ear.'

The doctor went away.

Time went away. Nothing happened. He slipped back into his dreaded state. A state in which he was entirely to blame for the disaster. He'd try to sleep. Hours would pass. Nurses would arrive, take his blood pressure. Check his eyes. Worried about brain damage. This went on for three days. Not that he'd be completely asleep, but retreated into a place where you are both asleep and awake. He'd been able to hear sounds and occasionally, voices, and feel movement and even hands. One night, he was sure someone was washing him. On another, he was being rolled onto one side, and later onto the first side. And on yet another, young women saying: One, two, lift!

When he did wake up, he did it suddenly—as if he'd had a long sleep after a hard day's work. His visual focus was better, his hearing too. A woman came and tested his hearing. Put earphones on his head. Made squealing noise. 'Can you hear that?' she'd say. Then she'd change the frequency. 'Can you hear that?' He'd lost eighty percent in the left ear. It seemed that he'd been saved from complete deafness in that one, probably by the cortisone. She said his hearing in the left should improve as the split drum healed itself. The other ear was better. The drum was intact and the loss was only fifty percent. It should soon improve as the concussion wore off. It was improving already. He could now distinctly make out what was being said to him, if only in his right ear.

The woman packed up her gear and went away. Chook had been present, watching.

'The local constabulary have been in to see you,' she said. 'I told 'em to piss off. You weren't in any condition. An inspector and a sergeant. The sergeant said he knows you.'

Becker didn't want to see anyone. The concussion had worn off and his hearing, at least in the right ear, had improved.

'I'm okay.'

'I told 'em all they needed to know.'

'There was a girl,' he said.

'Dell? You saved her. You fell on her, then the roof fell on you. You saved her. She's been discharged. Came around to see you, but you were out to it.'

'Anyone else?'

'Old Bob,' Chook said.

'Bob?'

'He had a heart attack.'

'Serious?'

'He's dead. The funeral's tomorrow, Thursday.'

'I should be there.'

'You're not fit to go.'

'And Muriel?'

'Shocked but not hit.'

'Anika?'

'In the kitchen at the time. A wall blew in. Bits fell on them, two caterers and Anika. Nothing serious. One of the caterers is dead. Another badly cut.'

'Children?'

'All outside at the time, playing with Nutty. As for everyone else, they were on the verandah. Most hit by flying boards, or glass. The house blew out on one side. The western,' she added.

'And you?'

'Blown off the verandah, straight down the steps. Jumped up and saw Robyn, curled up, gasping. Both arms over her belly. As if holding the child, protecting her. Searched around, checked everybody—'

'Where is she?'

'Robyn? In the morgue, mate. They're waiting for you. To make a decision. Funeral arrangements.'

'The baby?'

'In a crib, doing fine. No damage at all, they think. You want to see her? They'll get her for you.'

He did not answer. He didn't want to see the child. He didn't want to see anyone ever again.

'The other kids?'

'Wendy and Terry? They're with Muriel. Said she'd take the baby too, when she comes out.'

'She can keep her.'

'Hey, don't be that way. Your little girl's not responsible for anything.'

'If she'd not been pregnant—'

'Yeah, well, she was pregnant, happily pregnant.'

They fell silent. A nurse came and a nurse went.

'Laura was cut up a bit,' Chook said.

'Laura?' He had to think.

'Hit by flying glass. Had her back to it at the time. Copped it in the head and neck and on one ear. Nearly cut it off.'

'What?'

'Her ear. They were able to stitch her up. Has a big surgical pad taped to her head.'

'Yeah?'

'She's taken time off, so I'm running the shop. I hate paperwork.' Chook was trying to make conversation. 'I give it all to Dave. He's very grateful. Takes it as an act of faith. In his ability, that is. He's only a clerk. I don't know how he came to be a cop.'

Becker did not reply.

'They grilled him,' Chook said, 'the local cops. Thought he might have been responsible. He knew the time and place. He has a craving, you know.'

'Yeah?'

'For nicotine, chews it all day, drives me mad. Sometimes I wish he'd smoke instead. Stop all that chewing, like a cow.' A nurse came in pushing a trolley. 'He didn't do it, though. Didn't tip anyone off. Dave is too stupid to be nasty. Wouldn't hurt a fly. Goes on marches.'

'Marches?'

'To save the planet.'

Conversation fell flat. They watched as the nurse took his temperature and blood pressure and pulse. She looked very young, probably not long out of school. A trainee. She said nothing and he said nothing, while she notated on a chart. Then she went out with the trolley. Becker lay there, eyes almost closed, looking like he was going to drift back into sleep. Not real sleep, but some sort of incarcerating daze. Chook shook him.

'Wake up. Don't give up. You have a daughter, remember. Her name's Roberta. She's quite beautiful.'

Becker was not listening.

'They let me pick her up,' Chook said. 'In the nursery. She smiled at me. I wondered why she was smiling at me, an ugly bitch like me. Then I realised. I was smiling at her.'

Becker blinked, shook himself out of it.

'He did it,' he said.

'Who did what?'

'Bert, I showed him a copy of the letter.'

'What letter?'

'Addressed to Caitlin.'

'Who is this Caitlin?'

Becker did not bother to explain. His head ached. His ribs ached, his left leg in a splint. Each time he tried to move, it hurt like hell.

He remembered now. He had *not* shown Bert the letter. The old bastard had refused to look at it, but he'd told Bert what was in it. Something about a mountain. Someone getting killed on top. A Jap soldier, spilling his guts. No, that was not it. Mount Elephant, that was it.

'He knew Bob'd be there. Knew the time. Did it to kill him. Kill us all.'

'Kill who?'

'Old Bob.'

'No, no, mate, the local cops have interviewed him. When they heard it, he and Ray came running. I was there, I saw them. Ray was the first one in, helping people out.'

'When I get out of here, I'm gonna to kill 'im.'

'You ain't goin' anywhere, mate. You've got a broken leg. It's in a splint.'

'Ah, Jesus.'

'They've put a guard on your place,' she said.

Becker did not answer.

'What do you want done with the house?'

'What do you mean?'

'It's busted. It blew out one side, the western. They must have placed it under the living room, by the old fireplace, almost right under the table. Laden with food.'

'Burn it,' Becker said.

Late that day, the local police came and interviewed him. He was out of bed and doing some physio, trying to get used to crutches. His leg had been put in a cast that morning. His hearing was better, but he could not help them. One of them was the sergeant named Jack Jackson, the one who'd arrested Barnes. The other was a detective inspector named Quinn, or Quinlan, Becker was not sure. Who said very little. Contented himself by leaning against a wall and sniffling, and scratching, and frowning, and wriggling and exhaling. As if he'd run a long way. He had strangely round eyes, slightly protruding like intrusive nobs. And thin, black hair, slightly greying. And slightly distraught.

'What'd they use?' Becker asked.

The detective looked as though he were going to answer, but changed his mind. He seemed to be the kind of man hard to get information off.

'Gelly, by the look and smell of it,' Jackson said.

'Gelignite?'

'Yeah, two or three sticks. Wired,' he added. 'The Army's had a look at it. Found some bits.'

'Bits?'

'Of a mobile phone. Cable too.'

Becker was still shocked, but not medically shocked. He was not deranged or terrified. He felt nothing but sorrow. He wanted to get out of this kind of life, where you can be wiped out at any minute by people you do not know. They could be friends or neighbours. Or people who came out of your past, looking for you. Like figures in a dream, which does not make sense. Is not meant to make sense.

'What's happened to Barnes?'

'In this hospital,' Jackson said. 'In the mental health unit.'

'What's he got to say?'

'Nothing intelligible. Reckons you've always had it in for him.'

'Did he do it?'

'Can't see how he could. He was in here at the time.'

'He could have arranged it.'

'By phone? He didn't have a phone. We took it away from him. So we could trace the calls he made that day, when that old man was killed in your car.'

'Who did it?'

The detective inspector said: 'Your neighbour says he saw two blokes at your place one day, when you were absent.'

'What neighbour?'

'The old bloke with the cattle dog.'

'Two blokes?'

'With a van. Electricians from Griffith.'

'How did he know they were from Griffith?'

'There was a sign on the side, Terracini Electrics. And a phone number.'

'Terracini? What was the number?'

'Same as the one that called Barnes just before you were shot at on the road.'

'Barnes's wife—,' Becker said. He wanted to say that it must have been revenge. Trying to kill him because of the caper with Angelina Cosco. Except that he could not remember her name. He gave up.

'What did they say?'

'Their radiator happened to boil at that point. They had to get some water. So they went into your place and got some from a tap. They knocked on the door first, but no-one answered.'

'And Barnes? The phone call? Highway?'

'They say that was some personal matter, nothing to do with you and that old guy in your car.'

'He was a witness to a murder.'

'Keaton? Yeah, we know.'

'You think they did it?'

Jackson shrugged. 'Why would they use a van with their own name on it?'

'Why would they want to kill me? Kill my wife, my friends?'

'Any ideas?'

'Cosco,' he said. 'I helped the Feds to get his daughter out of Griffith. Maybe they think I'm hiding her.'

'Cosco? He's dead.'

'Maybe it's the family, for revenge.'

The plainclothes man had a different idea.

'Maybe you were not the target? Maybe it was your mate.'

'What mate?'

'The tall one that looks like a woman.'

'She's a cop, you know.'

'A Federal cop, yeah. For a cop, she's pretty hairy.'

'Hairy?'

'You know, hair-raising. Takes risks. Bends the rules. Likes to set people up, likes planting a bag of coke on someone.'

'She didn't plant anything. Barnes's wife knew what was in it. She asked for it.'

'Some people don't like his or her ethics.'

'She gets results.'

'Yeah? Well, maybe someone doesn't like him or her.'

Yes, Becker thought, Chook does take risks, and bends the rules. Plays around with lives. Like that caper in Griffith, very clever. Now Cosco was dead. And Barnes was in a psych ward, no doubt still raving about everyone bein' against him. Still couldn't think too well. Wished he were dead some days. Why was he there? He had accepted a bag of coke, but he had not been charged. They had compromised him just in case the caper with Angelina did not work, Chook had said. But it did work, Becker had protested. Yeah, well, Chook had said, rolling a reefer and lighting up and stretching her legs one day at the Hovell. She did not care who knew. By now she was some sort of law unto herself in Wagga Wagga. Why? Becker had insisted. Chook had just shrugged: No reason at all. Then, why don't you get him out of there? She'd shrugged again as she'd studied the toe of her boot. As if it was one one of the great questions you never dare to ask yourself. Then she had smiled, just a flicker. He's there, she had said, because he wants to be there. Why? Becker had said again. Look at it this way, if you were married to Maria Terrachini, would you want to be in a nice cosy place where everyone treats you with respect? Listens to your every complaint? Takes you seriously? Or would you want to be at home with Maria? Screeching her head off at you every day of the week?

CHAPTER 31

NEXT DAY WAS Thursday. Bob Elliott was to be buried that day at eleven o'clock. Chook offered to take him. Becker knew he should attend, but he was afraid to go. His left leg now being in plaster. The fibula was broken, but it was a stable fracture. Which meant he could put some weight on it if he wore a boot, a lightweight canvas thing. He could have used crutches, but he found them too difficult. So he did not go to the funeral. In a way, he was glad. He could not face Muriel, not yet. She would blame him for the disaster. Robyn should never have married him. So he let it slide, did not go, telling himself he was not capable. Muriel would understand. Her religion made her understand. But, at heart, she would know he was afraid to face her. He didn't know how she would know. But she would know. If he were any sort of man, he'd get up and go, no matter how much it hurt. But, he knew, he was not any sort of man.

He did nothing on Friday, except exercises with a physiotherapist. And when she'd gone, he kept trying. Determined to learn to walk with crutches, even though they hurt his right shoulder, the one that had taken a bullet one dark night back in Sydney years ago.

On Saturday, Chook drove him out in the office car, a medium-sized Mazda sedan, the one Laura Langley drove. She was a major in the Army's legal service in Sydney on transfer to the Federal Police. To get more experience in crime, real crime. She'd got sick of driving a desk, preparing briefs for court-martials. Soldiers hitting officers, getting too drunk to go on parade, selling Army equipment to criminals, that sort of thing. She was still shaken. Had never expected anything like this. The Army was much quieter, safer. She might go back there, take it easy for a while.

It was a shock. The eastern walls were more or less standing, so was most of the roof. The western side was blown out, boards flung across the verandah, across the lawn. Windows blown out, broken glass everywhere. Chairs tumbled and tilted and upside down, even on the lawn. Someone was going to pay for this. Becker did not know how he was going to do it. He was up against big and ugly and mean forces. They might be big, but he was going to get even one day. One way or the other.

There was a blue and white plastic ribbon around the whole house, or what was left of it. A sign saying: Police Line Do Not Cross. Chook lifted the ribbon and they went up the side steps. Robyn had been blown down those steps, headlong. Instinctively hanging onto her belly, trying to protect the child. Not her head. That was a mistake. Or not a mistake, depending on how you saw it. Protecting herself or the child within.

The living room was open to the sky. Some of the ceiling and the roofing iron had been blown upwards and then had crashed down. Floorboards lay everywhere at any angle. Some intact, others split and jagged, lying criss-crossed on exposed bearers. That's where Becker had fallen on the girl. They had to step carefully from one bearer to another or on some uncertain tangle, to get around. The kitchen wall had blown inwards, around the stove, the refrigerator, the cupboards. The bathroom was intact, useable, and in the last room on the western side, the laundry, the locker was steady and safe and unbroken and probably unbreakable. He thought of the Winchester stowed in there. Perhaps it would come in handy one day.

They were about to check the three bedrooms on the eastern side, when someone spoke outside. Or shouted or yelled or cried, aggrieved.

'I never done it!'

They hobbled and slipped and stepped their way back to the verandah. Bert Henschke was standing at the bottom of the steps, his dog at his heels. It was snarling quietly, curling its lip. They were strangers. It did not like strangers. Bert and the dog came up the side steps, gingerly. As if anything could happen at any time. Like a wall coming down. Becker went out, too quickly, the crutches slipping and sliding on the debris. Chook took one arm and helped him out, so that they were all on the verandah, the dog too. The dog didn't like what he smelled. He could smell the anger. Becker raised a crutch like a spear, went for Bert. The dog went for Becker. Bert stepped back, startled. His hair was a fright, so was his face. He looked tired and deranged, just hanging on. Hanging on to his reason and the dog.

'What do you mean?'

'I never blew you up!'

'Who said you did?'

'All because of Bob Elliott. I never blew 'im up.'

'Because he got the money? Caitlin's money? Instead of your old man?'

'It weren't my flamin' idea!'

'Whose idea was it?'

Becker got down the steps, on one crutch and hanging onto a post. He went for the mad old bastard.

'What are you trying to say? You know who it is?'

'Wouldn't do nothin' like that. Just 'cause that feller got everythin'.'

'You know who did it, don't you?'

'Ah, shit, I dunno.'

'Tell me, tell me!'

'Ah, Christ, ah Christ, ah—'

'I'm gonna kill you,' Becker said.

The dog barked again.

Chook intervened, pulling him back. Becker elbowed her away.

'You killed her, you fuckin' mad bastard!'

'Eh?'

'You killed her, because you didn't get it, didn't you?'

'Eh?'

'Didn't get what Caitlin got!'

Chook tried again. 'Leave it,' she said.

'So you got even, didn't you?'

The dog was struggling against the collar, the black belt and old clasp and studs and the grease and hair and the hands of time.

'You killed her son, didn't you? Killed his daughter. You killed my wife!'

'Harry, take it easy!'

'I'm gonna kill him.'

'Take it easy!' Chook was holding him, keeping him back.

Old Bert was pop-eyed. 'Never done it,' he said.

'You blew up this house, didn't you?'

'No, I never!'

'You spiteful old bastard—'

Chook hit Becker, on the right shoulder. His bad shoulder. Not hard, though.

'Stop it, Harry.'

'What?'

'Stop it, he didn't do it!'

'What?'

'Tell him, Bert!'

They calmed down, stepping back, relaxing. The dog relaxed, sitting. Bert's hand still on the collar. Its eyes flicking this way and that, the way dogs' eyes flick and fix and dart and see everything in a flash. Scanning the surroundings, for danger, for food.

'What?' Becker said again. His heart was pounding. He wanted to kill Henschke, but he could not. The dog would kill him for it. Then Chook would kill the dog. And where would all that all end? He gulped air. The crutch was beginning to slide. He was beginning to slide.

The old man looked around, his face screwed up in a mad sort of smile, as if about to burst. 'Two blokes was 'ere,' he said. 'Coupla days before.'

'I know that.'

'Electricians.'

'I know that. In the house?'

'Eh?'

'Did you see them in the house? Under the house?'

'Out on the road, when I seen 'em.'

'What doing?'

'Sittin' there.'

'In their vehicle?'

'Yeah, then one got out and went to the 'ouse.'

'We know all that. What did he do?'

'Couldn't see f'the trees.'

'Did he climb under the house on this side? Your side?'

'Couldn't see.'

'You could see the van all the time?'

'Yeah.'

'When the man got out of the van, was he carrying anything?'

'Could of.'

'What sort of thing?'

'Could of been a can.'

'A can?'

'To get the water.'

'They could have had sticks of gelly in it, couldn't they? And a phone and a battery and a lot of electrical gear. They were electricians. They could make a bomb.'

Bert didn't know. Chook shrugged.

'As the cops say, Why would they use a van with their own name plastered all over it?'

Becker did not know. He was beaten. If the Terracinis did not do it, then who else? Who hated him enough to do such a bad thing? Deliberately killing or wounding a lot of innocent people to get at only one man, himself?

Bert released the dog, which wandered off, sniffing. Searching for scraps. Bits of food lay here and there. A dropped plate in a corner, a crust under an upturned chair.

'Anyway,' he said. 'Ray's got somethin'.'

'Got something?'

'Yeah.'

'Got what?'

Bert twisted and turned, his feet not moving. He was like a gnarled old tree that seems to have legs, but somehow could not get going.

'What is it?'

'Didn't say.'

'Where *is* Ray?' Chook said.

'Gone.'

'Gone where?'

Bert shrugged. 'Griffith.'

'Why's he gone to Griffith?'

'T'see a bloke.'

'What bloke?'

'Dunno. Might be somethin', but.'

'What do you mean somethin'? A contact?'

Bert did not answer. Just looked around. Then looked at Blue. Blue had found some chicken bones. Chewing noisily, *snap, snap, crack.*

'When'll he be back?'

'Later.'

'How much later?'

'Didn't say, exactly.'

Chook's phone went off. She put it to an ear.

'Yeah?' She listened for a few seconds. 'Who? Who did you say? Giuseppina?' Listened some more. 'Giuseppina who? Ray? Ray?' She looked at the others, shrugged. 'He hung up.'

'What did he say?' Becker asked.

'Her name's Giuseppina.'

'Who did he mean?'

'Didn't say. Sounded in a hurry. And scared.'

'He's in Griffith?'

'Didn't say that.'

'Is he coming back?'

Chook didn't answer. 'Giuseppina?' she said, as if to herself.

'Giuseppina who?'

'I think he meant the lady,' she said. 'The one they call *La Donna.*'

CHAPTER 32

IT WAS NOW Friday, the day of Robyn's funeral. He got up early and got himself discharged from hospital and went out ot the farm and got to work. Dragged out whatever he could carry, using only one crutch. And one hand. Hopping on the other foot. At about nine o'clock, he noticed something sniffing at his plastered heel. It was Blue. Behind him was Bert. They soon got on top of the problem. Knocking down any hanging iron and loose timbers up top and dragging them out to a spot on the western side, the dog watching. Hank joined them and then Lucy Beerbohm and her partner from up the lane, gathering any valuables. Cars stopped now and then and watched, then drove off. At twelve, Becker called it a day. The church service was set for two o'clock. He and Bert were having a beer on the verandah when Chook turned up.

'Any word from Ray?' she asked.

Bert paused, thought about it. Then shook his head.

'You worried?'

'Should've 'eard b'now.'

'Did he say he'd be home yesterday?'

'Sort of. Y'never know.'

'Comes and goes, doesn't he?'

'Always been like that, bit of a law unto 'isself.'

'Well—' Becker finished his beer. 'I've got to get ready to go, Bert. That's been great.'

'Yeah, well—' They both stood. Strangely, Bert held out a hand. They shook. 'Never been invited to a party before,' he said. 'Not 'ere, anyway.'

A figure was approaching. They could make it out through the young pepper trees.

'This looks like Ray,' Becker said.

'Ain't Ray,' Bert said. 'Ain't 'is walk. More like Jase.'

'Jase?'

'Jason, they call 'im. Might 'ave some news.'

Bert walked out slowly in his stumbling way to meet the boy at the fence. He was a grinning redhead with hair all over his face. Becker went into the house, searched around for the makings of a sandwich. Chook had brought fresh bread and milk. He'd begun to eat, when she called from the verandah.

'It don't look good,' she said. 'Tell him, Jase.'

Bert and the boy were standing at the bottom of the side steps. The boy looked about twenty. He was one of those simple fellows who would always look young and silly, even when he was an old man.

'Tell 'em,' Bert said.

'Gone,' the boy said.

'Gone where?'

'Just gone. Was havin' a beer with him at this pub in Griffith an' he wanted a leak. Waited a while. Never come back. Looked for him high an' low. Looked out the back. No sign, nothin'.'

'You had a car?'

'Yeah, wasn't there, but.'

'The car?'

'His ute was there. He wasn't, but.'

'Reported this to the police?'

'Nah.'

'They'll find him, Jace.'

'Ah—'

Obviously, he didn't like reporting anything to the police.

'I'll call 'em,' Chook said.

'Chook will look after it,' Becker said. 'Hope nothing's happened to him.'

'Might 'ave,' Bert said.

'What do you mean?'

Bert was standing the way he used to stand at the fence, arms crossed, head up and looking at the sky. Or, not at the sky but at something beyond the sky, where all would be revealed. But usually it wasn't. Looked as though he were thinking about something deep, something confessional. To get it off his chest. He'd stop breathing for a few seconds, then explosively change his mind. Gasping, like a lawn mower you can't get started. Then, at last, he punched at the ground, or stamped on it. Two or three actions all at once. Hard to say what he was doing, throwing himself around like that, indecisively. Like a string of firecrackers going off, *bang, bang, bang,* one after the other. Jumping all over the place. Scaring the wits out of the kids. Everyone laughing. Suddenly he gasped.

'It was Ray!'

Becker and Chook stopped dead in their tracks. 'What do you mean?'

He did not reply. Becker could only guess.

'Ray blew the place?'

'Nah, not 'im. Wouldn't do nothin' like that!'

'What the hell do you mean?'

'Told 'em.'

'He told someone?'

'Could've.'

'Could've told who?'

'They was 'avin' a drink an' they got talkin'.'

'Who got talking?'

'Ray and these blokes in Griffith.'

'When was this?'

'Fridee, after you told's about the party.'

'What did he say?'

'Said he 'ad a neighbour that 'ad a nice place. Said you was gonna 'ave a birthday.'

'And a party?'

'Yeah.'

'And lots of people?'

'Yeah.'

Becker was disgusted. 'Ah, shit! Ah, shit!'

Chook stepped up, fists on her hips.

'So, Ray knew the day?'

'Yeah.'

'And the time? One o'clock?'

'Yeah, reckon.'

'Who were these blokes?'

'Ah, dunno. One was called Dom.'

'Dom? Just Dom? Was it Domenico? Domenico Gotto?'

'Could've been.'

'The fucking idiot.'

'Who is he?' Becker asked.

'One of Ray's suppliers,' Chook said. She turned back to the young bloke. 'And he talked? This Domenico?'

'Looks like it.'

'Who did he talk to, Bert?'

'Dunno, I don't fuckin' know.'

Chook seized him. 'Where is this Domenico?'

'Don't know. Don't fuckin' know.'

The boy piped up. 'In Griffith. The cops've got him.'

'Why?'

'Dunno.'

Bert was swaying, arms crossed as if rocking a baby to sleep. As if he knew something awful had happened. Or was about to happen. His eyes were closed now, shut tight. He began to sing to himself. It was a slow, crooning song, a song without melody or even rhythm, but was a song of his body. The kind of song you would hear from a witless child in torment. Then he began to cry. 'Sorry,' he said. 'I'm fuckin' sorry.'

Chook said: 'It ain't you fault, Bert.'

'Didn't mean 'im to tell no-one.'

'They were after me,' Chook said.

Becker said: 'After you?'

'Yeah, I'm pretty sure.'

'Because of Cosco?'

'Something like that.' She got to her feet. 'So now we know. See you at the funeral, Harry.'

'Where are you going?'

'Out to Griffith.'

It was a good service as far as funerals go. Becker drove himself. It was awkward, but he managed. The BMW was automatic. He did not have to use his left foot, so he managed well enough. Robyn had a lot of friends. She was the kind of woman who could not walk down Baylis street on a busy day without stopping several times to chat to passers-by and those in shops she knew or strangers looking lost. She'd have to stop to ask if she could help. The church was half full. Muriel sang her heart out, and the priest was at his best. He had bright, shining eyes. Much like her father's eyes, when first Bob had seen her holding a damask rose in her father's garden in Lockhart forty years ago. They sang heartily and thankfully for her life and gathered outside afterward, shaking hands and speaking low.

There was no funeral procession. Only Becker and Muriel were at the burial at the lawn cemetery out by Lake Albert. As well as Chook, who'd turned up late, on her Harley. Robyn had not indicated what she wanted if she died. Not even told her mother. Becker had thought cremation would be best, short and clean. It wouldn't be final if she were buried, at least not to him. She'd be there in the ground, thinking about him. But Muriel had objected. Did not want her daughter to go to the flames.

So they went to the cemetery and saw her lowered down. He stood there, thinking he was now the loneliest man in the world. If he'd been there alone, doing the job alone, he would have felt comforted. But he was standing there, watching with only three other humans and two funeral men and a grave-digger leaning on a tractor, waiting. Becker felt embarrassed, as if watching someone cleaning up after a traffic accident. Fascinating, but nothing to do with him.

Walking away, Becker asked, 'Any news of Ray?'

It was now close to four o'clock. There was to be no wake.

'They found him, the Griffith cops,' Chook said. 'In a ditch, face down.'

'Drowned?'

'Head bashed in.'

'Jesus. Did you talk to this Domenico bloke?'

'Tried, but got nowhere.'

'What are the local cops holding him for?'

'Nothing much, association with known criminals. Unexplained income.'

'Scared?'

'Not scared at all. Just sat there smiling at me and the locals, smiling like a bloke who agrees with everything you say, and knows you'll never break him. Like a bloke that says you'll never win. Because *they* are going to beat you. They'll always beat you.'

They had reached the car park.

'Does Bert know?'

'Called there on the way back.'

'What did he say?'

'He didn't say anything. Sat down, put his head in his hands and cried again, but not so loud this time. It seems he's had three wives and seven kids over forty years. Ray was the last of 'em. At least the last one who'd speak to him.'

That night Becker himself cried. Chook was there, sitting with him in the lamplight. They'd eaten some stuff they'd picked up in town. Roast chicken they could not reheat and some salad in bowls. And had had a couple of beers. Suddenly the tears began to roll, so he got up and went to bed. Chook said she'd sit up with the Winchester. He was dozing off when he felt her get into bed with him. When she put her arms around him, he tried to push her away, embarrassed. It was like being held by a man.

'It's all right,' she said. 'It's all right.'

CHAPTER 33

THE NEXT NIGHT, Saturday, he stayed in the ruins, alone. Someone had to keep an eye on the place. The evening was cool, trucks grinding past on the long trip from Wagga to Adelaide, 900 kilometres across one short stretch of Australia. He had no power. It had been cut off, probably by the fire brigade. He found a hurricane lamp and lit it. Then he sat in the soft yellow glow, a rug wrapped around his shoulders, eating some cold ham and chicken and salad and rice and dry biscuits and cheese. He sat in the gloom and the distant stars, looking at him through the roof. A soft south-westerly was coming through the walls and holes and the emptiness of a house, which was not all there. He would start cleaning it out tomorrow. Clear out the wreckage, build a heap until he decided what to do. Rebuild or demolish? He had little to build for now. His great rural dream had failed.

After a while, he decided there was nothing to do but to go to bed. The main bedroom had suffered little damage, only a few cracks in the walls. He undressed by lamplight down to his underwear. He might have to get out quickly if he heard something in the night. He was sure there would be a disturbance. A footstep, a gasp, a cry or some sort of moaning, if only the wind. He thought he heard footsteps outside. He listened for a while, ears wide open. Then he heard a car door slam. Or a truck door, or a van door. Hard to tell. Then an engine started. The sound died away. He got out of bed and found a torch and checked around. Could see no difference, but it was hard to see in the dark even with the torch. So he went to the storage cupboard in the laundry. It was a big locker, hard timbers. Unbreakable. Untouched by the explosion.

He unlocked it, reached for the Winchester, loaded it, seven 30-30 cartridges.

Even took the box with him, placed it on a bedside table. Propped the rifle against the wall by his head. Turned down the light, and waited.

Becker used to be like this in Canberra. He'd thought he'd got over it, fearing death at every turn. He'd been getting somewhere with the farm, with Robyn, with her children, and one of their own on the way. Now he was afraid again. Someone was out there, thinking about him. And he could do nothing about it.

He snapped awake. Someone or something was in the house. A light was dancing around, a torchlight. The steps came closer, crushing and wobbling on the boards they'd put across the bearers, uncertainly and yet safe enough if you were careful. Becker reached for the rifle. He even put a hand to the lever action, ready to pull it down, load a round. The steps stopped, the light came up off the floor and hit his eyes. It held for a moment, as if pin-pointing. He didn't know whether he was going to be confronted or be shot, *bang*. Straight through the heart.

'There's blokes,' Bert said.

'What?'

'Down the road.'

'What do you mean? How many blokes?'

'Dunno, got a truck, but.'

'You mean at the highway gate? Not the lane gate?'

'Highway.'

'How many?'

'Two or three.'

'Duffers?'

'B'the sound of 'em.'

'How do you know?'

'Heard the chain drop.'

'They cut the chain?'

Becker was out of bed by this time.

'Give me some light.'

Bert flashed the wardrobe and the chair where he'd thrown his clothes and his boots on the floor. One normal, one canvas. He pulled them on and picked up a torch and then the Winchester. They found their way to the front door. 'Where's Blue?'

'Down b'the fence. Told 'im to shut up an' keep watch.'

They walked down and hobbled down to the creek, then got across the weir or causeway or casual pile of rocks and moss and lichen and sticks and leaves and whatever else had gathered there, both blocking and not blocking the seeping stream in which there was very little water now, it not having rained much throughout spring. But there was still hope, because it was only September 1996. They managed that without using the torch. But with a hand from Bert. And got off the weir and sneaked and crept across the paddock and watched. Searching for shapes in the moonless night. And joined Blue at the fence. They opened the gate carefully—not a sound, not even a snort or sniffle from Blue. And slipped in. Feeling for the ground with their feet. The only light being the light of the stars and the afterglow, which, way out there on the everlasting plains on a clear night, is almost as bright as day. But only on the horizon. Right around, it glowed. As if the sun were trying to get around the whole globe from all directions at once and failing feebly. But you could see shapes against the pale, almost blue, light on the horizon in each direction. And occasionally and suddenly, against the lamps of some thundering Christmas tree, a great B-double heading for Adelaide and all points west. And you could see shapes now and then, human shapes. Darting and not darting like unseen gods in an underworld of ghostly illumination.

They watched and waited. Then they heard voices, real low. Then a cow being disturbed, snuffling and skittling out of the way in the dark. A rustle of hooves and answering snorts across the paddock.

'Get that one,' someone said. They had torches. You could make out the truck against the afterglow. Then, against the glow, even when there wasn't any moon. Nothing but the stars, stark and sharp and glittering in the immense darkness, which looked the blacker the more you looked. Then, there was a black shape, a truck. Another big B-double came rolling toward them, its lights blazing. Against it, they could see a silhouetted truck at the gate. On the tray was a wooden frame. The back would be down and there had to some sort of ramp. How were they going to get an eighteen-month-old heifer up a ramp without a lot of pushing and prodding?

Becker and Bert and Blue were walking slowly, carefully. Following the sounds, then the lights, dancing around like giant fireflies. Something came down with a crash. Must have been a tail gate. They must have had a ramp, but if they did, how the hell did they get it here?

'Look out, someone!' a man said.

'What?'

'Listen.'

'Listen, what?'

A torch swept across, but did not reach Becker and Bert and Blue.

They stood stock still.

'Must've been a cow,' someone said. 'Here, push this a bit more.'

They must have been pushing some sort of ramp.

'Bit more,' he said.

A man came out of nowhere and said, 'How's it goin'?'

'Gettin' there.'

They did a lot more pushing and shoving. Then someone said: 'That's good enough. How many you got?'

'Two for a start. Let's get 'em on board.'

Bert resumed walking in that slow, sloppy way of his, dragging his feet. So that he was skimming across the grass. Blue was a foot or two ahead. They were about a hundred yards away from the gate.

Becker couldn't resist any longer.

'Hey you!'

Two torches searched for them, did not quite reach. Becker had the Springfield up and sighted. That's exactly what he wanted, torches on him. It gave him a target.

'Get out of there!'

'Jesus,' someone said, a young voice, a big kid by the sound of him.

'Blue,' Bert said, softly restraining. Blue did nothing.

'Get!'

Becker fired. Up high, but not too high, right into the afterglow over their heads.

'Christ!' someone said.

Then Bert fired. It was his shotgun. The blast was like a lightning strike only a few yards away. Something hit the truck, a few pellets. They stung and whistled off metal.

'Get out quick,' a man said. They ran for the truck.

Bert fired again.

Becker tried to stop him. 'No, no, you'll stampede the cattle!'

They were jumping for the truck. A door slammed, the engine fired, then roared. They got it going—up a bank, clawing at the highway.

Then Bert let Blue go. He was very fast for a clumsy-looking dog with short legs. Caught one of them, one who'd tried to jump in but too late. Blue got him by a leg. Hung onto him, snarling, biting, chewing. The fellow screamed, fell off the truck. The truck was edging onto the road and turning westward. Becker and Bert ran to the gate. Blue was through the gate, following the truck, biting at something, worrying it. Trying to bring it down, the way a Queensland heeler brings down a calf. By the back leg.

The truck kept going.

'Blue!' Bert yelled. 'Here!'

The bitten man cried and cried. He was howling. The truck stopped, waited for him. Becker was sighting up on it up there on the road. He took one shot, straight at the engine outlined darkly. The bullet zinged and whacked and something broke, maybe glass. Maybe a window, maybe a mirror. Someone said, 'Jesus! Get out of here!'

The truck went off, gasping at first, then picked up real speed. It went on down the highway, heading west, showing no lights.

They went to the gate. It was wide open, but blocking it was a ramp, a cattle ramp. The kind you can put together section by section. Too steep for a full-grown animal to get up in the dark. But a weaner could do it if prodded.

The chain holding the padlocked gate had been cut, very neatly.

Becker flashed around, but it was impossible in the dark to see whether any had been taken. He guessed not. Not time enough.

He was going to close the gate, but the ramp was obstructing it.

'Leave it there,' he said. 'They won't get around that thing.'

He meant the cattle.

They went back to the house and had tea and some biscuits he found. Special biscuits, brownies with a thin layer of chocolate. Robyn had made them, always ready to stock up. Becker looked at his watch: just gone half-past three.

'Thanks, Bert,' he said.

'Blue heard 'em.'

Blue was panting like he'd run a mile. He had the smallest eyes for a big dog you ever saw, and he was probably the ugliest dog. But he had his purposes.

'Police'll know,' Bert said.

'Know?'

'Who they was, b'the ramp.'

Becker was not so sure. 'At least they got none. And they won't be back. Not after what Blue did to one of 'em.'

'Might be,' Bert said, chewing.

'Why?'

'Y'never know, do y'? The way some blokes think.'

A few days later, when checking his box for mail, Becker found a note. It was hand printed and simply read: We'll be back, you bastard! With a few misspellings. That did not matter. The meaning was clear enough.

* * *

On Sunday, Becker drove to Wagga and picked up Muriel. He was getting used to the pain. In fact, he liked it. It was a good sort of pain in his lower leg. It was stiff when he woke in the morning, but once he got moving, he enjoyed it. Like a war wound, one you could show your mates and talk and laugh about. Even drink to it. Together they went to the hospital, collected the baby, now registered as Roberta Becker without a second given name. As far as the medics could determine, she had suffered no injury in the fall. She and Wendy would stay with Muriel more or less indefinitely. Terry too. He went to town and joined Wendy and the baby. He had not finished at the small primary school at The Creek, but he soon got used to one in Wagga, not far from Railway Street. He would be in high school with big sister next year, so he might as well stay there. Becker did not know how he was going to look after a baby, even if he did rebuild a home for her. Finally, he told Muriel to engage a daily help. He would pay for everything.

'Thank you, Harry,' she said.

She was a modest woman, never demanded praise.

He tried to say something else. It was needed, he knew. Muriel had lost her husband and only child in the same shocking moment. Then had stepped up and taken on Wendy and Terry. And now a beautiful girl, blowing bubbles.

Not that she had any alternative. It was expected of her, a good Anglican widow. She did it because it was expected of her—not as a duty or a burden or a penance, but as an honour. She was English to the bones. It was her place to help. Without complaint. She could have feelings and disappointments and her regrets, but she must never complain. No Englishwoman of any breeding would ever complain. Not about God, King or Country. As her dear father would have said in his sincerity and faint hope and fragmentary sense of mission: We must carry on as best we can, now that dear Mother has gone. As he had said as he had crossed Her hands upon Her pale and tubercular chest, nineteen days before they had sailed.

He could not find the words. But she knew.

After lunch, Becker went back to the wrecked house.

Sat on the verandah, thinking and not thinking. What would he do? Raze the house to the ground and rebuild another on the same site? Or leave it without a house and live elsewhere? Give up? Sell the property, sell the stock? Quit altogether? Get out of farming. Admit another failure? If so, where would he go? Wherever he went and no matter what he did, he had a new responsibility—his newborn daughter. He was getting nowhere. He felt gutted. His life had gone wrong again, collapsed. He felt as bad as he'd done before he'd met Evelyn Crowley. As mysterious and as dangerous as she may have been, to be with her or to think about her had kept him going then. All because he'd found a handbag in a litter bin in Garema Place…

'Hullo,' a young voice said.

He looked up. It was Dell or, more accurately, Deloraine Duffy. She was smiling tentatively, perhaps afraid to shake him free of these thoughts.

'Hullo,' he said, surprised.

'I thought I should come and, you know, thank you—'

She came closer, step by careful step.

'You fell on me,' she said nervously. 'Stacey said you covered me, as the roof came down. You took the full force.'

'I don't remember much about that.'

'You were unconscious when they picked you up, picked me up.'

He rose slowly. His body aching, not so much with injury but with the whole problem of trying to live without one damned thing leading to another. He was think-ing of Ray. Found in an irrigation ditch, face down, head bashed in. When would it ever end? Probably never.

'It was only instinct,' he said.

He meant falling or flopping on top of her. He'd not thought about it. There'd been no time. It was one of those things you do, if you are a decent type of man. Not because she was pretty and delightful to dance with or young and happy and friendly and worth saving. It was instinct. Either you have the instinct or you do not. If you are a cop, you have the instinct. If you haven't, you shouldn't be a cop. The people who had killed Ray Henschke had no such instinct. With them it was kill or be killed.

'So, er,' she said awkwardly, looking back and beckoning. 'This is—this my friend, Hedley.',

'Hedley.'

'Hedley?'

'Hedley Devenish.'

'Devenish?'

A young man appeared. He was tall and slim and looked about sixteen, his face was so fresh. His voice was young too, when it came. He was probably about her age. 'Hullo,' he said. Nervously, his eyes flicking from Dell to Becker and back again.

'So,' she said, 'we thought we'd call in and see how you are going.' She glanced around. 'It's so terrible, isn't it? Such a lovely house, a joyful house. Are you going to rebuild?'

'I don't know, Dell.'

'Oh, you must, Harry. It was such a distinctive house. A historic house, John Kettle's own house. It's famous. Hedley has passed it many times, haven't you? He'd wondered who had such a smart place. He's doing engineering, aren't you? At the uni,' she added. 'He's in his third year. His father's an architect, isn't he, Hedley? And I'm sure that if he saw this house—'

'I'm sure he'd say, Get rid of it.'

'Oh, no!'

'I'm thinking of demolishing it.'

'Oh, no, Harry, please don't do that!'

'I'm going to get someone to flatten it.'

'Oh, no!'

'If I may make a suggestion, sir—'

'It has to be demolished. If a strong wind came up—'

The young man tried again. 'If I got my father to look at it—'

'He'd say pull it down, as soon as possible.'

'Let me speak to him.'

'Oh—'

'Please, Harry!' Dell said.

Becker hesitated. She was such a lovely young woman. Probably madly in love. Her eyes were those of a woman who is no longer a virgin, and wants to tell the whole word her big secret, but dares not. Certainly not her parents. She being only nineteen. There was no doubt about beautiful women. The more you looked at them, the more beautiful they became.

The boy pulled out his phone. 'I'm sure Father would give you a professional opinion.'

'Is it awfully wrecked?' Dell asked.

'Have a look for yourself.'

He was going to let her do it alone, but remembered. Some of the roofing iron was not secure, possibly some of the timbers too. So he went with her. She was holding onto his hand and dancing across the bearers and the loose boards, making a makeshift path through the remains of a party that would never come again. Food scraps and overturned plates and cups and glasses and cutlery, they lay in corners or splashed on boards or down in the deep recesses below the bearers. And on the table, the dining table on which the food had been placed and about which the guests had served themselves, but had gone out into the sun and were tasting it and talking and smiling and laughing. When suddenly—.

'This is where I fell,' she said. 'And where you fell on top of me. And saved me.'

Maybe she was right. He was lying face down when they were hit. But she was face up. One piece of timber had hit his left leg, low down, on the ankle or near it. The fibula was broken, but it was a clean snap, no fragmentation. Other timber had hit him full on the back, cutting deep, jarring his spine, cracking ribs. Fracturing two. If it had hit her, it might have smashed her face. Other bits and pieces had come down, hitting his head. Bits of plaster. Hitting Dell too, but nothing serious.

'How's your chest?' he asked, not really interested in her injury. She had survived and Robyn had not. But he had to say something.

'Oh, I'm fine. A few sprained ribs, but nothing is broken. Thanks to you.'

He showed her over the place, including the main bedroom. She stepped delicately, hands in case she stumbled. Fingertips touching almost nothing. Just the presence of things, rather than the things themselves.

'Oh, how amazing? Nothing damaged. And what a lovely room. She was a good decorator, wasn't she? Robyn, I mean. She told me she loved the house. Nearly as much as she loved you.'

She prattled on—desperately, it seemed. As if she did not want *Nil Desperandum* to disappear. But it was the name of the property, not merely the house. The land would remain, long after the human race had gone.

'Are you sleeping here?'

'Yeah, I am.'

'In the bed? Oh, how lovely! So, you are still with her, aren't you? Even when you are asleep.'

Her young man came in. Light footsteps, youthful, quick but respectful.

'He can come out this afternoon, late. After work,' he said.

Becker was not pleased. Didn't want some architect poking around, touting for a job.

He wanted to be quit of the place, although he did not know where he'd go, with a baby. He'd need a woman to live with, to look after the little girl, hopefully to be a companion. But could think of none. He was bad news. No woman worth having would want him now.

'All right,' he said.

Dell rushed at him. Threw her arms about his neck and kissed him.

'Oh, wonderful,' she said. 'Oh, good, good, good!' And kissed him again, followed by a big squeeze. 'Thank you,' she said. 'Thank you!'

The young man laughed. He loved her, you could see.

Late that afternoon, Darryl Devenish came with his son. Dell was not able to do so. She had a lecture. They walked all over the house and agreed with Becker. The house was not worth saving. It should never have been renovated. It was too old, the timbers not strong enough. Also, termites were still a problem. You could smell them when you got down on your hands and knees and sniffed in corners. They were in the joists and bearers, the frame. And another thing, a storm was brewing. If he were to keep it, the house would have to be covered with tarpaulins to stop bits and pieces blowing away, possibly across the road. Dangerously.

That decided him.

Late on Monday, a bulldozer moved in and flattened the house in a few minutes. An emergency job. The contractor had to cancel another job to do it. A storm was predicted for late that day. The debris was removed by truck and dumped somewhere official and out of sight. Anika and Hank had helped, moving in early. Bert and Chook helped. Young Dell came out with her young man to give a hand. Removing all remaining clothing, the utensils, the vases and pictures to their house for the time being. Packing everything precious. Even Robyn's clothing. Becker was not sure what he was going to do with it, but he could not get rid of it. He couldn't throw her away, not a woman like that. The furniture went to a storage depot. The Nissan was locked away in the barn. They'd finished by lunchtime.

Chook went down to the little store at The Creek and came back with a whole lot of chicken and salad and cold slaw and beer in tins, coffee in cups and they all sat around and toasted *Nil Desperandum*, which was looking pretty sick by now. Nothing but stumps and pipes sticking out of the ground. And bits of timber and joists and bolts and nuts and trivia you never thought was trivia, when it was holding a house together. The storm was building up fast. Angry black clouds rose and writhed to the south-west.

Heavy rain, they could see it coming, great columns of it.

The wind lifting, the lightning flashing.

They all cleared out. Chook had gone back after lunch. She had things to do.

Becker took one last look. Sitting in the BMW, watching as the storm hit, lightly at first. Then the force behind it lifted quickly, lifted everything in its path. Leaves flew, twigs snapped, branches thrashed. Big drops came down, hitting the land, the cattle, the house which was not there, and the BMW. Thudding on the roof like soft hailstones. He started up, drove away in the rain.

Goodbye, he said. Not to the house, but to his second wife, Robyn the Good.

CHAPTER 34

HE MOVED IN with Hank and Anika. He hadn't wanted to do so, but it was for the best. He could keep an eye on the property from one side, especially on the cattle. After that incident with the duffers, he was anxious. The local police had not been able to locate them. They must have come from far away. The police checked with every local hospital and doctor, but no medical help had been sought by the young fellow who'd been bitten. The dog's teeth must have gone in deep, cutting to the bone. He would be at risk of infection, perhaps amputation, if he left it too long.

Becker had not decided what to do with the property. If he were to keep the cattle, someone had to live on it, keep an eye on them. Bert had offered to watch the place from the other side. He was now grumpier and less articulate than ever, deeply hurt that his last son had been murdered by some scum of the earth for asking too many questions. But he didn't blame Becker or even Chook. It was part of living, in Bert's opinion. The bastards always beat you in the end.

Devenish, the architect, had advised rebuilding. He could design a simple house, quite commodious for a reasonable fee. It would be modern from the ground up, built to the highest possible specifications. Becker was not certain. Still did not know what to do, stay or go? There was always the problem of Roberta, who had a cot in Muriel's room. She was a good baby, who never cried and drank all her milk and blew bubbles. If you said 'Booh!' to her, she'd smile and say 'Booh!' back at you. Or, at least, she'd try.

Chook had been sour when she'd heard about the boyfriend, as if she'd been betrayed, misled, or led on, used. She'd snarled, when Becker told her. He did it gently. They were having a couple of Jacks at the William Hovell. On the floor by her chair was her helmet. This was about a month after the disaster. They'd been talking about Dell.

He was walking fairly well now. The canvas boot had been removed and he could put weight on the ankle still in plaster. He had short Canadian crutches now and used them. Or used only one. Or he did not bother. He had another two weeks to go before the plaster came off, possibly longer. Possibly four weeks.

'So that's why she'd been avoiding me?'

'Take it easy. Did she say she loved you? She was probably fascinated. I mean, what a great story to tell all her friends.'

Chook was still snarling.

'Story is right. I told her my life story, she wrote it up. The horror my father saw in Odessa, when the Germans and the Rumanians hauled out the Jews and the Communists, shot them in the streets, left the bodies propped up against walls and fences. He saw what happened in Aleksandrovsky Prospekt, where about four-hundred people were hanged. At another place, columns of hostages were either shot or burned alive. He saw such sights, the bodies burning. He had to. His mother had been killed in the shelling before the Germans broke in. Each day, he stuck with his father. He had to, no-one else would look after him. His father was a policeman, who had to do as the invaders demanded. He joined in these outrages. He helped to burn the hostages. He helped to kill the victims. If he'd refused, he too would have been shot.'

'How old was the boy, when he saw this?'

'Ten or eleven.'

'Did he have to shoot anyone?'

'If he did, he never told me.'

'The poor kid.'

'When the Russians came back, the same fucking thing happened—only it was the pro-Germans and any sort of Fascist, who were killed that time. His father was condemned as a collaborator, and shot. Why did they collaborate? Ukrainians had no reason to love the Ruskis. Do you know, in the thirties eight-million Ukrainians died as a result of the forced collectivisation of the farms. Eight million! That bastard Stalin did it. Then, the long, slow and degrading conditions after the war. They starved, my father and mother. They were street urchins, homeless. They stuck to each other, they had no-one else. They had to eat raw potatoes and garbage, whatever they could find. Even rats, sometimes uncooked. After the war, they tried to get out, right out, out of Odessa and out of the whole Ukraine. He was nineteen by then, she seventeen.

'They tried to get on a boat, flee to Turkey, anywhere. It took years and years. My mother had to prostitute herself to get to Istanbul. They were there a long time. Mother worked in a house of an old man. She did the cooking and cleaning, then she had to get into bed with him now and then. She told me all this before she died. He was quite kind to her. He found jobs for father, working at street cleaning, then on the waterfront cleaning and scouring boats. Then in 1959, they got on a fishing boat, thinking it was going to Greece, but it went to Cyprus. They landed at Limassol, still under British control. Put in a camp. At least they had food and medical help. Then, someone decided to send them to Australia.

'They reached this country in 1960. They struggled again, but in better conditions. A Greek gave them some work in a shop. They worked, they worked hard. He was a storeman, she a cleaner. They got together some money, had a few rooms somewhere in South Melbourne. In 1963 they had a child, me. For a while we were happy, relatively happy. Things looked up. Eventually, they scraped enough money together to buy a little stone house in Hawthorn. I went to school; I had warm clothes and good food. Then, in 1975, Mother died, cancer. It was a slow and awful death. Now it was just me and Father.

'It was a bad time. He was angry and lonely and always struggling to make himself understood. His English was bad, it still is. He's become a total loner. He works alone, at a night job, an awful job. But, at least he's still alive. When I was eighteen, I couldn't take it any longer, the sheer misery. I was angry and alone, the butt of jokes about my height. And my skinniness. And my resentfulness. So, I lit out and joined a gang of bikies. I think you know the rest. I told all that and much more to the little bitch—but not so savagely.'

Becker couldn't help smiling.

'Serves you right. She was not in love with you. Just fascinated.'

'I thought bloody journalists were supposed to do some digging, talk to people, find the facts and produce deathless prose—all their own work! But what did she do? Nothing! She took it down with that little recorder of hers, word for word, then claimed it was all her own work! And got a fucking distinction for it!'

'Calm down, people are looking at you.'

'Ah, shit on 'em.'

'You're hurt, I know. These beautiful young things, they like to play with you, don't they?'

'Little bitches, I'd like to piss on the lot of them.'

It was late afternoon. Chook raised a finger. Bruce came over.

'A Jack, if you don't mind, Bruce.'

The barman looked at Becker, who nodded.

Bruce went off as silently as a mouse. He was always on duty, except when he was not. He worked in shifts, which seemed to change every time you saw him. Chook was sure Bruce had a problem. He kept glancing at Chook as though he wished she were a man. A man who knew all about it.

'He has a problem,' she said. 'Asked me all about it.'

'About what?'

'Whether he should have an operation.'

'What kind of operation?'

'Apparently he's a bit of both.'

'Bit of both?'

'Male and female.'

'What did you tell him?'

'I said it was up to him. Apparently he thinks I'm a kindred soul.'

'Are you?'

'I've had an operation,' she said. Then added: 'But not the kind he's thinking of.'

'What kind is that?'

'He wants to be a woman.'

'What did you tell him?'

'I said to forget it. Unless he wants to get the rough end of the pineapple.'

'You said that to him?'

'He should know being female is not all it's cracked up to be.'

'You'd rather be a man?'

She shrugged. 'Too fucking late for that, isn't it?'

Neither spoke for a moment. It was getting on for four o'clock. The bar was starting to fill up. The tradesmen would be soon knocking off for the day. They would be followed by the clerks and other professionals like the bank staff and the teachers. Then the rest after shops closed. The day had begun to close down. Suddenly, it all came out.

'You've been wondering about me,' Chook said. 'Haven't you?'

'Have I?'

'Been wondering all sorts of things. For example, what I did with you know what.'

Becker almost said, 'Bodies?' In fact, it did come out, but only in a stumbling sort of whisper. No-one in the room would have heard.

'Yeah, well, it's best you don't know.'

'And the other things?'

'Whether I am a bit each way, anatomically.'

'You mean a—'

'Hermaphrodite? No, no, not at all. No—' The whiskey came. Chook nodded. Bruce slipped away.

'Whenever I see your baby,' she said, 'I know what's wrong. I want a child. A child, who'd be *my* child, someone to love and fondle and help and watch and guard and encourage. Preferably a girl, who'd grow up the way Dell has grown up. I suppose that's why I fell for her. She has everything. She has it now. But I? I don't have what she has.'

'Youth, you mean? Beauty?'

'A baby factory.'

'A uterus? You mean you don't have one?'

'Correct, they took it out.'

'Who took it out?'

'The doctors at the Austin Hospital, after I was rescued by the Feds.'

'In Melbourne, when you were young?'

'Yeah, I had a hysterectomy just before I turned twenty.'

'Hell, Chook.'

'I was as sick as a dog, rotten with disease. I had blood poisoning. They had to do it immediately.'

'Gee, I'm sorry.'

'So am I. I'd fucked up my life good and proper.'

'How long were you in hospital?'

'Nearly four weeks. I was riddled with disease. I'd been bleeding badly because of what that bastard did to me. Tore me to bits inside. As well, they feared blood poisoning, among other things. They had to fix that before they could do the op. They cut it out, my baby factory. Then I was taken to that place out at Greensborough, the rest home. Where the shrinks worked on me, and the psychologists and the physios and the social workers and the rest. They fed me well, a glass of wine with dinner each night. Treated me like I was worth saving. Treated me like I was a woman, even though I didn't have a uterus. As if they wanted me to get better. Become someone different. Someone better than the piece of shit I was or had been. The old man with the bow tie came now and then, smiling. For progress reports, he said. Held my hand one time. He said, Anastacia, you've had a bad time, but you are going to make it. Never give up, my dear. Never give up. It was a nice speech. I heard a few months later he had died. I cried then. I still don't know his name, except I called him Roof. He asked me to call him that. I said, 'Why?' 'Roof as in Rufus,' he said. He might have had red hair at some time, but his hair was silvery when I knew him. Thinking about it later, I was sure that Red was his son. They'd killed Red. For some reason he must have thought I was worth saving. He'd told me get out, run for it. But I'd not been able to run. Not then.'

'What was Red's name?'

'I never found out.'

'What did people call him?'

'Just Red.'

'And what about your benefactor? The old man?'

'I think his name was Redmayne.'

'You think?'

'A nurse said to me one day, 'Your friend is in the building.' 'What friend?' I said. 'Mr Redmayne,' she said. So, when he came in, I said 'Mr Redmayne?' to him. And he smiled and patted my hand. And said he'd found a spot for me. In Canberra.

'Why all the secrecy?'

Stacey took another swig of Jack. Thought about it.

'In the Feds, we don't have names, only code names or numbers or tags. Out in the field, you're in a world, where no-one knows who you are. You're trying to look like a someone you're not. Like a tax consultant or a real estate agent or a barmaid with big ears or a fitter and turner in a sweater shop in a backstreet where they don't fix motor vehicles—they remake them with a different plate. At the same time trying to save this fucking country from all the cheats and liars and political manipulators and thieves and crims and moral maggots, who'd like to take over. But maybe that's what I like about being a Fed. I'm someone at last, even if I still feel like a piece of shit at heart. I like the work I do—no uniform, no identification in any way. And I don't have to call in every time I've carried out an order and ask: What do I do now, boss? They give you a lot of leeway, let you decide for yourself. I can sit in a bar and let people stare at me and think about me and try to guess who or what I am. I don't tell 'em. I let them stare and wonder. Then I think back at them: You don't know me, pal. But I know you. So let's leave it at that.'

CHAPTER 35

BECKER DID NOT know what to say. In a way, there was no need to say anything. It explained a lot about Chook, why she was aggressive and resentful, so pissed off with the world. And yet determined to do something to put it right, if only to catch the scum and the creeps and the vile bastards who lived off others. And especially those who had killed Polly Politis in Canberra. The only person she had really loved, she'd said at Evelyn's funeral. And now, those responsible for killing Robyn the Good.

It explained why she behaved like a man, working out in gyms and building up her body and her effectiveness. Her fierce handshake, her kick-arse mentality. And why she let her jacket hang open, zipped only at the last inch or two. So everyone in a bar could see the butt of a Colt .38. Everyone in Wagga now knew she was a cop of some sort. And wondered why cops hung out in the Commonwealth Building. Pretending to be inspectors, who chased free-loaders on pensions.

'So, now you know why I can never have kids,' she said.

'I'm sorry, Stacey.'

'So am I.'

They sat there a while, not speaking but relaxed, as if something had changed their world. Although neither knew exactly what.

'I'm taking some time off,' she said.

'Where are you going?'

'You don't need to know.'

'South?'

Chook nodded.

'You're making this personal?'

'Very.'

'Don't be stupid. Leave it to the right people.'

'They do it by the book. That's too slow for me.'

'You've got more information?'

'I think I know who *La Donna* is.'

'Ray said Giuseppina.'

'Yeah, Giuseppina.'

'You know her other name?'

'I've been given a name.'

'Who by?'

'Silvano.'

'Silvano Cosco? In hospital? You believe him? He's crazy.'

'Yeah, he sure is, but maybe not all the time. Keeps saying some guy in Melbourne did it.'

'What guy?'

'Salvatore somebody.'

'You mean he was not responsible?'

'Oh, he was responsible, no doubt about it. But he's in denial.'

'Salvatore who?'

'Our people in Victoria have done some checking. They looked up every name in Melbourne that includes Giuseppina. It's quite easy with the electoral rolls and a computer. They came across one married to a Salvatore.'

'Yeah?'

'Salvatore Pisano. It turns out that this guy has had a stroke. He can't speak.'

'Yeah? That's why people have to talk to his wife?'

'And that's why they call her *La Donna*.'

'But, it may be someone else named Pisano.'

'Listen, mate, that creep, Adams, phoned someone in Melbourne early that evening before Polly and Evelyn were killed. We checked his calls next day. One of them went to a house in Richmond. That house is owned by Salvatore Pisano. That's more than a coincidence.'

'If he's had a stroke, he may be dead. She may be running the whole show.'

'In that case—' Chook leaned across. 'I'll kill her instead. I'll kill her real slow.'

'Jesus, Chook, you're mad.'

'I'll cremate her.'

'Cremate her?'

'Yeah, alive. I want to hear her screaming.'

'Oh, Christ, don't do it.'

'Just a thought.'

'Don't do it. They'll catch you one day. The police, I mean.'

'Ah, fuck 'em.'

'Maybe the Feds would cover up for you. Keep it out of the papers. But the State cops won't. They don't like you.'

'Ah, fuck 'em.'

There was a pause. Chook was tapping her unfinished whiskey on the table, thoughtfully.

'Why are you really doing this, Stacey?'

'For Robyn. For Polly.'

Becker was going to say that revenge breeds revenge. She was playing games with the Mafia. They would kill her, one way or other, one day. No matter how long it took.

She seemed to guess his thoughts.

'Not a word to anyone, Harry.'

He did not reply.

'Remember,' she said, 'you owe me one.'

He didn't reply to that either.

'When are you going?'

'Today.' She tossed down the whiskey, the last drop.

'It's gone four already. It'll be dark before long.'

'Good, no-one notices a dyke on a bike in the dark.'

She signalled Bruce, who came over. Chook put money on his tray. 'I'll get you the change,' he said.

'Keep it.'

They walked out. 'Where's your bike?'

'Up here a few steps.'

They strolled along the street, dodging people. At least Becker tried to do so, but he was slow because of the crutches. Chook gave way to no-one, not even women with children. As she walked, she pulled off the band holding her hair back in a tight knot. Her hair fell down in short, curling tresses. Just below the ears. She was good looking in a fiercely foreign way. The high cheekbones, the insinuating eyes, crinkling at the corners. As if daring you to smile at a freak like her.

They reached the bike.

'So long, Harry,' she said. And kissed him on a cheek. Passers-by laughed. One almost cheered. She put on the helmet, got on the bike, pressed a button, revved up the engine, then let it idle. And gave a smile, which was a smile and a wink and a smirk and kiss, all wrapped up in one.

He said it at last: 'You murdered him, didn't you?'

She was surprised, and he thought for a moment she was going to deny it, but she did not. Instead, she grinned. It was a smug grin, but not insolent or unfriendly or evasive in any way.

'The kid? Yeah, I killed him.'

'You deliberately killed him, didn't you? You could have called on him to drop the weapon.'

'Yeah, I could.'

'That's murder.'

'A piece of shit like that kid? Murder? No, mate, that's business.'

She patted him on an arm.

'So long, Harry. Don't wait up.'

She revved up the bike and, without a wave or another smile, rode off. Don't wait up for me, she had said, as if they were married.

That was the nub of it. He was bound to her. If she went down, he would go with her. Most likely charged with being an accessory after the fact.

On the other hand, Chook was some sort of friend. He was not sure what kind, but she wouldn't have told him she was going to Melbourne to kill someone if she didn't trust him. They had something in common. It was not just that her girlfriend had been killed trying to protect his girlfriend, Evelyn. It was something to do with the way humans got tangled up with each other.

That's how it had been with Evelyn. The more dangerous she was, the more you wanted to tangle with her. As a result, he'd been blown up twice. And he'd lost his wife. Who had done that? Someone in Sydney? Or Melbourne? Or someone much closer to home?

Harry Becker got in the BMW and drove around to Railway Street. He was going to pick up his daughter, five weeks old, and ask her: What the hell are we going to do?

You and me?

Shawline Publishing Group Pty Ltd

www.shawlinepublishing.com.au